Love at War

Love
at War

SANDRA HOWARD

The Book Guild Ltd

First published in Great Britain in 2022 by
The Book Guild Ltd
Unit E2 Airfield Business Park,
Harrison Road, Market Harborough,
Leicestershire. LE16 7UL
Tel: 0116 2792299
www.bookguild.co.uk
Email: info@bookguild.co.uk
Twitter: @bookguild

This work is entirely fictitious and bears no resemblance to any persons living or dead.

Typeset in 11pt Adobe Garamond Pro

Printed and bound in the UK by TJ Books LTD, Padstow, Cornwall

ISBN 978 1915122 131

British Library Cataloguing in Publication Data.
A catalogue record for this book is available from the British Library.

For Michael, always

I know not if we two should love
And blindly take,
A road that's scarred with dreams that die,
And hearts that break.

The path lies hidden from our eyes,
But this I know:
The magic whispers in our hearts
And we must go.

Iain Macleod

PART ONE

CHAPTER 1

Hamburg, November 1938

The scream woke me up. It was piercing, haunting, carrying, a woman's scream and such a pure distillation of pain and horror that I pressed on my ribcage, trying to stop a scream of my own from rising up in my throat. There were more screams, vicious jeers and yells. Whatever was going on outside, right below my window, sounded terrifying, all too horribly real to be a nightmare. I shivered and pulled the bedclothes more tightly round.

Had that poor wretched woman been thrown to the ground, the cold, gritty tarmac, and had a jackboot raised above her head? Or been forced to watch the SS beating up a loved one, rupturing his spleen and leaving him in a bloody pulp? I'd been in Germany long enough to know the kind of thing that went on.

The Stormtroopers, Hitler's bullyboys in their steel-capped boots, had been rampaging through cities further south, beating up Jews and hurling bricks through their shop windows. Were they here in Hamburg now, lashing out at a few more Jews, tired workers coming off a night shift?

Another piercing scream… The old Jewish cobbler had warned of them coming only last week when I'd taken in my shoes for re-heeling. We always had a little chat. 'Don't leave collecting these shoes for too long. The Brownshirts will be here any day and they'll torch this shop for sure, plenty others too. Folks have been queuing up to leave – the ones that can afford to.'

'But Hamburg's a liberal city, not like Berlin and the South. Won't we be safe enough here?'

'Far from it, the SA's assault division will see to that.'

He'd heaved a bitter sigh and tucked a thin red scarf more closely round his neck, hunching his shoulders against the chill of his little shop. His face was sunken and spattered with moles, he had small brown eyes like raisins, buried deep in the creases, but lively eyes, taking everything in.

They'd had a fierce spark of defiance that day and I shuddered to think of his shop being torched. It was his domain that shop, with its tang of resin and piles of repaired shoes in brown paper bags. He was a good, kind man eking out a living, but hearing those haunting screams it was hard not to fear for his life.

Hamburg was beautiful with its many church spires that rose above the city like tall trees in a garden. I loved its vast parks and the two, great silvery Alster lakes where I'd taken my study books in the summer. There was the appalling propaganda against Jews, toby jugs with hideously caricatured Jewish faces in every shop window, swastikas, despicable posters, but I'd made good friends on my course and never felt threatened or insecure.

It was very different for Ava, the Jewish doctor who'd become a good friend. My mother was a doctor too, and we'd found a rapport. Ava had silky dark hair, strong handsome features, yet a softness about her looks as well. She was kind, conscientious and considerate, always extremely cautious in what she said.

It was only when we were somewhere completely private would she ever open up. 'Jewish doctors are losing their practices,

Laura,' she said, walking in the park one day, 'and if I were ever to speak of what's really happening, I'd be shot. My brother was in a concentration camp for a few weeks and meeting him off the train, he was so altered I barely recognised him. He went straight to book a passage to America saying without that time in Buchenwald he'd never have got to know Germany.'

'Will you go too?' I asked, feeling spine-chilling fear for her, but Ava had just shaken her head with a small smile. She had to stay; her mother was very ill.

How would they cope if she lost her practice? There'd be no money, no one to help two poor defenceless Jewish women…

How long would all the vicious beatings go on before the good Germans stood up to Hitler and did something about it? Was the nation losing its sanity? I had a real feeling of the forces of evil at work and shrank inside my skin.

The sounds of rioting were fainter, it was eerily quiet now. I felt no less terrified, sleepless, with an early lecture next day, and had to try to see what was happening outside. Climbing out of bed shivering, shrugging on my blue hooded dressing gown, I went to do battle with the window, it was small and mullioned, always stuck fast. It still wouldn't budge, but with my face pressed sideways against the cold leaded panes, I could see quite far up the street.

The sky was lit up in the distance with an angry conflagration; billowing smoke and vermillion streaks like livid scars were flaring out against the blackness. There must have been at least one building on fire, but no sound of sirens. Where were the police, the fire engines and ambulances? Was nobody taking charge?

I woke to see faint diamonds of light slanting in over the counterpane. The hiss and gurgle of the radiator filling up was comforting warmth and I stayed hunkered down in bed, glad it was morning at last. My landlady, Frau Stürber, would be downstairs stoking the huge sooty boiler, sleeves rolled up on her ample arms and a streak of grime on her forehead. She was a cussed, cantankerous old soul, not a woman to cross, a widow with a married daughter who lived down south and never seemed to visit.

The sickening violence in the night sprang back into sharp focus like scenes from old wartime newsreels. It was twenty years since that terrible war, my whole lifetime, but the trauma and pain of loss were still branded on the nation's psyche. Mum had lost both her brothers; Dad's memories of Passchendaele never left him. Surely there couldn't be a chance of another war like that, it was too terrifying to imagine.

I sighed and looked round my room, which was narrow and scrimped as a scullery, on the top floor of a tall rickety old building that without the support of its neighbours would have tottered like a drunk. Right in town, though, and a just about affordable rent. Frau Stürber had the upper four floors; the ground and basement were a furniture shop.

A wood painting on the wall opposite my bed was of a child in a tight blue bodice with ballooning sleeves and a lace cap. It was trite and sweet, very different from the framed photograph above my bed that I longed to turn to the wall. That was of Frau Stürber with a group of women at some official event and they all had swastikas dangling on cords round their necks like necklaces.

I liked the small desk under the window with its flowered china inkwell, sloping green-leather surface and a top ledge just wide enough to hold my double silver photograph frame. Mum and Dad were on one side, Harry on the other and he was giving one of his special smiles that reached in deep.

I hadn't heard from him in weeks. Surely, he wasn't trying to cool things, not after Bavaria when we'd seemed so emotionally close. He'd been staying with his aunts, Frieda and Else, and would he really have asked me down for a few days if he cared so little as to stop writing? My stomach flipped, remembering sheltering from a storm in a hut high up on the Alpsplitze, Harry's mouth hard on mine...

Perhaps he was just very hectic with all the preparations for Uganda.

Suppose I chased after him, all the way out there? There must be jobs I could do with a music degree and fluent German, and my French wasn't so bad. Mum and Dad were open to new ideas and surely liberal-minded enough to let me go. My adrenaline was fizzing like fireworks. It was that or ending up stuck at home in Edinburgh with life passing me by.

Best to write ahead and tell Harry, not just arrive. He could have met a nurse, some girl on the voyage out, be engaged or even married already. I clutched at the slippery eiderdown, feeling physical pain at the very thought. But Harry was decent and conscientious; wouldn't he have written to tell me? Perhaps he had. Perhaps his next letter would send my world crashing down.

Did Harry ever think of himself as German? His parents had been, after all, before becoming naturalised British out in Malaya in 1911 where his father was doing forestry. They must be proud of Harry reading forestry at Oxford and joining the Forest Service like his father.

His parents had had to lie low in Austria during the war and still farmed there, in a remote bit of Carinthia called Eis. How safe was it for them in Austria now?

God, the time... Frau Stürber was a stickler for punctuality; we all had to be little church mice; quiet, polite and never a second late for breakfast.

I washed, flung on a cream shirt with ties, brown pleated skirt, lisle stockings, and shoehorned on my newly re-heeled brogues. Brushing my hair with a silver-backed brush – a present from Mum and Dad – brought back a sixth-form boyfriend's ham-fisted, backhanded compliment and I smiled to myself. 'You're like a beautiful thoroughbred mare, Laura,' he said, 'with your silky chestnut locks.'

He hadn't lasted; none of them had. There was only Harry now.

I threw my bed together, had a last look round and raced headlong down the three steep flights of stairs to Frau Stürber's small over-furnished dining room.

CHAPTER 2

The Aftermath

Breakfast never varied. Slices of *Schlackwurst*, *Liverwurst* and *Limburger* cheese, a dish of plum jam, neatly stacked slices of pumpernickel on a board, all spread out over a rust-spotted cream lace tablecloth. There were bowls of yogurt – Frau Stürber made her own – sour-tasting stuff, from a culture that multiplied daily, and she always doled out over-large portions, watching balefully like a yellow-eyed owl, challenging anyone to leave an unfinished bowl.

'*Guten Morgen*, Frau Stürber,' I mumbled, sitting down quickly at the heavy oak table and smiling at the two other lodgers. They were an ill-matched pair: Frau Metzger, a solid stony-faced matron and Herr Spreckels, a nervy, helpless kind of fellow of around thirty. He was thin as a stick of celery with a pronounced Adam's apple and a quality of poverty about him that touched my heart. His jacket was shiny, frayed shirt cuffs, too-short trousers, and the threadbare socks showing were no protection for the poor man's bony ankles.

No one ever said much at breakfast; the only sounds were a self-conscious clink of cutlery and the loud ticking of a wooden wall clock. But after all that had happened in the night, the silence felt shocking and wrong. I had to speak out.

'It was terrible, whatever was going on outside in the streets overnight, those harrowing screams, so heart-rending and unbearable to hear…'

I dried up, feeling the instant tension in the room. Frau Stürber had come in from the kitchen. She was leaning against the doorpost, bulky arms akimbo, chin raised, lips pressed together in a thin, tight line. 'Got what they deserved then, didn't they,' she sneered, with a hostile animal glint in her eye. 'Scum, they are, we don't want their kind round here. The Fuhrer will see 'em all off soon, you mark my words.'

'Pigs, the lot of them,' Frau Metzger agreed. 'Only fit for the slaughterhouse.' Had they no shred of compassion in their bones, bloodless hearts of stone?

Herr Spreckels had stopped spreading plum jam, quietly rested his knife, and was studying his plate with his head bent. Did he have some Jewish connection, a close friend, or possibly be Jewish himself? I hoped no one else had noticed his hands trembling before he slipped them down into his lap.

'Must go, got an early lecture,' I mumbled, pushing in my chair, feeling a mute, inchoate rage. Grabbing my coat from its hook in the dark hall and stumbling downstairs, I couldn't wait to be out of the door and into the bright light of day.

The postman was bicycling along the road. He was a good-natured, comfortable sort of fellow who always seemed to know how many letters he'd delivered for me. When there had been none earlier in the week, he'd said cheerily, 'Ach, wait till Sunday and I'll bring you something lovely!'

It was only Friday, but he dismounted and called over. 'I have a letter for you today, young lady. I hope it's one you want.'

I crossed the street with a quickening pulse; it wouldn't be from Harry. It would be a bill, a circular, a long, boring letter from an old school friend… The postman took his time sifting through the bundles before handing over an airmail envelope with Harry's writing and an Egyptian stamp. 'Yes, it is the one I want,' I said, smiling, my heart leaping with the feel of it in my hands.

The postman was staring at me with thoughtful eyes. 'Bad business last night,' he muttered, glancing quickly up and down the street. 'They're imported, you know, the SA, up from down south.'

He touched his cap, remounted and bicycled on. He was a decent man, embarrassed and anxious to reassure me that the people of Hamburg weren't like that, but Frau Stürber and Frau Metzger were, and they weren't lone voices.

It was a milder day after a recent icy spell, but I still shivered in my coat, trying to be braced for all the awful devastation there must be to see ahead.

The ground-floor furniture shop's windows were intact. The bank next door was fine too, but an acrid smell like burnt-off paint filled the air and further down the street the teenage boy from the fabric shop was sweeping up piles of shattered glass. He had on a thin sleeveless pullover and was pushing the broom in a desultory, despairing way. Coming closer, I saw him lean his head down to the broom handle and his shoulders begin to shake.

Seeing the shopfront, my hand went to my mouth. The window was one great jagged hole, the few shards of glass still clinging looked like stalactites or shark's teeth and the interior was a horrifying sight; the counter overturned, chairs smashed, bales of cloth all blackened and charred. The boy's poor mother was sitting on a couple of steps to an upper level with her arms crossed, hugging herself, and she was quietly keening, rocking from side to side.

'The SS took my father last night,' the boy said, following my eyes. 'I don't think he can still be alive after what they did to him, he has a weak heart.'

'I'm most terribly sorry. If there's anything I can do…'

'Don't get involved. It only draws attention. No one can help us.' He brushed over his eyes with an arm and lowered his head to the broom handle again.

It was wretchedly frustrating to feel so powerless. But what help or comfort could I give? What use were words?

Carrying on, I caught up with a small crowd of people walking the same way, and a thin plume of smoke in the distance seemed to be where they were headed. It had to come from the Bomplatz Synagogue, which I passed every day.

The immense, handsome building was still standing with its gracious dome intact, but it was a gouged-out shell, the interior a mountain of rubble. The once magnificent carved doors were charcoal, all the fine woodwork charred or burnt down, and the jewel-coloured stained-glass windows that had glowed so vividly in sun or rain lay in myriad splinters on the ground. Pale wafts of sunlight filtering in through all the smoke and dust looked like wisps of cloud.

Some in the crowd were hurling bits of brick and stones, mothers yelling at their kids not to pick up any glittering shards while brown-shirted SA soldiers stood about looking on with hard, satisfied faces. Three elderly Jews scrambling in over the rubble, probably desperate to save any last religious treasures, caught the soldiers' eye and sensing blood like a pack of wolves, they picked up bricks and took aim. Someone yelled out, 'Filthy Jews!' and there was a rush to join in.

A few people keeping well back, as I was, looked uncomfortable and two firefighters standing by their parked fire engine were staring at the ground. When a white-haired man went to speak to them, I edged closer, trying to listen in.

'We were told not to use any water, only watch for stray sparks reaching neighbouring buildings,' one of the firemen explained. Who had given those orders? Their boss at the fire station? Someone higher up the chain?

'It feels wrong to be standing by while the House of Prayer burns,' the other firefighter muttered, looking warily around. 'I mean, whose turn will it be next? Will the same thing happen to our Protestant and Catholic churches?'

The two men stiffened and snapped their heels to attention as a group of marshals arrived, but they were after the elderly Jews, quickly rounding them up and prising the blackened silver from their wizened old hands.

Seeing the marshals kick the poor Jews' legs forward, marching them away, seemed unbelievably cruel. What evil had Hitler unleashed? What hope for Germany when men in authority turned into rabid dogs?

I half ran the whole way down Mittleweg to the upstairs overspill restaurant room where my tutor, Frau Blohm, held her lectures. The room could hardly ever have been used, the restaurant was so uninvitingly gloomy, smelly and cavernous.

I was doing a course on Rudolf Steiner. Hitler, who didn't approve of him, had recently banned all Steiner schools and centres of medicine, so Frau Blohm's lectures were now strictly illegal. I was keeping that from my parents, enjoying the frisson of clandestine studies and keen to finish the course.

I was early, even with the wretched detour, and only Frau Blohm and one other student were there. I hung up my coat, keeping hold of Harry's letter, and said my good mornings, but the student, Gertrud, didn't look up from her book. We were a friendly class, Bertha and Anna my special friends, but Gertrud, who was overweight and moody, never mixed in.

I went to a table at the back and had my finger under the airmail flap when there was an influx of students and the moment was gone. Frau Blohm waited patiently for everyone to be seated. She was impassive and unreachable in class, a slim, sallow-skinned woman with short dark hair, but having got to know her a little, I'd seen her kindness and sensed she had inner strength.

'A word about the distressing events of last night,' she began. 'We will have the morning session, but then please disburse quickly and go straight home. There is always a possibility of more violence. And you would be wise to avoid getting into discussions or writing of these events to relatives or friends. Letters are sometimes censored, I believe. However, I'm sure things will soon be back to normal and we will resume our classes as usual after the weekend.'

Gertrud raised a hand and stood up, brushing back a strand of lank brown hair. 'Aren't you proud of our fine young soldiers, Frau Blohm?' She was flushed and expectant, looking round for approval, though no one reacted at all.

'My feelings are of no consequence, Gertrud. We are here to study Rudolf Steiner's anthroposophical theories, and I would prefer that we stay wholly focused on our work. Today, we shall discuss the clarity necessary for an exact knowledge of natural science; concentration and meditation, the essential disciplines needed if we are to have any concept of the spiritual…'

Gertrud looked unbowed. Odd that she was on the course at all, given Hitler's disapproval of Steiner, but perhaps her parents were followers. Who knew?

I felt claustrophobic, longing for the morning to end, to be back in my room, despite having to see Frau Stürber, and able to read Harry's letter at last.

As we went for our coats Bertha slipped her hand into mine. 'Can you come home with me now we've got a free afternoon? My parents are at work and I so hate an empty house. Oh, do say yes! We can have a snack, play some duets…' I had to go, she was looking so hopeful with her sweet heart-shaped face and eyebrows that flew almost to her hairline. Bertha's little rosebud mouth was often primly pursed, but not now.

'Love to!' I said, and squeezed her hand.

We set off to get the tram. I'd been home with her before. She lived in a residential area, a ground and first-floor maisonette with a front garden laid to paving. It was a modern and light with feathery, ferny pot plants, slightly lacking paintings and colour, but very different from the creaky dark of my centuries-old lodgings in town.

We didn't speak as the tram trundled past the many shattered shop windows. People were loitering, looking tempted to do a bit of looting. The city was crawling with police and soldiers, but they didn't seem to give a damn.

There was a tram stop outside the cobbler's shop and it was like looking into a gaping wound, the sight of it broke my heart. His tiny shop had been torched, smashed, all the shoes in for mending, the new leather soles, jars of adhesive, the old Jew's ancient anvil and last, everything ruined, heaped in a pile, even the charred remains of the shop's signboard, *O.J. Goldstein Schuhreparaturen*, and a tin of red paint chucked up over the lot. There was no sign of that proud, defiant good man. Was he lying in an alley with his head bashed in, hunted down and left for dead? He'd have nothing now, no livelihood, no life, even if he'd survived.

My fists were clenched, nails biting into palms with the effort of containing my emotions. Bertha and I walked from her tram stop in silence, but once inside the apartment, the dam broke and I had to let rip.

'What happened last night was unspeakable, horrific, and nothing, nothing, was being done to stop it! What's happening to this country, Bertha?'

'You must have been kept awake half the night, right there in town. We only heard about it on the wireless this morning.'

Was I hearing right? How could she sound so callously disinterested? Was it worry about the upstairs neighbours? There'd been no open window, no signs of life. 'Our maid goes home at lunchtime on weekdays,' Bertha said, 'but we can hunt about in the kitchen. There's pumpernickel and cream cheese and half an apple strudel. Not much, I'm afraid.'

15

'Thanks, it's plenty.' I was struggling to stay civil. We shared a love of music and Bertha did seem quite agonised; anxiety was written all over her face. Perhaps there was more to it than simply a cold hatred of Jews.

We managed. Discussed what to play, settled on some Bach arias, but something had to give, I couldn't just let things lie.

'Surely it was the most mind-numbing shock, though, hearing about it all on the morning news? You and your parents must have been truly appalled.'

I'd met Bertha's parents. Her photographer father had a military bearing and spoke in staccato barks, but he wasn't in the army, the police or government, wouldn't he be more likely to have liberal views? Her mother, mild-mannered and a bit mousy, gave the impression of having few opinions of her own or any that she felt able or inclined to share.

'My parents don't care much for Jews, actually,' Bertha murmured, sounding acutely pained, her flyaway eyebrows giving an unfortunate look of astonishment.

'But they can't possibly condone such vicious, violent evil acts, can they?'

'Look, I understand how you feel, I didn't like what we saw in town either, but it's best we don't talk about it, really…' Her eyes were full of pleading; she was in no doubt of my feelings, and clearly struggling with her own.

We sat at the piano, which was perfectly tuned, but even the glory of the Bach arias and the joy of singing in harmony, couldn't lessen the strain.

The maid had returned from her lunchtime break and brought in tea and cherry cookies. 'Will Harry be in Uganda by now?' Bertha asked, searching for safer ground.

'I should think he's about mid-voyage,' I said, biting into a rather soggy biscuit, sensing that without knowing him, Bertha wasn't especially interested. 'I had a letter from him this morning, actually. Saving it up for later! How about you? How are things with Hans?'

'I'd love some advice,' she said eagerly. 'I think he's keen, but it's so hard to be sure. We've been to concerts and had walks together, but he never opens up. I don't know whether it's shyness and I should be forward and encouraging, or whether he's just very serious-natured and that would be a mistake.'

'Gosh, I do see it's a bit tricky. He's taking his accountancy exams soon, isn't he? Couldn't you ask him questions, like whether it's going to be his future career? You could ask about his long-term ambitions and interests, anything to help give you a clue as to his feelings and character.' Hans struck me as formal and boring, but he didn't to Bertha, and wasn't that all that mattered?

I left soon afterwards, keen to get back in daylight and all the more impatient to be alone with Harry's letter. I felt confident of his character but, like Bertha, longed to know how much he really cared.

CHAPTER 3

The Journey Home

My dearest Laura,

I'm writing this at sea and hoping to post it in Port Said, so goodness knows when it will reach you. There's an awful lot to tell and of course answer from your lovely mail, which caught up with me when on a busy round of goodbyes. I'd have written sooner otherwise, so forgive me, it's been a hectic time.

I was very moved, reading of your unhappiness when we parted and the tears streaming down your face. It was hard saying goodbye, wasn't it, after our lovely time together, but how could you have thought you were intruding on my "precious little time" with the aunts! I was still hoping to be able to come to Hamburg then, and now, alas, we have all this distance between us. Perhaps we'll find a way to meet, you never know, though I'm unlikely to get any leave for a year or two.

We've had ten days at sea and are halfway to Africa. I'm enjoying the voyage, feel a little as if I've been blindfolded and spun round several times, though, quite without my bearings, but expect Port Said will shake the feeling out of me with all the new sights, sounds and smells. From there, we go on to Port Sudan, Aden and Mombasa.

I feel lucky to be travelling first class on my first appointment. There are a hundred and twenty of us, mostly civil servants from Kenya, Tanganyika and Uganda and they're good company. Most love the colonies and their work and are eager to be back, although one or two make resigned remarks like, 'Another two tours and we can retire and go home for good.' What a tragic life!

A few of us are learning Swahili and one of the old hands offered to give us classes, which is a great help. He's even marking our homework. Another bit of luck, there's a forest officer from Tanganyika on board who's given me wonderful advice, and his wife has even promised to take me shopping in Mombasa. She's going to help with stocks for a primitive household in the Budongo. Help I certainly need!

Life on board is very pleasant, time passes quickly. We play the usual deck games and change for dinner. Last evening, mangoes were on the dessert menu and the tall, very dignified-looking waiter said, 'Well, Sir, if you've never eaten a mango before, I suggest you take it to the cabin and try first in your bath!'

We had a fancy-dress ball one night and a kind elderly lady dressed me up as a Chinaman. There are a few unattached girls, nurses mostly, so I have dancing partners and we enjoy each other's company, but I keep wishing it was you in my arms on the dance floor.

Lord and Lady Baden-Powell are on board, travelling to Kenya. I was out on deck with them as we went through the Straits of Messina and Lord Baden-Powell turned to me with a twinkle in his eye.

'I know this coast on either side very well,' he said, 'spent quite a bit of time here, way back, studying and drawing butterflies. The local military were very suspicious, as there were fortifications to guard the Straits, but I'd swotted up on all the local species and they couldn't question my lepidopterist credentials. What they failed to notice, however, was that the patterns on some of my butterflies' wings exactly matched the outlines of the fortifications!' Baden-Powell grinned. 'That was in my very early days in intelligence, no longer a secret, as it was at the time.'

I must close now and go to my Swahili lesson, but I worry about you, dear one. We only have the occasional bulletin, but what's happening in Germany sounds very troubling. I will write more and send my next letter to Scotland, since you must be nearly home for Christmas by now.

Write very soon. I miss you and long to see you again.

Your loving Harry

I gazed out of the train window. I was on my way home for Christmas. Harry seemed excited about Uganda, unfazed at the thought of coping alone in a remote bungalow in the heart of the Budongo Forest. I felt such a deep ache, yearning to be there with him, sharing and easing his load. To have the thrill of travel, see East Africa and realise that secret dream, what joy it would be. My married friend Irene, who now lived in Tanganyika, said that Uganda was a bit provincial and Kenya was the place to be, it had so many glamorous British settlers.

But it didn't have Harry.

The times I'd read his letter I could have recited it. It was chatty, interesting, solicitous, but '*Perhaps we'll find a way to meet*' sounded hardly more than a pleasantry. If only he knew the strength of my feelings, how I lay awake at night with my heart feeling as battered as a carpet against a wall. I sighed and tucked the letter into one of the hidey-holes in my smart new tan leather handbag, bought specially for the journey home. It had a lovely rich redolence and would have looked quite the part in Bond Street.

The fields and dykes and windmills of Holland were flashing by; tidy, peaceful and bland as the new white bread that was all the rage with the Dutch. Anna, my other good Hamburg friend, often stayed with her grandparents in Holland and had told me that. The countryside looked calm and unchallenging after Germany's industrial north – Bremen and the swampy Weser River, the smelly coal mines of Borken belching out thick yellow smoke. Further south, there'd been quaint, delightful turreted villages and immense stretches of dark forest that brought waves of nostalgia for Bavaria and Harry.

Thank God, we were through the border now with its thicket of soldiers and station guards. Their treatment of a group of Jewish children from Berlin had been shocking. Slapping them about, chanting the new Nazi edict, "All Jews barred from using any tram, station or port", with snarling satisfaction. The kids were due to board the same train and to everyone's relief, the Quakers chaperoning them had had the relevant papers. They'd stood their ground and won through.

The Dutch cheered the children at every station, shouting hurrahs, handing out steaming food, and the brightening of those sad little faces was a joy.

A few of the kids were in my carriage, and the small girl beside me with fat dark pigtails held by rubber bands, was writing a letter on her knee. It was hard not to glance down and read over her shoulder.

'… *We are received everywhere in Holland with joyful hellos, it is so comradely and nice, and the ladies have handed out hot meals, French beans and beef. And we've been given*

21

sodas, a bar of chocolate and apple for each …Forgive the bad writing, but the train is jolting so much. Love and ten thousand kisses…'

At the Hook of Holland, the children were huddled on the quayside in the drizzly mist, tearful, staring up miserably at the vast bulk of the ferry, *The Amsterdam,* with her towering Devon-cream and black funnels. They were leaving everything familiar, the only life they knew, how easily would they settle in?

I was sharing a cabin. It was Hobson's choice who it would be with and once on board, I went straight to find the cabin, crossing fingers for someone friendly and nice. Being first there gave me a chance to bag the upper bunk, though both had short black velvet curtains to draw round for extra privacy.

The cabin door swung open and my heart sank. The woman standing there was the size of a tank, nip and tuck whether she'd even get through the door. Perhaps, she'd be enormously nice, I thought dubiously, giving her my best smile.

'Hello, I'm Laura Jameson.'

'Viola Maddox, pleased to meet you. Mind if I take the lower bunk?' She'd never have made it up top. 'Been tutoring a little brat in Rotterdam.' She continued in a deep bass voice. 'English mother, Dutch pa.' Miss Maddox pushed a tiny pair of steel-rimmed spectacles further up her nose. 'Ah, well, it's off back to my lodgings in Neasden now to sit out Christmas.'

Had the poor woman no family? I felt a lurch of sympathy, aching to be home as I was, being hugged by the family and seeing Mum and Dad's new house. It was modern and a bit further out, but still in easy reach of Edinburgh.

Miss Maddox opened her battered suitcase and began to undress. The air in the cabin became intolerable, thick with the odour of stale talcum powder, and the ship was beginning to roll. 'I'll just go up on deck for a bit,' I said, feeling claustrophobic and queasy, grabbing my handbag and edging past. 'Sleep well. I'll try not to disturb you later.'

There was hardly a soul out on deck. A man in an oilskin and sou'wester was striding the boards, and two of the older Jewish boys were leaning over the rail staring out to sea. I leaned on the rail further down, glad of the whip of wind and squally rain, enjoying the surging waves that looked pewter in the wash of light from the ship, black and frothy as a pint of Guinness in the distant dark.

Would there be a letter from Harry waiting at home? I took his photograph out of my bag. It was just a small faded square and the light minimal from the iron-encased lantern on deck, but I knew the honey-brownness of his eyes, the tawny lights in his unruly hair. Thick eyebrows, straight nose and a firm well-shaped mouth that was unquestionably male. He had a way of cocking his head sideways and rubbing behind his ear. Was that the kind of habit that began to irritate in later marriage? I was willing to take the chance.

Staring at his photo brought quivery sensations of urgency like a feather trailing the skin, feelings that were hard to handle. It brought back sitting in an Edinburgh café with my sister, Lil, listening to two pinch-faced women having a bitch. 'She's such a hussy, that one!' the woman in a maroon hat had sneered. 'Make-up thick as paint, eyes for every man in the street. Disgusting, she's got no shame.'

'Oversexed,' her friend had said succinctly, slurping her tea.

Could I be "oversexed" too? A girl at school had once brought in a health manual with pictures of a naked man and woman standing face to face; the man's penis was sticking out and we'd giggled, speculating on how it could possibly *fit*. One girl said the very thought of it made her insides crawl, but I'd been more fascinated than shocked. I knew about boys, had bathed my younger brother Jack when he was little and accidentally burst in on Dick, the elder one, in the bathroom and seen him with an erection, the thing sticking way out in front, stiff as a splint. Dick had spun away, blushing a deep cochineal red, hissing at me to get out. He hadn't been able to look me in the eye for days afterwards.

I went back to the smelly airless cabin. Miss Maddox was asleep, snoring lightly, and didn't stir as I climbed up into the top bunk. I lay awake for a long time, tense and uncertain, with wishful thoughts of Harry and Africa filling my head. Not long now, nearly home, and he'd said he would write.

CHAPTER 4

Christmas in Edinburgh

Dad was on the platform, anxiously scanning the train. 'Daddy, Dad!' I yelled from the train door, jumping down, quickly tipping the steward bringing my case and racing headlong into Dad's arms. It was such emotional heaven, burying my face in his greatcoat, drinking in the ferny, tweedy smell of him, the lingering waft of pipe tobacco and coal dust. 'Oh, Dad, I've missed you so much!'

He beamed. 'Welcome home! You must be worn out from the journey, but you had a good lunch? The food on the *Scotsman* is usually top-notch.'

'Lunch was fine! Can't wait to see everyone and the new house, Dad. Sad Dick's in Canada. It'll be a great experience, working in a Newfoundland hospital, but rather him than me with those bitter winters of theirs, even worse than here.'

'We must get a porter,' Dad said, looking round. No Mum at the station, which hurt. She was always off somewhere, so obsessed with her work. I'd miss Dick over Christmas, but Jack and Lil would be home. Jack was only fifteen, but we were very close while Lil and I had our differences. She was ahead of me in so many ways, a year younger, doing medicine at Cambridge and having a ball. My future was all about getting to Africa and Harry, just a blur of uncertainty.

It was a pitch-black winter's night, our breath steaming. Hanging onto Dad's arm going to the car park, my fingers were numb. 'The new house is much smaller and modern, of course,' he said, 'but it's lovely countryside round about. The garden slopes down to the Union Canal towpath and you should be able to go skating if this hard frost holds.' He sounded a little on the defensive, but after living in the heart of Edinburgh, must be finding it hard to adjust.

I squeezed his arm. 'I'm going to love it, Dad! It's near where Granny and Gramps lived, isn't it, and people round there were very friendly. I loved all the competitions they had, like whose haystack had the best tassel on top!'

The porter lifted my suitcase into the boot of the old Hillman Minx and left looking pleased with his tip. The car wouldn't start. The engine kept turning over. 'Old girl's past her best, like me,' Dad said dryly, but she finally spluttered into life. 'Mum's at a psychoanalysis conference in Oxford. She's dying to see you, Fudge, but can't be back till tomorrow.' He glanced, looking anxious. 'Her work is important, you know, she's even doing a little broadcasting these days.'

Shouldn't she be thinking more of him for a change, and less about her career? I minded how neglected he was. We were very close, Dad the only one who still called me Fudge. His own nickname, Buffy, was a hangover from his army days that had stuck fast; did anyone even know his name was Andrew now?

His job at the Edinburgh College of Art was ill paid but seemed to interest and absorb him. It was wonderful how he'd settled into it uncomplainingly, after India where he'd had rank and position and led a privileged life.

'I'm very proud of Mum,' he said, breaking into my thoughts.

'It's a great thing, women going into medicine. There'll be a desperate need for doctors soon, the way things are going.'

'You don't actually think there could be another war?'

''Fraid so, Fudge. I can't really see how it can be avoided. People are buying gas masks and even camp beds to be ready to take in evacuees.'

Had Mum been trying to blot out the pain of the last war, throwing herself into a career? Losing one brother at Verdun and the other at Amiens must have been heartbreaking, I should try to be more understanding. 'There was no talk of war in Hamburg, Dad. No shortages, no anti-British feeling. The treatment of Jews is horrific, Kristallnacht will be branded on my mind forever more, but my Hamburg friends are good and kind, and really make me feel at home.'

True, but I was paving the way for my return.

'Don't be so naïve, Fudge. It's Hitler, not the German people, you need to worry about.' That was annoyingly patronising, but he was understandably concerned. Dad had aged, his slightly protuberant, cornflower blue eyes looked tired and watery, the creases in his face deeper and there were tiny red thread veins in his cheeks, but the warmth of his humanity shone through like the evening star. 'Here we are,' he said, turning up a steep lane and in through an open white gate, 'so wonderful to have you home.'

Out of the car the air didn't feel quite as cold, almost as if it was about to snow. It had been a bleak heavy miserable day the sky entirely clothed in clouds, as if to show even a chink of blue would have been improper.

We went in through a small chilly outer lobby untidy with boots and umbrellas and hung up our coats. The hall was warmer and Lil and Jack were there with big welcoming grins on their faces. 'Give us a hug then!' Jack said, open-armed.

'Goodness, how you've shot up,' I laughed, standing back. 'You must have grown at least an inch a month!' He was lanky, with our

Mum's dark hair, sweet-natured and sensitive. He'd once confessed to a terror of having to go to war. 'I could never kill a man, even if it meant facing a firing line…' Thank God he was only fifteen.

'I suppose you're bilingual now,' Lil said, dryly as we parted from a hug.

'Well, I can read my Goethe in the lingo, but still think in English so not really.' It felt best to play it down; we were always getting at each other.

'Any mail for me, by the way?' I looked over to the refectory table that had been in the Edinburgh house; it looked good in a modern hall, still with our old blue leather visitor's book, the telephone and a big brass bell.

'Nothing I haven't posted on,' Dad said, raising an eyebrow, sussing me out. 'Can you get in Laura's case, Jack, and show her up to her room? I'll mix us a welcome-home cocktail then, warming whisky and ginger, I think.'

'Sounds good!' Any drink that wasn't neat spirits was a cocktail to Dad.

Jack led the way down a wide first-floor passage. 'Mum says pastels are all the rage,' he said, opening the last door. The room smelled of fresh paint, the colour on the walls not bad, a kind of pale seashell pink. I wasn't mad about a new walnut dressing table with a tall mirror, but pleased to see my old patchwork bedcover and pine desk. 'Now, come see the bathroom, it's all black and white tiles, black bath panels, very geometric and modern.'

Hardly modern with the laundry drying on an overhead pulley, how life had changed. In India, we'd had *ayahs* and *dhobies* and the washing always whisked out of sight. Crisply uniformed *sepoys* had snapped their heels and stood smartly to attention. I'd been eight years old when we left, but could vividly remember the heady scents, cumin, cardamom and cloves, the carmine reds and hot yellows of tropical plants, wandering cows, all the dirt and dung. India had felt like a second skin. We'd come home to a tall, dark house in Edinburgh with one young maid and a cook, Mrs Hodges, who was a gem.

It was good to be back. Dad's cocktail burned as it went down and Max, his beloved cocker spaniel, made a satisfying fuss of me. Tabitha stayed tight-curled in a fireside armchair, her head buried under a protective paw, and didn't trouble to stir. The sitting room looked lived in with a sofa table covered in newspapers and books. There were bookcases, royal blue lamp bases and parchment shades, loose-covered armchairs on either side of a modern pine mantelpiece. And my Challon baby grand piano was there too, which gladdened my heart.

'Have you had to find a new cook, Dad?' I asked. 'You must really miss Mrs Hodges, but I suppose it's a bit far out for her now. Can I help with supper?'

'Don't be daft, you can't cook for toffee.' Lil grimaced. 'Try living in digs like me. Anyway, supper's done. It's in the oven keeping warm.'

Jack said, 'Mrs Hodges still comes. She stays till three and leaves supper ready. It's chicken, ham and leek pie tonight, which she says is one of your favourites.'

'Dear Mrs Hodges, she never lets us down.' Dad smiled fondly. 'There's heavy snow forecast, so she's gone to her sister who lives in the next village.'

The postman would never make it…

Lil was looking irritatingly glamorous. 'All this make-up, thick mascara, scarlet lips, and you've had a perm! Not thinking of chucking in medicine and going on the stage, by any chance?'

'Oh, do shut up, you should wear a bit more makeup yourself with all the Christmas parties ahead – which I'm going to have to miss.'

'Lil and I are off skiing,' Jack explained, looking embarrassed, 'leaving early on Christmas Day, but at least we'll have Christmas Eve all together.'

He was obviously thrilled to be going while sweetly conscious of how miffed I'd feel. He was right; no letter from Harry and now being in for a lonely time. 'Where are you two off to then? Switzerland?'

'Yes, Unterwasser. Our railway tickets would make you laugh, they're covered in adverts for things like Carter's Little Liver Pills.'

The snow was over a foot deep in the morning. I dressed in a heavy tweed skirt and Fair Isle jumper and went downstairs with my head drooping like a wilting rose, sure there'd be no post for days.

Mrs Hodges was stirring a pan on the new electric stove, unaware of me at the kitchen door. 'How do you like this swish new Hotpoint kitchen then, Mrs Hodges?'

She jumped and turned, a great big grin breaking out on her creased, chunky old face. 'Oh, Miss Laura! My, you do look bonnie, and away so long in *that place*.' Resting her spoon, she came hurrying over and took both of my hands. 'It's just grand to have you back safe and sound. I wouldn't trust that Mr Hitler as far as I could throw 'im.' She pursed puckered lips, giving small sideways shakes of her head as if to confirm his badness.

The grooves in her plump, kindly face were as deep as plough tracks, iron-grey hair permed to a frazzle unlike Lil's soft curls, but no one had a bigger heart than Mrs Hodges. 'Mustn't let the porridge catch,' she said, returning to the stove. 'I'll get used to an electric kitchen, what all the knobs do, and the new refrigerator is very fine, but what if there was a power cut? I don't know. Breakfast is nigh on ready, dear. I expect Miss Lillian is sleeping in, but can you call to your father and Mr Jack? They're out shovelling away the snow.' Her eyes went to the window. 'Ah, here's the postman now. He'll be glad of the cleared path.'

I looked out with a quickening pulse. His trousers were tucked into his boots, snow clinging right up to their rim. He handed

Buffy a slim bundle, touched his uniform cap and trudged off looking stalwart, if cold.

'You're popular today, Fudge,' Dad said, coming in with Jack, their breath steaming and in stockinged feet. 'Two from Germany and a letter with an East African stamp, which I suspect is the one you're hoping for.'

'I like the stamp,' said Jack, 'very jolly with the lion and palms. Isn't it strange seeing the new King's head on the stamps now, he does look young!' The words, *Kenya, Uganda and Tanganyika* encircled an oval profile of the King.

I wanted to hear all about Uganda and the Forest, but from the Mombasa postmark Harry had yet to get there. Bertha had written, and the other letter from Germany was from Frau Blohm.

'Breakfast,' said Dad firmly, 'you can read those later.'

A fire was laid in the sitting room, no one about, and lighting it, watching the kindling flare, I put on some coal and went to an armchair with jangling anticipation. I saved Harry's letter till last. Bertha's was all about Hans, who was still being un-communicative, but she lived in hope with all the festivities. Frau Blohm sent Christmas greetings, but her letter was mainly to forward one that my university tutor had sent to Hamburg.

He said an American mission school in Cairo was looking for a female graduate to teach music and languages, if that was of any interest. I would be required to pay my own passage, but it was a live-in post, to begin in October 1939.

My pulse wouldn't slow down. Cairo was over halfway, the same continent… Would Mum and Dad help out with the voyage? I could go third class.

The school was bound to have found someone else by now. I forced down my hopes and opened Harry's letter, with my pulse beating just as fast.

He was still very full of the voyage out.

…At Aden, we leaned over the rail and dropped pennies into the murky dockside waters and watched all the lithe little Arab boys dive down into the depths to retrieve them. They darted about underwater like shoals of little brown fishes and found every single one thrown!

Mombasa is teeming, such a fascinating, stimulating place, despite the steamy heat and stench. I love the wobbling, clattering carts (think rag and bone men) piled high with pineapples, mangos, pomegranates, guavas, every exotic fruit you could name. The city pulses with life. Narrow streets of rundown buildings, Arab in style, overhung with decorative wrought iron balconies and stupendously handsome carved doors…

He sent Christmas wishes and had enclosed a colour picture of Mount Kenya, with such a glorious richness of light and shade that it looked like it was winter, summer and autumn on the mountain, all at the same time. Little about missing me, which was desperately deflating, though his distress at my returning to Hamburg was a small comfort. Kristallnacht was only the tip of the iceberg, he said. There was sure to be censorship soon.

…Perhaps we should have a code for Hitler, something like "Mr Harvey and his team". We can't have our letters censored! Not long now till I'm in the Budongo and hopefully finding a letter from you waiting at the post office there.

He ended with love and a row of kisses. It wasn't enough. I wanted more.

I decided to wait till Jack and Lil had gone skiing before bringing up Cairo. But what chance of the job still being available, of even getting there with all the depressing talk of war? And if it actually happened? Dick joining up and the daily dreaded fear of a telegram, brave young pilots shot down. Bertha and Anna would be on the other side, unable to write. How many of us on either side would even survive?

It could be a short, sharp war and the mission school job still be on offer. Everything was possible; there had to be a way. Cairo was a stepping stone to Uganda and if you wanted something badly enough, you just had to persevere.

CHAPTER 5

Buffy and Edith

Buffy chucked *The Scotsman* back onto the sofa table. It was hard to concentrate with all the bickering going on, Laura and Lil jabbing away at each other like a pair of boxers. He looked out through the French doors at the snowy garden, half listening, hoping all his new planting would survive.

'How can you not believe, Lil! I mean, how can your life have any meaning? Believing in the soul is what keeps me going.'

'Well, it doesn't me. The concept of the threefold being leaves me cold, I don't need a soul and spirit to keep me pure. I know my right from wrong and believe in the end we simply peg out and die. And you can bet all those people in church every Sunday go out of sheer habit. They sit there feeling smugly virtuous, sneering at some hideous hat two pews down, thinking of their roast beef lunch waiting at home and not hearing a word of the sermon.'

'I don't see how you can possibly feel anything *profound* without the need of a beyond,' Laura said, ignoring the belief or otherwise of Sunday churchgoers. She sighed. 'Suppose I'll just have to accept having nephews and nieces who've never even heard of the soul.'

'Why do you have to be so *intense* the whole time? And just for the record I don't plan on having children for years. My career and partying come first, making the most of life. You need to go to a few parties yourself, Laura, have a few hot dates and be a bit less boringly serious.'

'Well, just for the record, I have got a date. Hamish Drinkwater is taking me to the Campbells' Christmas party.'

Buffy was pleased to hear that. He worried about Laura mooning after this Harry Werner, whom she hardly really knew.

'You do always have to have the last word,' Lil said cheerfully. 'The Campbells give great parties, it should be fun. Hamish has plumped out a bit, but he's no bad dancer. She held up the percolator. 'Any more? How about you, Dad? Coffee?'

Buffy shook his head. The truth was, Lillian had her life all worked out. She partied into the night but always did well in exams. He would have liked her to believe in the soul, but she was resilient and if life dealt her a few knocks, she'd soon bounce back, he felt sure.

Laura, for all her steely determination and keenness to travel, was an innocent, too trusting by half, vulnerable and insecure. She was passionate about her music, enjoyed singing and dancing, but was completely dead set on this man. Buffy trusted her and was sure Werner's aunts would have been good chaperones, but Laura clearly felt herself to be in love and he didn't want her hurt.

She was still chipping away at Lil. 'You'll marry one of your Cambridge doctors-to-be, have kids before you know it, be talking gallbladders and little Tommy's tonsils over candle-lit suppers, but *I* at least know you've got a soul.'

'And you'll pop off to Africa and marry your Harry,' Lillian laughed, sensibly not rising to the bait. 'You'll have loads of babies, live in a mud hut and fight off all those tigers and baboons.'

'Little chance,' Laura muttered, 'even without a war.'

Buffy resisted mentioning the absence of tigers in Africa. 'I think that's Mum calling you, Laura,' he said, 'And, Lil, you need to round up Jack if we're going.'

He was taking Lil and Jack into town for some last-minute shopping and still had to buy a few presents himself. Edith always had her Christmas shopping done by early November, all beautifully wrapped and stored on top of the wardrobe. She did it with a slight air of martyrdom, reminding him, not very subtly, that it was on top of a very demanding job. Buffy was proud of her medical career, never complained, but resented being made to feel inadequate. He had a job too.

He appreciated Laura going into bat for him, but with she and her mother both such strong characters it didn't help much. Edith was off to London again soon too, right after Hogmanay.

He took the coffee tray out to the kitchen and found Mrs Hodges screwing the mincer onto the worktop. 'Afraid it's only shepherd's pie tonight, Mr Jameson.'

'Nothing nicer. We'll be eating ourselves into the ground in three days' time.'

*

Edith was sitting at her dressing table staring into the mirror. Her lips had got thinner; it was distressing, the business of ageing, deep lines above the lips and bracketing her mouth that drew the eye. Catching sight of Laura in the mirror then she felt embarrassed to be caught peering so intently at her own reflection.

'Did you want me, Mum?'

'Yes, sorry to drag you upstairs.' Edith couldn't help a smile, Laura was looking so suspicious and guarded. 'I thought as you're not going into town and with all the Christmas parties coming up – Hamish was asking when you're back – we should possibly talk clothes.'

'He's called already. I've agreed to go to the Campbells' party with him.'

'Actually,' Laura said, coming more into the room, 'I'm rather regretting it. Lil says he's put on weight and he's so koala bearish with those large brown eyes.'

'Don't be hard on him! He's bright and decent, he'll be a good lawyer, and he's not in the least overweight.' Edith sighed. 'It's awful to think of young men like Hamish with their whole lives ahead of them joining up if there's to be a war.

'Anyway, these parties. There's the Campbells' do, the usual highland reels at the Fosters', the Greys have asked us over… Have you got anything to wear?'

'Not much, there was so little room in my case with all the presents.'

'I wondered if you'd like to try on one or two things of mine. You'd look lovely in that appliquéd velvet jacket I've put on the bed. The holly green would echo your eyes, and you'd be glad of the warmth at the Greys'. I've died of cold in that house, nowhere chillier than that vast great dining room of theirs with the stag heads. It's like dining on a station platform in a January gale.'

'Won't you want to wear the jacket yourself? It suits you very well.'

'Absolutely not, it's far too tight under the arms now.' At least Laura hadn't flown off. It was difficult enough to reach her at the best of times, and party frocks hadn't seemed a likely medium. 'There's a mauve chiffon cocktail dress that would suit you too, and what about that beaded ruby shift?'

Laura eyed it in a way that was difficult to read. 'I'll try that on just for fun, but wouldn't I look a bit of a… hussy in it?'

'I shouldn't say so.' Edith laughed. 'I used to wear it to parties both in London and Edinburgh in my day.'

It felt best not to make encouraging remarks when Laura held up the slinky number to the mirror and slipped out of her skirt and jumper. Seeing her shimmy into the glittering tube, Edith felt a flicker of envy, wistful memories of her own partying days.

Laura didn't need any perm or make-up; with her creamy skin and burnished hair, she looked ravishing just as she was. She had shapely bosoms too, shown to advantage peeking out of the scooped neckline.

'You look beautiful in that, elegant with just a touch of the hussy…'

'Mum! Anyway, it's so skin tight, no good for eightsome reels. I'd probably split it right up the seams.'

'But you could do reels in this,' Edith said, taking a midnight blue satin cocktail dress with padded shoulders out of the wardrobe. It was figure-hugging down to the lower hip before flouncing out in chiffon layers. 'It's far too tight on me these days and just the job for Hogmanay.'

It fitted perfectly and Edith felt a considerable sense of achievement. Wry as well when Laura accepted both dresses and the velvet jacket and, aware of her own contrariness, grinned in a self-deprecating way as she went to hang them up.

Downstairs, Edith stared out from the sitting-room French windows. There'd been a hard, overnight frost; the snow was crisp and crunchy, glittering like Christmas tinsel. She remembered being called a beauty herself, aching for the romance of travel and love. The year she'd had as a medical missionary in India, meeting and marrying Buffy, had been so rewarding. Then had come the agony of war, Buffy sent to France, she alone in London, pregnant with Laura, mourning her brothers. Building up a career in medicine had been her salvation.

Laura appeared and Edith said, privately smiling, going over to the drinks trolley, 'I think we've earned ourselves a small glass of sherry now.'

'I don't know, it feels very louche, drinking sherry on a weekday with one's mother…'

Was this the moment to bring it up? It was treading on

eggshells, but Laura had to know. 'Um, I'll be in London for a few days, right after New Year's, darling, giving a talk on Jung and attending a conference on child guidance. It's an important advance in family medicine, there's a serious need for community clinics to support struggling families and I'm determined to set one up in Edinburgh. It would mean battles with bureaucracy and long hours, but I'd be living at home.' Edith smiled cautiously. 'Can I leave you to look after Dad?'

'Sure. I'll fill the hot water bottles and stoke the fire…' Laura's face was a mirror to her conflicting emotions, whether to be judgemental or impressed. Like most of the world, she felt that being a good wife came before a career, much as she might admire the cause and enjoy time alone with her father. Edith heaved a sigh. How long before women were encouraged to go to university and have careers?

'I'm interested in Jung,' Laura said unexpectedly. 'What's the theme of your lecture, which part of his teachings?'

'Spirituality and the search for God.'

'Lil's stopped searching for God, if she ever did. Pity she'll be away, you should give her a copy of the text. Do you really think there's going to be a war, Mum?'

'Afraid so and I can't see it being short-lived, Hitler's amassing a vast armoury and he's far too chummy with Mussolini by half. We're not prepared enough. It's a sickening thought, but this is a war we could lose.'

'No! We're built of stronger stuff than that. We'd fight to the last.'

'That's my girl! And there's the car back now, just in time for lunch.'

CHAPTER 6

The Campbells' Party

Mum was in London. Dad and I were huddled over the fire, the cold was sawing into my bones. I was halfway through a letter to Harry, sitting on the hearthrug, leaning against an armchair with a writing folder on my knee. No point mentioning Cairo, it would only tempt providence.

Tabitha snuck up onto my lap, digging in her claws. 'What's wrong with the bloody chair?' I muttered, lifting her off and twisting round to use the foot stool.

Dad looked up from his book. 'Language,' he said routinely. 'You'll get chilblains sitting on top of the fender like that, but while you're there, how about toasting some crumpets? I'll bring some and make the tea.'

'Any excuse! And I'd love a cup, thanks, Dad.'

He was soon back and shifting my folder so he could rest the tray, I pronged a crumpet and held it up to the fire.

'Dad, is this a good moment to talk?'

'None better. I guess it's about your young man?'

'No, well, only obliquely. My university tutor, Mr Kennedy,

has been in touch about a job, teaching music and languages at a mission school in Cairo. It wouldn't be till the autumn and very little pay, but I'd really love to put myself forward. It's living in, no boarding costs, but there is the voyage out…'

Dad poured the tea and took a cup back to his seat. 'I can understand how much you want to go, and of course we'd help with the voyage out, but it's not that simple, love. We could well be at war by then. There'd be no civilian travel, the Med far too dangerous and anyway, all the liners commissioned to carry troops. Cairo could have become unsafe and the school have to close its doors. I know it's a thrilling offer, but you mustn't get your hopes up too high.'

'I don't see why the school should have to close,' I muttered, feeling stupidly close to tears. 'Children need an education whether or not there's a war.' I buttered a crumpet with fierce concentration. Could fate ever be as cruel?

Struggling up, I took Dad the crumpet and kissed his cheek. 'You're right, and I'll only get my hopes up medium high, but I'm not giving them up altogether.'

'No,' he smiled up and squeezed my hand, 'I never thought you would.'

I finished my letter, wrote a couple of thank-yous and went up to change for the Campbells' party. Hamish was due in half an hour. Mum's blue satin dress was having an outing, I'd rejected her silver-fox fur cape with its art deco clasp, which would have definitely looked too dated. The beaded sheath would have caused a stir, but I was wistfully saving that up for Harry.

The doorbell rang. I heard Dad go to the door and took my time, peering at my make-up in the better light of the bathroom. It was embarrassing, going downstairs with Dad and Hamish watching, felt like making an entrance, and it didn't help when Dad gave me a peck, whispering audibly, 'Fun, seeing that dress again!'

'It was one of Mum's,' I said, turning to Hamish. I felt good in the dress and didn't really mind that much.

'It's very glamorous, suits you beautifully. You look lovely in it, Laura. It's wonderful to see you again after so long and you must be very glad to be home.'

'Yes, very. It's good to see you too, Hamish. Thanks for coming for me, I wouldn't have wanted to miss a Campbells' party!' That was hardly a vote of confidence and I felt my colour rise.

Dad said, 'Quick drink before you go, a nip of mulled wine?'

'Sounds excellent, Mr Jameson, how kind.' Hamish's politeness was ingrained.

Dad went to the kitchen while I took Hamish into the sitting room and stood leaning against the mantelpiece, my back to the fire, smiling brightly, trying to make amends. Hamish's usual well-bred way of making conversation seemed to have deserted him. He was looking pinkly self-conscious in his crisp white shirt and dinner jacket, marooned on an Indian rug in the middle of the room.

'I hear you're a fully-fledged solicitor now, Hamish, and about to join the family firm,' Dad said, returning, pouring the steaming wine with its tangy aroma of spices into heatproof glasses. 'You'll be showing the old guard how it's done.'

'Making a hash of it more like,' Hamish said rather sweetly, accepting the proffered glass. 'I'm supposed to start in a few weeks…' He hesitated. 'It's just that life seems to be speeding by rather fast. I'd hoped to take a year off to go travelling, but if there's a war I'd want to enlist and there'd be no chance of that then.'

'There can't be a war,' I said passionately, childishly, 'there can't be!'

'It's looking bad, Fudge,' Dad said, with a slight frown, 'but no talk of war when you're away to a party! Off you go and have a grand time. Got your key? I won't wait up. Take care on the ice, Hamish. The lanes are lethal round here.'

Hamish took my arm on the frosty path, helped me into his father's car, a stately blue and black Morris, carefully spreading a musty, tartan, doggy-smelling rug over my knees. He drove dutifully down the hilly lane at a snail's pace.

'I've never seen you look more beautiful,' he said, once we were out on the open road. 'Don't know why, but somehow I expected you to be showing more of the strain with all that's happening in Germany. It can't have been an easy time.'

'No, Kristallnacht was truly horrific, it's indelibly printed on my mind.'

'Lil said you're going back at the end of the month, but is that wise? I worry about your safety. You surely can't carry on as if nothing had happened.'

'Things have settled down. It's fine, it's just to finish my course.' Hamish was right, I knew, which brought me low. And Africa seemed even more beyond reach, like losing a ring in the sea, glimpsing a flash of gold, seductive and shining before the swamping waves crashed down over it and swept it away.

We were in the suburbs of Edinburgh, turning up a street of slate grey Victorian houses, tall and forbidding where the Campbells lived. Hamish drew up right outside their house. The twins, Angie and Rose, had just turned twenty and with their birthday so close to Christmas, the party was an annual bash.

The front door was ajar, party chatter spilling out like a meeting of starlings, excitable and shrill, and we hurried in out of the cold.

'Laura! It's way great to see you,' Rose exclaimed. 'We're dying to hear all.'

'Great to see you too, Hamish,' Angie, the more sensitive twin said, smiling at him. 'The drink's in the dining room, it's all happening in there.'

'Thanks,' Hamish said, beaming back and taking my arm. 'We'll plunge in.'

We stayed in the doorway, absorbing the scene. The dining room, papered in a burgundy flock, was a dark, gloomy room by day but looking more like a jazzy nightclub now with the thick haze of smoke and throbbing music. The carpet was rolled back, a glowing fire in the grate, but there was no disguising the dank, fusty odour from visible patches of mould creeping up above the skirting.

However, would the Campbells heat the place if coal became rationed in a war?

'I'll get us a drink,' said Hamish. 'Don't move, be right back. I'd love to have you for a few minutes before you're claimed.'

'I'll stay rooted,' I said, glad to hear I'd be off the leash. Still, looking round there seemed no one I was keen to talk to, which made me feel a lack of connection, distant from my old Edinburgh friends and a bit lonely. If Harry joined up and anything happened to him, would life cease to have all meaning? Would I end up leading a passionless existence, pining for what couldn't be?

'Penny for them?' Hamish said, handing over a sticky glass of punch.

'I was just slightly wishing I hadn't agreed to go to a panto on Saturday with the Stewarts. Would you come, awful as it's bound to be?'

'Sure, love to, much as I'd rather be seeing a flick alone with you.'

He clinked glasses, meeting my eyes. He was tall, well built, and had a good face, open and engaging with regular features; floppy, mousy hair. I was fond of Hamish; he was just a little too over-keen and part of the life I longed to leave behind.

'Here's to having you home,' he said. 'Sorry about the spillage, bumpy route back. So, how about that film? *The Citadel*'s had terrific reviews. It's on at the Palace with Dick Donat and Rosalind Russell. Ralph Richardson's in it too.'

'Thanks, yes, I'd like that, good plan.' Was that to be my

lot, seeing films with Hamish, who was acting more like a shy eighteen-year-old tonight than a man of twenty-four? 'There's David and Margo,' I said. 'Let's go over.'

They were by the bar, the dining table pushed to the wall, where people were jostling to ladle out punch from a huge double-handed centrepiece bowl. There was food; hot dogs, cubes of cheese and ham, chicken vol-au-vents.

David and Margo, sweethearts since childhood, asked eagerly about Hamburg, shouting to be heard. Talking about it all didn't come easy and it was a relief when Rose cranked up the gramophone and put on a smoochy Hutch number, *These Foolish Things,* then a Jack Hylton, *She Shall Have Music,* which got us all going.

I jitterbugged with David, jived, did the Lindy Hop, till finally, breathless and hotter than a blazing fire, flopped against the wall. 'Enough! Let's get a drink.'

Waiting with David at the bar a carrot-head in a green smoking jacket stared at me, leering nastily. 'You're the Jameson girl back from Germany, aren't you? Sounds like there's a lot going on out there. Good on the Krauts, I say, having it in for all those pig-faced Jews, it's what we should be doing here.'

'Are you being deliberately vile or was that just an attempt at a very bad joke?

I glared, feeling shocked and disgusted and David made hasty introductions, trying to cool things down, 'This is Iain Hench, Laura, as in Hench whisky.'

Iain Hench ignored him and went on staring. 'Ooh, touchy, aren't we! Hitler's got the right idea. Who needs the bloody Jews? They're a stain on a civilised society.'

'So, you're a Fascist fan of Hitler then? Mussolini too?'

'He's drunk, best leave it,' David pleaded, and Hamish was shaking his head as he and Margo came closer, but I wasn't having it, boiling with fury.

'So, you're a paid-up Fascist then, in love with Franco as well?'

'I've a lot of time for Hitler actually. He's built up Germany, given it some spine, and Franco's a good man, good for Spain. The Jews are scum. Everyone knows it and you do too. You'd be lying if you said any different.'

I slapped him hard across his drunken, leering face, my hand stinging, tingling as it came away, leaving a deep red mark. Iain flinched and staggered back.

'Bitch,' he hissed, holding his hand to his cheek. 'Cunt. Fucking bitch.'

In the lull of a record being changed the slap had sounded like a thunder crack and people came crowding over. Hamish reached us and took my arm, steering me through the crush with Iain still swearing and cursing in our wake. 'Fucking do-gooding bitch. She knew I was right, couldn't take a few home truths, could she!'

He could say what he liked. I felt better, cleaner, after living with such an extreme sense of impotence in Hamburg, never able to risk speaking out.

We reached the hall and I said, 'Sorry, thanks for not disowning me!'

'Iain's rich and a bully and no one ever challenges him. What you said takes guts.' Hamish gave a quick smile and I felt a new respect for him.

The twins' parents and a few of their friends were in the sitting room across the way. It was overfilled with bulky loose-covered armchairs and heavy mahogany furniture. There was a free small sofa against the back wall whose springs creaked as we sank down onto it, but no one gave us curious stares. They seemed unaware of the drama across the hall.

Vlirich Luft was over by the fireside. I was pleased to see him. He was a German scientist who'd been living in Edinburgh for years, whom everyone liked and called Vli. We often got together and played chamber music, he was a good friend of the family, a friendship dating back to when his grandparents used to drive out from Edinburgh in a coach and horses to visit mine.

Vli caught my eye and came over and Hamish rose. 'I'll leave you in Vli's good hands for a moment, just better check on the state of play next door.'

'And please tell Angie and Rose how very sorry I am. Then perhaps we should leave.'

Vli raised his unruly bushy white eyebrows. 'What have you got to apologise for, Laura, dear? That doesn't sound like you.'

It was hard to explain; Vli was German and any talk of Jews and fascism was a delicate area. 'This man called me a liar, you see,' I ended, embarrassed.

'It's difficult, isn't it? We can only hope that somehow a miracle of sanity will prevail.' I saw the understanding and sadness behind Vli's intelligent eyes. They were deep cobalt blue, piercing in his gaunt, weather-ravaged face. I admired him enormously. He was one of only two survivors of the disastrous Nanga Purbat expedition, the most tragic in climbing history, which he'd once told me all about.

The highest mountain open to German mountaineers was Nanga Purbat. They could never attempt Mount Everest, which had to be climbed from Tibet and only the British had access there. They'd all been strong climbers on the expedition, but with limited experience of the Himalayas had become trapped in a ferocious storm. All the others had eventually succumbed to frostbite and perished in the snows, Vli and a Sherpa were the only ones to survive.

'It's such a shame we can't get together as usual this January,' he said, 'I shall miss your beautiful singing, but have to be on the other side of the North Sea.'

'And I shall miss your piano playing very much too. It's sad. I never imagined anyone could play with such exquisite devotion. *Hingabe*,' I said, showing off my German. 'I so love listening to you.'

Vli smiled. '*Danke, das lar eine Schöne Sache zu sagen.* Thank you, that was a beautiful thing to say.'

His piano playing was unlike any I'd heard; it simply wasn't Scottish to play with such devotional emotion. Being half English, I felt the Scots earned their reputation for being reserved, but Mum said they simply needed to be understood – and a certain amount of restraint was only decent after all.

'I saw your mother in town yesterday,' Vli said, 'and heard that you're shortly going back to Hamburg. You're enjoying your studies there?'

'Yes, I'm fascinated by Rudolf Steiner, though at times his ideas do seem a bit weird!' It was a slightly evasive answer, but there was much that couldn't be said.

'Here's Hamish back, and it's long past my bedtime. I'm glad to have seen you, Laura, dear, and hope very much we can meet up again next year.'

If war broke out what chance of that would there be? Uganda seemed more of a distant dream than ever. What would Harry be doing now? Reading a book in his primitive forest bungalow? Seeing other expats? Taking out a nurse…?

Hamish touched my arm. 'Rose said you absolutely mustn't worry, you added some exciting spice! But it is a quarter to three. Had we better be going?'

'We better had! Good thing Dad's not waiting up.'

I didn't speak in the dark of the car, frustrated to have let in thoughts of Harry. Shouldn't I be planning to stay at home anyway and do war work? See films with Hamish and stop clutching at stars?

'Can we talk?' I turned, surprised by Hamish's serious tone. He looking straight ahead, driving slowly. 'There's something I need to say.'

'About the terrible scene? You were marvellously kind not to be cross!'

That didn't need an answer and Hamish was lost in some deep, disquieting thought of his own. I had the sense of a swallow-like swoop and rise of emotion in the chill of the car and waited, wondering what was troubling him, what leaps and dips of the heart, and if it was anything he wanted to share.

'Lil told me,' he said, still looking ahead, 'which I knew very well anyway, how much you care for Harry Werner and hope to go out to Africa. But if war is declared, that wouldn't be possible, and things aren't looking good.'

'I know, it's too awful to contemplate.' I gave a warm smile. Hamish was stating the obvious, yet radiating tension that I couldn't miss.

'I vividly remember when you and Harry first met. He'd been touring the highlands and islands with Alan Woods, remember? They stayed a night or so with Alan's parents in Edinburgh and asked a few of us in for drinks. You were just seventeen, I was in love with you, saw the instant spark of connection that night, and Alan told me later that Harry had asked for your address. I've known about your feelings for him ever since and quite how much he means to you.'

A film of cloud over the moon had cleared and as Hamish turned, I could see his expression, the intensity of his own feelings, the torment was clear in his face. He'd always been keen, that had been obvious, but now he was laying bare emotions that were real and raw. I was deeply shaken by his intensity, his moving declaration of love, but there was nothing I could say or do to ease his pain.

'It was actually two years before I saw Harry again,' I said, trying in vain to lessen the contact and connection, 'and now it seems there'll be no chance to meet again for years to come.' Memories flooded in, of Bavaria, Harry's urgent kisses, his nervous, needy hands on my breasts. I felt wrenched in two, hating to think of Hamish being caused such a depth of hurt, but unable to help, as he knew.

'I feel so fearful for you and full of angst, living under these black clouds as we are, the circling dogs of war, and dread the cruel hand we're likely to be dealt. War can change people, Laura dearest. Soldiers see colleagues being killed, which leaves scars, guilt about surviving, bitterness and insularity. Forgive me for talking like this and please forget we've ever had this conversation. I just needed to have it before joining up, needed to feel that you completely understood how much I only want your happiness, however painful for me.

'This isn't easy to say, but if anything happened to Harry I'd know, more than anyone, the immensity of your suffering, and as long as there's breath in my body I'd be there for you. I could be a prop, a shoulder to cry on, some little speck of comfort, nothing more.'

We were going up the snowy lane, turning into the drive. Hamish switched off the engine and glanced quickly with a piercingly gentle smile. 'That would be enough for me.'

I laid my hand on his. 'Thank you, from the bottom of my heart.'

He took my hand, held it tightly, brought it up to his cheek. 'You mean everything, you see.' He was silent for a moment then gave another small smile, all the more agonising for me. 'But now we carry on as before. And it's bloody cold in the car, time to say good night and let you go.' He kissed my cheek, bringing exquisitely sad shivers of connection that reached into every corner of my being. 'Come on!' He grinned. 'I'll see you to the door.'

CHAPTER 7

Hamburg, Summer 1939

The lake was looking like polished glass, silvery and still. Hamburg's great lakes were its lungs, where the city breathed. It was such a peaceful place. I watched the ducks waddle to the water's edge and flop down in, rippling the calm, gliding off jauntily to join their mates. They had nothing to ruffle their feathers, no one encroaching on their territory. Austria and Czechoslovakia had been taken over; Spain had a dictator now with Franco winning the civil war; the map of Europe was changing colour fast. Hitler and Mussolini had signed what they called a friendly alliance and the newspapers more accurately described as a Pact of Steel. I sighed with the sadness of it all, knowing it was really time to go home, while there were still many reasons to stay…

The trip up the Elbe with Bertha and Anna had been heaven; farmland and pastures as far as the eye could see, the trees in leaf, scintillating emeralds and limes of spring, sunlight on the meandering river. I'd played the piano at the inn where we'd stayed, but just upriver, all that time, Nazi soldiers had been stalking the streets of Hamburg in their droves.

My poor tutor, Frau Blohm, had been despairing over her temperamental Russian mother, who was feeling suicidal and threatening to put a bullet through her head, and I'd taken her mother out walking one weekend. It had been invigorating and rewarding, being out on the heathery moors in the clean, fresh air and seeing Frau Blohm's emotional, overwrought mother brighten and smile.

The weather in Hamburg had been filthy ever since that weekend, chill as a Scottish winter, dank and murky as an Irish bog, but now with a little pallid sunshine and the chance to be out, I was writing to Harry by the lake. We'd given up on using any risky code for Hitler and I'd hoped talking of the gloomy weather and fading chance of the mission school job in Cairo would give a clue as to just how dire things in Germany really were.

My doctor friend, Ava, had lost her practice, but she and her sick mother had managed to board the *St Louis*, a German liner bound for Cuba. Now, only yesterday, I'd read that the Cuban authorities had rescinded almost all the valid visas of those 900 mostly Jewish passengers and turned the *St Louis* away. The ship's captain had tried to dock at ports in the US, but even his direct pleas to President Roosevelt had fallen on deaf ears.

Ava, her sick mother, all the pretty young teenagers and families I'd seen boarding, must be weak with terror, and the conditions on board unspeakable. The *St Louis* was bound for Antwerp now, but would any of its passengers find shelter in Belgium or France? Would any of them even survive?

It had got late, a cold wind whipping up, dusk falling fast. I set off feeling brought further down with the dread of having to pass Frau Stürber on the stairs. Mealtimes were bad enough. On my return in January, she'd offered me a larger room at little extra cost, which I'd had to take with no other affordable lodgings around. I'd been glad of the extra space, but worried about Herr Spreckels. He hadn't been at breakfast, and when I asked after him, on finding a shirt button at the back of a drawer, a sock under the bed, I learned it had been his room.

'Gone and good riddance,' Frau Stürber had sneered with satisfaction. 'I wasn't having any Jew scum here, bringing disrepute. Saw the back of him fast.' She must have been snooping in his room and tipped off the authorities. Yet, however shocking, her views were commonplace. My heart bled for Herr Spreckels.

I took the tram back and was walking the last half-mile down Mittelweg when two soldiers stepped out from a doorway and blocked my path. They leered menacingly, salaciously, and my heart pounded. Was I about to be arrested, raped? I had no escape and the blood froze in my veins.

'You will come with us,' one of them said, gripping my arm, 'we show you a good time…' His greasy, leering face was right up close, foul-smelling breath, his fingers digging in painfully.

I felt trapped, weak at the knees, facing two lecherous, loathsome soldiers, but whether from instinct, pride, adrenaline or foolhardiness, wherever bravado comes from, I drew myself up and found some fight. 'How dare you proposition me!' I hissed, yanking my arm free. 'You let me pass this very minute.'

They stared, smug, drunken and aroused, not giving an inch, still blocking my path. 'Not so fast, we have authority. It is an order, your duty, the Führer's wishes. Arian women must help to breed the Super Volk.'

'What rot! I'm a British citizen, a guest in your country, and you're supposed to be keeping order. You should be ashamed.' I stepped off the pavement shaking with fury, into the dark unlit street, and strode away. My heart was hammering, nerves clattering like cymbals. They followed for a bit, laughing self-consciously and calling out obscenities. I didn't turn, kept striding on, and they soon got bored and tailed away like the bullies and cowards they were.

CHAPTER 8

Home Again

Mid-July. My trunk was packed, last debts settled, a taxi waiting, but I still had to return my key. I found Frau Stürber in the steamy kitchen, which was stultifying in the July heat with a heavy pot releasing a disgusting odour of greasy mutton. 'I'm off now,' I said, leaving the large key on a dresser top by the door, 'just saying goodbye…'

'Another empty room,' Frau Stürber muttered, coming over, but even as I breathed out, almost free of her, the hateful woman grabbed my upper arms and kissed me wetly on both cheeks. My horror was complete.

The taxi drove past Hamburg's fine old terraces, the handsome courthouse, the docks. Was I seeing the city for the last time? A vast swastika poster hanging down from the top of the railway-station wall was impossible to miss, a jolting reminder of the need to leave. Bertha and Anna were coming to see me off. We'd be on the opposite sides in a war, so hard to imagine and unutterably sad.

They were there already, looking out for me. Bertha was in tears. We hugged in a threesome, clinging with the pain of parting. 'We'll miss you so, so much,' Bertha cried. 'I'll write, tell you how things are. There are rumours…' she whispered '…terrible shortages, hard times coming, so if I talk about pride in our fine soldiers, you'll know to read between the lines…'

Anna was standing back shyly. She was a tall, fair-haired girl, self-conscious of her height, which made her a little round-shouldered, but it wasn't easy to tell her to stand up straight. 'We've got you a present,' she said, holding out a package, which was beautifully wrapped in gold paper with silver ribbon.

'You shouldn't have!' I exclaimed, embarrassed. 'I'll send something tartan and Scottish from home…' The book was a copy of *Baedeker's Egypt,* the kindest, most thoughtful choice, but Africa wasn't going to happen now, and feeling like a child denied a promised picnic I couldn't stem the tears.

Bertha hugged me close. 'Baedeker describes a journey from Cairo to Masindi Port in Uganda,' she said. 'Is that anywhere near Harry's forest?'

'Think so,' I said, wiping my eyes. 'The Budongo Forest is hard to find on a map, but Masindi's the nearest town.'

My trunk was on the train, the whistle blowing furiously and everyone scrambling on board. 'I'll write,' I shouted from the corridor window, words lost to the squeaky grinding of the train's rusty wheels. As it gathered speed, Bertha and Anna were soon engulfed in steam and lost to view.

*

It was late August. The weeks at home had been dragging interminably. I drank in the beauty of a summer evening – the countryside bathed in an amber glow, the sun casting long shadows – and tried to feel more positive. I was learning to drive, thanks to my enlightened mum and dad, but with the Cairo mission school job on hold, too much uncertainty at the moment, they said, there seemed little to be positive about.

My hopes of a teaching job at the new Rudolf Steiner School in Edinburgh had fallen through. The head had been apologetic, explaining that with a key teacher coming from Switzerland he hadn't the means to take me on. I felt dejected and low, staring out at the garden, and took Harry's crumpled letter out of my cardigan pocket to read for yet another time.

…I'm to take over from Jim Murray soon, who's staying on a bit to show me the ropes. He picked me up from Masindi, twenty-five miles away, and by the time I was climbing the forty steps up to the bungalow, I was too strung up to speak! There's a bedroom and living/dining room with an open-hearth fire, and the garden has roses, canna lilies and bougainvillea, a Christ's thorn hedge just yards from the veranda where there's a sheer drop; very handy for the avoidance of drunken slips! The climate up here is little warmer than an English summer, except in the dry season, and a fire in the evenings is a cheery sight.

The office is in a separate building with two rooms and I'm sleeping in one of them till Jim goes. Jim's a Scot, he and I have got on splendidly, despite the fact that he's older, tougher, stronger and didn't go to university, but his knowledge of Uganda is amazing, and he brilliantly applies in practice all the theory I learned at Oxford!

I have a camp bed, a chair and a washbasin mounted on two packing cases. It's all I need. The loo is in a tiny thatched mud hut all of its own, just a deep pit – few jobs for plumbers out here – and there's a separate primitive kitchen. The cook and houseboy's huts are a short way behind. It feels very incongruous, having servants to cook and wait at table in surroundings like these! The food is basic, they have a limited repertoire and we bachelors haven't a clue!

Nor had I… it was hard to picture myself trying to teach the natives good cooking skills and recipes, perhaps better ask Mrs Hodges for a few tips, possibly saying it would be good for running my own household one day…

…What wonderful news about the mission school in Cairo! I'm delighted for you, dearest, and who knows? If all goes well, perhaps we can manage to meet, but I fear we must dampen our hopes of that with this dire threat of war. I was extremely relieved to hear you were on your way home. Keep safe, I think of you, miss you greatly and send my love…

Dad came in, making me embarrassed to be caught reading Harry's letter yet again, and I was shocked and fearful to see how drawn Dad looked. There was strain and anxiety showing in every crevice of his face.

He said, 'I've just heard on the wireless that Hitler began firing on Poland at dawn, the German troops are killing indiscriminately and Chamberlain will issue an ultimatum now, to which Hitler will never comply. We'll be at war in days.'

It was the 1st of September, a day I would remember for the black wall that came down, closing off all we knew and loved. War would tear through our safety net of peace and stability. Dick would be quick to join up, Hamish had been going to, and Harry said he would too. What chance of any of them surviving? I couldn't swallow for the lump in my throat, and tears pricked in my eyes.

Dad gathered me up, smoothing my hair. 'We're better armed, Fudge, thanks to Churchill. He foresaw this, one of the very few who did.' Dad smiled, releasing me. 'That's the car, Lil and the boys back, and Mum will be home tomorrow.'

On Sunday the 3rd of September, I woke to see soft pleats of sunshine slanting across the counterpane. It looked a beautiful day after yesterday's leaden skies, but at breakfast the silence hung heavy. Buffy rose. 'I need to tune in the wireless. There's to be an announcement at the start of the eleven o'clock news.'

With minutes to go, we all assembled in his study, Mrs Hodges too, drawing up chairs round his cumbersome old Murphy set. When Big Ben sounded, my heart pounded as loudly as the chimes. 'Here is the news and this is Alvar Liddell reading it. The Prime Minister will make an announcement now.'

Chamberlain spoke briefly about Hitler's refusal to withdraw his troops from Poland, before concluding in his familiar weary way, 'And consequently this country is now at war with Germany.'

There were no words to fill the void, the only sound the grandfather clock in the hall steadily ticking the last minutes of peace away. Life as we knew it had irrevocably changed with the Prime Minister's few chilling words.

'I need a cigarette,' Mum said, taking one from the box on Dad's desk.

'Me too.' Lil held out her hand.

A high-pitched wailing whistle reached us from somewhere far outside.

Jack said excitedly, 'Listen, listen, that's an air-raid siren, I'm sure!'

'More like it's just a siren being tested.' Dad smiled fondly. 'We'll all have to learn to tell the difference between the sound for *Take Cover* and *All Clear*, which I remember as being softer, more like the whine of a spinning top.'

He'd been through all this before, lived through the Great War and survived. We had to hold on to hope.

The rest of the morning passed by slowly in a sort of faux normality. We went for a family walk after lunch. With the mellow cloudless day there was the scent of warm grass cuttings, a charcoal tang of garden bonfires, and beyond the village, the timeless beauty and perfect peace of the rolling Scottish countryside.

*

By October, little had happened and there was an eerie calm. We were kitted out with gas masks and had been warned about German bombers; Scotland's factories, its coalmines and shipyards being key targets, but so far, life just chugged along. It didn't feel like being at war. Lil and Dick were back at university, Jack at his school, soon to be evacuated, Mum and Dad busy in their respective jobs. I was the only one still at home all day, fed up and lonely.

The telephone ringing gave me a start. It was the head of the Rudolf Steiner School in Edinburgh. 'The teacher due to come from Switzerland has been refused permission to enter the country,' he said, 'and I would be delighted if you were still able to step in. I'd need you to take lessons in German and French in addition to the singing, piano and flute. Oh, and a little craftwork would be good.'

'I'd be delighted to step in,' I said, resisting the temptation to say that I wouldn't be exactly idle.

Dad congratulated me, looking extremely relieved, which was hardly surprising. I'd been mooching about, wearing my misery like a ball and chain. What could he expect, though, with not a peep out of Harry since a letter in July?

'Your French isn't up to much,' Mum grinned, 'but you're resourceful. You'll get by.'

A letter finally came from Harry, post-stamped 30th August, so I had no idea whether he'd been called up, or any word of the situation in East Africa. He chattily described settling in, forest workers squabbling and asking for advances, although he still felt safe as houses, going about alone, weighed down with bulging money bags on payday.

I wrote back immediately, full of my new job.

…It's such a relief to have a job, and teaching at a Rudolf Steiner school feels like a sort of lingering link with Hamburg. I'm living in and we've been evacuated from Edinburgh, to a gaunt Victorian pile in the country, which isn't great, but thankfully it's not far from home. There's only the head, myself and the children. I have eleven kids to teach, six to eight-year-olds. They're quick to pick up languages and love the German poems I make them act. One parent said her son calls me Fraulein and I shouldn't be surprised if I'm imprisoned as a German spy!

There's a little German poem, by the way, that I particularly love.

"Du bist mein, ich bin dein, Dessen sollst du gewiss sein, bid eingeschlossen in meinem Herzen, Verloren ist das Schlüsselchen: Du musst auch für immer darin bleiben."

It lost the rhythm a bit in English. "You are mine, I am yours, of that you may be certain. You're locked in my heart; the key is lost. You will always remain there…

You're always in my thoughts too, closeted away in the tenderest part of my heart…" I wrote, which was overdoing it.

I asked after his parents' safety, living as aliens in Austria now, and wound up saying how much I longed for a *Wiedersehen*. There was no chance of meeting for years, it was wretched, but I felt in my bones it was going to happen one day.

CHAPTER 9

Buffy

Buffy looked across to Edith. She was knitting a sturdy sock, taking up knitting-needle arms like most of the women in the country. 'Do we really have to let her go?' He knew Edith wasn't really on his side, yet still forlornly willed her to agree that Laura couldn't possibly go to Cairo. It was far too hazardous, whether the mission school wanted her now or not. 'I mean, this isn't going to be a short, sharp war. Things could get seriously bad out there, and the thought of her sailing through the Med with all the risks, even of being torpedoed…'

Edith set aside her knitting and rose to give the fire a jiggle. 'It is a bit risky, of course,' she said, looking back at him, 'but Hitler's biding his time. There was the Luftwaffe raid on the Forth Bridge, that bomb on Edinburgh Zoo, though it only killed one poor giraffe, this must be the best time for her to get away.'

Tabitha had bagged the momentarily vacated seat and Edith had to shoo her off to sit down. 'Chasing after Harry is almost certainly a lost cause, but on balance, I feel Laura will be safer in Cairo. Isn't it better that she's far afield, meeting young officers and having new experiences? Who knows what lies ahead, after all? We could even be invaded, God forbid.'

Buffy wasn't swayed; young officers moved on or got themselves killed, and he had a distressing image of Laura being wooed by an Egyptian sophisticate and persuaded to settle in Cairo. 'There's really nothing for her here,' Edith pressed. 'Even poor smitten Hamish is about to go to France now he's through his training. I've always had a soft spot for him, but Laura's focused elsewhere. She's so dead set on Cairo now that the offer's back on the table. We can't stand in her way.'

'She's only seeing Cairo as a stepping stone and I worry so much about her mooning after Harry Werner. There'll be no chance of her getting to Uganda in wartime, and he's joined up anyway, Laura says. I only hope he doesn't go and get himself shot. She'd be inconsolable.'

'You can't think like that. And surely it's better she's run off her feet at the mission school with all the distractions of a lively place like Cairo.'

Edith was being realistic and resilient as ever. But could there ever be a bleaker picture? Laura alone and vulnerable in an alien land, Dick risking his life in the Royal Marines, Lillian at Cambridge with Spitfires flying overhead… At least Jack's school had been evacuated to a country mansion quite nearby and Edith working hard to establish her medical centre in Edinburgh. It was an immense relief, having her close and at home.

She looked up from her knitting with a smile. 'Time for a drink? Whisky? Don't move, I'll do it.'

'Thanks. I'll call P&O and confirm Laura's passage then, shall I? Before we lose the reservation?' He ran a hand over his brow, feeling the deepening furrows and struggling to contain the pain in his heart. 'God, this bloody war!'

CHAPTER 10

March 1940, Voyage to Cairo

It was a fine cold spring day and Lil and I were out for a walk, she had come home from university to say goodbye, which had warmed my heart. I was feeling more and more emotional: 8th of March, twelve days to go, Cairo in touching distance of Uganda… If only Dad wasn't so miserably sad. I was already feeling a thudding ache of homesickness myself, never closer to him or more aware of how much I'd worry and miss everyone at home.

'You're really sure, deep down?' Lil said, turning with an anxious un-Lil-like smile. 'No qualms? I'd be scared as a cat, travelling all those thousands of miles in wartime. You could still change your mind. I'm sure Dad could get a refund.'

I looked down, avoiding tussocks and cowpats. The fear had seeped into my very psyche; fear of the unknown, of being torpedoed and a cold, agonising death in the Med. I could almost smell my own panic. I was even terrified of being seasick in the Bay of Biscay. I had to go, the longing was pulling, luring me on, but what hope of ever reaching Harry? The way ahead was incredibly strewn with boulders.

'Cairo's supposed to be a great sexy hotspot,' Lil said. 'Masses of nightlife and partying, plenty of glam young army officers, but that's hardly your scene, is it, Sis? And how are you going to meet up with your Harry when he's off fighting in the war? Isn't it all a bit of a pipe dream?'

'You're right, of course. I'll just have to survive on hope.'

We stopped and had a hug. I was feeling very tearful. I'd always resented Lil with her prettiness and sense of fun, the career she had all mapped out for herself, but hugging in that field, the envy felt very surface deep.

'You know, I've always been a bit dead jealous of you,' she said, as if mirroring my thoughts. 'Your music and spirituality, feeling such a depth of passion. I can't imagine chasing someone across continents on such a fragile little flame of hope.'

'You'll fall in love soon enough. It'll hit you for six and leave you reeling.'

'Poor old Hamish, he'll be pining his heart out for you over in France. It must be pretty scary there, waiting for the full-on attack. I hope you gave him a ginormous hug and kiss goodbye to keep him going.'

I wished she hadn't said that, so casual and irritating. It changed the mood and made me feel overcome with guilt about him. I'd been far too self-obsessed to give much of a thought to Hamish, out there, hiding in fields, risking his life.

'You take good care now, Miss Laura. When I think of that Mr Hitler, our young lads laying down their lives,' Mrs Hodges blew through her lips, 'doesn't half make me blood boil. Well, you'd best be off then.' She wiped away two fat tears with a corner of her apron. 'Safe journey and see you come home before long.'

'You take good care of yourself too…' I bit on my lip, kissed Mrs Hodges' flushed, onion-scented cheek and fled.

It was harder to put on a brave face at the station and Mum

was weepy-eyed as well. 'It'll improve your French at least,' she said, with a wan grin. 'Look after yourself, darling, and write!'

'I'm going to miss you lots,' Jack said gruffly. 'Be sure to send plenty of photos to keep you near.' That did for me and my tears became a torrent.

My trunk was on the train. Dad came on board with me and held me tight. 'We're always here for you, darling, any problems, anything at all…' The whistle was blowing and, turning to go, he put the back of his hand to his eyes.

'Oh, Dad!' I clutched at his arm, but it was time.

I waved from the train, kept waving till the train rounded a bend then found the strength to wipe away my tears and go to the carriage. It was full and the tension was palpable. Two soldiers were taking quick puffs of their smokes, a strained-looking woman dragging on a cigarette too; she had mud on slackly hanging lisle stockings and a noticeable whiff of the farm about her in that stuffy space. A young private was wedged between an older couple, the three of them silent and sitting rigidly upright. I imagined those poor parents returning home inconsolable.

I had a window seat and looked out, seeing nothingness. Would I ever get beyond Cairo? I had such an aching need to love and be loved, share secret hopes, embarrassments and fears, but all without really knowing if Harry had any of the same feelings.

Dad, who knew about such things, had suggested that my Hamburg friends write to neutral Lisbon, addressing any mail to Box number 506 at the Thomas Cook office. They would forward any letters onto London, he said.

I'd set that up before leaving Hamburg and just had a letter from Bertha, but she made no mention of receiving mine. She talked censor-consciously about *"our wonderful Führer and fine soldiers"*, but the hardships they were suffering sounded far worse than ours. Most essentials were rationed but still available while Bertha said they had no soap or toilet paper and a desperate shortage of food.

'...*We have a sort of imitation coffee made from barley, oats and chemicals, but no butter or jam, and we cook rice mashed with mutton fat for an ersatz taste of meat...*' It was heart-breaking; those happy times with Bertha and Anna in Hamburg felt like a trick of memory now.

At Tilbury Docks, there was scurrying and confusion; kitbag-toting soldiers; porters heaving trunks, looking harassed; a reek of tar and pervading smell of damp. As I waited out on the grimy dockside, black clouds scurried overhead and a strong wind cutting in was bitter. The liner, the *Strathnaver*, looked huge with three tall funnels, handsome even painted in wartime grey.

'Only one of them funnels is functional,' said a sailor, following my eyes.

'Gosh, yes, only the middle one's got soot. Why's that?'

'Makes folks think she's more powerful.' He grinned and doffed his sailor's hat. Staring up at the ship, I remembered the frightened Jewish children at the Hook of Holland leaving all they knew and loved behind. My nerves were bad, I was shivering with cold, longing to be on board and the die finally cast.

We were inching away from the dockside. Tearful passengers crowding at the rail, waving large white hankies. They soon scurried inside, beaten by the cold. I stayed out on deck, gazing out, bent almost double with the wind, till the coastline had completely disappeared and there was only the frothing gunmetal sea and stark black line of the horizon.

I was physically and emotionally exhausted to the point of collapse and reaching my single cabin, must have fallen asleep even before unpacking my bag. I woke with a furry mouth, still fully clothed, creases in my cheeks... I'd slept for ten hours. I'd missed dinner, probably breakfast too, but opening the cabin door to go to the bathroom, almost fell over a tray with a pot of tea and two digestive biscuits. Very welcome, if stone-cold.

By evening, I felt ready to meet my dinner companions for the voyage. The dress code was formal and I wore Mum's midnight blue satin. The *maître d'* instructed a waiter to show me to my assigned table; being escorted through the splendid art-deco dining room with many diners already seated made me feel very self-conscious and conspicuous. The waiter held out the only empty chair and, looking round shyly, I apologised for my non-appearance the previous night, explaining about catching up on sleep.

'And now you emerge like a butterfly breaking free of its chrysalis,' said a grinning army officer across the table. 'I'm Paddy Boyd, 11th Hussars. Let me do the honours and introduce you to us all. This is Lady Tufton on my right, who's joining her husband in Cairo. He's doing lonely duty with the military police out there and must be panting for her to arrive.'

She was matronly, looking extremely affronted at that, and said pompously, 'My husband is working hard, trying to keep order in these very difficult times.'

Paddy Boyd grinned and carried on. 'Next to Lady Tufton is Sir Stanley Russell, the renowned archaeologist. He's going to be overseeing the return of artefacts from Tutankhamun's tomb to the Cairo museum. This is his wife, Margaret, on my left. It's a great honour to have them both at the table.'

Sir Stanley was gently self-deprecating. He was shrunken and white-haired, and Margaret, who was quite as elderly, gave a charming smile. She was dainty as a bird with twig-like arms that looked frail enough to snap. Paddy continued. 'Next, Lieutenant Colonel Archie Williams, who's with the Black Watch and joining his brigade out in Palestine. On your right is Bob Sims, who's a war correspondent, and on your left, Major Sir Egbert Carter-Smith, both of whom are bound for Cairo, like me.'

I smiled round, 'I'm so pleased to meet you all and apologies again.'

'Welcome to our table, Laura, if I may call you that,' said Bob

Sims. 'It's a delight to have you joining us now, beautifully filling the empty seat.'

'I'll second that,' said Lt Colonel Williams loudly, leaning forward. Lady Tufton gave him a dragon look. He was a heavy drinker from his colouring and the choleric impatience he displayed, failing to catch the wine waiter's eye.

'You mustn't mind these cheeky cooped-up men,' said Bob Sims. 'I'm afraid the ship is full of us. You're going to Cairo?'

'Yes, I have a teaching job there at an American mission school.' I felt myself redden; others round the table had stopped talking to listen in.

'You will find Cairo's a very jazzy place,' Paddy said, 'and may need a little chaperoning, but there'd be no shortage of offers for that, you can be sure!' He twinkled at me before giving his order to a waiter standing patiently by.

The menu had tried to mask the inevitable wartime shortages. A fish course of kedgeree, chicken curry or beef bourguignon, sure to be a near meatless stew, and treacle tart or fruit jelly, probably thinly dotted with tinned peach.

The chicken curry wasn't bad, and I warmed to Bob Sims. 'Being an unarmed war correspondent must take almost as much courage as soldiering,' I said.

'The men doing the fighting are the brave ones, I only have to bear seeing the terrible casualties. I do other journalism. Human-interest stories, pieces on defence. This is actually my first wartime foray since the Spanish Civil War.'

'Which must have been the most desperately harrowing experience.'

'It was, unspeakable, villages being torn apart, neighbours burning each other's houses – people hardly knew whose side they were on half the time, and atrocities being committed on all sides. Democratic intellectuals like George Orwell viewed a Franco Fascist regime as morally calamitous, but Russia was arming the communists too who poured in. Hitler and Mussolini were supporting the Falangists… At least Franco seems to be taking a neutral stand in this war, just as Spain did in 14–18.'

'Some of our own communists went out to fight, didn't they?'

'Yes, I did a piece on a lad from Glasgow who'd paid his five pounds, eight shillings, got on a bus in George Square and, to quote him, "fetched up in Paris via London and had a day there like a Celtic supporters' outing." But that was before he got to Valencia, where after hanging around for weeks, he'd been packed off, poorly armed, to defend some strategic valley. They'd hidden in olive groves, he said, but were soon captured. By the strangest coincidence, his mother had seen him on a Movietone newsreel – prisoners of war being paraded for the benefit of the cameras – so knew he was still alive.'

'What a happy outcome, which can't have been true for many.'

I warmed to Bob with his saturnine looks, pitch-dark hair and deep delphinium-blue eyes. His face was lean with high cheekbones, harshly defined, but with a softness about the eyes. Probably early thirties with a wife back home?

'I'm talking too much and monopolising you,' he said, with a gentle smile.

'No, the opposite, but perhaps I had better turn…' Which I did regretfully, drawn by Bob's very arresting eyes.

Major Sir Egbert Carter-Smith on my left was pushing bits of gristle to the side of his plate and looking down morosely. In profile, his bushy gingery moustache looked like the tip of a red squirrel's tail. I felt he'd be hard to take seriously. He sensed my gaze and looked up, assessing me carefully with small, inquisitive eyes.

'Tell me, Miss Jameson, where's home, where are you from?'

'I was born in India, but Edinburgh is really home. My mother's a Scot.' I resented his need to know my pedigree and had almost said, *You mean which drawer am I out of?*, only just stopping myself in time.

'Ah. Beautiful city, Edinburgh, though I'm Hampshire-born. However, Scotland has always seemed a rather untamed place to me and, I'd say, with a hugely disproportionate number of dukes from the Highlands.'

He really was the most ridiculous man. Not to Lady Tufton, it seemed, who was openly listening in. 'Indeed, I do agree!' she said fervently. 'Even more dukes than marquesses.'

I soon got to know my fellow diners, their quirks and the various nuances, and began to look forward to mealtimes. Archie Williams was perennially drunk and tactile; Paddy, good, light-hearted fun; Major Sir Egbert, pure PG Wodehouse; Bob, interesting and appealing. There was the miserable business of the blackouts, but the days slipped by and despite the fear of being torpedoed, that plume of anxiety hanging over us all, I enjoyed the voyage enormously.

I started a letter to Harry on a bitterly cold day in Marseilles, where we'd been advised not to go ashore. I described how my days were measured by meals with the dragon, Lady Tufton, regularly giving us the dining equivalent of a cold bath. Our arrival in Cairo was looming large, my sense of panic building, and I wrote wistfully about my dinner in London with Dick the night before sailing.

…I had my last evening on English soil with my brother Dick. He's a lieutenant in the Royal Marines now, calls himself a "lute", and looked extremely smart, if only in khaki (I'd hoped for navy blue). He said I was looking "magnificent"! I've never had such a compliment from him before, or as big a kiss. He'd come to the hotel where I was staying, and that kiss raised the hairs of everyone in the lounge! I'm sure the waiters wouldn't have been half as attentive had they known we were brother and sister. Dick was about to be off on some top-secret mission and I'm sick with worry about him now.'

He was due to sail for Norway, though said he shouldn't have told me and the secret hung heavy.

…The blackouts on board are a bore, but no worse than at home. When I asked my class to draw a picture of their houses, one little boy did a lovely colourful drawing then smeared it all over with black crayon. 'That's the blackout,' he said proudly…

I wrote about Hamish and hinted at his keenness. With the sense I had of Harry drawing back a bit, had to rein in my feelings. I left the letter unfinished, we were going ashore in Malta and would write more later.

Malta was a first taste of the east with all the bartering, and to feel the sun on my bare arms was heaven. There were glorious glimpses of the Mediterranean down steep, cramped little streets, tiny stone houses all hugger-mugger, fishy smells less than glorious, but the sea was as brilliant an azure blue as I'd only ever seen in Impressionist paintings.

Valetta overflowed with soldiers, donkeys and cats, and there was a mass of warships in the harbour, but it was a Sunday with much of the town closed. I saw the cathedral, which was magnificent, could have been in Renaissance Italy, and stayed for part of a service. It was dauntingly Catholic, but I left that bit out, finishing my letter back on board again, since Harry was Catholic, I knew.

My lasting image of Malta, I told him, with the familiar red telephone boxes, pillar boxes and statue of Queen Victoria, would be of a vivid little outpost of the British Empire.

At Port Said small craft were darting everywhere. Rowing boats and gondola-like canoes, whose boatmen wore rounded white skull caps and crowded and bobbed round the *Strathnaver* as she dropped anchor. Out on deck with field glasses, I could see a man in a bowler hat strolling along a slatted-wood jetty; natives, glistening with sweat, bent double as they heaved great sides of beef and baskets of coal up on board. I saw two European women in floaty dresses and wide-brimmed hats strolling along a pavement. All life was there.

Paddy Boyd appeared at my side, his arm resting lightly on my shoulders. 'I hope you'll allow me to take you out in Cairo. There's always plenty of action and you can't stay cooped up in that mission school forever and a day. Remember *One Thousand and One Nights? "He who has not seen Cairo has not seen the world"*? I know your heart is elsewhere, but can we stay in touch?'

'Thank you,' I said, flattered and privately amused, since others, even Sir Egbert Carter-Smith, had already made similar overtures. Paddy was engaging; with his sandy hair and height, he fitted my image of a charming, fun-loving young army officer, but I felt Bob had greater depth. He hadn't said more than how much he'd enjoyed our talks and hoped we'd see each other in Cairo, but, guilty as I felt about Harry, I was really hoping for that too.

CHAPTER 11

Cairo 1940

Could I really be here, on the same continent as Harry? Africa had its own special smell, like a person's skin; it was unique. I had a sense of belonging here, of the caressing, clinging orange-scented air becoming a part of me, and felt sure that if ever I were brought back to these shores blindfolded, I would know that I was on African soil.

The train to Cairo was packed. Half the ship was on it; families with excitable children; sweating, nervy-looking soldiers; a few resigned Egyptians squeezed in amongst them. I watched the countryside slipping by, the donkey and camel traffic on mud roads, women washing clothes on slabs of stone, men working the fields, buffalos drawing water or threshing or doing something where they went round and round in circles. Rural Egypt seemed very primitive.

We arrived in Cairo close on midnight, but the station was still hot and steamy with fetid smells. No shortage of porters, though, and I was soon in a cab. It was a very dark night and with the street lamps painted blue, the light they gave was eerily dim.

There were no women to be seen, only a few men wearing long white nightshirts and who in the blue nocturnal light looked like wandering ghosts.

The cab driver didn't speak a word of English, but I'd written down the address and we eventually drew up beneath a sign saying, "*American Mission College for Girls*" to my relief. He unloaded my bags and left. I felt slightly panicked, standing outside the heavy brass-studded door, clanging the bell and praying it would be answered. It soon was and a servant in a red fez silently let me in.

A woman coming up behind him hid her yawn with a smile. 'Hi there, welcome!' She had a strong American accent. 'It's Laura Jameson? I'm Gloria Parker, one of the teachers here. I'll show you to your room. There's sandwiches and fruit there for you, but then forgive me, I'm dead on my feet.'

'Of course, I'm really sorry, arriving so late. It's very good of you to wait up.'

We climbed a wide, polished-wood flight of stairs, tiptoeing to avoid a clatter, and Gloria led the way along a carpeted passage to a door towards the end.

'Here we are, sleep well, see you at breakfast.'

The food was under a muslin cover on a table, but my eye went straight to the high wood-framed bed, swathed in mosquito netting. I was exhausted.

Waking with a start, it was a relief to know I wasn't lost in a dark forest, that it was only a dream, but I couldn't for the life of me think where I was. Then it all came flooding back; the intoxicating foreignness of Port Said, the pungent spices, piquant unknown fruits, the stench. That long train journey in the cloying heat, the Egyptians in the carriage reading their newspapers from the right.

Faint light was filtering in. I looked at my watch: half past six. Pushing back the folds of mosquito net, I swung my feet down onto dark stained boards and crossed to open the shutters. It was barely daylight. There was an apartment block opposite. We must be in a residential area. A single horse-drawn cart piled with dates going by was pulled along by a skeletal old man in a nightshirt.

A cautious knock on the door made me start and, shrugging on my new peach silk dressing gown, I hurried to see who it was. It was a slight shock to see a burly, bearded Egyptian standing there. I smiled encouragingly. He looked very anxious.

'I am Mahmoud, your chamber man, Madam. I greet you. I bring tea? Coffee?'

'Thank you, tea would be lovely. It's good to meet you and could you tell me what time is breakfast? I don't want to be late.'

Mahmoud shook his head vigorously. He had his hat on in the house, like the man last night, and its little tassel was dancing. 'No, no, is all right. Breakfast in one hour. On table is book with information.'

'Ah, yes. Thanks, that's a great help.' I smiled again and Mahmoud looked sweetly relieved, as if sensing I wasn't the type to bite his head off. He was wearing a grey-striped nightshirt, altogether smarter than the ghostly white shrouds I'd seen so far, and he had a very cherubic smile.

'I bring tea each morning at six o'clock,' he said, bowing and backing away.

The booklet contained a formidable list of rules and regulations, times of meals and chapel, and there was a note of welcome from the head, Miss Wilcox.

I chose a subdued navy dress and went to the dining hall feeling nervous, with sweaty palms. Three long tables, just like my old school in Edinburgh, and a horizontal top table where a small group, presumably the teachers, was seated and all watching my progress down the hall. The stern-looking woman who rose had to be the head, Miss Wilcox. She was formidably tall, wearing a black skirt and white blouse with a cameo brooch at her throat. Her dark hair, scraped back into a bun, was thin enough for patches of scalp to show through.

'Welcome to the Mission,' she said. 'I trust you slept well after the long journey?'

'Like a log, thank you, and it's wonderful to be here at last.' I smiled self-consciously, taking her limp hand, worrying about my sweaty palms and the crumpled state of my frock. She had a voice to command respect and discourage platitudes, and an unsettling air of fortitude, as if feeling her time would be better spent elsewhere. She said, 'Now, let me introduce you to your colleagues. This is Gloria Parker, who takes math…'

'We met late last night,' I said, smiling at her. 'Thank you for waiting up.'

Miss Wilcox continued seamlessly. 'Betty Horne, who teaches religious studies, Mary Draper is our Arabist, and this is Dolly Swanson, our geography teacher, who will be helping you to settle in. Have your breakfast then come to my office directly. Dolly will show you the way. We need to discuss your schedule.' She pronounced it *skedule* and, inclining her head slightly, turned to go.

The teachers were mainly young and apart from a Swiss girl, Nina Biser, all were American. Dolly grinned. 'I expect you're starving after that journey. The scrambled egg's good. I've got a lesson at eight, but I'll point out the staffroom, where we can get together afterwards and have a good old gas and some coffee – or is it tea? We Yanks love our coffee. It's the only thing to get me out of bed.'

'Tea gets me up; coffee keeps me going,' I said. Dolly with her giggly warmth and dimples was fun. I was sure we'd soon be good friends.

I knocked on the head's door. Miss Wilcox looked distant behind a vast mahogany desk, whose papers and leather blotter were arranged with military precision. The room was spacious, fragrant with furniture polish, cooled by a fan. She indicated a chair and I sat down, trying to look alert and obliging.

'Lessons are from 8 am till 4,' she said, skipping the preliminaries, 'and you will be teaching girls of all ages. We have students here who marry in their teens and return to continue their studies – some even into their twenties.'

'Do all the girls speak English?'

'We teach in English, but it is rarely a girl's first language. As well as music, and you may choose your own pieces to teach, I should like you to take a beginners' class in German. Now, if you've no further questions…' I thanked her, wondering whether she felt a spattering of German would come in handy if, God forbid, we were defeated in the war.

I hurried to the staffroom. It was small, poky and airless with a central table, a few upright rush chairs and a very ineffective fan. No Dolly yet and I was glad of a moment alone; the session with Miss Wilcox had felt like a first day at senior school. All the same, to have a free hand with the music was an unexpected boon.

Dolly burst in and collapsed onto a chair. 'You okay, still in one piece?'

'Just about! But it was interesting. I hadn't expected to be teaching girls of all ages.'

'And all shapes and shades and sizes. I'm still nothing like clear about all the nationalities, even after two terms. Cairo's like that. Brits, Italians, Greeks, French, Swiss, Russians, even an Egyptian or two! And soldiers pouring in from all over, of course. A bunch of New Zealanders are giving a party on Friday night, by the way. You must come to that.'

'Thanks, I'd love to.' I was still trying to get my head round it all. 'So the girls must be all different religions as well then?'

'Most are Muslim, the servants too, but being on a Christian basis here, they have to attend chapel whatever their faith. Not the servants, of course.'

'It was quite a surprise, a man doing my room.'

'The maids only serve at meals. It's the fellows who do all the housework, just as it should be!' Dolly roared with laughter. She had reddish blonde hair, freckles and dimples and a bouncy sense of fun; we'd hit it off from the start. She said the other teachers were a friendly bunch, always good for a giggle.

The first few days took all of my energies, there wasn't a moment to write letters, but I stayed up late one night, needing to get one off to Harry.

> … *There's only one girl in my class whose first language is English and a little brat of eight who said she couldn't possibly learn music in any language except French! I wasn't having that. Most of the girls are easy to manage, though one or two of the older ones can be a bit uppity. I have good laughs with the other teachers. It feels a bit irresponsible in the circs, but it's a release of a kind with all the wretched news. It's so terrible about Norway. Is our precious island going to be next? Please not. I've had no word from home, no letter from you, and I'm worried to death about Dick…*

Two tears dribbled down; the thought of the Germans taking Oslo, invading Denmark, and Dick on his secret mission. I was sick with worry.

> … *We had a half-day yesterday in honour of the newborn princess. Poor little thing! I doubt any child was ever so unwanted. Everyone's saying, 'Bad news, bad news,' instead of happily welcoming a new princess, but women can't rule. The king can have four wives, but only the queen's children count, and the country wants an heir.*
>
> *Anyway, it means we have a free day and there's the "Eastern Easter" coming up. Much needed, we're rushed off our feet! I have a good friend, Dolly, one of the teachers, and*

we went to a party given by some New Zealander soldiers. A couple of our chaps were there too – just arrived, very young and pasty. We all drank a lot and danced, but I so wished you'd been there… The Palestine Orchestra put on a concert too, which was a treat.

Dolly is terrific fun. She's taking me to Groppi's café, which she says is the height of Anglo-Egyptian society, so it's best hat and frock forward for that. Cairo is ritzy and glamorous, hot and smelly. The cigarettes are filthy, cheeky kids press for piastres, but we eat like kings: meat, fresh veg and fruit and even wine. It's hard to think of the hardships at home without being overcome with guilt.

It was late. I was emotionally overwrought with the worry of Dick, fearful that Harry was drawing back and couldn't help laying my feelings bare.

…It's a wonderful thing to feel such love for a person. I dread all my desires and dreams being unfulfilled but cling to that glimmer of hope. So, my dearest, this letter comes with my undying love sealed in. I long to see you.

Your Laura

Should I talk about being *his*? Wouldn't that make him step back still more?

With every day that went by, my hopes of letters from Harry and home rose and sank again. I began to feel angry as well as sad.

Dolly said, 'Don't be glum, not when we're going to Groppi's!'

It was a new experience and I wore my best summery dress, cornflower blue with a square-cut neckline, and a wide-brimmed, navy-banded white hat. Dolly hailed a taxi, typically dilapidated and creaky, and we agreed to split the fare; the mission school housed us, but the pay was a pittance and I was flat broke.

'Midan Ismail Pasha, please,' Dolly said. 'Where are you from? Born here?'

'Sudan.' The driver – dark-skinned, bulky, reeking of garlic and weighing down his tinny taxi, clearly didn't share her American need to communicate. I'd sooner he concentrated on the driving, You took your life in your hands in a Cairo cab.

We walked down a wide street whose grand buildings had seen better days.

'It all happens at Groppi's,' said Dolly, not for the first time. 'It's where Cairo's elite do their deals, as well as flirting, splicing and splitting up. You'll see your elegant army top brass chatting up charming urbane dudes – probably German spies they're keen to haul in for interrogation – and you can just feel all the political undercurrents. Here we are, Talaat Harb Square. The ice creams are smothered in crème Chantilly and the cakes are to die for!'

A beaming gold-toothed waiter found us a tiny wrought iron table in the packed café, brought glasses of sweet, syrupy tea and long, lavish menus. We ordered strawberry ice creams, the cheapest thing to be had.

'Most of the locals look obscenely rich,' I said, 'those flashy gold watches, and the women are just too gorgeous by half. And don't they know it, crossing and flashing their slender legs the whole time!'

Dolly wasn't listening. 'Do look! Two of the most dishy-looking Brit officers coming in… Mine's the tall, fair one. You can have the older guy, who's got more pips.'

'You're in luck, I know yours. He was on my table on the ship coming out.'

Paddy had spotted us instantly. 'The lovely Laura!' he exclaimed, bounding over, 'what serendipity. And you must introduce me to your charming friend.' He was able to nab the next-door table, whose occupants were vacating it after an obvious tiff. 'Convenient!' Paddy grinned, as the woman charged off, tossing back glossy dark hair under a cloche, the man with her hastily following.

Paddy's companion, who'd now caught up, was his senior officer, Colonel Brett. 'They don't breed 'em like you guys back in the States,' Dolly said, with sparkling eyes. 'You Brits are something else!'

Colonel Brett smiled a little absently, looking towards the glass revolving door. 'Ah, here's Simon… Forgive me, Paddy, we've got a slot for tennis…'

Paddy was busy joining up our tiny tables. 'I've been *aching* to get in touch, Laura, just had to nip off to the desert for a bit. We 11th are old hands out here. We know what sand does to the armoury, stuff like that. Have you seen much of the city?'

'Not yet, they work us hard, but I seem to remember a rash mention of taking me sightseeing.'

'Laura's dying to explore. And I am too,' Dolly added hopefully.

'It's a pity, but with the holiday coming up, I'm off to the Delta to stay with some medical friends of my parents. They have a farm out there. Dolly's a bit miffed, being left all on her ownsome…' I was trying my best for her.

'Then we must go sightseeing this very day,' said Paddy, not taking the hint. 'How about doing the Khan el Khalili bazaar then a drink at Shepheard's? It'll do my stock no end of good, walking in with you two on my arm.'

'The bazaar's near the tenth-century mosque, isn't it, the Mosque of el Azhar?'

'I'm for the bazaar,' Dolly said firmly. 'You'll love it, Laura. They sell gorgeous silks and cotton, perfume in jewel-coloured bottles, alabaster pyramids…'

Paddy grinned. 'We'll do the mosque some other day and I'm in touch with the Russells, those dear archaeologists on board. I'm sure they'll give us a special tour of the museum and Tutankhamen treasures.'

'That would be amazing, the greatest thrill.'

We took a taxi to the bazaar. I climbed in first to put Dolly next to Paddy. We chatted a bit before I mentioned how worried I was about my brother Dick.

'You'd get a telegram, mustn't fret,' Paddy said cheerfully. 'The mail's taking weeks too with the ships having to sail all the way round the Cape. The war could be going better,' he said, 'Germany invading the Low Countries and Calais's just surrendered, I hear. Belgium too, and there's to be a huge Allied evacuation.'

How bad could things get? I turned to look out of the window with a silent sigh. It felt a black day under the blistering Cairo skies.

We were in a poor quarter with narrow, dark alleys and rows of brick and mud shacks pressed as tight together as playing cards in a pack. Filthy little children played in the dust; such poverty. When the taxi dropped us off in the midst of the sad squalor it was astonishing to see the magnificent entrance arch of the bazaar and all the colour and throbbing activity beyond.

All Cairo was there; tourists, shoppers, pink-skinned soldiers, the chic elite. Great shiny bales of cloth rolled out, richly patterned rugs hung on hooks, rickety stalls with tatty souvenirs, craftsmen squatting, battering out designs on brass. There were small shops; many selling jewellery with trays of uncut gems and some exquisitely intricate and beautiful pieces on display.

'Those will have belonged to refugees,' Paddy said. 'It's awful for them, having to part with their most precious treasures to survive.'

We explored the stepped alleys, walked under Moorish arches and looked into garishly lit interiors, absorbing the sights and sounds as if by osmosis. A ragged youth with melting brown eyes tried his best to sell Paddy some amber grease. 'Is aphrodisiac, Sir, make you very good lover.'

'A slur on my manhood,' Paddy grinned, and slipped him a few *piastres*.

Taxying to Shepheard's Hotel we were soon back in the broad streets of the city centre where chauffeured cars purred, elegant women crossed their legs at smart café tables and the nightmare of war seemed as distant as the Antarctic. Dolly chatting excitedly about the hotel's fame and history, all of which I knew from Dad. 'Founded in 1841, would you believe, which I guess means much more to us Yanks!' She was ebullient, bubbling over, but the poverty we'd seen and the dreadful news of the war were inescapable.

How would all the young soldiers, arriving daily, cope? Wobbly-kneed and homesick after weeks at sea, bombarded by sellers of grapes, dates, velvety apricots, lured by all the cheap alcohol and cigarettes, the dozens of open-air cinemas, the Gyppie boys leading them by the hand to brothels and nightclubs.

Velly good belly dancers, I find you nice lady. Would the soldiers be blind to the shocking poverty, the dark-shrouded women with sick babies covered in flies…?

There were palms in grand urns at Shepheard's Hotel. A balustraded terrace ran along one side of the entrance steps and since it was the cocktail hour, was buzzy and packed. A few smartly dressed Egyptians and chic women in glamorous hats there, but the terrace was a sea of khaki. Army officers sprawled in wicker armchairs, legs outstretched, hats resting on kit bags, one with the smart red band of a brigadier.

'I'm in my seventh heaven,' Dolly said, clinging to Paddy's arm as he'd typically managed to spot a free table. 'Gins and tonics and all these handsome chisel-faced army officers!'

I'd been privately hoping we might happen on Bob Sims. Shepheard's, where officers drank enough to be indiscreet, must surely be a war correspondent's natural stamping ground.

'Mind if we join you, old sport?' Two subalterns drew up chairs, unasked.

'If you must…' Paddy sighed theatrically.

'And perhaps you'd introduce us?'

'If I must…Peter Phillips and Richard Smith, both in the Hussars and need watching.'

Peter turned to Dolly with a very attentive smile. 'This is wonderful! Tell me,' he said, gazing into her sweet, open face, 'where are you from in the States?'

'I'm an East Coast girl, New York born and bred. But tell me all about *you!*'

With Dolly and Peter locking eyes, Paddy and Richard giving the drinks order, I had time to look about. Out in the street, a white-helmeted policeman was waving on horse-drawn carriages while letting army trucks park. A dress shop opposite had a proudly displayed sign, "*By appointment to her Majesty, Queen Mary*". The clothes in the window looked way out of range, definitely for the Cairo elite.

Turning back, I had a quick glance round the terrace. No sign of Bob. One or two women were hatless and I took off mine and shook out my hair.

'You should do that more often,' said Paddy, before being distracted by the very grand waiter in *galabiya* and red fez, trying to make space for the drinks.

I saw Bob come up the entrance steps then, and go straight into the hotel. 'Just nipping to the Ladies',' I said, pushing in my chair, hoping Dolly wouldn't come too.

The hotel lobby was massive, Moorish, marbled and deliciously cool. A splendid central staircase curved upwards with two barebreasted ebony caryatids at its base. Bob was just leaving the front desk, about to disappear further into the interior, and I was about to miss my chance.

'Goodness, is that you, Bob?' I called. He spun round, with his face breaking into a very reassuring smile. 'So good to see you,' I said, feeling my colour rise. 'I'm with Paddy and a few others out on the terrace. Can you come to join us?'

'Nothing I'd like more, but maddeningly I'm a bit late to meet a chap in the bar. And it's only men in the Long Bar, I'm afraid, or I'd steal you away. Silly rule, but the chaps knock back a good few jars, which is often quite helpful.' Bob looked at me with such warmth that I felt quite quivery, my heart beating hot and fast. 'It's lovely to see you. Could we perhaps have dinner one evening and catch up?'

'Love to,' I said, a bit too quickly and eagerly.

'I don't suppose you could make next Saturday? I'm told they have regular dances in the garden here, wonderful if you can.'

'The trouble is, with the local holiday, I'm just off to stay with friends of my parents down the Delta. I may be able to be back… can I let you know?'

Bob tore out a page from a small black notebook and scribbled down a number. 'Always someone there to take a message. Please try to come.' He studied me warmly with his soft smile, apologised again and hurried away.

I was looking forward to seeing the Delta. It was hotter by the day in Cairo, grimy and dusty and sand even getting into the food. But my hosts, the Wilsons, weren't returning till Sunday and giving me a lift back. It would be difficult to leave early, wrong of me too, I felt, with a flash of guilt about Harry.

A flunky directed me to the Ladies' room, where I bolted the colossal door of a mausoleum-like cubicle and where, whether from the glacial gloom or thoughts of Bob, I couldn't stop shivering. Quivery feelings, electric sensations, but how could simply seeing him again make me feel this way? I had such a yearning to lean my head to his chest… He was at least ten years older, could be married, even a father, though had given no indication of that in all our talks on the ship, and I'd been too shy or embarrassed to ask.

I'd been writing long, loving letters to Harry, upset and irritated at not hearing a word, but the post was probably to blame. I should stay the full week and make my excuses to Bob. I thought of his angular face, the soft look in his arresting violet eyes...

There was a war on, no possibility of travel, and any long-term hope of it felt very distant indeed. Was it so terrible to be longing so much to see Bob on Saturday night?

Couldn't I look on him as a friend, even a sort of father figure, someone to give wise advice? It was no good, didn't wash. The way I was feeling, seeing him would be a very disloyal and bad idea.

I pulled a comb through my hair and hurried back out to the terrace.

CHAPTER 12

The Delta and a Date

Harriet and Ronnie Wilson were younger than I expected. Harriet was tall and lithe with cropped fair hair and Ronnie, who was a surgeon, stocky and swarthy, with appealing brown eyes. They seemed very social; I'd hardly walked in the door before Harriet had mentioned a big party in the week and said they had friends coming to dinner that night.

'How should I dress? Will Ronnie be in a dinner jacket?'

'No, just wear whatever you like. I'll be in short.' Would others be in long then? I'd packed little for evening, only the blue cocktail dress in case of weakening about Saturday night and having to go straight to Shepheard's.

Harriet showed me round before we went to change. The house was fresh and airy, uncluttered. Modern cubist paintings and geometric rugs, coolly elegant after Cairo's dinge and dirt. There was a manservant called Hassan and silent maids who glided between rooms with their sandals gently slap-slapping on the marble floors.

The blue satin felt a bit overdone for a Sunday. I wore a pink scoop-neck dress with a sash. It was only cotton, quite becoming, though, and would have to do.

Harriet was in short black silk, but as the first guests arrived, a Lebanese couple, Anwar and Faisa – leading lights in Cairo, Harriet said – my heart sank. Faisa was in full-length pearl silk with dangly diamond earrings. The other guests were an Englishman in the Egyptian civil service, whose glum, pale wife was pole thin and wearing long green chiffon, and a bloated Scottish irrigation inspector, Fraser Gordon, my notional date.

Fraser was highly opinionated about the political scene but clearly well informed. I was grateful to Ronnie for forsaking the insider chat and charming me all through dinner, talking of their farm, which he clearly adored, and the apartment he and Harriet had on Gezira Island in Cairo. He had to be off in the morning, he said, back to his hospital work.

He was gone by the time I was up. There was breakfast on a shady veranda: chilled fruit, delicious croissants and coffee. Harriet said, 'I thought we could take in the Ptolemaic and Roman antiquities at Athribis tomorrow, and would you like to come for a ride this morning, see a bit of the countryside? We have a couple of donkeys and I ride out most days.'

'I'd love that, but never ridden a donkey before. I'd hate to hold you back.'

'You won't, you'll be fine. I'll put you on Juliette, she's the stodgy one. Romeo is a bit contrary and inclined to bellow.'

'For stodgy, read: reasonably safe?'

Harriet grinned. 'You'll be fine.'

Juliette had a comfortingly broad back and I soon relaxed. 'You must really love it here,' I said. 'The house is so elegant and beautiful, and I could read a whole library of books in that hammock under the trees.'

'I sure do, Cairo's fun, but one can only take so much of all that bloody sand.'

The heat and platinum-white glare of the late May sun were blinding, but the neon-green fields, minarets, distant lines of palms and the countryside were breathtaking. So rural, and the poverty was everywhere; the women scrubbing clothes on the riverbanks, carrying hefty pitchers with infants astride their shoulders. I felt for them.

I said, gripping the reins with one hand and pointing, 'I love those cone-shaped pigeon towers. They're like helter-skelter towers with portholes. This is heaven and it will be a thrill to see Athribis tomorrow too. I haven't even got to the pyramids yet, they work us so hard.' Was this the moment? 'I, um, hope you won't mind, but a friend has asked me to dinner on Saturday night. Would it put you out at all if I left a day early? I could get the bus.' My cheeks burned…

'Of course, you must go! I'm sure we can fix you up with a lift into town. People are always in and out, as we're only an hour from Cairo.'

It had taken twice as long, coming by bus, with all the army trucks and line of unhurried camels in our path.

"We've got lunch with a good friend of mine today,' Harriet said as we turned for home. 'She's a poet, called Samira, and wildly exotic! And another friend, Hakim, is giving the party on Friday, which I'm glad you won't miss. It'll be a glamorous bash. Hakim is immensely rich, very into modern art and surrealism.'

'I'll be way out of my depth then,' I laughed, relieved to have packed the blue satin. 'I don't know a sausage about surrealist art.'

'Nor do I. Nor does anyone else much in Cairo, so don't look so worried. We've been fossilising away here in art terms, and people find the new surrealism hard to take. It's a sort of protest against Fascist and Nazi atrocities, a growing movement imported from France, a carry-on from Dadaism. It's causing offence, very frowned on by the authorities, but Hakim funds all these daring young artists and there's sure to be one or two at the party.'

I even felt out of my depth at lunch. Samira, with her long tapering fingers and red-painted nails, the heady scent she was wearing, would have made any man swoon. I was overawed too by her sumptuous house that was marbled, gleaming with silverware and hung with huge, glorious tapestries.

It was a large lunch party and in a yellow halter-neck summer frock, I felt a country bumpkin all over again, right down to my block-heeled sandals. Samira, though, gliding about in her flowing embroidered robes, made every one of her guests feel they personally mattered to her.

She couldn't have been more charming and said, resting a cool, elegant hand on my bare arm, 'I hadn't expected Harriet's house guest to be quite as young and beautiful. Hakim's going to be mad for you, you'd better watch out at his party!'

*

Having called and left a message for Bob, I was in an adrenaline-fuelled fluster, dressing for the party on Friday night. Was it so wrong, a pleasant evening with a friend from the voyage out? Not if it stayed that way…

Ronnie was late back from the city and we arrived to find the party in full swing. Hakim greeted us in the thronging marble hall, kissing Harriet's hand expansively, mine too, and giving me a flattering eye. 'Champagne, we need champagne!' he shouted, and a waiter magically appeared with a tray held high.

Hakim was short and heavily built, around fifty, at a guess, with crinkly black hair and a neatly clipped moustache. Ronnie and Harriet were busy looking round, seeing friends and Hakim, linking arms with me, said airily to no one in particular, 'I'm going to borrow this lovely girl, who everyone's dying to meet.'

He forged a path through the crush of guests, who folded away like the parting of the Red Sea, and took me out into an exquisitely tiled courtyard with a fountain and water lilies, lush tropical plants. 'You're a beautiful breath of fresh air,' he said, 'how lucky we are to have you. Now, come and meet some of my more talented young friends.'

Three arches led in from the courtyard. Hakim took me in through the central one, into an interior that was a palace, an Aladdin's Cave of delights. Mosaic floors, life-sized sculptures, chests glowing with lapis and inlaid brass, gleaming silver urns. Rooms meandered into rooms like a beautiful garden with secretive corners – proposal points I'd once heard them called – alcoves were screened with intricately appliquéd arrases and the many vast dominating canvasses were violently colourful, unmissable on the walls.

'They're mostly done by artists like those two young men over there,' Hakim said. 'Come to meet them.'

The two were arguing, gesticulating furiously, both extravagantly dressed with silk cravats and flashy jewel-coloured waistcoats. 'We need innovation, brutal honesty, free expression of passion and desires,' the more flamboyant one said, snapping off abruptly to kiss my hand with an elaborate flourish before carrying on. 'What has anyone got to fear from the liberation of Eros?' Even his clipped black beard seemed to have a ferocity of its own.

The other artist was sickly-looking, his turquoise jacket only adding to his pallor. He said, 'I accept that there's an interesting challenge in depicting human longings, but never forget the supreme beauty of flame-red lotus flowers…'

'You abhor modernity then? Like Hitler? Shame on you! Long live surrealism and degenerate art!'

'Bravo, magnificent!' Hakim exclaimed, clapping enthusiastically and moving me on. 'He's in a Trotskyist group, that one, *Art et Liberté*. I love the rawness of his experimental art. Now, here are two very dear friends of mine.' Hakim beamed at two heavily bejewelled matrons with feathers in their coiffures.

'When I was last in London in '33,' the purple feathered one said, after the introductions, 'I had the honour to meet the Prince of Wales. He was *such* a charming man, so gracious.'

Her companion was nodding vigorously. 'Shocking, his having to abdicate, such a *terrible* loss.'

'Still, George VI is proving a good, dutiful king,' I ventured, 'in time of war…'

'Oh, for pre-war London!' Hakim laughed, elegantly cutting off the conversation while leaving the elderly pair quite charmed.

'We should have a little rest,' he said, walking me to an alcove where small groups were lounging about languidly. We sat down on a banquette and he patted my hand. 'Now, I want to know all about you, all your innermost secrets.'

'No secrets, no skeletons!' I laughed.

Samira, seated on an emerald velvet pouffe nearby, was looking as exotic as a peacock in a richly embroidered gown with jewel-studded gold bangles going way up her beautiful arms. She was with a couple of wizened old men speckled with sunspots and turned round to prod Hakim in his broad, white-robed chest.

'Now, now, none of your predatory designs on this beautiful young girl, you old bear. You should be introducing her to some of your more respectable artist friends – as if there were any.'

Hakim reached out to rub his thumb over Samira's full red lips. 'I have done, and now we're having a nice quiet chat.' He was tracing round her jaw, giving a slight smirk, which made me feel like a voyeur; he fitted the image of middle-aged predator, but with his lavish charm and flattery was hard to dislike. He flicked Samira's luxuriant hair while drawing me closer to his side. 'I am enjoying this wonderful little threesome,' he said, chuckling, looking from one to the other of us. 'It's the perfect *ménage à trois* of my imaginings…'

Samira frowned at him. I knew it was a suggestive phrase but had never quite understood why. *Ménage* translated as housekeeping or household after all. Feeling quite bold, I was tempted to ask. 'Sharing a house together?'

Hakim threw back his head and roared. 'No, darling, sharing a bed,' he said, still laughing, kissing my cheek wetly. 'Sharing a bed together, my little ingénue, but a house would be a good start! Oh, would that I could be the lucky man to initiate you,' he kissed me again, 'into all the sweetest pleasures of life yet to come.'

The party ran its course. I kept looking round for the Wilsons, impatient to be gone, fretting, wanting to look my best for Bob. Hakim had left me blushing as crimson as the banquette we'd been sitting on, and the scarlet embarrassment of my naivety wouldn't leave me. I thought of Lil, younger and way ahead of me, while I was about as savvy and worldly-wise as a nun. I felt desperate, humiliated, overcome with shame, but in an odd way, exhilarated and more alive to my own sexuality. I should never have agreed to see Bob, longing to as much as I did... Harriet had mentioned a possible lift into the city, but nothing had come of that.

Still no letter from Harry; suppose there was one waiting for me at the school? A loving letter that would renew the hope that, with no end of the war in sight, had dimmed like a dying candle. Harry was away fighting and the war could only get worse. Did I really have any serious hope of ever seeing him again?

Ronnie turned up, seeming as keen to leave as I was, drumming his fingers on his cigarette case, eyes skinned for Harriet. She came hurrying up then with a crazed-looking young man, apologising and introducing him. 'This is Yehia. He is driving into Cairo tomorrow and happy to give you a ride.'

'That's amazingly good of you,' I flashed him a glowing smile, 'thanks so much.'

'The pleasure's entirely mine.' His hair stuck out like a rag doll, and he was swaying steadily from side to side like a metronome. 'I'll come at three.' He bowed very low, almost losing his balance. I hoped he'd be sober by the following afternoon.

It was nearer four o'clock when he arrived, looking as green as stagnant water. Was he safe to drive? I said my thanks and goodbyes and followed him out to an ancient little Fiat, fervently hoping he wouldn't throw up all over me or pass out at the wheel.

We'd hardly driven a mile before his hand was on my thigh. I returned it to the wheel and moved as far to the edge of my seat as possible, gripping on, sure the door was about to fly open; the car was very old. Yehia leaned over with his wandering hand and the car swerved and careered across the road. How we avoided crashing into an oncoming horse and cart…

We got to the mission school, God knows how, and I almost fell out of the car in my relief to be back, intact and alive. I was seeing Bob in hours.

CHAPTER 13

Shepheard's Hotel

I waited by the door, anxious to slip away quietly without being seen and avoid any fascinated questions about Bob. Dolly and others knew all about Harry.

Bob was on time and gave me a heart-stopping smile. We settled into a taxi, 'I'm so glad you could come. I haven't been to one of these dances before, hope it won't be a bun fight, but I've asked for a table well away from the band, we should be able to hear ourselves speak. You're looking very lovely…'

I thanked him, embarrassed, and talked about the Delta. 'The fields planted with clover were the most brilliant emerald green, and there were egrets and herons…' I was wittering, showing my nerves.

'It sounds as if you had a great break. It's always good to get out of Cairo.'

'Yes. My parents' friends took me to glamorous parties given by rich Egyptians. It was quite an education!'

'They sound an enlightened couple. The Gezira Sporting Club has a few Cairene members, but there's not a lot of mixing, more's the pity.'

'You know Cairo well?'

'Not really, I was here once before, briefly, but you pick these things up.'

'You journalists, you mean. We hear so little news and I haven't had a single letter from home for weeks. I feel dreadfully worried about them all.'

'And you must long for a letter from Uganda.'

I nodded, wishing he hadn't brought up Harry, and felt more subdued.

We were at Shepheard's. Going up the steps, Bob said, 'You may not hear for a while yet. His battalion could be anywhere with who knows what difficulties of communication. And I'm afraid things are going to get worse. But no more talk of war, it's too depressing. Let's shut our minds to it for tonight.'

A three-piece band was playing, people dancing, and there were lights strung up overhead. Some of the women were in uniform, some in long evening dress, probably officers' wives, and there were younger girls, probably secretaries and nurses, wearing short cocktail frocks like mine.

A waiter in white pantaloons showed us to our table and asked about drinks. 'Gin slings? What do you say?'

'Sounds good!'

'And can we see the dinner menu?'

'Dinner is served in the dining room, Sir. There's no dining out here.'

'Could we perhaps just have chicken sandwiches or something? We'd be very grateful…' The imposing waiter inclined his head, yielding to feminine wiles, but left looking filled with alarm.

'Thanks, that was inspired of you. I should have done my homework better! You're looking so very beautiful. I remember that dress from the ship and loved it then, just as now.'

'It's a bit old-fashioned, it was my mother's actually.' I reddened, never finding it easy to accept a compliment. 'Can I disobey instructions and ask if you've had any late news bulletins? People down the Delta were saying that our troops in France are in full retreat, heading to the coast, but won't that make them sitting targets? I worry about a friend of mine from Scotland who's there.'

'It's been the most miraculous thing, a whole armada of private little boats and craft crossing over in dreadful conditions to rescue them. They were stranded on the sands at Dunkirk, the Luftwaffe picking them off like flies, and now nearly a quarter of a million saved, so there's every hope for your friend.'

'But many too who will have lost their lives...'

'You can't think like that when there's every hope, the odds are very good. On other news, I heard only tonight that Italy's declared war on France, us too, of course, and with the Italians right on our doorstep here they'll be pushing hard. I'll go to the front and file my report, but it's standing on the sidelines, and I feel more and more now I should go home, tie up loose ends and join up.'

He couldn't, mustn't; I felt jolted. 'But you're needed here! People have to know what's going on. Your reports, the job you do, it's vital.'

'Hardly! I'm very expendable, no shortage of war correspondents.'

'Not ones like you, brave and experienced...'

I tailed off as Bob laughed out loud. 'Flawed, bad and a coward, more like! We'd better change the subject fast!' I loved his laugh, his voice, and felt desolate.

The waiter brought our cocktails. Bob said, 'When you were in Hamburg two years before the war, did you get any sense of what was coming?'

'Kristallnacht was inhuman, still wakes me up at night, but to imagine the madness of another war, it seemed impossible, no one could let it happen.'

I looked down at my pink drink, feeling embarrassingly close to tears.

Bob leaned to touch my arm and I felt the light brush of his fingers deep within. I wanted more of his touch. I loved Harry, couldn't and didn't want to forget him, only to forget about feeling disloyal. I'd talked so much about him on the ship. Wouldn't Bob feel the need to keep his distance? He was a decent good man.

I wanted to be held tight on the dance floor, swaying to the music, moving as one. I wanted to feel the length of him and lift my mouth to be kissed. Even if the war ended with miraculous speed, what chance of getting to Uganda then? And even suppose I did, would Harry really expect me to be a virgin at nearly twenty-three?

The waiter came with the sandwiches, chicken and beef, crisps on the side, and managed to find room for them on the tiny table. He poured the wine and left. I stared at the gleaming burgundy liquid in the glass for a minute before looking up. 'Can I ask personal questions? I know nothing of your home life, even if you're married.'

Bob smiled. 'Not married, much as my mother would love me to be. She longs for grandchildren. My father was killed in the last war and my sister died of leukaemia when she was seven.'

'How unbearably sad, and losing your father too, I'm very sorry.'

'The trouble is,' Bob held my eyes, 'close as I've come to marrying, I've never quite felt able to take that final step. Plenty of marriages do rather seem to miss a beat. It's probably being too idealistic to hope that I'd know instinctively when the love was real and that marrying was meant to be.'

'But,' my cheeks flamed as I tried to frame the question, 'are you near to taking that step? Is there someone at home who you think about with marriage in mind?' My blood was racing. Did that perhaps explain his need to join up?

His expression hard to read, except for the softening of the hard-etched lines, it was almost as if he could read my thoughts and understand.

'You're asking very perceptive questions. There is someone at home, a girl I see and get on with. We're good friends and she gives heavy hints about wanting to be married, but it would feel – and this is an awful thing to say, terrible analogy since the relationship has its physical side – almost like marrying my sister.'

He reached for my hand. 'I'm escaping, you see, coming out here. I love the job, reporting from war zones is challenging and worthwhile, but needing my freedom is a part of it.' His smile arrowed straight in. 'I feel a cowardly heel, but that's how it is, I'm afraid. Now I think we should eat our curling sandwiches, and I'm longing to take you to dance. After that, it's my turn to ask questions.'

On the floor with Bob's hand firm on my back, I felt inhibited, holding myself stiffly, desperate to press my body, but resisting. The need of his touch was too overwhelming, a shock to my system, like an electric current. His hand was warm, directing, and he chose not to notice any reserve. I gave in, melted, couldn't not, and soon there was little more than a hair's breadth between us.

A couple of rhumbas then a waltz that brought us even closer. Then a faster number, which made Bob laugh. 'It's Bing Crosby, *Don't Fence Me In,* and right after my guilty confession!' I smiled uncertainly, not sure what to make of that.

We jived to Glen Miller and Fats Waller. It was eleven o'clock, still little let-up from the heat in the enclosed garden and the airlessness was getting to me. 'Can we sit down? I need a breather.'

'Me too, and a drink.' Bob held my hand as we went back to the table. It felt natural after dancing for so long and I'd begun to relax. I thought of Lil's summer balls at Cambridge. Were they still happening in time of war? Lil had no moral boundaries, jumping into bed with her student friends. She wouldn't have made such an ass of herself with a wicked old roué like Hakim.

Bob ordered iced water and another bottle of wine.

'I'll be under the table!'

'We'll dance it off. No need to finish the bottle, I'd just like to sit here for a while, looking at you and knowing more.'

'You know plenty already. I talked far too much about myself on the ship.'

'Only about your family and Scotland, not about you. Tell me how you met Harry. You braved torpedoes, chasing out all this way after him. Have you known each other a long time? Did he ask you to come?'

'No to both questions. He neither asked nor tried to put me off. We first met years ago, when he was holidaying in Scotland. I was very young and never imagined seeing him again, although had felt an attraction. We met once more with mutual friends then when I was about to go to Hamburg, Harry wrote saying he'd be in Germany briefly, seeing his aunts in Bavaria, and asked me to come to stay. He was on his way to say goodbye to his parents in Austria.'

'So, you holidayed in Bavaria with Harry, chaperoned by the aunts?'

I met Bob's gaze. 'Yes. It was a romantic few days, climbing mountains…'

'And did you make love, high up on the slopes?'

His eyes were teasing, which was irritating, and I answered primly, 'We stopped short of that, but have corresponded ever since.'

Bob had a dubious, maddening look on his face, which got me really riled.

'I didn't need any say-so from Harry. I was determined to get to Africa and see him again, and not even the coming war was going to stand in my way.'

'Such strong will,' Bob murmured, with one of his irresistible smiles. 'You mustn't worry, sure you'll hear from him soon. The army probably dropped the letter into the wrong bag and it'll have been twice round the Cape by the time it comes. But can I just say one thing?' He searched my face, making me ache for him to rub his thumb gently over my lips as Hakim had done with Samira.

'It's probably a bit out of turn of me, but you and Harry hardly seem to have been together very much. We're in for a rough time, but if, God willing, we get through this war and things eventually work out, my advice is to try not to rush into marriage. Take a little time, discover one another. You'll probably feel all the more certain, but just in case… I must confess I'm rather in the opposite camp, feeling I know Coral almost too well!'

I was silent. We'd drunk most of the second bottle of wine and I was feeling tactile, emotional and uncertain; dreaming a little less about being married to Harry and living in a remote malarial forest. I couldn't say that, though, battling with my powerful attraction to Bob. It was a feeling like being in the path of an avalanche. I felt transfixed, waiting, terrified of how deeply I could become submerged.

We were almost the last couple there, the band playing slow romantic numbers, time to go. Bob held out his hand. 'Let's have a last dance before they turf us out then I'll see you safely home.'

As the taxi drew up outside the school, he put his lips to mine. 'Can we do this again next Saturday? And perhaps see a film on Wednesday? Please don't think I'm pushing too hard, it's just that I'm negotiating to join a convoy out to the desert, which is likely to be the week after, and it's a bit superstitious of me, but things happen in wars, there's never the luxury of being able to plan ahead.'

'I'd love to do both,' I said, meeting his eyes. 'I finish a bit earlier on Wednesdays too, sometimes it's not until nine.' Where were my loyalty and sense of commitment? The flutters of guilt were gathering like falling leaves.

Bob saw me to the door, kissed my cheek and left. I turned the front door key and went inside, leaning back against the warm wood of the solid door, knowing I would lie in bed sleepless, imagining his non-return from the desert, lying there with the spectre of loss playing notes on my spine. I shouldn't be seeing him next week. I felt frightened for the future, and wet-eyed.

CHAPTER 14

The Cinema

Gloria Parker, the maths teacher, was speaking passionlessly about helping the needy in time of war. The small chapel was airless with an odour of dusty prayer books and candle wax, overheated bodies too, and a fly was buzzing persistently close to my ear like an alarm clock. The students in the front rows with their covered heads, most of whom prayed to Allah at home, must sit through these services in a stupefied daze.

There was a rota for giving the address, my turn next week, and I should be putting my mind to that, not thinking obsessively about Bob. Was my need of him purely physical? Was it the same with Harry? Had that passionate urgency I'd felt high up on the Alpsplitze, the need that had propelled me across continents, simply been all about physical pull? How well did I really know Harry? Well enough to recognise the deeper feelings needed to last through thick and thin? Feelings to lead to a lifetime of loving? The seeds of doubt were in me now.

Dolly was grinning behind her hand. We were sitting near the back, damp with the heat, and stifling yawns. She'd be dying to hear about Bob and I was longing to talk about him and ask advice, but wouldn't even Dolly be a bit shocked?

'Masses to tell,' she whispered as we filed out of the chapel. 'I've been getting it together with Peter while you were off doing your pastoral thing and I'm hooked! In love! Gotta dash, got a lesson, unlike you with your free day, but let's go out for tea later and catch up.'

'Sounds great, but not Groppi's. I haven't got a sou to my name. Longing to buy a new dress too…'

'Ooh, that means you've got another date lined up with Bob!' She hurried off giggling and I went up to my room. The bed was made, everything spick and span. Mahmoud had left a plate of fresh fruit; figs, melon and slices of orange. He knew I'd been late in and skipped breakfast; he was a wonder.

The heat was oppressive and the thought of the long summer break with no holiday job, nowhere to go, was infinitely depressing. Confined like a prisoner in the empty school, feeling spit-roasted in the August heat… Dolly was going to Alexandria to help friends with their new baby. Gloria, with her rich parents, had a flight booked to America; everyone seemed spoken for.

I had work to do, letters to write, but they could wait. I went down the corridor with its fresh tang of beeswax to closet myself in the white-tiled bathroom and have a good long soak. The tub was a solid old thing with claw feet and a long green stain down to the plughole. I turned on the huge brass taps, undressed while the water thundered out and climbed in, loving the sense of luxury.

My body was white, arms and legs tanned. I cupped my chalk white breasts, imagining Bob holding them, fingering them. The nipples became hard and erect and I had an urge to rub and feel between my legs, sensations that felt indecent and improper. But would feeling be such a terrible thing? Hakim had opened my eyes, awakened me to my own sexuality.

I'd asked Bob if *The Times* arranged where he stayed and he said they gave him an allowance, but left that down to him. He rented a one-room, top-floor apartment from a French family whose maid brought him breakfast and took messages. He paid an extra whack for that, no flies on the French, but the apartment had steps up to his own private bit of flat roof with a fantastic view of the city.

Bob would be so experienced, I wouldn't know what to do… But it wasn't going to happen; he had a relationship with a girl called Coral, and what greater betrayal of Harry could there be?

At lunch, everyone talked about holiday jobs. I said something would turn up but with little hope in my heart. Dolly suggested El Horreya for tea, where we'd been to one evening, a café with ochre walls, mirrors with gilded slogans like *"Votre Boisson Préférée, VIMTO!"* and a powerful aroma of Turkish coffee. I hoped it would be quieter in the afternoon; there were questions I needed to ask.

We took a tram downtown. The reek of stale cigar was more evident by day, but there was hardly anyone there. A few locals who eyed us curiously soon returned to their newspapers, and two papery-skinned old men, engrossed in a game of chess, stared so long at the board that I imagined cobwebs forming.

We ordered *karkade*, the deliciously tart hibiscus tea that went all the way back to the pharaohs, and Dolly leaned in close. Her sparkle was astonishing; she was always giggly and fun but had a new aura about her with a new man in her life, a luminous glow, a shine to her red-blonde hair.

'I've been getting it together with Pete ever since Shepheard's! Do I owe your friend Paddy one ginormous thank you!' She tweaked the skirt of her turquoise frock and carried on in a loud whisper. 'Pete's the best thing that's ever happened to me. He's based at the barracks but has a friend with a flat here who's had to go to Palestine and given him the key. Miss Wilcox wouldn't approve!' Dolly's open face suddenly clouded. 'I only hope it isn't all about seizing the moment… Pete's off fighting in the desert next week and said if I'm the last girl he sees in this life, at least he'd die happy! Which was kind of heartening and not…' Dolly's every emotion showed on her dear face.

The tea arrived and as soon as we were alone, I said, blushing, 'I shouldn't ask, but, well, is he the first?'

'God, no! I've had the knickers off more than once back home. It was never like this, though…' The locals must have been eagle-eared behind their newspapers with Dolly's carrying accent; too much to hope that they didn't speak English… 'Now, I want to hear all about this mysterious Bob who's got you so all shook up, and don't spare the blushes.'

'I do really like him, but he's ten years older and it feels dreadfully disloyal to Harry.' I stared at Dolly, trying to pluck up courage. 'But, well, I'm seeing Bob again and don't really trust myself. I'm, um, terribly inexperienced…'

'No way! Then you gotta go for it, girl. What the heck, it's wartime. You're real sweet on this guy, it sure shows, and the Germans and Itis will be bombing Cairo before we know it. Just see he wears a condom.'

I stared, feeling even more nervous. 'I, um, don't know what that is…'

Dolly stared back at me in wonder and set about telling me in every last embarrassing detail, and when I thanked her, blushing, she said cheerfully, 'Anything can happen. Will we even be here tomorrow? And now you must definitely buy that new dress, more than one. I'll lend you the money.'

'Thanks, Dolly, you're a brick! Just for today, though. I'm in the money as of the lunchtime post, a letter from home at last and Mum had put in a cheque! Quite a handsome one too, so I can pay you right back.'

'You must be real glad to hear from your folks, I'm so pleased for you!' Sensitively, Dolly hadn't asked a word about Harry. Still no letter... 'Better get the check,' she said, 'and go buy that dress. This is definitely your day!'

*

On Wednesday, sitting at the back of the open-air cinema under a gloriously starlit sky with Bob, I felt heart-pounding happiness. *Goodbye Mr. Chips* was showing. 'It's a weepie,' Bob said, 'we'll need our hankies.' I needed one anyway, dreading his trip to the desert.

The cinema was full; hairy-armed soldiers in front of us, loud-mouthed and drunken with thick red backs of necks; sloe-eyed Egyptian youths looking on the make, after company of either sex; hawkers pacing the aisles, being bawled at by Tommies and ushers alike.

I'd bought two new frocks, egged on by Dolly, one, figure-hugging cream silk with a low cowl, I was keeping for Saturday, and a wine-red dress with black lace on a low-cut bodice. Bob had admired it and asked if it was new. I loved the way he noticed things.

'It feels close to heaven, in both senses,' I said, leaning into him, 'being out here on such a balmy beautiful night. How well are you up in the stars?'

'I'm not, haven't a clue, you'll have to give me a class on constellations.'

'You must know the Plough and North Star – and that's the Scorpion stretching right across the Milky Way. I love its shape with the curling tail...'

'I'm going to need a lot more lessons like that.' He squeezed my hand and the credits began to roll.

The film was unbearably moving. The wartime scenes made me think of the uncles I'd never known, and when poor Mr Chips' young wife died in childbirth, my cheeks were wet with tears. Bob held my hand and tucked it under his arm, wiping away a tear or two himself. I was surprised and touched that he had a sentimental side.

Coming out blinking into the neon-lit exterior, the redneck soldiers who'd been in front of us were being harassed by a couple of ragged little boys.

'You like filthie ladies, Sirs? You follow?'

One of the soldiers spat into the child's face and Bob rounded on him. 'How dare you! Letting down your country like that, you're disgusting, a disgrace.'

'Fuck you, shitface. Shit in yer fuckin' eye!' They swaggered off, sniggering.

'Sorry you had to hear that,' Bob said, putting his arm round me as we looked for a cab. 'I've booked at a kebab place downtown for a quick bite. I know you won't want to be late, midweek.'

I did want to be late on Saturday, though, whether lessons on Sundays or not.

The restaurant was friendly and atmospheric with tomato-coloured walls and decorative fretwork. French, Greeks, Egyptians; the only British there were a couple of subalterns conferring like businessmen with their heads close.

I asked for the latest war news and Bob's expression clouded. 'France has surrendered now, right after the armistices signed between Italy and Germany and when we'd hoped and believed they'd fight on. German tanks just across the Channel, it doesn't bear thinking about.'

'Are we losing this war? Will there be swastikas flying over Parliament?'

'We're not going to lose, we'll fight on for as long as it takes. It's going to be bloody, we badly need more air power, but we're in for the long haul.

'Let's talk about anything else.' Bob's violet eyes were on me, warm, smiling. 'I called on an eccentric White Russian colonel today, one of life's originals, who distils vodka in his bath. He showered me with bottles of the stuff that I could hardly refuse and told me about another ex-pat Russian, guy called Vladimir Peniakoff, who knows every dip and incline of the desert like a black-cab driver knows London, and who's keen to do reconnaissance trips for the army.'

'See what you can discover with your journalist skills!' I laughed, but from the way Bob had spoken about the war, my every instinct told of his seriousness about joining up. I passionately didn't want him to. Was this falling in love, this need that eclipsed all other feelings? Harry seemed more distant in every way. Still no letter. Why hadn't he written? Had anything happened to him? Was there someone else? My emotions were in turmoil.

I looked at Bob, aching for physical contact, and said, knowing the need to keep things light, 'I had to take ten teenagers to a concert yesterday, and needed eyes in the front and back of my head. With half the girls having to marry their cousins or uncles to keep the money in the family, you wouldn't believe all the prospective suitors masquerading as relatives!

'It was such a relief having a letter from home.' Did it matter, Bob knowing I hadn't heard from Harry? 'Everyone's fine, thankfully, and all I need now is a holiday job. It's going to be a long hot summer, cooped up in that deserted school!' Bob was attentive but with a tender, contemplative look on his face, his thoughts elsewhere. Were they near or far distant from Cairo?

I must have been staring. He felt my gaze and raised his eyebrows. 'You were far away,' I said, embarrassed. 'I was just wondering about your thoughts…'

'They were on you, how contented and happy I feel.' His face could look hard and etched as a woodcarving, but not now, and my heart turned over.

We finished the tiny demitasses of lethally strong Turkish

coffee and the waiter brought sweetmeats and the bill. Bob reached to brush over my lips with his fingers. 'I must get you back, much as I'd love to keep looking at you across this little table. It's going to be a long three days till Saturday.'

'And for me too.' I smiled, feeling the blazing heat of my elation. How could I possibly let him know what I wanted to happen on Saturday night? I was ten years younger; wouldn't he be too decent to lure me to his top-floor apartment and make love? Wouldn't he simply take me back to the mission school, put his lips to mine and drive away into the night?

CHAPTER 15

The End of Term

'I would like a word later, Laura,' Miss Wilcox said at breakfast, rising from the table. 'Please come to my study at break.' She pushed in her chair and strode down the dining hall, straight-backed, dressed as usual in a high-necked white blouse and black skirt. Her peremptory manner was no more than normal, no less unnerving when it came to an unexpected summons. I'd been back very late the previous Saturday, but we were free to come and go after hours and it was Friday already. Surely a bit late in the day to be raising eyebrows over that?

I had two lessons before break, German, which was a bit of a bind, since the girls were stubbornly disinterested, and my music class. I'd asked a teacher from a connected school to visit, a jolly woman in her forties, and we were going to play a duet; Miss Bonsor on the recorder, me on my lute. I wanted the class to see that music was to be enjoyed, not all about working for diplomas. None of those could be taken anyway with the war on, apart from a diploma in teaching. I was giving extra coaching in harmony and theory to girls sitting for that who were older than I was.

Playing together for the first time, we were a bit wobbly, but the class entered in, one girl even saying cheekily that they should hand round a hat. A couple of them asked to learn the lute afterwards too, which was gratifying.

Break came all too soon and I hurried to the head's office. Miss Wilcox was blank of expression as well as looking physically remote on the far side of her vast desk. She gestured to a chair and I sat down cautiously, trying to slow my speeding heart.

'I've had a call from a Colonel Harvey at Abbassia Barracks,' she said, 'who asked whether there were any British teachers on my staff available to be a governess to his children during the summer break. He wanted a three-month commitment, however, which would mean missing the start of the fall term.'

My heart-leap of hope faded like the sun veiled by a cloud. Was I being told as a mere courtesy? 'They live in officers' quarters at Abbassia, have boys of eleven and nine and a girl of five, and a governess would be required to live in.'

'I'd really love to be considered,' I said, wondering at Colonel Harvey asking specifically about British teachers. 'Would it be at all possible to miss a few days at the start of term?' I held my breath, sensing the door was a fraction ajar.

'I could consider accommodating a late start. It's hard to know what the situation will be by then, even whether we will be able to reopen at all.'

To my utter amazement, her face broke out into a smile. 'This does seem fortuitous. Word had reached me that you were concerned about the summer break and it will be quiet as a morgue, here in the school.' Miss Wilcox picked up the telephone and asked to speak to Colonel Harvey. 'No time like the present,' she said, leaving me further dumbfounded, and arranged an interview for me with the Harveys, at five o'clock that very afternoon.

I got a bus to the Abbassia Barracks and found the house; square, redbrick and identical to its neighbours, typical of the married officers' quarters I remembered from childhood. All had gardens, many with sprinklers working furiously, struggling to beat Cairo's heat and the thin sandy soil.

Colonel Harvey came to the door and shook hands. He was tall with thick, slicked-back fair hair, a large moustache, and stood as ramrod-straight as Miss Wilcox, as crisply formal in his dress too. His khakis looked fresh out of the press, shoes polished to a mirror shine.

He took me into the sitting room where his wife was waiting. 'I'm Mary Harvey,' she said, holding out her hand. She was fairer than her husband with light blue eyes and a slightly faded look about her face, which was finely lined, though she was probably only in her thirties. The room was unimaginatively furnished – a beige three-piece suite, hunting prints and a carved camphorwood chest – and they seemed a very proper couple, as safe and conventional as the furnishings in the room.

A maid appeared with a tray of tea. 'I'm off now, Mrs H, see you tomorra then.'

'Thank you, Maisie,' Mrs Harvey said, looking pained at the informality.

'We are hoping to go to Palestine,' Colonel Harvey said, while his wife poured weak tea into flowery china cups, 'but awaiting events, since accommodation is scare in Jerusalem and it isn't a safe time at the coast. You would come too, of course, to attend to the children. And here they are now, I do believe.'

He looked over to the door. 'Come on into the sitting room, boys, and look sharp about it. I want you to meet Miss Jameson. And pull those socks up at once!' he said, before introducing his two sons, Arthur and George. I warmed to them, loving the familiar whiff of hot sweaty boy about them that brought memories of my brothers. I felt an acute stab of homesickness.

The boys' five-year-old sister, Alice, followed in, skipping about, looking very pleased with herself. She had blonde curls that clung damply to her small heart-shaped face and was wearing shorts. 'I've changed into a cock!' she said jauntily.

It was an arresting statement and her parents looked at each other, embarrassed. 'I think not, dear,' Mrs Harvey said emolliently, sliding me a quick flustered glance while Alice pouted and stuck out her small jaw. 'You're our little girl and you must change quickly back into your pretty dress.'

She wanted a daughter in her own mould, but I enjoyed Alice's feistiness and liked the boys; I was less taken with their disciplinarian father, but that was a small price to pay.

Back at the mission school, I couldn't stop pinching myself. A holiday job, everything fixed up in hours, and Miss Wilcox had actually smiled. The war was raging, but providence had intervened.

The chance of going to Palestine was a thrilling possibility, but there'd be no Bob, and I felt the wrench of parting as keenly as if it had already happened. And the germ of a seed he'd sown about how little I really knew Harry nagged. I knew Bob almost better after two weeks at sea, dinner sitting next to him every night, long talks during the day. He was completely familiar to me, to the point where I felt able to share innermost secrets and fears.

But I would get to know Harry too, given half a chance…

Bob was so much on my mind. The times left to us to meet now, with Palestine, were precious few. I dreaded his need to join up, the dangers Harry must be facing, Bob joining a convoy into the desert, dreaded him returning to Coral.

Lying in bed that night, I thought obsessively about making love with Bob. Would he continue to hold back? Feel it was taking advantage? I could hardly say, *'Please, Bob, will you take me to bed?'* But didn't these things just happen in the heat of the moment? I sighed and settled on my side; either way, it would help not to be looking like a washed-out rag.

*

Bob had borrowed a friend's car for the night and we drove to Shepheard's.

The band were playing as we went out into the garden and he took me straight onto the floor, dancing cheek to cheek. I lost all my inhibitions with the unnerving sensation of Bob's warm breath on my skin.

'You're beautiful, Laura,' he whispered. 'It's not just this slinky, silky dress, lovely as it is, or your fresh, light perfume. It's you, your own special smell, it stays with me.' He lifted up my face and held my eyes. 'You're going to have to work hard to keep me in check tonight.'

We left the dance floor arm in arm and I leaned into him freely, feeling a shimmering current of communication, sure that he did really care. 'I've got some amazing news,' I said happily, as we sat down. 'It came completely out of the blue, a holiday job as a children's governess with a family at Abbassia. I'm in a complete daze. It was all fixed up in an afternoon.'

'You heard from the Colonel then?' Bob had an amused grin on his face, which got me riled.

'Is this all your doing? How would you know about that?'

'Don't look so deliciously furious! I just happened to overhear a conversation in the Long Bar the other night, an army colonel saying they needed a holiday governess for his children. He had the sort of prejudiced attitude that I knew you'd mind, said he couldn't be doing with any of these darkies, that sort of thing, but I reckoned you could handle that and guide his children's views.'

Bob being so sure, and right, about my reactions gave me a warm feeling. 'So, you butted in and mentioned the mission school? But why should Colonel Harvey have asked specifically about British teachers? We're an American mission school after all, and American girls are hardly "darkie foreigners".'

'Not far off in the Colonel's eyes. I simply suggested that there may be one or two British teachers at the school. And you must see that you'd fit in better at the barracks.' Bob grinned. 'Anyway, he thinks you're "top hole" and even rang at dawn today to thank me, which I could have done without.'

'You don't know what he thinks, but I think you're a complete marvel.'

'Just don't find me out. Here's the waiter. Same as before?'

We danced into the night, close as pages in a book. I was dimly aware of other couples dancing more decorously and giving us sniffy looks. It made me feel a bit anxious, but I couldn't see anyone I knew.

Bob gave a light press on my back. 'What's wrong? You've tensed up a bit.'

'Nothing, just someone walking on my grave.' I leaned back with a smile and suddenly saw the Major from the ship, Egbert Carter-Smith, on the floor. He was dancing with an ample middle-aged woman, but his eyes had been trained and his expression said it all. My heart plummeted. He'd telephoned the school twice to ask me out and I'd refused, saying it would feel disloyal to Harry, feelings of disloyalty that were buried deep, out with Bob.

'You've really tensed and frozen now, someone you've seen?'

'Yes. Egbert, from our table on the ship – who's looking suitably shocked. He's asked me out, you see, and I've made excuses.'

Bob nestled his cheek back onto mine. 'I'm sure he's used to rejections and he's unlikely to come storming over, telling me to unhand you or be put in chains, but perhaps we'd better go back to the table.' Bob sensitively kept his distance as we left the floor, for which I was very grateful.

We sat in the dark of the garden, sipping drinks. Bob's foot touched mine and he met my eyes. 'I need to talk to you…' He stopped, looking beyond me with a frown. 'Damn and blast, here comes the Major. No escaping now.'

I turned to see Egbert making his way over with a purposeful scowl on his face and determined hunch to his shoulders. I was already feeling chilled by how serious Bob had sounded and now, with Egbert, had to try to sweet-talk my way out of a self-dug hole. He stumbled, stepping onto the grass, and reached us still looking irritable and disconcerted, trying to smooth out his expression.

'This *is* a pleasant surprise, Laura, seeing you here. I had to come to say hello.'

'Quite a surprise, seeing you too, Egbert,' Bob grinned. 'How's life?'

The Major harrumphed, keeping his gimlet eyes solidly on mine. 'You're looking as lovely as ever, m' dear. Attracting a lot of attention too, I may say.'

'Won't you sit down a moment,' I said, feeling politeness necessitated it.

'Thank you, but I should return to my table. I only came to greet you and offer a word of advice. You're a beautiful, innocent girl and there are people, journalists included,' he glowered at Bob, 'here in Cairo, who have a different code. You would be wise to bear that in mind…'

'Steady on, old chap,' Bob laughed, 'it'll be pistols at dawn at this rate…'

Egbert ignored him, fingered his squirrel-tail moustache and kept focused. 'People do talk, d'you know, dear girl, best to remember that. Well, I've said me piece. Always a delight to see you and I shall hope to do so again while in Cairo.' He turned on his heel, giving off waves of self-righteous disapproval, probably uncomfortably aware, too, of our eyes following his back.

'You should have biffed him one for that monstrous slur,' I said hotly. 'He hadn't even been making a joke, the pompous ass, incapable of any humour.'

'Don't be too hard on him. He's a sad case, sweet on you and lonely. It makes me a bit ashamed of being so cocky.'

'You weren't, you were a model of restraint. And sad case or no, he was appallingly rude and had no business invading our privacy like that.' The wretched man, we'd been in a blissful bubble of intimacy on the dance floor and to know Egbert's eyes had been glued… I stared at Bob. 'And on top of it, he interrupted you when you were sounding alarmingly serious. What had you been about to say?' My stomach was tight with dread. Had he been about to say that tonight had to be goodbye?

'Tell you later. Let's have a last dance and to hell with Egbert, then perhaps a stroll somewhere more private where it's easier to talk.' He leaned to touch my face as he often did, and I felt such a surge of emotional and physical pull that my lips set up a tremble.

The three-piece band were playing a slow waltz and we danced like lovers. His hand was on my bare back, thighs brushing as we moved, and my knotted nerves, being gently massaged, were unravelling. I couldn't have cared less who was watching, not Sir Egbert, not his companions, not any army gossipers there. I was lost to the moment, lost to the world.

We were arm in arm, walking away from the hotel and past Bob's borrowed parked car. There were taxis lined up, trees shading the pavement, awnings and smart shopfronts. A few white-robed Egyptians about, but the darkness of night lent a cloak of anonymity.

We turned down a deserted side street whose substantial buildings, banks probably and business premises, looked silent and shut up for the night. Bob slowed and leaning against a stone wall, drew me close, taking my hands and bringing them to his lips, kissing each in turn, staring over them into my eyes.

His steady gaze seemed to confirm my fears. I was unsure, terrified, but didn't flinch, staring back into their indigo depths. 'What had you been about to say before the interruption?' I asked again. 'I need to know.'

'Only that there were things I wanted to say, but not at a table at Shepheard's. Like how very much I longed to kiss you properly and ask you back to my two small rooms and show you my rooftop view, but that I cared too much to press you – too much for my own good. So, shall I drive you back to the mission school now? Is that for the best? We don't know what's going to happen,' he said, entwining our fingers, 'and if we take this too far, it gets harder, which wouldn't be easy for either of us. So, shall you stop staring with those enormous eyes of yours and I take you back now? I'd entirely understand and respect your feelings, couldn't bear you to feel beholden or under any sort of pressure.'

I kept on staring, feeling on fire, burning to be kissed, knowing what I wanted to say but not how to put it. My heart was racing, I was desperate, had to find the words, say something, anything… 'It's not that I'm hesitating – well, I am, but I've, um, never been in this situation before…'

Would he realise what that meant? He could hardly imagine I was quite as innocent and naïve as for this to be the first time. There was a war going on, girls grabbing the moment, shedding their inhibitions, and nowhere more so than in Cairo. I breathed in, un-entwined our fingers and lifted my arms around his neck. 'But I know how much I want to be with you,' my heart was pounding, lips quivering, 'however hard it gets…'

His mouth was gentle at first then hard and searching, his tongue meeting mine. I thought for a fleeting second of Harry, the thrilling kisses and ache of longing that had brought me chasing all the way out after him. But I'd been much younger and nothing had ever felt as overwhelmingly earthy and real as now. I was drowning, drawn further and further in deep with the sensation of Bob's mouth on mine, wanting only to lock out the world, yield and give of myself.

He held me close as we walked back to the car. I felt protected, less panicky about my naivety. He drove fast and drew up outside a large walled property in a mimosa-lined street, helped me out and found the key to a tall wrought iron gate in the wall. It opened onto a floodlit courtyard with statues, palms, spiky plants.

The house beyond had fretwork shutters, ornamental balconies. Bob took me round to the back and up several flights of an exterior staircase. 'There are a number of entrances,' he said, 'probably for the original owner's visits to his various wives, which means I have my own front door.'

'It's a very handsome one with all this intricate carving. She must have been a very favoured wife.' The door swung back creakily on its hinges and we went into the dark interior.

Bob felt for the light switch, shot home a huge iron bolt and kissed me. 'Here we are, my beloved, welcome to my lonely bachelor pad.'

There was no hall; we'd come straight into a room that was sparsely furnished, a rattan sofa and chairs, a brass-studded coffee table. I waited uncertainly while Bob closed the shutters. 'Have a look round while I fix us a drink. It's vodka or vodka, I'm afraid, courtesy of the mad Russian colonel.'

The Arab-style coffee table was long and low; there was a painted chest, an untidy desk with a swan-necked lamp and a battered old Remington typewriter. I pictured Bob hammering away on the keys, scrabbling round for scribbled notes among his jumble of papers. 'That's where I burn the midnight oil,' he said, coming up behind me, 'thinking about you, and this, and all the while knowing I shouldn't bring you here.'

'I asked you to, wanted you to…'

'Yes. That helped a bit.'

He grinned and kissed my lips, putting a chilled glass into my hands. 'It's good strong stuff, needs the tonic and ice.'

'Have you brought other… friends here?' I asked, my cheeks flaming.

'Girlfriends?' He eyed me. 'I have asked one or two girls back on past trips – ships in the night – but not to here, not on this trip. The only people to have huffed up all those stairs have been a few old bores prepared to take the *shekel* of my booze in return for a few titbits of info.

'I was a bit depressed for the first few weeks after we arrived, actually, worrying about the need to sort out my life, whether to give up all this,' he eyed the typewriter, 'and join the war effort. Whether it would be right and proper to have given you a call.' He downed his vodka, lifted my chin and kissed me. 'Enough of that. Finish your drink and come to see my rooftop and the stars.'

There was a door out of the galley kitchen, a fire-escape staircase up to the roof space where there were dusty geraniums in terracotta pots on top of a low protective wall. The view was spellbinding. All Cairo was there, spread out, sprawling in all directions as far as the eye could see. The city in wartime was in near darkness, as if eclipsed by the brilliance of the stars, but the brooding, silent pyramids were still dimly visible in all their haunting awesomeness.

Bob was standing behind me with his arms round my waist, lifting my hair, kissing my neck. 'You're distracting me from this miraculous view,' I said, still staring out, my heart pounding violently as his hands found my breasts. The panic was there while my whole body felt hollowed out with craving, I couldn't help turning into his arms.

'Come downstairs, I want to undress you and make love to you. We'll take it slowly. I'll be as gentle as possible, so much want it to be as good for you.' He searched my face. 'You know it may hurt a bit first time?' I nodded and leaned my head to his chest, drinking in the salty tang of his damp shirt, feeling the hardness as he pressed me close. I didn't want him taking it slowly, I wanted more of his fierce earthy kissing, all the love he could give.

A faint, ominous sound like rumbling thunder rolled in on the still warm night air. It was very distant, somewhere miles out in the desert, but there were faint, terrifying reverberations that made my skin crawl. Was that mortars? All the straining, urgent anticipation of lovemaking was draining fast. The war was being fought somewhere out there in all that relentless sand, body parts being tossed, heads severed, twisted limbs, mutilated bodies, brave young men breathing their last. I thought of being one of the loved ones left behind…

Bob had stiffened too, his arm tightening round me, and I could feel his fast-beating heart. He was joining a convoy in days. Was he thinking of being jolted about in a Jeep, trying to make headway through treacherous mine-strewn sand? Imagining his life being measured in hours?

He took my face in his hands and gave voice to the thoughts. 'We have to live our lives while we can. It feels like a miracle, being here with you. I knew I loved you on the ship and that you felt something too, but had to stand back when we got here, feeling as possessive and close as I did, for your sake. And there was Harry. So, if this feels wrong, you must say so. Don't think I wouldn't understand.

'But it doesn't.' I put my hand to his hair, his roughening cheek, and stared into his eyes, glistening in the starlit dark. I traced the contours of his face, feeling such an intense force of urgency with my longing to be held and in his bed. My body was liquid with need. 'I want you to make love to me – for my sake.'

His double bed dominated the low-ceilinged top-floor room; the pristine sheets looked white and virginal as a nun's mantle. There were still my unspoken fears, the panic building… Before leaving home, Mum had asked if there was anything I needed to know. 'Just in case you've managed to see Harry,' she said, 'or become involved with anyone else.' What would I have done without Dolly?

Bob's mouth was on mine, powerfully, passionately, as he slid down the cap sleeves of my cream silk dress. He was kissing and caressing my shoulders, feeling for the back zip of the dress.

I murmured tensely, 'I've never been seen naked by a man before…'

'Surely by a doctor?' He raised his face and looked at me with a quizzical smile.

'My doctor in Hamburg was a woman, she was Jewish, I pray she survives, and my mother's a doctor too. You're the first, you see, in more ways than one.'

'*How do I love thee, let me count the ways…*'

'I'm, um, between periods. Isn't that a bad time?'

'Terrible! Don't worry, I'll wear a condom, won't take any risks.'

I was holding on to Bob, mentally thanking Dolly, stepping out of the dress, feeling self-conscious as he took off my bra and pulled down my best lacy pants.

I wasn't wearing stockings and suspenders with the heat, couldn't have afforded nylons, and standing naked felt both defenceless and brazen.

Bob was still fully dressed. He stared openly at my body before cupping my breasts, holding my eyes, lowering his head to one of my nipples, circling it with his tongue, squeezing the other one hard between finger and thumb. I couldn't help the sharp intakes of breath with the intensity of the competing pain and thrill and fumbled urgently with his shirt buttons. As he shed his clothes, I had to adjust, seeing the dark line of hair from belly button to the depths of his groin, and followed the line down cautiously. Bob took my hand, covering it with his, moving mine up and down, moving us nearer to the bed. I was lost to the moment, lost to the heat of my desire.

The sensation of his tongue trailing my stomach was like being borne up on feathers alone. I froze as he took his kisses further down, but he stayed my hand and we were soon locked together, bodies slippery with mingled sweat. I felt an unimaginable exhilaration, a sense of empowerment too, with his need of me. Our mouths were joined, limbs entwined…

They were still entwined, lying with sweat drying and cooling on our still bodies. I could never undo what had happened, I'd chosen and lived the moment. Regret may set in, but I didn't think so, feeling loved and whole as never before.

'How was it, losing your virginity to a journalist with a different code?'

'Not so bad. I like your code. Can we do it again?'

He kissed me tenderly, but his eyes were half closed. Mine weren't when every fearful instinct told me I was about to lose Bob. I had to give the address in chapel in the early morning and take lessons. Adrenaline would carry me only so far, but how could I care when every minute of the night had been so infinitely, unforgettably precious?

I looked round the room; a fretwork cupboard, tall chest of drawers, our clothes chucked onto a peacock-backed chair. I didn't want to lose him, didn't want Bob to go…

'You know what I'd like to do more than anything else in the world?' He wasn't asleep; his fingertips were trailing my arm. He hitched up on an elbow. 'Marry you tomorrow. Find a way, find someone to do it.'

'There's a but coming, isn't there? That's just a lovely dream.' I was fighting tears, knowing it was Bob's way of saying what couldn't be. I loved and adored him and it shredded my heart to think that this was his prelude to goodbye.

He hitched up further and stared into my eyes piercingly, as if the pupils were a route into my mind. 'I'm far from dreaming, just craving the moon. But it's a moon that wouldn't be fair or right for you. We've found this love and sense of rightness. I believe I could make you happy, but I have to go home, see my mother, enlist and play my part. I'm not built to cling to the skirts of a war correspondent's exemption. And even if I make it through the war unscathed, the work I do, the only thing I'm any good at, would take me away from you for too much of the time.

'I'm ten years older and it wouldn't be much of a life for you. You came out here, braved torpedo-infested waters looking for someone you felt in love with, and there'd always be a tiny mouse-hole corner of you, thinking what ifs and having flashes of guilt.'

Was he right? How could you see into the future, feeling as I did now, so deeply, profoundly, emotionally in love? He kissed my eyes as the tears spilled out, and caressed my damp hair. 'I have to go home and do my duty. I dread all the training, the orders and discipline, but can't stand by. Can you understand?'

My tears were coming thick and fast. 'I can, but it's just got horribly much harder, just as you said it would, harder in every way.'

'I'll give you my mother's address and phone number in Oxfordshire. It would help me to know you had that means of contact. I need you to feel that I'd always be there for you, whatever the circumstances, wherever I was with my life.'

'And if you'd married Coral?'

'Maybe we'd both have married. Being there for you would still hold good. Life takes many turns, it can slip through your fingers like silverfish. We just have to hold on to what's real and meant to be. There was a Chinese philosopher, Lao Tzu, who said, "*Being deeply loved by someone gives you strength, loving someone deeply gives you courage.*"'

I wept into his chest, desolate, aching with misery. Life was taking one of its many turns and I yearned for it to be any other. It broke my heart.

I moved my head down to his stomach, licked his skin, told him he tasted and smelled like a Cairo market. He pulled me on top of him and the sex was gentler, more familiar the second time. He made me reach my own orgasm. 'Do this when I'm gone, don't feel coy, enjoy your beautiful body and think of me once in a while.'

'And will you think of me too, once in a while?'

'All the time, loving you, dreaming of the silky sweep of your eyelashes, your amber, green eyes that seem lit from behind. I love the dell of your clavicle, these fine cheekbones, the gold lights in your hair…'

'Stop, stop! And it's nearly dawn. I've got to go, got to give the address in chapel in three hours' time and somehow string a few words together.'

Bob jumped up and held out his hands. 'That's terrible! Will you get by?'

'Do my best!' I looked down at the stained sheets and up at him, anxious.

He grinned. 'It's a French household. Can I see you Tuesday? I go to the desert Wednesday then home. But never a word about goodbye?'

'Never a word.' Unspoken words, but the pain would be overpowering with the crushing finality of goodbye. Would the pain ever really go? I loved Bob and knew I always would do. For a lifetime, the love would live on in my heart.

CHAPTER 16

Abbassia

Moving in with the Harveys and adjusting to the very British way of life at Abbassia Barracks had taken a little doing. No more American whoops of 'you don't say!' and talk of "doing the math". Now it was 'righty-ho,' 'piece of cake' and 'crikey!' There were even more rules and regulations than at the mission school, greater eagerness to conform, but the very Britishness was as familiar and easy to slip back into as a pair of old brogues, provided, of course, I could see my face in the polished sheen.

I was lonely without Dolly and the laughs; missed her badly. All being well, we'd meet up the following term, but had still clung together in tears on the last day of term. Pete would be back soon, all being well, but Bob was gone.

Living with the Harveys for over two weeks now, I knew the routine. I taught the children music, maths and French in the mornings, took them swimming in the afternoon. I put the youngest, Alice, to bed, before joining the family for supper, although the Harvey parents were out socialising most evenings.

The best moment, after helping clear the meal, was escaping to my room. It was like a railway carriage with its narrowness, an unfortunate reminder of my first room, lodging with Frau Stürber, but still a precious private space where I could cry and try to hold on to my sanity.

Three letters had arrived from Harry on the day I'd been seeing Bob for the last time. I could no more have read the letters beforehand than forego that last chance to say goodbye. When I faced reading them later, Harry's letters had wrenched me apart, but I had yet to answer them, couldn't, not with my thoughts and heart so completely elsewhere. Suppose they'd arrived a week earlier? I had to live with the guilty truth of my passionate relief not to have been faced with that decision.

Bob had given me a silver bracelet that night. I fingered it on my wrist. It was delicately worked, chosen with care and engraved with the words, "*Remember me*". I'd wanted him to have something of mine, my book of Shakespeare's sonnets, and written in it, "*For Bob. With love, always*".

Would I ever see him again? I still shivered with the sense of his touch, still saw the connecting depths in his eyes. It was all too recent to be a softening memory. I felt disloyal and gouged out, an empty shell, but my feelings for Bob would always be part of me, never forgotten, sealed in and hidden away like an image in a locket worn close to the heart, parcelled up and locked in a safe hideaway. I had to write warmly to Harry, speak of love that was genuinely felt, but only after one last night of tears.

The morning lessons weren't too bad. Alice's speed at picking up French was a marvel. She put her older brothers to shame and was very cocky with it. She asked, 'How do I say "stupid" in French?' then pranced about the house, saying, '*Mes frères sont stupides!*'

On the way to the officers' swimming baths, Alice whined, '*Je veux une glace.*'

'*On verra ça!* Which means, Alice, we'll see about that!' The heat was extreme and we all had one when we arrived.

I pushed Alice in her rubber ring till she found a friend, and leaving them bumping rings, hitched up onto the side, I dangled my legs and kept an eye. The water was full of squealing, splashing kids; George striking out, Arthur, the elder, more phlegmatic, of them, was practising his belly-flopping dives, stoically persevering. Mothers and minders, the occasional father, sat under sunshades, gossiping and sipping long fruity drinks decorated with mini parasols. Mrs Harvey's world, but she couldn't take the heat and rested of an afternoon.

I thought of the caring words in Harry's most recent letter. '*My darling one, I haven't heard from you in weeks. I'm terribly worried. Are you all right? I desperately long to see you, there must be a way…*'

Alice was tugging on my feet. 'Can you give me some more pushes?'

'How about a go without the ring? I'll keep my hand under you, you'll be fine.'

'Yes, yes!' She splashed the water excitedly. 'Mummy never lets me.'

'Don't worry, I'll make sure you stay afloat.'

I slid into the pool, but George was struggling and in trouble. An older, ferret-faced boy was forcing George's head under water and holding it down.

'Bully!' I hissed, hauling him off. 'You do that again and there'll be trouble. George could have drowned.'

'Pity he didn't,' the boy muttered, kicking off up the bath, thrashing water back into my eyes. Alice, who loved any drama, was open-mouthed.

My mixed age and race classes at the mission school were a piece of cake compared with looking after the three of them.

The Harveys were home for supper. I bathed Alice, read to her, kissed her and put out her next-day's clothes. Only then did Mrs

Harvey relinquish her gin and tonic to pop up to say goodnight. Governess felt an elastic term.

'We can go to Palestine,' Colonel Harvey said, lining up his knife and fork and lifting a starched napkin to his moustache. 'Temporary accommodation has been found for us near Jerusalem and I'm able to bring my family.'

'Gosh, how exciting, Father! Jerusalem is three thousand feet high.' George was lit up, while Arthur looked nervous of the unknown.

'So, it should be a little cooler at least,' said Mrs Harvey. 'This summer heat is unendurable. Will we have a house, dear? What sort of accommodation?'

'Not very satisfactory, I'm afraid. We are to stay temporarily with an elderly spinster in a mountain village, five miles out of the city. All I know of her is that she has built a threefold temple in the garden, so I fear could be a little odd.'

I asked, 'A temple for the three religions?'

'Yes, indeed. I'm told it has a cross with an altar for the Christians, crescent and star for the Muslims and double triangle star for the Jews. She is said to believe that at her temple the world is come to peace.'

'What a beautiful thought… Do you possibly have the address yet?' I should write some letters tonight and would be glad to be able to include it.'

'I'll hunt it out for you.' He managed a smile, a rare occurrence and a short-lived one, since he immediately, snappily, ordered the boys up to bed.

Mrs Harvey looked peeved. Did he seldom smile and "hunt things out" for her? With my newly awakened sexuality, I was aware of a hint of boredom between them, aware of the looks I'd been getting from officers and troops at the barracks, some mentally undressing me, while the Colonel's smile, just now, had been simply friendly and appreciative. He was straight-laced and prejudiced, but honourable, I believed. The Harveys, as Bob had suggested, weren't really so bad, just dreadfully conformist.

'There'll be all the packing up…' Mary Harvey sighed rather irritably. 'I assume we won't be leaving for a few days?'

'No, dear, not till the weekend,' her husband said, patiently.

She was like a wilted flower, drooping at the thought of an exciting trip to Palestine. I said I'd do all I could to help, and her cool half-smile seemed to imply that was the least she expected. She turned to the Colonel. 'And dear, you have remembered about the Wrights coming to dinner on Thursday? I'd actually thought of asking that nice major as well, since we have Laura with us.'

'Of course I remember.' It was Colonel Harvey's turn to be irritable.

The 'nice major' was sure to be Sir Egbert. I'd just have to put up with whatever sidelong swipes and injured looks he sent my way.

I said good night and went upstairs as soon as possible, looked in on the boys, kissed the tops of their heads and crossed over to my room, closing the door with a sigh. Having found the courage to reread Harry's letters, I couldn't leave answering them a moment longer. His first two were mainly about army life, the first weeks of his training and wry little anecdotes that he obviously found easier to write about than any deeper feelings.

…Everything has to be done so strictly by the rulebook, we are in the King's African *Rifles after all, and know our native species, but still have to refer to a mango tree as a bushy topped tree! And I must tell you about falling in for church parade! First, the Anglicans ordered to fall in to one side, then it was us Catholics and other denominations, till there were just three chaps left. The red-faced regimental sergeant major glared at them and hollered, 'What church are you?'*

'We're Jews and it's not our Sabbath today.'

'We can't have that! Fall in with the Anglicans!'

We are out in the field now and had a few skirmishes near the border (can't say which). We intercepted an Italian report about an enemy aircraft attack, which was a mystery, having no bombers in the area, till a white settler flying a light reconnaissance plane confessed to lobbing a small homemade bomb over the other side. It gave us a good laugh.

Harry's second letter was similar, but with a chink of his feelings creeping in.

… The battalion has two black officers whom the white NCOs have to salute. We accepted that, but the white South Africans kicked up. The Ugandan officers have such dignity and charm that they tactfully turned a blind eye to breaches of saluting and soon won the grudging respect of even the South Africans.

I've had a bout of malaria and longed for a letter, but had my thoughts of you to keep me going. I hope so much to hear soon. Please, please write!

The thought that he'd been shivering with the high fever of malaria, nauseous, lonely – and all the weeks I'd avoided writing…

His third letter was still more painful to read. He wrote passionately of his longing to see me, of giving anything for the chance to be together. I'd had that same need in the past, wanting nothing more than to be reunited, which I'd only hinted at shyly and now, feeling such sad, loving remorse, could at last pick up a pen and write from the heart.

Dearest Harry,

Three letters from you, all in the same post! I'm so relieved. I'd been wondering and worrying, not knowing where or how you were. It made you seem ever more distant, a remote figure,

but now you're real again, alive and well and aside from the
awfulness of malaria, making me smile…

That much I could write openly and genuinely, but it was no answer
to why I hadn't sent a flurry of letters needing to know if all was
well. Wouldn't he be asking himself that now, feeling suspicious and
forlorn? I carried on, wrote about the Harveys, Palestine and the
threefold temple, and how I wished he could change places with one
of the sergeants escorting us through the desert.

I wrote of Lil's May Balls at Cambridge, still happening; the
pyramids; going out at dawn with Dolly and being overawed at
the magical wonder, especially the Great Pyramid looming up in
the morning mist.

…The sight of the Sphinx squatting there, so still and
inscrutable, it had us transfixed. It had a serenity about it
that seemed to defy everything worldly, even with its knocked-
off nose. The dragoman explaining how the pyramids had
been built made me weep for the thousands giving of their
all and their lives. It wasn't for nothing, building something
of such monumental enduring beauty, but such sacrifices felt
inhumanly cruel…

I signed off lovingly, leaving the letter unsealed to add the address
in Palestine.

I wrote to Mum and Dad, to Bertha in Hamburg via Lisbon,
though doubted that would get through. Then, late as it was, gave
into a desperate urge to write to Bob. Would he get back safely
from the desert and find it before leaving for home? I would never
know. I craved hearing from him, ached for the tactile contact of
a letter to press close to my heart, but knew Bob wouldn't get in
touch. He was doing the right, brave, dutiful thing, and it was
time for me to move on.

CHAPTER 17

Palestine

The Harveys' dinner party, just before leaving for Palestine, didn't happen. George went down with chickenpox then Arthur too. The Wrights had children and understood, while the Major – it had been Sir Egbert – had seemed quite put out, Mrs Harvey said. 'He sounded really disappointed, mentioned that you'd travelled out together, Laura, which was quite a coincidence, and I suppose would have liked to see you.'

It was a lucky escape and made up for the last frantic days of being nurse, packer, laundress; not an easy last week and tempers were frayed. The war felt closer too, with sirens dragging us from sleep to take sick children down to a rabbit hole of a shelter to suffocate in a sandy space the size of an oven with an inescapable whiff of hot bodies. I couldn't wait to be getting away to a mountain village near Jerusalem; it seemed a dream.

Colonel Harvey was going ahead, Mrs Harvey and Alice following on by plane, the boys and I crossing the Sinai Desert by train, rumbling across the desert by night to arrive in Jerusalem by morning.

We left early. Arthur and George, who were more or less recovered, climbed excitedly into a truck with our escort of two sergeants: Collins and Jones. We set off for the coast. The countryside was dusty and barren with little to hold the boys' attention except for a long caravan of camels, so overladen that it was a wonder their knobbly knees didn't buckle. It was incredibly hot. The sergeants, big friendly fellows, tanned and solid-chested with hefty biceps, did a great job of keeping the boys entertained, and when we finally reached the Suez Canal and were handed over to two other sergeants, I felt quite sorry to say goodbye.

We crossed the Canal on a ferry being serenaded by croaking frogs. The temperature hardly dipped as the sun went down, and the blast of heat that hit us on the other side was like standing in front of the open door of a furnace. The two new sergeants were Wilson, lanky and shy, and McKay, wiry and pugnacious with a broad Scotch accent. They handled the passport checks and officialdom efficiently before hurrying us to El Kantara to board the train.

It was packed with Arabs and soldiers who made cheeky, fruity remarks and got an earful from Sergeant McKay, but it was all in good part. Then, pulling away with clouds of black steam billowing out and a jolt that sent us all sideways, the train chugged on into the night. The dark descended like a blackout blind and all the annoying flies dropped away, but the temperature hardly dipped; how travellers in biblical times could ever have crossed the Sinai Desert on foot and without refrigeration seemed an incredible feat.

While the boys slept, I stood at the corridor window looking out over the vast desert blackness. The silence of night was echoing; it seemed magnified 10,000-fold in that lonely place. Had Moses heard the silence, alone on his mountaintop, receiving the tablets of the law?

I loved Palestine. The little village of Ain Karim nestled at the foot of a hill covered with silvery olive trees, a profusion of wild flowers. Church bells sounded; it was all in stark contrast to Cairo with its dirt and din. Miss Miller, our charming, frail old landlady, lived at the top of the hill. Her mellow-stone house was tall and flat-fronted, with the tiny threefold temple in the garden.

The children and I were sardined on the top floor but could go out onto the roof, where there was a glorious circular panorama. A golden strip of sand to the west, the eastern shore of the Mediterranean, Bethlehem was to the south and further east were the suburbs of Jerusalem with the towers of the Mount of Olives. Looking north, I could see the burial place of Samuel and the hilltop where the Ark of the Covenant had rested for so many years.

I took the children sightseeing. Alice was bored, but we all loved an exquisite twelfth-century crusading church, restored by some French Benedictines. They made excellent wine and delicious honey, which they gave us on hunks of crusty bread, along with their light fruity wine, even a little to Alice.

Inevitably, we couldn't go to any German or Italian monasteries but visited a colony of Russian sisters, captivating little ladies with sweet faces, whose church was covered in passion flowers. Everyone took great pride in their race and religion; even the poorest people wore exquisitely embroidered costumes.

There were evident tensions. Apart from the early Jewish arrivals, a small settlement of the Pica who had good relations with their Arab neighbours, it was a sad situation. Rumblings and nurtured grievances being held at bay in time of war, but they were sure to erupt before long.

In mid-August, we moved into a flat in Jerusalem. I was sad to leave Ain Karim for an impersonal modern block, but the tight-packed old city within the city walls was exhilarating to see. Grimy little alleys, so narrow that a man could lie across them, his head in one shop, feet in another. There were swarms of flies, beggars and cripples, donkeys and goats; time had stood still in the market.

Fusty sacks of grain; the piquant aroma of citrus fruits; rosy apricots; fat, spotty watermelons. The shops – small shacks with dark interiors too black to see into on a bright day – sold trinkets, carpets, brasses and fine silks. I bought a length of lilac Damascus silk for next to nothing. As I walked in the little garden of Gethsemane, the sun going down over the city, glowing and shining through transparent red leaves, was like the light of Ethiopian rubies in the Bible.

Everyone looked colourful and individual: Greek priests; Bedouins in flowing gowns; Jewish men wearing flat hats over their long, straggly hair; Arab women in headdresses as exotic as Claudette Colbert's in *Cleopatra*. I fingered Bob's silver bracelet wherever I was, missing him dreadfully, but writing to Harry again was healing and brought a sense of hope. He'd been adopted by a kitten, he said, and I told of the bears and elephants of Alice's imagination. Her favourites were a bear called Nose and his brother Snub. They came to tea but weren't allowed to speak unless spoken to; such was the influence of her strict parents.

The children had invitations to friends' houses and, on one occasion, the Harveys took me to lunch at the King David Hotel. It was a lovely change to wear a pretty frock and sweep up to the huge pink-limestone hotel in a sleek military car.

The hotel, swarming with army top brass and dignitaries, was almost as buzzy as Shepheard's. Colonel Harvey, who went in for hierarchy, was impressed to see a gracious straight-backed woman with a girl in a grass-green hat. 'That's the High Commissioner's wife, Lady MacMichael, and one of her daughters.'

At lunch, he warned we were at greater and growing risk. 'I was up at Haifa yesterday. It's been badly bombed by the Italians, shocking to see their deadly aim; body parts strewn over the market place, noxious clouds of black smoke from an oil tanker and the stench of all the dead fish in the harbour…'

'It's ghastly, of course, dear, terribly worrying, but we are at lunch…'

I said, 'Can I just ask? Is London still under siege and being as badly bombed?'

''Fraid so, m'dear, but our pilots are fighting back and our superb radar is hampering their range. Apparently, Göring is even accusing his fighter pilots of cowardice! But I heard only today, so extremely vexing, that we've lost Berbera in British Somaliland to the Itis. Our chaps had to flee to Aden with their pants down – literally, don't give me that look, Mary – some even in their pyjamas.'

Had Harry been helping to defend Berbera? There must have been casualties…

'You're looking worried, Laura. Is it about your young man in East Africa?'

'Well, yes, I'm hoping he isn't in British Somaliland. He wasn't a regular, due to start training for his commission soon, but not quite yet…'

'Doubt he'll have been up defending Berbera then. Colonel Harvey smiled. 'Don't you fret. Now, we really must order, I haven't got long.'

Fears of an invasion of Britain continued to haunt me. Colonel Harvey said that with the Luftwaffe failing to break down our defences and Churchill's magnificent speech about our brave pilots, the country's resolve was positively *Bunyanesque*, valiant against all disasters.

We were packing up to return to Cairo when the Italian planes, their so-called "Green Mice", bombed Tel Aviv, with many dead. I thought of Harry fighting the Italians and said a prayer.

I had another letter from him before leaving. It was a new

passionate Harry. He said he loved me and I'd be hearing from him almost daily now. He had things he wanted to say but would keep them for the right moment and another day.

CHAPTER 18

Dolly

'You look disgustingly healthy, you mean old bean!' Dolly poked me in the ribs. 'A gorgeous tan and me a washed-out old bat after such weeks of night feeds.'

'That was fishing for compliments, you look blooming. Must have seen Pete or heard from him at the least. So, tell all!'

'Sailing, partying with Australian soldiers, dining with lonely army officers, Alexandria wasn't so bad! I got the train to Cairo one weekend, saw Pete and flew back in a small plane very late on the Sunday, only just in time for a feed! 'Now, let's hear about Palestine and you,' she said, without drawing breath. 'Pete thinks Bob's really decent and virtuous going back to enlist, but guess it hurts bad?'

She cocked her curly head sympathetically, was all ears, but it wasn't easy to speak about Bob and keep my heartache contained. Palestine had been a bridge to the future. I'd mentally left the special corner of Cairo reserved for Bob; he was locked in my heart, but I'd crossed that bridge.

The staffroom door opened and others came in, longing to hear about Palestine. I said, 'There were such beautiful places to visit. I loved the little Church of Perpetual Adoration in Jerusalem with its candles and fresh flowers and a French order of nuns. They worshipped night and day, completely veiled and in white robes with beautiful blue borders…'

'Oh, how wonderful!' Gloria sighed.

'Then there was Nazareth with Capernaum in the distance and the severe bare hills of Transjordan. And the Sea of Galilee was awesome with the sun casting glorious rays of light, magically shadowy with the moon. But, nearly 700 feet below sea level, it was sweltering!'

The bell rang and we filed back to lessons. There had been a huge number of new registrations, despite the desert war coming closer by the day. Returning students had hugged me as close as if I'd been their mother, saying how much they'd missed me. There were more loving letters from Harry, one from home with Mum asking gently how things were going.

Dolly missed lunch; she was nowhere to be seen. I went out for toothpaste, was cornered by a student, desperate about her arranged marriage, looked for Dolly, but still no sign. There was a letter from Dad in the lunchtime post, which I joyfully took to my room to read.

Dad spoke of the war, the Battle of Britain still raging, which brought me low, but he asked, with an uncanny sixth sense, whether there was someone new.

> …I just had the feeling from your last letter. I remembered you spoke of a war correspondent whose company you'd enjoyed on the voyage and have a sense that he's someone you've grown to care about very much. …If you ever need to feel your way or be reassured, you know it would never go further. I'm always here for you, darling Fudge, with such little advice as I can give…

The letter brought him so close, memories of being hugged tight, his special tweedy smell, his pipe... I felt blown off course, in a blizzard of homesickness. I missed him dreadfully, longed to pour my heart out about Bob, but the supper bell was ringing and I wiped away the tears.

Dolly was at supper, but she looked wretched and wasn't entering in.

I worried and wondered, and when she hurried from the table, chased after her. 'What's wrong? Is it Pete?' She turned, shaking her head with the limpid hurt in her eyes of an animal in pain, and I hurried her to my empty classroom.

'It's my dad. He's had a heart attack and may only have weeks. I don't want him to die... There's not many planes, I've got to get home...'

I took Dolly into my arms and hugged her. 'Your mother will need all the support you can give. We'll find that flight, get you on the first plane.'

'It's Pete too, out in the desert and I can't see him before I go. He could be killed, like, tomorrow. They're trained desert fighters but so outnumbered, and you Brits only have a few old, worn-out tin trucks...'

'Well, your President Roosevelt needs to stop worrying about the election and send us some reinforcements...' I bit my tongue, longing to take back saying something so stupidly thoughtless and insensitive.

She wailed, 'You don't get it! I'll never see Pete again. He won't stay in touch.' She was inconsolable. 'And even if, please God, my dad pulls through, I won't be able to come back. They'll say it's too dangerous. I'll lose Pete...'

And I was losing Dolly, may never see my best friend again. I hugged her and urged her to try to get some sleep; we'd find a flight in the morning.

I wrote to Dad, telling him about Bob, feeling emotional and desperate for Dolly, then went to bed and cried into the pillow. I lay awake thinking of the change in Harry, his letters now, so loving and full of wild ideas of places to meet, Khartoum the most recent. But he'd never get leave and I'd never get in or out of Cairo. I tried to imagine seeing him again. He and I had grown closer, but how changed would I be in his eyes? How affected would our relationship be by what had happened with Bob? My eyes were more open now. I knew about sex, and needed it now, but wouldn't Harry still think of me as an innocent? Wouldn't that make him suspicious and wondering?

The siren sounded. Doors opened and someone yelled out, 'Summons to our subterranean parlour!' The school shelter had a concrete floor and didn't send up clouds of sand with every shuffle of feet like the rabbit hole at Abbassia, but was still a furnace. The sirens went twice more in the night. It was exhausting.

We learned in the morning that as well as bombing Cairo's Maadi district, the Italians had hit the American-operated oil refineries in Bahrain, which caused far more outrage at school than any bomb dropped just up the road.

CHAPTER 19

Farewell to Cairo

I went with Dolly to the Almaza aerodrome to say goodbye. We swapped contacts. I gave her my address in Scotland and Harry's holding address, and we clung to each other like prisoners about to be shot. We sobbed so hard that everyone near us in that crowded place looked down at their feet in embarrassment, and we ended up laughing through our tears.

It was physical pain, watching Dolly walk out onto the runway and board the huge plane. I stayed on, staring up as it soared away into the hazy blue of an Egyptian sky, finally having to accept the reality of her going and feeling only emptiness. We'd opened our hearts to each other; Dolly had been a true friend.

Taxiing back to school, huddled in the back and miserable, I tried to be positive, thinking of friends in Cairo and at the barracks, lessons, activities, knowing all the while how unbearably lonely I'd be, running on empty, emotionally and physically exhausted. As well as the long hours at school, I'd been asked to organise and play in Saturday concerts at the YMCA.

The concerts had an audience of two or three thousand men.

How I ever got through the first one… God must have had a hand in it. The place was packed, the lads cheering and lewd. 'Show us yer knickers then!' But my adrenaline flowed, the concert a success, and I began to feel more on form.

The Principal of the American University was at the second concert and asked if I'd play the piano at a university dinner he was giving, which was flattering.

It would be a pick-me-up. I looked forward to it and, when the evening came, dressed in the wine-red frock I'd worn to the cinema with Bob.

Seated between the Principal and a New Zealander soldier with twinkly eyes, I listened to the mood music round the table. The Principal's wife, sitting opposite, had a carrying voice. 'Tell me,' she said to the American next to her, a lugubrious post-grad fellow with over-long hair, 'what's your particular interest? What brings you to Cairo?'

'I'm studying philosophy and the Pharaohs,' he replied complacently, clearly feeling himself to be on a laudably erudite path.

'You don't say!' my New Zealander neighbour shouted over. 'Well, the army is my philosophy. There is a war on, you know.' It was typical of the chasm between those on the frontline and the uninvolved. The Yanks looked uncomfortable and as soon as the coffee was served, I was invited to give my recital.

Life dragged on. I missed Dolly terribly. My music lessons were solace and I suppressed irritation when Miss Wilcox appeared at the door, probably bringing bad news. 'There's a telegram for you, Laura. Do come to my office if you need to.' I had ice in my stomach as she handed it to me with the class looking on, all agog.

Telegrams in wartime were like staring into the abyss, bearers of news to nudge you over the edge. My skin shrank as I forced myself to look down.

'DARLING – STOP – WILL YOU MARRY ME?'

I smiled back up at the class. 'Now, we'd better get on with our notations...'

My concentration wasn't at its most focused for the rest of the day. Even supposing Harry and I made it through the war, did I really want to be Mrs Harry Werner, living in the depths of a forest, with mosquitos and prowling wildlife? Would I ever forget Bob? Would the "what ifs" he'd warned about lurk deep inside my heart? But he'd told me to marry, wanted me to have a life; it needn't be Uganda forever... The colonial forest service could post Harry elsewhere, give him a spell at home. There were forests in Britain...

How were we possibly going to meet, let alone marry? I thought of his honey-brown eyes, unruly tawny hair... Had the army chopped it all off? I smiled to myself and worried about getting to sleep that night.

It was impossible. Lying wide awake in the small hours, my mind was speeding like the hands of a clock gone awry. Would Harry send a ring? Cairo was the place for gems. I'd had a fanciful longing for an Ethiopian ruby ever since Palestine – or did those only exist in the Bible? Would we have a church wedding – if we married at all? Would I wear white? Should I write to tell Bob? No, that would be unbearable. Should I even tell Harry about him? No, far better not...

I had just enough time to get to the post office after lessons and send a one-word telegram saying, "*YES*". The deed was done, my heart pounding like a crescendo drum roll, but now came the strain of waiting. It would be weeks before a return letter, and would it answer all the questions pouring into my head?

It felt best to tackle Miss Wilcox about my contract, to know the worst, and I went to her office in the afternoon break, convinced she would dig in her heels.

She gestured to a chair. 'I trust the telegram you received wasn't bad news?' Despite my affirming smile, her face was, as ever, hardly an open book.

'No, actually. Rather the opposite! It was a proposal of marriage. I, um, wondered, in the unlikely event of me being able to get to Uganda, whether you could see your way to releasing me from my contract a bit ahead of time.'

'You realise the chasm you would leave in the music department?' I nodded, kneading my hands in my lap, biting my lip in frustration. Was she so unfeeling? Had she no blood in her veins? 'However, the situation with the Italian advance is sufficiently precarious that I shall not stand in your way. I have appreciated your hard work and contribution. If you do go, I shall make no unpleasantness about it.'

Her smile couldn't be called warm, but mine in return was river-wide. I promised to write out a music syllabus for the rest of the school year and assured her I'd be there at least until the end of term, probably longer.

I wrote to my parents, to Harry, and over the next days, made enquiries about travel to Uganda. Was Harry even there? Would he be able to get leave? Would we have a honeymoon? I checked the mailbox twice daily, even on Friday before remembering it was the Muslim day of rest. Another two weeks eked by…

Dramatic news was coming from the desert. The British and Indian troops had seen off the Italians, who had retreated back towards Libya with nearly 40,000 men lost or captured. The school probably wouldn't have to close now, though the Egyptian Government was threatening to stop Muslim children from attending Christian schools.

The news from home was terrible. Liverpool heavily bombed; Coventry Cathedral destroyed; fierce bombing raids on Southampton, Bristol and Birmingham. What about Edinburgh and the family, Lil in Cambridge?

On Monday evening, my mailbox was full. Two letters from Harry; one from Dick, who must be safe and on leave, thank God; one from my friend Irene in Tanganyika. There was also an official-looking communication, which I opened first. It was the immigration permit that I needed, a single sheet of paper stamped with a bright red wax seal. I was being allowed to enter Uganda, *"for the purpose of marrying Sergeant H.A.R Werner"*.

Seeing an official mention of my impending marriage seemed unreal; it was setting my star, casting the future in stone. My pulse was racing like an Olympian runner. Was Harry still at the front or given leave to return to Uganda? Going by the permit with its seal, he must plan to be there.

Reading his letters, all became clear. He'd been granted ten days' leave in which to marry and have a honeymoon. Married friends of his were offering to host the reception and he and I could have a church wedding, as long as I was prepared to become a Catholic... Was I okay with that?

Was I? I'd been christened by a Presbyterian padre in some remote Indian settlement, but never joined a church or taken Holy Communion. I believed that the church as people knew it would eventually become far less important, the role it fulfilled now overtaken by modern post-war needs and anyway, weren't Christian values, honour and decency what people had to work out for themselves? I loved the Russian orthodox services without understanding a word, but was hardly ever going to convert to that faith.

Writing to him late that night, I confirmed my willingness to become a Catholic, while a bit unsure of what was demanded of me. I sat back then, worrying, rocking on the hind legs of my chair, but if I wanted to be married and buried by the church, I may as well take the plunge. Mentioning a ring, though, however incredibly cheap the gems in Cairo, could touch his pride, and every penny was needed to pay a fare. Neither of us had any money.

Harry's letters had many censored lines, but he must be somewhere near the Nile. He'd said in one letter that it was "…*not particularly beautiful at this stretch*".

I'd taken thirty-nine girls to see some eerie caves up in the hills that morning. Dolly would have taken them, but there was no Dolly. The caves, one of the most ancient places in Egypt, had huge pillars that gave the feeling of a nature temple, and the Nile seen from on high had looked such a delicate streak of silvery grey-blue. I loved to think of the great river snaking a path all the way down from Uganda, passing Harry wherever he was, gliding on through fertile banks to where I could look down on it far below.

The girls had got overheated and were badly behaved, but I stopped the coach on the way back to buy forty bottles of Gazzoozza, as the Arabs called any sickly fizzy drink, which calmed them down.

Christmas came. I had a cable from home. "*Greetings to you both – stop – Good luck in New Year – stop – Mum Buffy Lil Dick Jack*". I felt tearful, lonely, continents away from my family. There was a lot going on at school, festivities, concerts, services; Gloria was sweetly making nightdresses for my trousseau, but after the stifling summer heat, Cairo was chilly and dark as night from five o'clock on.

I had no Dolly, not enough money, and had drawn a blank on civilian flights. Harry sent £30, all he could manage, which he hoped would help me on my way. Imperial Airways no longer ran commercial flights; I felt in despair.

I couldn't appeal to my parents, struggling to survive the war, and there were four of us, but I'd always managed, even arriving back in Hamburg from Harry's aunts with a single German mark to my name.

The Harveys asked me to dinner in the New Year. I accepted with apprehension, convinced that Egbert would be there, twiddling his squirrel-tail moustache. I wore Mum's old blue cocktail dress and set out to get the bus, putting a brave face on it. I hoped that Mrs Harvey, who'd seemed almost more delighted at the news of my engagement than my own mother, would tell everyone all about it.

It felt quite like old times, walking in the door. I popped up to say hello to the boys, peeked in on sleeping Alice and came downstairs just as the other couple, the Wrights, were arriving with Egbert. He gazed at me with doleful eyes before turning to greet his hosts.

The evening got underway. Colonel Harvey looked at his wife, smiled and raised his glass. 'Celebrations in order tonight, my friends. We must drink to Laura on her recent engagement. Many congratulations, dear girl.'

Egbert looked momentarily shocked, but quickly recovered, composed his features and said with studied politeness, 'I wish you every happiness, long life with your journalist friend, whom I haven't actually seen around in a while...'

I flashed him my warmest smile and gave a little laugh. 'Oh, no, Egbert, not Bob! He went home to enlist, months ago. I'm marrying my dear friend, who's now in the army, who went out to Uganda before the war.' Egbert stared, almost forgetting his manners as he visibly digested the news.

'I wouldn't have expected that of a war correspondent,' he harrumphed. 'Takes a bit of guts. Good man.'

I smiled again, impressed with his magnanimity. 'But travelling to Uganda is proving hard, if not impossible, even to marry! Imperial's not running any more civilian flights and I'm running out of ideas.'

'Why not go by flying boat?' Egbert said. 'I can give you the name of someone at BOAC who I'm sure will help if he can.'

Two weeks later, I was saying weepy goodbyes to the teachers, my students, friends, Miss Wilcox, saying goodbye to the city. It was looking its best; the gum trees in blossom, the days fresh and cool. I felt wistful as well as elated. Cairo would always hold poignant, beautiful memories, but it had to be farewell.

I travelled to Uganda by flying boat, climbing high, soaring up above the barren winter desert with Cairo becoming further and further distant, a tiny fading sprawl. Then completely lost to view. I was winging my way with trepidation and high anticipation to come to rest on Lake Victoria and find Harry waiting there.

PART TWO

CHAPTER 20

Harry

Harry was hours early at Lake Victoria. Uganda was a minefield of mishaps and potential disasters; stampeding elephants, punctures, potholes, but his ancient old sky-blue Chevvy had been fine. It was in impressively good shape after lying idle in the Budongo for two years. With no back seat, it was called a "box-body" and was deceptively powerful, taking the forested north, all the perpendicular hills, mud tracks and hairpin bends in its stride and so far never letting him down.

The lake, whose extraordinary vastness and silky depths were hard to comprehend, was absolutely silent and still in the sultry January heat. Weaver birds were twittering round their hanging-basket nests, as lightly attached to swaying boughs as to make one hold one's breath. Long-billed pied kingfishers, distant clusters of marabous on their nests looked like white handkerchiefs spread out over the trees.

A flight from Nairobi was just arriving, bustle and animation at the jetty. General Sir Alan Cunningham was on board. He had recently taken over as Commander of the East African forces.

Harry liked the sound of him. He was an original thinker by all accounts, an exceptionally intelligent man. Word was that his predecessor, General Dickinson, had been virtually sacked.

The General, who was waiting around for the luggage with his aides, glanced over at Harry, looking rather confused. 'Are you here for me, Sergeant?'

'No, Sir, I'm on leave actually, meeting someone off the Cairo flight.'

'Why the full uniform then? You're very smartly dressed.'

'I'm about to be married, Sir, and it's all a bit of a rush. It's the problem of women only able to travel as army wives, we have to go straight to the church if she's to become one and be allowed to stay.'

'Well, I do see you'd need to be in your best kit.' He grinned round at his aides. 'Great news, eh, chaps? Congratulations in order, I'd say.' There was a bit of ribaldry and backslapping before their bags and transport arrived.

Not long to wait now. Jostling locals and porters were fighting to get close to the barrier with the Cairo flight's imminent arrival. Barefoot boys were laying out more of their excellent woodcarvings, cranes, hippos, elephant bookends; busty women in their colourful headgear draping swathes of *kangas* over branches of trees. The *kangas* mostly came from Kenya and had Swahili slogans, and riddles, bordering the designs. Harry read one. "*Mole ibariki dil ndoa isipate doa ila lpate poa*". "*Lord bless this marriage so it does not get a blemish*", which seemed uncannily apposite. It felt like a sign.

General Cunningham, he thought, was going to have his work cut out if, as rumour had it, we were planning to invade Italian East Africa. A 300-mile desert to cross and not a dribble of water between the bordering rivers, Tana and Juba, Italians guarding the crossing points… No easy task. There wasn't the transport to move all the men and equipment, and the water carriers were famous for leaking most of their load.

The sun was beating down, Harry's uniform sticking to him. Laura was having to marry in her crumpled travel clothes. Suppose she changed her mind, seeing him again after so long? Suppose he changed his? They'd had so little time together… No going back now. It was the 24th of January 1941, his wedding day.

He had felt so hassled by her keenness, unsure, rather dreading her ever making it out to Uganda. Then when her letters had stopped coming, the sense he'd had of her slipping away, his feelings and need had grown. Laura was writing warmly, their relationship more equal, intimate and loving. Marriage had felt like a rock, a place to shelter.

But still with gunfire to be dodged along the way… To have proposed after so little contact, without even really knowing each other… Was it the war, grabbing the moment, the sense of his life being snuffed out at any time?

Harry squinted into the glaring distance; the flying boat was a small speck on the shimmering horizon. He quivered with anticipation watching the cumbersome machine grow large in the sky before skimming the silvery cobalt lake and coming to rest by the jetty.

The passengers climbed down: Ugandans, army officers, two missionaries, a sawmill owner, a provincial commissioner whom Harry knew. No Laura. Had she missed the plane? Not coming? He saw her then stepping down carefully onto the slippery boards, the sun burnishing her hair to a coppery sheen.

'Hello, stranger,' she said, pushing through the barrier with a golden smile. 'Are you as nervous as I am? I never imagined marrying in a short, creased frock with no father to walk me down the aisle. But I have got a white hat…'

He took her hands and she leaned to kiss his lips, which brought a great surge of desire. He couldn't speak, couldn't take his eyes off her. She'd grown into her looks, amber green eyes, arched eyebrows; she looked wiser, more mature, infinitely more alluring.

'We'll have to hurry a bit and get to Kampala, we need to be at the church before three,' he said, finding his voice. 'It's this way for the car. I had a nostalgic moment yesterday, collecting it from Budongo and reuniting with the sounds and scents of the forest. Better than the stink of army latrines! I'd left the car with my nearest neighbours, a mile or so away. They're a Dutch couple, Luuk and Anke Janssen. He's a sawmill owner, she's a homely soul. You'd like them. Everything's a bit of a distance, but Masindi and the shops are only an hour's drive.'

Silly to mention the isolation… They'd reached the car and holding the door for her, putting his damp cheek to hers, he caught the scent she was wearing; it was light, lily-of-the-valley perhaps, or summer jasmine. Her cheek was velvety, soft as the first light, and the heat of his desire was uncontainable. All his fears, how little they knew each other, whether she'd stay faithful in the time he was away fighting, how she'd cope in a malarial forest; everything wiped from his mind.

He tipped the porter and climbed into the driving seat, weak with need. 'You don't even know where we're honeymooning yet. I couldn't book anywhere till you had a seat confirmed and it was too late to write by then.'

'We're lucky to have a honeymoon at all. Where are we going?'

'The Mountains of the Moon Hotel. It's near Fort Portal and at the foothills of the Ruwenzori Mountains, very remote and romantic with entrancing views. I've been to the town, seen the mountains. They're famous. Ptolemy is said to have named them the "Mountains of the Moon" back in the second century. They're the stuff of legends, always thought to be the source of the Nile, and there should be some lovely walks. Short ones – and early siestas…'

Laura grinned, to his relief, and he carried on. 'We're in Entebbe for only a few days afterwards then I have to be off on the officer training course, I'm afraid, and it's in Nakuru in Kenya. I'm busting a gut to get a permit for you to come too. The army say no camp followers, but I'm not giving up for one minute.'

'No, please don't! I'd love to be together for as long as possible. There must be some teaching job I could do somewhere near. Are we really going straight to the church? I should brush up and put my hat on.'

'I thought we could have a quick snack at Kampala's Imperial Hotel, which is right by the church. I'd rather leave the car there and tip a boy to keep an eye.

'I've had lovely letters from both of your parents,' Harry continued. 'Your father says you're inclined to be glum, but it doesn't last long, and your mother that you've got great gifts, including being more entertained by your own failures and mistakes than depressed by them.'

'She doesn't think I've got a gift to my name.'

'Cedric and Mary Barnes are the friends giving the reception. He's deputy commissioner for the province. And my boss, George Parker, has the honour of giving you away.' Harry glanced at her. 'I'm really sorry, you must feel sad about no father to walk you down the aisle, but George, who's head of the forest service out here, is a good man, so kind and helpful. He couldn't have done more for me.'

'And helping me now too.' Laura brushed Harry's cheek with the back of her hand, sorely testing his control.

They were at the hotel. He parked, reached back for her hatbox and kissed her velvety cheek and said, going in, 'George is a marvel, he's giving us the use of a small government bungalow in Entebbe after our honeymoon, before I have to be off on the course and wherever I'm sent to after.'

'Which means a long separation.' She smiled. 'Terrific to have a place of our own, though, even for a few days. I was wondering where we'd live, since it can't be at Budongo. Of course, if I can't come to Kenya, I'll have to find a job and somewhere to rent…'

That came as a shock. The thought hadn't even crossed his mind, terrible of him, so irresponsible; it should have been uppermost. Harry felt shaken and ashamed but said nothing.

'This place looks very modern and grand,' Laura said, linking arms.

'It was built about ten years ago, quite an addition to Kampala.'

The dining room was on the first floor and they went out to the balcony with its balustrade smothered in passion flower. They were too late for lunch, but able to have coffee and a slab of pound cake.

Laura rose and picked up her hatbox. 'Must go and get ready, then you can carry on filling me in, but there's the week ahead,' she gave another of her ravishing smiles, 'when I'd love to hear all about your friends and everything here.'

Harry didn't want to spend his honeymoon talking about friends. He felt in his pocket for the ring, the shock of Laura's need of somewhere to live out of mind. It was three years since he'd kissed her. Would she make comparisons? Would they fit well together? He was racked with physical and nervous uncertainties.

She came back wearing her hat, white with a sprig of white fabric flowers. It was wide brimmed and cast a shadow that gave her film-star glamour. He would rather see her glinting chestnut hair, such a perfect foil for her delicate face. Her dress was a deep peach colour, safe and demure, with rounded collars and pearl buttons; it hung a little unevenly at the hem, which he loved. It made her seem vulnerable. She looked pale, palely beautiful. Was she as frightened as he was of the enormity of the vows?

He reached for her hand, impatient for her to be his to protect. It would be impossible to forget that moment, Laura, pale and exquisite in her drooped-hem dress, who'd just stepped off a flying boat to marry him. In under an hour, they'd be bound together for life; he felt shivers of fear and portent, fear of human failings, of their very survival in a war-shattered world.

…Marriage is a sacrament, a permanent and exclusive bond between the spouses, sealed by God. …The sacrament confers on you the grace you need for attaining holiness and responsible acceptance and upbringing of your children. Marriage is God's doing. God himself is the author of marriage, His way of showing His love for those He created…

Was Laura finding the service too heavily Catholic? It wasn't ingrained, part of her upbringing as it was with him, it wouldn't just be washing over her… Why didn't the priest hurry up and get on with it?

Rows of his friends and acquaintances there, and with only a few hundred British officials in the whole country. Even two *gombololas*, local administration chiefs, resplendent in their flowing black white-bordered robes, who were always courteous and helpful. One of them, aware of a very bad road in Harry's pre-army days, had sent an *askari* to be there in case help was needed. A spattering of Kampala locals there too, probably regular attendees.

The church was a modern building that had a vaulted ceiling but wasn't ornate, more like a village hall. No flowers, why the hell hadn't he thought of flowers? Would Laura mind? Probably, women noticed such things. George's wife, Jane, had handed her a small posy of white carnations.

This was it, they'd reached the vows. The priest, a paunchy, wheezy Ugandan with bristling sideburns, was looking directly at Harry. *'Since it is your intention to enter into the covenant of Holy Matrimony, join your right hands and declare your consent before God and His Church.'*

He frantically summoned up his memorised lines. His thudding heart seemed to be counting him down like a stopwatch.

'I, Harold Albert Richard, take you, Laura Louise, to be my wife. I promise to be true to you in good times and bad, in sickness and health.' He stared at her, shaking. 'I will love and honour you all the days of my life…'

She began. 'I, Laura Louise, take you, Harold Albert Richard, to be my husband. I promise to be faithful, in good times and bad, in sickness and health, to love and honour you all the days of my life.' Her voice was clear and unfaltering; her eyes steady, holding his.

When the rings were exchanged, blessings done, Harry kissed her lips. The priest gave a slight frown. It wasn't always accepted practice, but the smile in her eyes said it all.

Walking down the aisle, his eyes were wet with tears. He smiled through them, hoping they'd go unnoticed, and clutching Laura's hand as tightly as a child's, they went out, man and wife, into the brilliant afternoon sunshine.

CHAPTER 21

The Honeymoon

Now after the shyness of meeting again, our futures set in stone, wedding vows taken with their shivery power to unnerve, Harry and I had to get to know each other. I was warmed by his obvious emotion, banishing those smallest of doubts, the panic in the pit of my stomach, and thinking ahead with positive excitement.

Our reception hosts, Cedric and Mary Barnes, lived in a modest red-brick bungalow in Kampala's tidy residential suburbs. Harry held me tight to his side as we went up the front path. The door was open and the welcome party spilling out with overdone congratulations. Harry said, 'This so good of you both, really appreciated! You mustn't ply me with too much booze, though, with a five-hour drive ahead…' I couldn't wait to be off and alone together.

The Barnes' small sitting room was packed, stiflingly hot. Glasses of fruit punch were pressed into our hands, Harry being slapped on the back while I stood aside feeling shy. I knew no one apart from his boss, George, who'd escorted me down the aisle, and his wife, Jane. The furniture was pushed back, but there was hardly room to breathe. Everyone was sweating and gulping down punch that was almost neat gin. I felt fuzzy on two sips.

Two of the wives there, Betty and Rita, cornered me and chattered unstoppably. Rita said, 'How simply *unthinkable*, being married straight off the flight! No wedding dress, no bridesmaids. You poor, poor thing!' She had a frizz of fair hair, a Pekinese snub nose, and was looking down it sniffily at my frock.

Betty said, '*Such* rotten luck, and missing all the lovely preparations too, poor thing.' She was prettily plump but had a girly, high-pitched voice that jarred.

'It's wartime,' I laughed, feeling a bit superior, yet knowing I'd have loved a white wedding. 'It's a miracle we could marry at all. There was certainly no time for second thoughts, getting straight off a flying boat and into the church!' That didn't go down well; they looked distinctly un-amused. 'Lovely to be walked down the aisle, though,' I added hurriedly, 'so good of George to step in.'

'Did I hear my name mentioned?' He was right behind us, talking to a bearded outdoorsman. 'This is Jock Hardwick,' George said, introducing me, 'he's prospecting for oil up near the Murchison Falls, not far from the Budongo actually. Can I leave you in his capable hands while I see to a few empty glasses?'

Rita and Betty eased away and from the looks on their faces, didn't approve of Jock Hardwick one bit. He saw me absorb the mood music and his mouth twitched. He had a thatch of straw hair, an earthy ruggedness and his sapphire-blue eyes, meeting mine, were all the more piercing for his deep tan. I liked him.

'Cairo this morning, married this afternoon,' I said. 'So little time and there's so much I'd love to know about Uganda. Are you being much affected by the war?'

'Hardly at all, certainly no shortage of food,' Jock looked over to the Barnes' table, 'no bombs, no blackout blinds, and the Ugandans are good people, very keen to contribute, do their bit and volunteer for the KAR.'

'Harry admires the Ugandan soldiers. He says they're brave, dignified men.'

'The farmers are decent and hard-working too, growing extra cotton, tea and coffee, for the war effort, raising money – upending British ideas of imperial patronage, I'd say.' Jock grimaced. 'Just hope we reciprocate after the war…'

'You sound very attached to the country. Have you lived here long?'

'Ages. I was saw-milling up north for years, where I met Harry, then I got in with an entrepreneur, convinced there was oil to be found. Not so sure about that myself, but I'm too old for the army and like being outdoors, so I'm helping a bit with the prospecting.' Jock twinkled his eyes. 'Harry's a lucky man.'

'I'm the lucky one, still pinching myself to have made it out here. It's a worry, though, not being back at home, training as a nurse or doing whatever I can for the war effort, feels wrong. It's different for Harry, right there in the KAR…'

'Relax, you're newly married and making him happy. You'll find something useful to do out here, think of the wonderful positives!'

'You're being very reassuring.' I smiled but looked down at my nails. Suppose I'd stayed home. I wouldn't be just married, never have met Bob… Was he away at the front by now? Had he got engaged? Married to Coral already?

'I'd love to know those thoughts,' Jock grinned, 'but Cedric's about to speak.'

'Order, order!' Cedric tinkled a glass. 'Time for speeches and telegrams!' The family had wired, Dick from wherever he was, but there was no cable from Harry's parents in occupied Austria. They couldn't even know he was married. I wanted to weep for the sadness of it all.

George gave a generous speech, talking up the groom's qualities, while it was left to Harry to talk up mine that, even if there were any, he had yet to learn. He told a pathetic joke about being a bag of nerves but sleeping like a baby – waking up crying every two hours. People laughed, but it was probably half true. He did a round of thank-yous before apologising for the drive and having to slip away.

Mary Barnes had made up a picnic basket and thanking her profusely, we made it out of the door. Outside, the Chevvy was festooned in blue and silver ribbons with a cardboard "*Just Married*" on the back bumper and we were sent rowdily on our way. They were a friendly bunch, wishing us well, but I couldn't help a small sinking feeling. Was I to be stuck with Rita and Betty all the months, years, that Harry was away in the war?

Clear of the city, we stopped to get shot of the ribbons and card. The dusk had held for a few glorious red-hued moments before a moonless night folded away the scene like a theatre curtain. As Harry drove on, it was impossible to know what was out there, whether mountains, forests, miles of savannah. There were no clues in the eerie blanket blackness; I felt a bit scared.

We'd shaken off a few ramshackle vehicles sharing the uneven road, and the noises of night were frighteningly loud. A percussion of screeches and screams, a lion's roar, chorusing cicadas and battering wings, huge whirring insects that hit the windscreen with such force that I instinctively ducked every time.

Harry laughed. 'You'll get used to it. I once drove into a vast swarm of locusts two miles wide, a humungous cloud, literally in the many millions. The road was slippery with them. It was impossible to see a thing, worse than a pea-souper fog. I very nearly collided into a planter who'd come to a complete halt.'

'I'll be terrified to ever open the windows now!'

'Swarms of locusts are very rare, promise! It's usually just a few flying ants.'

'What about all the lions, leopards and bad-tempered chimps?'

'The lions hunt out on the savannah. It's only the old ones who ever venture into the forest, hoping for an over-excited monkey to fall out of a tree for lunch. Don't worry, there's the cook boy, other boys too who look after the place, and the wildlife stays in the wild. A baboon has been known to pinch a few pawpaws from a tree at the bottom of the garden, but that's about it. I long to be taking you to the Budongo Forest,' Harry felt for my hand, 'and I'm desperate to stop and kiss you, but daren't risk the car playing up on these remote *murram* roads.'

'I'm with you on not stopping.' We'd stopped to fill up at the one pump in Mityana, a largeish village, the only place for petrol, Harry said, the whole way to Fort Portal. I kissed his cheek and reached for the picnic basket. 'Better have a sandwich and coffee to keep you going. Just don't go needing a pee!'

We weren't hungry after the party bits, which was just as well. The sandwiches were filled with a paper-thin slice of some dry indeterminate meat that would surely have been grey as ash if we could have seen it, two hard-boiled eggs that gave off a smell like a fart when peeled and two bruised bananas. The very milky coffee splashed up like a stepped-on puddle whenever we tried to have a sip.

Harry said, 'It's nursery food out here. Brown Windsor soup, meat and two veg, spotted dick pudding. The Africans learned at the feet of our *memsahibs* who taught British seaside hotel, not French Riviera, cooking, unfortunately.'

'Cairo was the opposite, all those food-loving French, Greeks and Swiss. There were great places to eat.' I moved on quickly; talking about Cairo felt wrong.

'The Mountains of the Moon Hotel. What could sound more romantic and mystical! It's a heavenly honeymoon choice and I love you.'

'Do you? Really? Can you say it again? Unconnected with the choice of hotel?'

'I love you. I love you, husband, dear,' I teased.

'You'll get lots of love-yous from me later on. I'm saving them up. Not far now, it's only about another half hour.' Harry drove on in silence, leaving me to wrestle with the enormous decision churning in my mind. It had been for weeks. He'd know anyway, wouldn't he? Surely honesty was best?

'Harry, darling, just so you know, I'm not a virgin. Sorry, if it's a bit of a shock.'

'Oh. Well, I'm not either, but nothing of any significance. Thanks for telling me. I'd rather not know anything more, though, not for now. The past's the past.'

I packed up the picnic detritus. Harry seemed subdued. Would it have been better not said? We were both understandably tense and weary. The road was better, which was a good sign. I felt so desperate to be there.

'How did you get on with Jock Hardwick?' Harry asked, as though anxious to change tack. 'He's a good fellow, rough diamond and gone a bit native. He has a Ugandan girlfriend, which causes a few murmurs and sneers. Does that rather shock you? Perhaps I shouldn't have said.'

'No, never don't tell me things. And no, it doesn't shock me. Being entirely honest, if I hadn't met and liked him, my feelings could have been a bit mixed. Rita and Betty were certainly very toffee-nosed, which is an understatement. But if Jock has fallen for a local girl and they love each other, isn't that all that matters.'

'I wish a few others round here felt like that. You, my dearest, are well ahead of your time. We're coming into Fort Portal. I can't wait to be at the hotel.'

The hotel was long and low with a veranda running the length of its frontage, and gardens that, as far as one could see, looked extensive and fine.

After ringing for what seemed like an age, a lean, lanky, youngish European came to the door stifling a yawn and smiling. 'Welcome, friends! I'm the manager here. Come on in, and congratulations are in order, I believe.' He sounded Polish, possibly Danish or Norwegian. 'A boy will bring the luggage. You're in room six,' he said, taking us down a passage hung with African spears and shields. He unlocked the door, handed Harry the key and flicked the light switch. 'The bathroom's next door, you'll love the view in the morning. I'm Adolf, by the way, but call me Dolf, makes life easier! I'm Polish and no fan of my namesake. 'Breakfast is from six to ten. What time for your morning tea?'

Harry raised his eyebrows.

I said, 'Eight o'clock? We're on honeymoon!'

Left alone, and Harry so obviously shy, I chatted lightly about not very much. 'Dolf was sensitive about his name, wasn't he, but awful being saddled with one so defiled by association. He's given us a good room. I love the four-poster, and all that white mosquito netting gathered into a tiara looks like a bridal veil!'

'They're called coronas,' Harry said pompously. 'Handsomely carved posts, they're ebonised teak. I know my trees!' He was moving closer when there was a knock on the door and the boy brought in the bags.

I looked round while he tipped the kid and closed the door. A dangling ceiling light was off centre to allow for the fan; there was a wooden standard lamp, blue-flowered curtains and an abundance of solid wood furniture. Harry flicked off the main light switch, which caused a large insect to buzz its annoyance, dive-bombing endlessly at one of the weak little bedside lights.

Harry shed his uniform jacket and chucked it on top of his stiff tropical hat on a chair. I felt less worried about my confession as he came close and held my shoulders, staring into my eyes. 'Happy?'

I smiled and nodded. 'Are you? Stuck with a wife now, for better or worse?'

'For ecstatic best! Welcome to my life and my arms. It's been so long since seeing each other,' he was tentatively stroking my hair, 'I don't want to rush you…' I lifted my face and he kissed me, cautiously at first, but his mouth was soon hard on mine, his tongue thrusting, his pressing body rigid with need.

I undid his tie, unbuttoned his shirt, slipped in my arms and ran my hands lightly up and down his damp back. He smelled of sweat and nerves and no mistaking his urgency. I wanted to encourage him and make the sex good. Bob had taken me to heights, awakened needs, and it was difficult to hold back, but I worried about making my sexuality too apparent. I wanted to be caressed, direct Harry's hand, to kneel and excite him; it was a fine line to tread.

I pulled back, lips smarting, and brushed lightly over his mouth. 'Can you undress me now and take me to bed?' He found the top of my zip, fumbling with sweaty, trembling fingers, and even with my help struggled with an endearing mix of carefulness and haste. Then edging us backwards, lifting the veil of mosquito netting, he scooped me up with little effort and laid me on the high four-poster bed. 'You're mine and I love you,' he said, ripping free of his own clothes and climbing up. 'Help me, say what you want me to do.'

He didn't wait for that and when we lay back and Harry's breath was slowly calming, he felt for my hand. 'I can't tell you how I've longed for this moment. I've thought of you while polishing buttons, hacking back the bush, aiming a rifle at a buck for the pot. I suppose it was inevitable, being so incapable of holding back, but don't give up on me, will you?' He turned with a sheepish smile and stroked my cheek with the back of a finger.

My head was in the dell of his shoulder and I kissed the wet skin of his neck. 'We've got a whole week, masses of time, every waking minute, in fact – apart from climbing a few mountains of the moon and marvelling at the view.'

'Not too many mountains, you just want to exhaust me and have a quiet time.'

'Possibly not…' I reached down and felt his twitch of arousal '…but if we don't get a bit of kip now, they'll be bursting in on us with the morning tea.'

Harry was bright and breezy in the morning, full of bounce. 'The boy will bring in the tea, saying, "*Jambo Bwana, Memsahib. 'Habari? M'zuri?*" which means, "*Hello, Sir, Madam, how are you? All well?*" Harry was leaning over me, encouraging me awake, kissing my lips. 'You'll soon pick up Swahili. I can speak some Lunyoro, the Bantu language up north, and knowing a bit of both is handy, but they understand a bit of Swahili too.'

I yawned widely. 'Too early for a Swahili lesson. You can give me classes, but not now and not on honeymoon either. We've got to get through this whole long ghastly war first anyway, before I'll ever need any of the languages up north.'

'God, how I long for that day to come.'

The thought of living in a forest surrounded by marauding wildlife, locusts, mosquitos and thieving baboons, had always seemed such a remote possibility as to really be only a dream. There'd be snakes too, and the nearest doctor an hour away. I shuddered to think how I'd cope if we had a child. I'd have to. People did.

*

'Solomon tracked the Queen of Sheba out here all those millennia ago,' said Harry, his fingers trailing my arm. We were leaning against a rock, legs outstretched, a light wind rustling the eucalyptus trees. 'I like to imagine him gazing up at the Mountains of the Moon, believing they were the source of the great River Nile. People thought that, right up till John Hanning Speke finding it less than a hundred years ago.'

'I'm sure Solomon would have been more preoccupied, searching for his queen, but he must have felt very humbled, seeing these majestic towering mountains, shrouded even then in the mists of time. The colours are so beautiful too, the reds and burnished yellows, every shade of green, and I love the flat, limp leaves of the banana trees.'

'There's such variety up here. The trees are mostly sub-tropical, in fact, with the cooler air.' Harry gave my arm a squeeze. 'How about that picnic? I'm starving.'

Chicken drumsticks; sandwiches; figs; slices of juicy, sweet pineapple wrapped in waxed paper; rich, moist fruitcake and a thermos of chilled, freshly made lemonade; it was certainly a step up from Mary Barnes' picnic. I leaned my head to Harry's shoulder. 'I was worrying about Bertha and Anna and feeling for you all the more, not knowing about your parents, whether they're even still able to farm. And your aunts in Bavaria… isn't it very difficult for you, fighting this war with relations still there?'

'The worry goes without saying, but defeating Hitler is the single most important thing we'll ever do in our lives, and my German ancestry could never stand in the way.' Harry laid me back on the picnic rug. 'But it doesn't help to brood and we're out here in all this glorious isolation.' He undid my shirt and slipped in his hand. 'How about making the most of it?'

We saw little of the other guests by day. Harry knew one or two, an English teacher at Makerere University and a bishop holidaying with his wife, who, we suspected, had quite a little thing going with Dolf while the bishop went off on long hikes. I played the piano in the evenings and because we were on honeymoon, people bought us drinks, which we gladly accepted with money so tight.

I had a few moments of lowness with Bob in my thoughts and tried to concentrate on the positives. Harry was happy, he'd seemed a bit subdued by my confession, but the sex was fine. He was seven years younger than Bob, in more of a sexual hurry, but we were on a path to the future, feeling our way and growing closer.

Harry said, thanking Dolf as we left, 'First, there's the war to be sorted, but we'll be back one day…'

Would we? Somehow, I doubted it. I liked Dolf, felt sad for him. He'd begged his pregnant wife to leave Poland with him, but she'd wanted to stay, and a week after he left, Hitler's invading troops had stormed in and war was declared. Dolf had never seen his baby son or daughter; didn't even know if they were alive.

I prayed they were, prayed that Harry, Bob, Hamish, all the young men and women risking their lives for their country and freedom, would see the end of the war and survive.

CHAPTER 22

Entebbe

The bungalow on loan to us in Entebbe was small, not unlike the Barnes', and quite as stiflingly hot. The best thing about it was a jackfruit tree with its vast pendulous fruit, right outside the living-room window.

We had driven the five hours back to Entebbe in scintillating sunshine. After the blackout outward journey it was bliss to see all the lush sunlit vegetation, it felt like Uganda's true beating heart. Dolf had organised a packed lunch and given us a whole fruit cake; we were working our way through it and loving the memories.

Harry was out, seeing George Parker, his Forest Service boss. I was recovering from Mary Barnes, Rita and Betty coming to call. Just popped in for the picnic basket, they said, then stayed gossiping for hours. They'd been pink in the face with excitement; high-society murders didn't happen every day.

Rita hadn't drawn breath, 'Of course, he'd had it coming, the amoral bounder, and a man of his standing! It's too, too appalling!'

'Josslyn Hay, Earl of Errol and High Constable of Scotland,' Betty exclaimed, 'can you believe it! Having such a *public* affair with another man's wife, he's a disgrace to king and country. And now a fine upstanding man like Sir Jock Delves Broughton being accused too. Terrible, he's no murderer, husband or not.'

'But the poor man *was* murdered,' I said, feeling Joss Errol deserved a little sympathy whatever his moral compass. None was forthcoming. The three ex-pat wives carried on, flushed with their pious indignation, feeding off every scrap of the meaty gossip like hyenas stripping a bone.

I'd seen a huge, crude black headline on honeymoon: "Passionate Peer Gets His". We weren't reading newspapers, but it had been the talk of the hotel and memorable for us, since Joss Errol had been murdered on 24th January, our wedding day. He'd been found slumped on the floor of his Buick with a bullet to his brain. Two milk boys out on their rounds had seen a car slewed off the road, peered in, told their boss at the dairy, who'd quickly alerted the police.

The muggy airlessness in the bungalow was getting to me. Windows were wide open, an ineffectual fan full on. I should get on, had thank-you letters to write for wedding presents I could have done without: a visitor's book, set of fish knives, a tiddly silver vase. Pity Harry couldn't have steered his friends in the direction of sheets and towels. We had none of the basics, were so strapped for cash.

I'd written to Mum and Dad, answered Lil's letter and was rereading it before facing the duty ones. Lil hadn't tiptoed lightly; she'd painted the most shockingly distressing graphic picture of just how bad things were at home.

...I went dancing at the Café de Paris and stayed over in London with Henry, my new beau (don't tell the parents), but the state of the city is dire. It looks toothless, like an old hag, with all the great gaping holes between buildings, interiors exposed, bits of wallpaper hanging off, the smashed spikes of a

baby's pram. And the noise! Sirens, bombs, and if you lie flat in a doorway like we're meant to, you get almost as bruised and knocked as with an actual hit.

Heartless crooks stooping as low as to cut the fingers off dead bodies for their rings, the vile thugs. They deserve to have bits cut off that I couldn't possibly name. Still, that sneaky trip to London was a break from Cambridge's Arctic cold, battling with the Siberian winds sweeping across the Fens. The university's a desert, no, an iceberg. There's no life, no night sport, few students, all the blackouts... I'm doing a bit of war work at an air force base at least, don't wear stockings, can't afford them, and my legs are as mottled as an old lady's, a horrible sight, whatever Henry says! Lucky you, perfecting your tan! Write soon.

Poor Lil. Such horrifying images of London in the Blitz. I ached to hear news of the whole family, felt worried to death, but had my own problems too, however insignificant by comparison – a rather urgent need of a roof over my head. We had the use of the bungalow for Harry's leave, but what then? Where was I going to live when he was gone?

He was being ages. George Parker's office was in Entebbe, conveniently close and where all Harry's mail and army communications were being sent. There'd be bumph on the officer-training course in Nakuru, but what chance of a travel permit for me waiting to be collected there as well?

I wrote a couple of thank-you letters, resisting the lure of the local newspaper on the coffee table, still with huge eye-catching headlines about the murder. A story about a blackmailing local politician, front-page news at any other time, had been relegated to an inside page. There seemed no let-up to the press' obsession, more salacious details appearing every day, and giving into temptation I went over to flop on the sofa and have a read.

Harry came in and leaned over to kiss the top of my head. 'I have been hard at the thank-you letters,' I said sheepishly, turning, 'but this story's like a foreign film that would never get past the censors. All these Happy Valley stories of wife-swapping parties and drugs, jokes about the Wanjohi River flowing with champagne. Can it all really still be going on with Britain being blitzed to the skies? Anyway, darling, what news?'

'No dice with a permit for you, I'm afraid. George has tried too. He's given me a letter certifying that you're my wife and I'm a government forest officer, which could help at the border, but you'd have no official status in Kenya, still be resident here. It's a real problem.'

'So, do we take our chances and I slip into Kenya unofficially? Couldn't I stay somewhere near your training camp and find a job in Nakuru? There must be places to rent, however broke we are.' Harry nodded vaguely, anxiously too, knowing as well as I did what little hope I had of finding parents keen for their kids to have piano or German lessons in wartime.

Even if I found work, what would I do when Harry had his commission and was back at the front? Stick around in Kenya or return to Uganda, where I was legal? There'd be no Entebbe bungalow, no place of refuge for stray army wives.

Harry grinned. 'We'll get you into Kenya. It's no good trying to plan long term when we're fighting Hitler and Musso, just have to live from day to day, but we're going to win this war. I'd put good money on it.'

'We haven't got any to put!'

What were my worries beside Harry's? He'd soon be back living on bully beef in some godforsaken desert hellhole, glad of every day he was alive.

I kissed him. 'Have some tea and cake. I made a Victoria sponge, which was just as well, since Rita, Betty and Mary were here. They never stopped gossiping. Didn't you say that Nakuru was near the Aberdare Mountains? That's Happy Valley country – do you think the partying really still goes on, even now, with the cuckolded husband, Jock Delves Broughton, under suspicion?'

'Haven't the foggiest, but I'd rather you didn't accept any invitations to wife-swapping parties around there.'

'That paper says Delves Broughton could soon be brought to trial.' I thought of Rita and Betty, hotly on his side. 'He had the motive, but it's no proof.'

'True, we mustn't damn the man yet. Still, whoever did it, the story's going to keep all the *memsahibs* in hot gossip for years.' Harry followed me into the kitchen. 'It's wretched about Joss Errol, I'm sure there were husbands lining up to put a gun to his head, but he'd been doing good stuff over the last couple of years and was no appeaser, like many of his kind. He'd joined the KAR, been appointed Military Secretary and become General Cunningham's right-hand man. I hate the fact that he was murdered on our wedding day.'

'General Cunningham will have a job to handle the scandal, won't he?'

'A bit, but I'll bet working on cunning plans to outsmart the Italians will be higher up his list.'

*

Our few days in Entebbe were over. Harry was boyishly excited, making lists and poring over maps like a scoutmaster going camping with his cubs. He piled up the car with our luggage then came bouncing back in through the kitchen door on a blast of muggy air. I was making sandwiches, dripping in the humid heat, and in no mood to be swivelled round with his burst of sweaty passion.

'We'll never get off at this rate and I'm sticky and clammy in this awful bloody heat.' I was irritated at his obliviousness to my tension.

'It's the hottest time of year here. Nakuru is higher and cooler,' Harry said, calming down, 'and it has a beautiful lake with flamingos. You're going to love it there, my darling, when we've got you sorted with a place to stay. Everything's going to be great. You'll see.'

CHAPTER 23

Harry

Harry was tensing up; he knew Laura was too. They'd been motoring for three hours, nearing Jinja, and she'd been in her own space, almost distant, for most of the time. He felt excluded, and depressed, all his excited anticipation draining away. He longed for the courage to ask what, or rather who, had happened in Cairo. Surely everything was fine? She'd come to Uganda, married him...

He kept his sighs to himself and turned with an awkward smile. 'Well, here we are in Jinja! I love Lake Victoria's northern shore and we've broken the back of the journey. I'm ready for that picnic too.'

Laura smiled. 'The lake's a perfect place for it, and good to stretch our legs.'

It was a glorious day, a soft light breeze. Harry took a track down to a promontory that looked out over the water and parked. Laura spread out the food on the rug he'd brought out from England, older and mustier than the one the hotel had provided on their honeymoon picnics. He sat down with her on the grassy bank and pointed out wallowing hippos, sly-eyed crocodiles, but Laura was preoccupied, unpacking the sandwiches. 'This is not much of a step up from Mary's,' she said, 'just sandwiches, fruit and the remains of Dolf's cake.'

'It's a banquet before all those tinned processed peas.' The fruit cake had lasted a whole week.

The swirling froth, the roar of the Rippon Falls crashing onto the great flat rocks nearby, was stupendous. Fishing boats were tiny specks out on the lake, fishermen casting their lines at the water's edge. Harry felt the beauty of it with an almost painful intensity. He felt intensely close to Laura, the more so for his unsettling thoughts in the car. He longed for her to be as much at one with the place and feeling the same sense of rightness.

'All this,' she said, 'and to be at this very place as well, the actual source of the Nile, it does make me feel very emotional.'

Setting off again, Harry felt better, still dreadfully unconfident about getting her into Kenya. He was glad to have a room booked for their night at the border. George had recommended the Tororo Hotel, having a job to keep a straight face, cracking up as he described it, and now, Harry too couldn't help his face from breaking out into a smile.

'What's so funny?'

'Guess how the Tororo Hotel's proprietor ends his letters to government officials… "*You* have the honour to be, Sir, *my* humble obedient servant!" He's a law unto himself, George, says, so we may yet be turned away and end up sleeping in a stable.' That took his mind to babies. Suppose Laura was pregnant and coping all alone when he had his commission and was gone?

"I seriously hope the place is a bit more than a stable,' she laughed. 'I'd kill for a long, cool, reviving bath.'

The Tororo Hotel was easy to find, small and red-brick with a wooden porch and mature jacaranda trees. It looked charming. A giant of a man with a greying frizz and substantial potbelly was standing in the doorway, sizing them up as they climbed stiffly out of the car. He had to be the proprietor.

'You booked a double room,' he said. 'Two singles only, this is a family hotel.'

'But we're married!'

'So you say. Two singles, seventeen shillings each. A charge of two shillings is levied against visitors who do not bath. Own servants cannot be catered for.'

'All right, two rooms, but that costs us three shillings more…'

'No reductions. Dinner is four shillings each person and it's nearly over, you'd better hurry. Breakfast, two shillings.' He peered past them. 'Good car. I help you in with the bags.' He carried in their three hefty cases – everything they owned, one case up under his arm – as effortlessly as if they were filled with air.

The two single rooms were clean and there was a large notice about pets. "*Dogs and other fleasome beasts & birds are not allowed into the hotel*".

The dining room was deserted. They had tasty freshwater fish with green beans and potatoes and wobbly red jelly and custard, all served at great speed by another enormous fellow in a grimy apron and chef's hat.

Harry went to put in requests for a bath and came back grinning. 'That's just saved us four shillings, we're a bob up.'

There were two bathrooms for the hotel's ten rooms. They could talk to each other through the partition wall, but it was one more separation. In his sparse single room, lying on the narrow bunk bed, waiting till the coast was clear and trying to handle his arousal, Harry felt desperately worried about getting Laura into Kenya. Suppose the course wouldn't allow him any time off. Was this to be their last night together for who knew how long, sleeping in separate rooms?

He had to get her over the border; so much better she was in Kenya. Better too if she were in Nairobi, in easy reach of hospital care, should she be pregnant by the time he had his commission and was back at the front.

He wanted a son. It was an intense need, a knot, an inner stab of longing that often caught him unawares; tiny fingers curling round one of his own, close-knit post-war family life in the heart of the Budongo Forest. He ached to be there, doing the job he loved. The imminent separation from Laura would be all the more painful for the togetherness and physicality of the past ten days, a gut-wrenching endurance test. Suppose he were shot up, blown up, dying in agony, never even knowing if he had a child?

Thoughts like that got him nowhere – and the hotel was silent at last.

He crept along the passage in his pyjama bottoms and eased open Laura's door. She beckoned him in with a crooked finger. He slipped into her bed and made selfish love but was burning up, and it had to be missionary style in a bed the width of two floorboards.

'You okay,' he said, lying on his side to avoid rolling onto the floor, 'apart from being squashed up against the wall like a zapped mosquito? Love me? Nothing making you anxious – apart from the obvious?'

'Of course I love you, silly old bear. And for God's sake, don't worry about me. I'm resourceful, remember. I'll find something to do that earns a crust. The proprietor's quite a character, isn't he?' Laura said, changing the subject in a way as to avoid serious conversation. It was a trait that Harry found very irritating.

'And nothing like laying down the law,' she carried on. '"Your tea will arrive at six!" No question of our having a say in the matter! But funny how even the Tororo Hotel is geared to our British early-morning tea habits. It was the same in Cairo, Mahmood unfailingly bringing me tea every morning. He was so sweet...' She trailed away as she always did when talking of Cairo.

She stroked Harry's cheek. 'Hadn't you better creep back now, or the 6 am tea boy will be telling on us...'

'God, I feel frustrated at having to sleep alone. See you at breakfast, Mrs Werner.' He kissed her lips. 'Six thirty? Good to be early at the border.'

*

They had no trouble getting into Kenya. The young, smartly dressed official seemed to brush over, or even be unaware, that a wife needed an army permit to accompany her husband over the border. Laura presenting her passport, still in her maiden name, explaining shyly about being just married, and the susceptible fellow had just melted. He congratulated her in Swahili, stamped their passports. Harry felt faint with relief. 'That was an unexpected piece of cake,' he said, 'one hurdle over, but you'll still need to lie low, I'm afraid.'

'Because I'm officially resident in Uganda?'

'Yep. We just have to hope our luck holds. Still, fingers crossed, it's a heavenly day and the gods are with us, I feel it in my bones.' Harry grinned, but he would be at the barracks by nightfall and no Laura, just the hard grind of training.

Motoring on through the savannah with his wife by his side, he began to relax a little. The tang of the parched grasses and dry dung, flashes of vibrantly coloured birds, lilac-breasted rollers, malachite kingfishers. 'The cactus-like plants that look like candelabra are actually a euphorbia,' he said, feeling more in his element, 'and all the massive baobabs can store enough water in their trunks to last right through the long dry season. And those bushes with the hanging black balls are called whistling thorns. They are always full of ants. The boys out herding cattle in the baking sun all day shake out the ants and eat the whole ball for a bit of energy.'

In Nakuru, they found a small hotel whose only free room had a distant view of the lake. He paid up front for two nights, took up the luggage and took Laura to bed. One precious hour of lovemaking before it was time to report to camp.

They set off to explore the town, with Laura driving, since he was leaving her the car. She spotted an outdoor café. 'Quick cuppa before we have to say goodbye?'

A hefty buxom waitress brought over their tea. She set down a tin teapot, chipped cups, milk and sugar on the small metal table that clanked with every touch of knees, and returned with two doorstep hunks of a violently orange pound cake.

Laura smiled up at her. 'I don't suppose you know of any schools round here? I teach and I need to find work and a place to stay too…' She sighed, a touch theatrically in a wistful bid to touch a chord, but Harry was beginning to worry about being late and drummed his fingers under the table. 'We've just got married,' Laura said, 'and my husband's had leave from the army but has to report back now…'

A sharp-minded person might have wondered at Laura being suddenly homeless, but she added quickly, 'I don't come from these parts, you see.'

'Well, girly,' the waitress said, wiping her pudgy hands on her flowered apron, 'there's a kiddies' school up dat hill beyond di church. You could try there. They may be short a pair a hands, now there is less men around to do di jobs with di war.'

From the way Laura thanked her, you'd think the woman had just saved her from drowning. Harry doubted it was much of a lead and slightly begrudged the generous tip that he felt compelled to leave on the table.

'Better stop some distance from the gates,' he said, as they reached the barracks. She rounded a corner before stopping and out of the car, pressing her up against the driver's door, he kissed her long and hard. It was time to go, but he felt like a lamb being torn from its mother, and it was Laura who gently pulled apart, giving a soft smile.

Her hand was on the car-door handle and he had to go. He said, 'It won't be for the first month, but I believe we get a bit of time off at weekends after that. Just be sure to leave a forwarding address at the hotel if you manage to find anywhere to rent, but for God's sake, stay on there if you don't. To hell with the cost...'

He kissed her again, needing to feel every pulse and bone, every curve of her body, to hold on to her scent, cling to the very essence of her and keep her near.

She said, 'If only you could give me a call and we could talk.' He touched her velvety cheek with the back of his hand. 'No chance of that, wouldn't be allowed even if you were legal. You must leave any new address, but I'll find you wherever you are.'

CHAPTER 24

Alone in Nakuru

I watched Harry hurry away. He looked back once with a forlorn smile, rounded the corner and was gone. Driving beyond the gates, I'd seen the rows of barrack huts. Solid brick, he should be fine, but would I be?

I sighed and set off to find the café again, get my bearings and try my luck at the school up the hill. I felt frightened and alone, yet a flicker of excitement too; a new country, new experiences, a sense of promise and adventure. Kenya had potentially more like-minded Europeans. It was more sophisticated and would, I felt, make beautiful Uganda feel like a provincial outpost. That was most likely unfair, and right now, all I had to look forward to was a depressingly blind search for work and long, lonely nights in a strange, unknown country.

Nakuru was a spreading town, but the café easy to find, not so far from the barracks as I retraced my steps. Driving up the hill where the waitress had pointed, passing the small church she'd mentioned, stone with a delightful square tower, I saw a long thatched wooden property. It was single-storey with the mandatory veranda frontage and sat side onto the lane, shaded by some immensely tall and beautiful umbrella acacias. There were smaller buildings in the grounds that extended out behind, and a large signboard by the gate: "*King George Primary School*". There had to be a chance.

I parked on the verge, took out my powder compact, dabbed at my nose, combed my hair, touched the Chevvy's polished-wood dashboard for luck and climbed out. It was dusk already, far cooler than Entebbe and I shivered. Six o'clock. Would anyone still be about? There would be separate schools for European and African children, and all fee-paying.

I went through a small gate and walked up a red-earth path flanked by straggly plumbago, to the main door. There was an old-fashioned bell pull that set up a jangle, and the sound cutting into the evening quiet was like an enormous dinner gong. I waited, shaking with nerves, and eventually heard shuffling footsteps.

A gnarled old Kenyan in a blue singlet and *kanga* eased open the rather flimsy panelled door. 'Yes, Memsahib, can I help you?'

'I was wondering whether it would be possible to have a word with the headmaster or headmistress. I'm a teacher, newly arrived in Kenya.'

'That will be Mr Long. You wait here, please?'

He shuffled off and I listened out, wiping clammy hands on my peach wedding frock. I heard a door open and bang shut in a draught, brisk footsteps, squeaky shoes. A stocky man of about forty came to the door. He had dark hair with a widow's peak and enquiring deep-set brown eyes. 'I'm Mr Long, the headmaster here.' He held out his hand. 'I gather that you wanted to see me. How can I help?'

'My name's Laura Werner,' I said, liking his firm, warm handshake. 'I'm terribly sorry to come unannounced, but I've just arrived in the area and saw the school sign. I'm, um, hoping to find a teaching job while my husband is at the officer-training station here, and when he rejoins his battalion too.' I gave my most winning smile. 'This is dreadfully presumptuous, I know. Do forgive me if I'm wasting your time…'

'Not at all, please come in. We can have a quick talk in my office, but I'm afraid my wife will be expecting me back for dinner. We live on the premises,' he explained, 'as do most of my staff. We're one big family here.'

His small office, whose walls were lined with books and watercolours, had just enough room for his large headmaster's desk that, unlike Miss Wilcox's, overflowed with disorderly piles of paper. 'Do sit down.' He indicated a wobbly-looking rush chair and leaned forward on his elbows, pyramiding his hands.

'We have a hundred or so children here, four- to ten-year-olds, mainly from the outlying European community. A few boarders, evacuees from Mombasa, where things are hotting up, but I expect you've just come from there if you're newly arrived, all the way round the Cape, I expect.'

'No, only from Uganda, where I was recently married. I was in Cairo before that, teaching music and languages at an American mission school and have a reference from there. I could teach other subjects too, to the little ones – even sport!' I reddened. Whatever had possessed me to throw in that?

'Ah, now you're talking! We lost our voluntary sports master when he joined up and I've had to step into the breach. But seriously, we are short on music. Our maths mistress tinkles away at assembly, but she doesn't always hit the notes! You play the piano?'

'And the lute – I, um, put on concerts for the troops at the YMCA in Cairo too.'

'Goodness. Impressive. You're staying locally? You'd be able to come in early?'

'As early as you'd like. I'm booked in at the Flamingo Inn, but do need to find more permanent accommodation rather urgently…'

Was that pushing my miraculous luck, making my circumstances seem as desperate as they were?

Mr Long rose. 'Can you come back at about ten o'clock tomorrow morning? I'll think on it meantime, see what I can do.' He saw me to the door. 'A pleasure to meet you, Mrs Werner,' he said, shaking my hand again warmly.

*

Two weeks on, I was still pinching myself. How could it be that I was living in at the King George Primary, playing the piano at assembly, taking music and singing classes, getting a show underway for Parents' Day at the end of term? It was a Mr Long-shaped miracle. I taught the older children a bit of basic French as well and stood in for him when he was too busy to lob a few tennis balls over the net.

He and I had come to a life-saving arrangement. He had little money for an extra teacher, but we'd arrived at the happy compromise of peppercorn pay in return for free bed and board, which seemed like a perfect solution.

My accommodation was a thatched hut that had its foibles. On the upside, it had a curtained alcove with shower, washbasin and lavatory and, since the previous occupants had been a couple – the bespectacled, crosspatch maths mistress, Mrs Smithers, and her husband, who had recently moved off campus – an enormous double bed. Harry would be pleased.

On the downside, the place having been empty a while, snakes seemed to have viewed it as a cosy retreat. I felt like one of the early settlers, checking every corner and crevice, but with none of their pioneering spirit. I twice had to flee to summon a houseboy to do the slaying. It had frightened the daylights out of me, a real live snake curled up where the sun had been concentrated through a window. That had been a puff adder. 'Very deadly,' the boy said with satisfaction, the other time a thin speckled yellow specimen that he dismissed as "not so bad". He gave me a broomstick to stun further invaders; I had more lucidity of mind with a weapon of sorts than allowed for a sound night's sleep.

The thatch smelled mouldy too, and leaked when it rained, which wasn't such a problem, since the school had provided a vast racing-green tarpaulin to spread over the bed. Nakuru, lying fairly high, was cool at night, so I didn't mind the extra weight and it hadn't rained much either.

I'd quickly got onto first-name terms with the Longs – Seymour and June – and gave piano lessons to their eight-year-old twin girls, which all helped to secure my position. I kept June company whenever possible. Even as the headmaster's wife, when you'd have thought she had masses to do, she always seemed at a lonely loose end. She had short fair hair, dry and split at the ends, and was a bit bloated and blousy-looking, her once pretty face puffy and showing all the signs of a heavy smoker and drinker.

June certainly loved her gin and ciggies, I soon discovered, and gossiping about the scandalous Erroll murder was like a quintuple of her favourite Gordon's with a splash of Roses lime. I worried about her; she seemed dangerously close to a full-blown depression.

Another week flew by. No sign of Harry, but it was still under a month and, snakes apart, I was in love with the country. The ebony nights, stars with the sparkle of a diamond tiara, the rich, terracotta red earth. I loved the sweet-scented early mornings, the profusion of familiar flowers; roses, canna lilies, zinnias. There was the pink silvery lake, pink with the thousands of flamingos, where I picnicked at weekends with my new friend Cyril, the shy English teacher who also lived in. Life was busy and good. It was unbelievable luck.

Cyril was middle-aged. He'd come out to the Belgian Congo with his missionary parents who, three years on, had been found hacked to death in the jungle. Poor Cyril, a child of eleven, he'd been pushed from pillar to post, but was intelligent and resilient as well as painfully shy, and had ended up teaching in Nakuru.

We took books to the lake. Cyril was reading an Agatha Christie, *Murder on the Orient Express*, and I was into *Testament of Friendship,* Vera Brittain's book about her great friend Winifred Holtby. My mother had sent out a very welcome package, care of Harry's boss, George, in Entebbe: paperback novels, a pair of silk stockings and a large, thistle-decorated tin of shortbread.

I wondered vaguely if I could be pregnant, but my periods had always been irregular and if anything, I was losing weight, not gaining it, lobbing and kicking balls about with energetic children and too busy to linger over meals. But just suppose… How would I cope? I shelved the worry, not one for now.

It was four weeks to the day since Harry and I had crossed the border. I was smiling, going into my first class with a roomful of six-year-olds chanting, 'Good morning, Mrs Werner,' in their very British young voices.

My big task was getting them to harmonise with *I Can Sing a Rainbow* for the end-of-term show; they were doing well and the lesson just finishing when I looked up to see Seymour in the doorway. He waited for the children to file out, chatting about school events, then said, 'How about coming to dinner tonight? We're grateful for all you are doing.'

'I'd love to, thanks very much.' I was giving a piano lesson to their twins at five when June would have started on her gin. What sort of state would she be in?

In the next break, I went down to the hut to hunt out something to wear. There was little space for clothes. Most had to live in the suitcase and be hung out in the sunny outdoors to kill off the smell of dank and mothballs. My navy and white with the wide belt would be best, certainly nothing as glamorous as the two cocktail dresses I'd bought in Cairo. But the sight of those, carefully wrapped in tissue paper, caught me off guard and like a match sparking a conflagration, brought a sudden electric flare of need of Bob.

Sanity quickly returned. I fingered his silver bracelet, which I often wore. It didn't feel wrong, simply a thread of connection, a link to a treasured memory.

The Longs' solid brick house, built very much in the British colonial tradition, had no veranda. They had a cook and Jimiyu, the elderly houseboy who'd answered the door on that first evening, At lunch, Seymour ate in the school canteen with the rest of us.

He ushered me into the sitting room and held up a silver shaker. 'Martini?'

'I can think of nothing better,' I said, perching on the arm of a lumpy armchair, watching as he poured out three martinis into stemmed glasses and popped an olive in each.

'Hope it's okay.' He smiled, handing me a glass.

'It's perfect, deliciously chilled.'

'We're lucky to have a decent icebox. Oh, by the way, your husband called just as I was leaving the office. He'd found your forwarding address and wanted you to know he has the weekend off. I told him you did too.'

'Thanks, that's wonderful news,' I said, feeling a bit caught out, the one day I'd let in thoughts of Bob... 'And Harry can be on snake duty!' I was anxious to establish that he could stay at the hut. 'I hope you'll be able to meet him.'

More martinis were poured, June downing hers in a gulp. I praised the twins' piano playing, a bit disingenuously, feeling at home in the room that I now knew well, teaching the girls at the quaint old upright piano with candleholder brackets and gold scrolls. It must have come out with an early Kenyan settler.

Jimiyu summoned us for dinner, dressed in a long white *kanzu*. He set down three bowls of brown soup very carefully, with a woman, as thin and elderly as he was, following with a bowl of croutons. There was an enormous contraption on the sideboard. Was it a wireless? It had matching square glass jars at each end, filled with a liquid of the most violent shade of green. I said, 'That's quite a piece of kit! What's in the jars? What do they do?'

'It's acid, helps to boom out the sound,' Seymour said. 'I can get what news they give us, though never feel we get the full picture out here. I can tune in later if you'd like, and hope to hear the nine o'clock news.'

'I'd be terribly grateful, feeling really out of touch since Cairo…' The clink of spoons took over. 'Are you old Kenya hands?' I asked, feeling unable to say anything positive about the floury brown soup, and curious; they didn't seem like the hardened ex-pats I'd met so far.

June, who'd been silent most of the evening, said, 'We came out in 'thirty-six for a four-year term and now we're stuck here for God knows how long.' She gazed blearily at her husband. 'I want to see my parents. I've had enough.'

'We're damn lucky to be here,' Seymour said, failing to hide his irritation. 'Don't whinge. Think of the Blitz, the terrible hardships, and count your blessings.'

'Sugar's rationed,' she muttered, 'when it's grown all over the bloody country. You're out all day, the twins are at school. What am I supposed to do?'

'The sugar's needed for the war effort, as you well know, and you could take more of an interest in the garden, *dear.*' I heard the sarcasm. 'Talk to the *shamba*, help me with my veg…'

'I'm not going near the *shamba* with that lethal *panga* he uses on the grass.'

'Why don't you register with the KWEO? That's the Kenya Women's Emergency Organisation,' Seymour explained, looking at me, embarrassed. 'It was set up by the last Governor's wife, with so many women here anxious to help.'

'What sort of things do they do?' I asked.

'Clerical work, running canteens, nursing, knitting… You should join a group and do your bit, June, dear,' he said, with a kindlier expression.

'I can't knit and don't drive. You say these things, but it's not that easy…'

'I can knit after a fashion, help you to get the hang of it, and I've got the car. I could try to find a local group we could join.'

Seymour thanked me profusely, and Jimiyu bringing in a dish of meatballs and one of veg was a welcome distraction. The peas and mountain of hearty spinach were fresh and good; Seymour knew his vegetables.

He tuned in his remarkable radio after the stodgy pudding and we listened to the news, with the airwaves crackling like dry bracken. Franklin Roosevelt had signed the Lend-Lease Act to give aid to Britain. German Panzers had arrived in North Africa with heavy armaments for a major offensive… 'Hell's bells,' said Seymour, 'they'll be sweeping up the Nile next.' The death toll for the bomb disaster at the Café de Paris had now topped thirty-four, the newscaster said.

June stared. 'What's wrong, Laura? You've gone white as a sheet. I think you need a sip of brandy.'

'My sister has gone dancing at the Café de Paris, she was going again…'

'That bomb must have hit a couple of nights ago or more. I'm sure you'd have heard,' Seymour said, 'but if you want to go to the post office, wire home and set your mind at rest, I can take your first lesson.'

He was a practical thinker and I thanked him gratefully, but it was hard to linger and enter in, and thanking them for dinner, I made my apologies.

The Longs saw me to the door, June swaying slightly and leaning against the bannister. My thoughts were all for Lil, but I felt June needed help rather badly.

Seymour said, 'I'll walk you back, check out the hut for you.'

I was glad of that, with all the scuttles and rustling leaves, feeling emotional and quite scared. Every sound was amplified; cicadas, hoopoes, nightjars and something tap-tapping along the ground, drum-like, that gave me the jitters.

'That's just a hornbill,' Seymour said comfortingly. He came into the hut, checked carefully around, and hesitated for a second. 'The odds on your sister being at the Café de Paris that night are remote. All will be well, I'm sure.' Then, squeezing my hand and kissing my cheek, he left me alone to my fears.

I eventually fell into a fitful sleep, dreaming of yellow and black snakes and ticking time bombs. I woke with a start. Bright early-morning light was filtering in, but the ticking was still there… I sat bolt upright, feeling petrified, then my heart slowed. Only the alarm clock… The buzzer soon went off and the day began.

CHAPTER 25

Harry

Harry was enjoying the course. It was more civilised than anything he'd experienced in the army so far, the men in his group were good company and there was tennis, making a pound or two at bridge – only to lose all his winnings again at poker. Annoyingly, to the one smart Alec among them, an over-Brylcreemed bragger, the sort of fellow you'd suspect of being a conman.

Calling the Flamingo Hotel and discovering Laura's whereabouts had left Harry in awe, her resourcefulness coming into its own. He couldn't wait to see her, felt continually aroused and in need of her. Two more days…

The military training was tough going but satisfying; plenty of advice on management skills, though the wisest guidance on leadership he'd received had come from a gruff old major, on his early KAR days in Uganda.

'Take these rules to heart, young man, and you won't go far wrong. Only give orders you would willingly obey yourself. Only give orders you can and will enforce. Lead by example. Look well after those you command and be sure your men have got their food before you begin on yours.' He was a curmudgeonly old fellow but with a heart of gold, and it was advice Harry hoped to try to follow.

He was stuck in a Swahili class, a compulsory course, no getting out of it and, knowing the language backwards, was bored stiff. He'd elected to learn Amharic too, which should come in handy if sent to Abyssinia or nearby, as was likely – hopefully with a second lieutenant's pip on his shoulder and a few extra perks.

Toppy was nuzzling his knee and he slipped down a hand to stroke him. He was a smooth-haired black mongrel with spaniel ears and adoring eyes who'd attached himself. Harry called him Toppy for the wretchedly frail condition he'd been in, almost toppling over on his four black paws. Harry had paid the vet bills and loved him from the start, and now his best mate, Tim, adored Toppy too. They shared the responsibilities and at some stage would have to find him a permanent home, but were putting that off for a while.

'Adjutant wants to see you in his office sharpish,' said a waiting private, nabbing Harry as he came out of the class.

He hurried across the yard, trying to think what rapping over the knuckles he could be in for, feeling a bit anxious. He said, 'Stay!' firmly to Toppy and knocked on the adjutant's door.

'Believe you wanted to see me, Sir?'

The adjutant was writing at his desk and rested his pen. 'Ah, Werner, yes, I need to have a word. Take a seat.' He was a young Irishman and competent by all accounts, a disciplinarian, though there were hints of a lighter side.

'Not easy this,' the adjutant said, staring thoughtfully, taking his time to frame the words. 'I've had the Nakuru district authorities on to me today. They've, ahem, discovered about your wife's unauthorised presence in Kenya and requested that I order you to see she returns to Uganda forthwith.'

'Oh…' Harry's insides felt concave, the disappointment hitting him in the solar plexus like a fist of iron. He hesitated, playing for time, determined not to give up lightly. 'Could I possibly try to find somewhere for her to stay in Uganda first? She'd only arrived in the country a week or so before we came here, you see. We actually had to be married on the day she flew, given travel rules.'

The adjutant eyed him balefully; impossible to read his mind or gauge the hardness of his heart. 'Well, I've done my duty,' he said, his mouth twitching. 'I shall enquire no further into the whereabouts of Mrs Werner.'

*

On Saturday morning, as early as was reasonable, Harry rang a jangling bell at the King George Primary School. An elderly Kikuyu took him out through the gardens, down a path with a few thatched huts on either side. Every blade of grass was shimmering with a dewy sheen; there were canna lilies, roses thriving in the more temperate climate. Harry absorbed the gardens but smiled absently as the Kikuyu talked about the various huts, until they came to the last. 'This one is the Memsahib hut. She be pleased to see you.'

Laura was sitting outside on a chair, sunning her legs, knitting. She glanced up, as if keeping watch, and seeing him, gave a big wide grin. 'Thanks, Jimiyu. This is my husband, Harry Werner, as I expect he explained.' The old man nodded, beamed happily and turned back up the path.

'God, I've missed you!' Harry nuzzled her neck, drinking in the intoxicating scent of her honeyed skin. He kissed her lips lightly, feeling self-conscious outside. 'Can we get inside, quick?' he murmured, kissing her sun-tinted hair.

Laura led him by the hand. 'Welcome to my home from home! A married couple had it before me. So how do you like the bed?'

'I'll show you how… Does the door lock? Will anyone come?'

He picked her up and dropped her, bouncing down, onto the bed, rolling her over, undoing her zip, kissing her all down her backbone; he was overcome. She was his beautiful wife; he couldn't get enough of her. 'Plenty of catching up to do,' he said, tearing off his clothes. 'Can we stay in this playground all day?'

They had most of the morning in it. 'You've got a job to do, snake duty,' Laura said, sitting up and peering carefully round. 'I've had some scares. This hut needs to be on stilts, so no more idling in bed.' Harry pulled her back down, doing his best to idle, which he felt he'd hardly been doing so far. Catching up, learning about her terrible fright over Lil, with her news, he worried whether to mention the adjutant's call from the local authorities. On balance, it felt best, though he knew she hadn't really taken to the Entebbe crowd. He had such a love of Uganda, it made him feel a bit resentful.

She said, 'Do you think there's any chance the authorities will forget about it now? I'm happy here, would hate to have to leave. I love the school and get on with the headmaster, Seymour Long. I long to help his wife, June, too, who's a drinker and I think close to a full-blown depression. There's a group in town, women working for the war effort, and I'm trying to teach her to knit.'

'And I thought that dangling strip on your needles was socks for me.'

'You'd be so lucky… Poor June, Seymour's a doer and a bit abrupt with her, which doesn't help. I've chatted up a pupil's mother who's in the group and I'm taking June to the next meeting. Trouble is, she doesn't seem to have a skill to her name.'

'Perhaps she can sing,' Harry said sarcastically, stifling a yawn.

Laura took him seriously. 'I wonder if she can… Either way, that's a genius idea. We could put on a concert to raise funds.' She kissed him and swung down her legs. 'Time for lunch. Come to the dining hall and meet my dear friend Cyril. Then I must give a child a piano lesson up at school. It's a way to make a few extra bob with my pay here such a pittance, but I do live free after all. Will you be okay on your own for a bit?'

'Just hurry back… Have we really got to have cocktails with the Longs this evening? God, what a yawn.'

After a meagre lunch of shepherd's pie and jelly, Harry strolled in the grounds, glanced up at the immense height of some umbrella acacias, as well as looking carefully where he put his feet. He was well aware of the danger of disturbing a sleeping snake. The birdsong was more muted in the heat of the day, but they were still twittering away like housewives; the place was alive.

He wandered back to the hut. Laura's dresses were hanging up on a couple of nails hammered into the wood and he fingered them, feeling close. Her shoes were on top of each other, the bed taking up every inch of space. A narrow ledge with a square of mirror nailed above held her brush and comb, bits of make-up, a scent bottle and a couple of bead necklaces and a silver bracelet.

Harry fingered the bracelet. It was one she often wore and rather beautiful, delicately patterned, probably a family piece. It had a slight quality of the East, like the jewellery he'd seen in Mombasa and hadn't been able to afford. He saw there was an inscription on the inside, *"Remember me"*, and stared down at it, feeling instinctively chilled. She'd been given that bracelet in Cairo.

Images formed of sexual encounters, tearful farewells – no question of her *forgetting* when that wretched bangle was never off her wrist. His head told him he was overreacting, while his heart thudded so loudly and monotonously it felt like torture. There'd been that long period of no contact, the subtly different tone when her letters had finally resumed. He felt a vicious, tearing rage; his whole body quivered with the force of his bitter jealousy.

Had her Cairo lover been a soldier? Possibly killed? Harry had an urge to stamp on the bracelet and smash it to pieces. Four weeks of longing, brimming over with love, emotionally and physically inflamed with his need of Laura, and now the crushing let-down.

Should he thrust out the bracelet as she came in and challenge her? 'Get this in Cairo by any chance? From your lover?' No, that would sound like a petulant teenager; better to be more restrained and ask casually over dinner about the past men in her life. He could be wrong. It could be a family piece after all.

He looked at the novels on a stool by the bed: *The Waves*, by Virginia Woolf; *Strong Poison,* Dorothy L Sayers; *Rebecca*, Daphne du Maurier. He was reading the blurb on the Sayers cover when Laura came in through the door, smiling, looking flushed with the heat of the sun, completely exquisite.

'Bad snake drill, this open door,' she said, wagging a finger. 'Have you read that? I've got other Sayers too. Mum sent me a huge parcel of books.'

She kissed him on the lips. The blood coursed through him and he pulled her head back by her hair, thrusting his tongue with such teeth-grinding force that he tasted the blood of a cut lip. He pushed her backwards onto the bed, rough and out of control, dragging down her pants, hearing her dress tear as he took her with violent, passionate forcefulness.

It was over so quickly and left him breathless, sweating, and he dropped his head to her chest. The sickening thought hit horribly home that he'd pretty much raped her and put himself entirely in the wrong. 'Sorry. Forgive me.' He took her hand, fingering it, kissing it, still breathless. 'It was just... wanting you.'

'What's to forgive? Hot passion on a Saturday afternoon, bit out of the run,' she gently retrieved her hand, 'but I'm not complaining.'

Harry half wished she were, so shocked he was by his own behaviour, but feeling no less determined to pin her down. 'Can we skip the school canteen tonight?' he said. 'Perhaps go to The Flamingo, where you first stayed? That seemed a quiet enough place. I doubt we'll meet the authorities there.'

'That's a lovely romantic idea. And I thought perhaps we could have a picnic by the lake tomorrow. You won't mind if we give Cyril a lift? He'd be frightfully grateful and would love to talk to you, I know.'

Harry could see no way out of that. 'Fine,' he said brusquely, letting his feelings show. They'd be stuck with that insipid fellow now for the whole bloody time at the lake. Didn't she want every minute, just the two of them, like he did?

'Don't put on that sour face. Cyril's had a miserable life and he's sweet; a good, kind friend and company for me with you away. You must see that?'

He did see, worried constantly about Laura having to cope alone, but it was wartime, fuck it, and wasn't he lonely too? It would be all the harder now. Why wasn't she pregnant? Shouldn't she be, by now? He wanted a son.

*

The headmaster mixed strong martinis. Harry had two in quick succession. He chatted civilly and accepted a third while seething internally. She was too bloody familiar with "Seymour", smiling, laughing, looking glowing in that revealing red dress and the man so obviously attracted to her, ignoring his sodding wife. And how far would Laura take her friendship with that sad case, Cyril? How close would she get? Jealousy coursed in Harry's veins. She was his wife. She should be knitting baby bootees, not helping June and flirting with that cocky headmaster.

He caught Laura's eye. 'Time we were off, sweetheart,' he said lightly, before turning to Seymour with a rictus smile. 'Many thanks, it's been great, but we have a table booked, I'm afraid. Sorry to drag her away.'

'I'll drive, shall I?' Laura said. 'You okay, darling? Nothing bothering you?'

'Just your friend, Seymour, who's a bit too bloody pleased with himself.'

'He's a good head, though, hard-working and a decent man at heart.'

They drove the short distance to the Flamingo Hotel in silence.

The dining room was small and square, with watercolours of Mount Kenya and massed flamingos by the lake. There was vegetable soup and chicken fricassee on the menu and a smarmy waiter hovering, asking what they'd like to drink.

They were the only diners, aside from a grey-haired woman with a bristly moustache who was reading a neatly folded newspaper. Harry ordered a bottle of red wine; he could have done without that woman flapping her ears, but to hell with that, he was determined to have it out.

Laura held his eyes. 'You are upset about something, aren't you, and it isn't Seymour. Tell me. No harbouring grievances, it never does…'

The waiter brought in the soup. Harry waited impatiently then stared steadily across the table. 'I was wondering about your lover before me. Was that in Cairo?'

She glanced over at the woman with the newspaper, slurping her soup now, not reading, before looking back at Harry with pleading eyes. 'The past's the past, darling. You said that yourself on the way to Fort Portal.'

'I also said that it wasn't for then, but it is for now. I need to know.'

'It was very short-lived. He had a girlfriend in England and went back.'

'He was a soldier in Cairo? He gave you that bracelet you wear the whole time?' She'd left it off that night irritatingly, but also tellingly, Harry felt.

'I wear it for no other reason than it's pretty. Look, darling, it's over. The past's the past. He was a journalist who went home to join up. You and I are newly married, I love you and I'm very happy, as I hope you are too. Isn't that enough?'

It wasn't. His stomach was ice-cold and clenched. The waiter came to clear and brought the fricassee and a dish of rice that he took an age to serve.

'Can't we just enjoy the evening?' Laura pleaded, when he'd left. 'I haven't seen you in over four weeks. It's our first weekend and extra special, an evening out after all those canteen meals – though this fricassee does smell a bit rank!'

How could he "just enjoy the evening"? Saying she loved him and was happy; there were different kinds of love. That man, whoever he was, had meant a lot.

And how was he going to handle the corrosive jealousy eating into him? It would be even worse when he had his commission and was back with the 7th. The battalion was based at Assab on the Red Sea coast now too, one of the hottest places in the world. On the frontier with Djibouti, which was occupied by the Vichy French and used as a base for German submarines. Blockading the territory was going to be grim.

Harry sighed openly; they were at war and Assab was his cross to bear.

He had to try to forgive and forget; he had a beautiful, kind, talented wife who'd crossed continents to be with him and whom he loved completely. Why couldn't he just let go, be grateful and cling to what they had? A future life together, children and happiness if they saw out the war. He wanted a family, a large one, sons and daughters… It mattered, it was instinctive, his religion. Harry had a fervent belief that his genes, something of him, should survive. It felt all the more vital in wartime with no guarantee of making it through.

He leaned over the table, took Laura's hand and was rewarded with a golden smile. He was conscious that the lone woman had been paying her bill and not seen their reconciliation, and after probably hearing every word…

She passed their table with her chin raised, leaving the dining room, and muttered, almost inaudibly, 'Loose morals.' Harry couldn't help feeling gratified; she was definitely on his side.

CHAPTER 26

Moving On

The weeks sped by. The end of term came and went. The school show was a great success, the children sang sweetly and Jane, my chosen star, played her flute solo to perfection.

Over the tea and biscuits after the show, parents who'd become friends asked me to lunch, games of tennis, swimming parties, picnics; my holidays had got very busy. I'd been taking June to the women's group meetings and as well as sewing and knitting, heard the constant gossip about the Earl Errol murder and the trial of Sir Jock Delves Broughton, which had yet to happen. Names of other potential suspects were tossed around like juggling balls, many furious at all the cuckolded husbands who could have done it, being able to walk free.

My tentative suggestion of a concert had caught hold, and managing the lesser talents was a delicate job, but Harry's throwaway line about June's singing abilities had been inspired. She had a clear, tuneful voice. It had taken some coaxing out of her, but she'd found the courage to mix with members of the group, found her feet as well as her voice, and even allowed me to take her to a hairdresser's. She had dry split ends no longer and was drinking less.

With the summer term underway, I had new worries. The school was thriving, new pupils, more boarders, and Seymour was in his element. He kept thanking me for the transformation in June, and hugged me so hard and long, seeing me back to the hut one evening, that Harry would have had a jealous fit.

I had to tell Seymour about leaving. I'd managed to find someone to take over my music class – one of the mothers; a competent pianist and warm-hearted – but I felt dreadful about letting him down. He'd been my saviour; I'd had the happiest of times at the school; a wonderful, supportive friend.

I had to leave, and before the end of term too. It wasn't only feeling fairly convinced I was pregnant. Harry's three months of training were almost up. He'd soon be rejoining his battalion, which meant going to Nairobi to await a convoy to take him to wherever they were. There was no neat timetable for convoys; he could be waiting weeks. He hadn't pressed, but I knew how much he would want me to be with him in Nairobi for however long or short a time.

First came the need to see a doctor and have the pregnancy confirmed, but either way it was time to move on. It made sense for the months, even years, I'd be on my own, to be living in Nairobi. There'd be more places to rent, more chances of paid work, and a baby in the snake hut would hardly be ideal.

It wasn't easy to ask to use the school telephone without good reason, so I'd quietly asked one of the mothers if she could make me a doctor's appointment in my lunch hour. She'd managed that and I was grateful.

Driving into town, I worried about the future. Harry's longing for me to be pregnant reached me in waves; he could have shouted it from the hilltops. I should have found the courage on honeymoon, suggested waiting a bit, but felt such a need for Harry to be happy. He'd talked so excitedly of his longing for children and I had been trying to bury thoughts of Bob.

I parked outside the surgery. The street was at a lower level and scrambling up the grass bank I had a near collision with a man coming along the side path who seemed to have a slight limp.

'Coming in here?' He held open the glass-panelled surgery door with an elaborate flourish and a big grin. He had sophisticated looks, fair floppy hair, open-neck silk shirt, linen trousers, and he didn't stop talking as we went in. 'This has definitely made my day! What have I been missing here in Nakuru! Or are you just a glorious apparition and I need to see the doctor after all?' It was hard not to smile and feel flattered.

We were shown into a small stuffy waiting room, the only people there. 'I'm just here to do a favour for friends,' he said, 'haven't got an appointment, I'm just hoping to get the doc to hand over more of their happy juice. The bugger's pulled the plug on them and they thought I'd have better luck, which is by way of saying that I'm hale and hearty and you absolutely *must* come for a drink, soon as we're done here.'

'That's very kind, but I'm taking a class in less than an hour and absolutely *must* hurry off.'

'You've got bags of time. I'll run you back.' He eyed my wedding ring. 'I expect your poor husband is *miles* away fighting this dreadful, dreary war.'

'Sorry, must go, and I have a car right outside.'

The doctor appeared at the door, a florid, overweight ex-pat. 'Do come in, Sir Edmund,' he said, adding, almost as an afterthought, clearly placing me well down the pecking order, 'won't keep you long, Mrs Werner.'

My turn came. I explained about having irregular periods and after prodding me about, the doctor said I was probably two or three months pregnant and he would have the result of the test in three days.

The glamorous Sir Edmund was chatting to the receptionist, waiting, and he left with me, taking my arm. 'Five minutes! There's a hotel bar right across the street. I can't let you go without knowing all about you. I'm Edmund Southan by the way.'

I gave in, mistrustful after the airy talk of "happy juice" and, disliking his flippancy, calling the war dreary, but that seemed to be just his way and needn't mean much, I supposed.

He ordered a pink gin, raising an eyebrow when I insisted on lime juice, and proceeded to flirt outrageously. A middle-aged couple further down the bar exchanged looks.

Edmund was persistent if nothing else. In a remarkably short space of time, he had got out of me that I wasn't a Nakuru housewife and was "possibly" moving to Nairobi. 'But that's heavenly news! I'm back there on Monday, back to business, but it's exhausting, staying round here with all the parties. Fun, though, and now I've met *you*! I live a bit out of the city, out in the sticks at Muthaiga.'

'You live at the Muthaiga Club?'

'Oh, no, Muthaiga's the district. The name comes from the bark the Maasai used to distil poison for their killer arrows. But the Club's very near. My parents were part of the group who built the place in the twenties. They wanted something exclusive, competition for the Nairobi Club and Torr's Hotel. Tart's Hotel, as it's called. There's the Norfolk too, still run by a woman everyone calls Queen Annie.'

'Nairobi seems well set up for nightlife. Must go now, thanks for the drink.'

'You can't possibly, not without giving me an address in Nairobi.'

'I don't know it myself.'

'You must have some idea!'

'We're possibly staying in the guest cottage of some army major, that's all I know. Now, there's a challenge for you, Nairobi's a big place.'

I left sensing the prudish watchful eyes of the couple sipping their lunchtime gins. There was the woman at the Flamingo Hotel…

It wouldn't take much for rumours of drinks with glamorous men to get back to Harry. He'd reacted so violently over Bob, sensitively known it had been a serious affair, but how could I have convinced him otherwise with the knot of my longing for Bob so tightly tied?

Harry had surprised me with the force of his jealousy, which felt instinctive, part of his nature, and wouldn't be restricted to a Cairo lover. I hated to think of him away for long stretches with the KAR; lonely, suspicious and disbelieving.

The war was escalating. Why couldn't he just accept that I loved him and believe, as I did, that we'd grow closer together and be happy over time?

How much time did we have? Would Harry survive the war? How would we manage the long months and years of separation? Would there ever be a future without tensions and with a real chance of normal married life?

CHAPTER 27

Harry

Harry had his commission. He felt quite proud and overjoyed too that Laura was coming with him to Nairobi and they could be together for however long he had. She was driving and he lifted her hand from the wheel, rubbed his thumb over her palm. It was their last weekend in Nakuru, only the packing up at the barracks, only a few more days…

It was a sparkling day and they were on the way to the lake, and without Cyril for a change. Laura had said it would be a special last time there together and he wasn't about to argue with that. A small cloud fogged his eyes; why hadn't she got pregnant? Was it biological? Something wrong? He felt irrationally angry, so badly wanting a child.

They found a good spot and spread out his old rug that lived in the car, enjoying seeing the great shifting pink mass of flamingos. They were literally in their thousands, fuchsia pink, wings flapping, wading and dipping their long swan necks deep into the shallow, alkaline lake.

Harry said, 'See the pelicans and cormorants and the little

grebes and white-winged black terns? It's amazing how the small birds can get a look in.'

'My handsome, knowledgeable birdman.' Laura grinned and gave him a kiss.

They idled around, strolled a bit, talked about nothing very much till the shadows grew long and she said it was time to be getting back. 'You'll take the car for your kit? I'll be all packed by early morning, Tuesday, and ready for the off. I just wish we knew whether it'll be days or weeks in Nairobi and, of course, to have some idea of wherever you'll be.'

'Well, it pretty much has to be north!'

Harry couldn't say more; secrecy and censorship were vital. His commission was all very fine, but he could hardly swallow for the lump in his throat, thinking of the length of their imminent parting.

Back at camp, there was a lot of backslapping and suppressing of fears and he was feeling carved up at having to say goodbye to Toppy, squatting to fondle his spanielish ears, almost about to cry. Toppy seemed to sense uncannily too that this was no short-term parting. His feathery tail drooped and he slunk into the shadow of a Jeep as Harry got to his feet. Tim, who was staying on for a week or two, had promised to try to find Toppy a loving home. There must be a family in Nakuru who'd be glad to take him on.

*

Early Tuesday morning, drinking in the heady scent of mimosa on the air, Harry drove to the King George Primary School for the last time. He had mixed emotions, wild impatience to be in Nairobi with Laura, bitterness at the thought of the fond farewells she'd be having with Seymour. If she were pregnant now, how could he ever be entirely sure that the baby was his?

He sighed, knew it was extreme of him, cancerous jealousy and eating into their relationship. Laura was leaving and before the end of term too, coming with him to Nairobi, and she seemed genuinely happy about it.

She was waiting outside the main door with her luggage and they made a quick getaway. They didn't speak much. He drove south, hard and fast, enjoying the dewy freshness before the day warmed, the sun beating down on the carmine-red earth. Flame trees in scarlet flower, the sound of the wind in the grasses, skittering impala, jewel-coloured birds; the beauty of it all took his breath away.

'It was a dreadful wrench, having to leave Toppy,' Harry said, as they stopped for a quick bite of lunch at Naivasha. 'I'd hoped the camp would adopt him as a kind of mascot, but no go. It's all down to Tim now.' Laura was sympathetic, but she didn't know Toppy. The school had a strict rule on no dogs.

'However did you find such an ideal place to stay in Nairobi?' she said.

Harry grinned, pleased with himself. 'One of the guys at the training camp knew a major, stationed in the city, but who had a sizable family house with a guest cottage. I telephoned, won through and he's being amazing about the rent.' Perhaps too much to hope that Laura could stay on there after he'd gone?

It was dusk when they hit the outskirts of town. Harry drove more slowly down wide streets whose suburban houses had provincial solidarity. They were built mainly in the Lutyens style with pillared porches and stone fireplaces. 'These houses have got so much grander,' Harry said, 'the mud and wattle of the old pioneering days making way for corrugated roofs, bricks, tiles and gables.'

Laura laid her hand on his arm. 'I'm glad we're having a night at the Norfolk and not meeting the Staffords till morning. We'd have been a bit tired and preoccupied, going straight there, and I have some news.

'I'm about ten or twelve weeks pregnant. I hadn't been feeling sick, only slightly faint, passed out once, momentarily, but my breasts seemed more swollen and tender and I was beginning to wonder! I've seen a doctor, had it confirmed… I hope it's a happy surprise, darling, not too much of a shock, but it must have crossed your mind as a possibility.'

Harry felt a glow of adrenaline flood his sky, a lifting and brightening of his spirits like the light of day. The baby couldn't be Seymour's, had to be his; they'd hardly arrived in Kenya three months ago.

He slowed down and stopped the car, leaning across to kiss Laura, feeling infinitely loving and whole. 'Our child!' The joy of it and the wonder was flooding in his veins. Fatherhood, it had happened at last. 'He's the future, darling, our child. We're fighting this war for our children and the freedom to see them grow.'

CHAPTER 28

Nairobi

The Staffords' house was in a wide avenue of properties with high hedges and pillars crowned with pineapples, eagles or solid balls. I had a wistful moment. The avenue seemed a far cry from Nakuru and the snake hut; I'd been happy there.

We had no trouble identifying the house; the pillars with lions and the tall wrought iron gates had S's entwined in the design. A boy hurried to open them. Harry took the sweep of a circular drive and drew up outside a very substantial property with wide steps up to an imposing black front door.

It was opened before we could knock and a houseboy in a white *kanzu*, very tall and elegant, escorted us through a high, cool hall, showing us into an enormous sunny drawing room. 'Do come in, won't you?' Mrs Stafford said, rather imperiously. She was a statuesque big-boned woman and shook hands with a gracious air. 'A little early for gin, but I'm sure you'd like a cold drink?' She inclined her head at the elegant servant, who melted away. He returned almost immediately with three fruity pink drinks on a large brass tray.

'Thank you, just the job.' Harry smiled, taking one of the frosted glasses and the proffered monogrammed napkin. 'And we couldn't be more grateful for—'

'Your luggage is being taken to the cottage,' Mrs Stafford interrupted, fixing him with hooded ice-blue eyes in such a way as to say that his gratitude was taken as read. No question of who wore the pants in that house. There were vases of peonies, heavy silk curtains with swags and tails, Royal Worcester figurines, a magnificent Blüthner grand piano. I longed to sit down and play.

We sipped the sweet chilled drinks. Mrs Stafford complained about the influx of expatriate troops in Nairobi, needless rationing and the crying need for some rain. 'Now,' she said, with a brisk change of tack, 'you'll want to see the cottage and freshen up. Come back at one o'clock for some luncheon, we can talk over any details then. There's a way to drive the car round to the cottage. Take the lane just left of the gates and the *shamba* will be there with the key.'

We found the lane and saw a barefoot garden boy waiting by a small latched gate. 'You park in lane,' he said, taking us up a short path then to a small brick bungalow. It was screened from the main house by some ornamental trees, and the extensive well-kept lawns and grounds beyond looked enormous.

The cottage had a veranda and a basic kitchen in a small separate hut, bare of any crockery aside from a couple of plates and cups. 'It's good to have the kitchen out here,' Harry said, 'keeps the smells away from the cottage.'

'Good to see there's an icebox! Mrs Stafford's a bit much,' I said as the boy left. 'So regal, I nearly dropped down in a curtsy. Bet she really queens it in her circle of army wives.'

'Careful, you're one of those too now and she'll have you in her sights.'

So annoying of him, I didn't think of myself as an army wife and felt frustrated and on the defensive. 'We're not army regulars like all those conventional types at Abbassia,' I snapped. 'The wives were so kowtowing, they'd be right up Mrs Stafford's street.'

'That's such a sweeping generalisation. So, a few army wives are conformists? Plenty others who are quick-witted, entertaining and even,' Harry glared, 'as enlightened as you are, my love. Anyway, there's not much you can do about it. Nairobi's overrun with the army, you won't be able to avoid the other wives.'

He seemed really touched on the raw. It had been a silly little sideswipe but surely hadn't put him in mind of Cairo? 'Try to think positively,' he said, 'army life may not be your thing, but the regulars round here will know the best doctors, that sort of scene, and you're going to need all the help you can get.'

That was true enough. 'You're right, of course, darling, sorry!'

'You'll need a houseboy for the cleaning and cooking. You're pregnant. You must look after yourself and rest. The boys tend to hive off a bit of food for their families, but try not to mind. People complain, but these local guys have so little, I never begrudged them at Budongo.'

'Calling them "boys" is very belittling.'

'That's as it's always been,' Harry said, sounding a bit pompous.

I could see the advantages of having help when I was the size of the Chevvy, but it would feel extravagant at this early stage. I sighed internally. Best go with the flow. 'This is certainly a step up from the snake hut,' I said, looking round. 'It needs a few home touches but smells a lot drier and fresher, and to have a proper door to a proper bathroom, glory be!'

'And such little rent too. I doubt you'd find anything as good in the whole of Nairobi. Could you manage here with the baby, if you were able to stay on?'

'Big if! You'd better try your charmingest with stuck-up Mrs Stafford at lunch.'

'Do me best.' He gave me a kiss. 'I'm still so over the moon, though God knows when I'll get any leave to see the baby. The little blighter will probably be in short trousers by then.'

Major Stafford had come home for lunch, which was unexpected. 'Archie Stafford,' he said, with a firm handshake. He was tall and thin with a high cerebral forehead, a little remote-looking, with tired, kindly eyes. He asked after our creature comforts as solicitously as if we were close friends, and I hoped his instinctive civility would carry through with my chances of staying on.

Lunch was tasty, slow-cooked chicken in a mushroom sauce. Mrs Stafford did the talking. Her husband's kindly grey eyes glazed over, probably habitually, as she gave orders and bossed the staff. Could her parents have been early pioneers when Nairobi was no more than a train station and a few tents, and staked a claim to the land? It would explain the Staffords' ownership of such a splendid property in that exclusive part of town.

'I know this is very premature and presumptuous of me,' Harry said, 'but I'll be joining a convoy any day and it would set my mind greatly at rest if Laura were able to rent the cottage on a more permanent basis. She's expecting a baby, you see, and new to Nairobi…'

Major Stafford looked at me with a heart-warming smile. 'But of course, you must stay on. We'd be only too delighted, wouldn't we, Beryl, dearest?' He fixed his wife with a surprisingly assertive eye. 'You'll be quite private down at the cottage and it's far enough away for us not to hear the baby's mewing!'

Beryl Stafford, who'd been silent for once, regarded me dubiously. 'Have you really got a bun in there? Doesn't show, you can't be very far gone.' She heaved a sigh. 'Our two boys are grown now, one almost through Sandhurst. We're hoping he'll be sent out this way. The other's still at Eton, missing out on holidays here with this wretched war. He's a trial to us, that one. Shows no interest in the army or the professions, far too obsessed with his clarinet and playing in a *band!* I mean, I ask you! That school needs to knock some sense into his airy-fairy head.'

'Does he play the piano as well, that lovely Blüthner in the drawing room?' 'Yes, he's very musical,' Major Stafford said with pride.

Beryl glared. 'The boy needs a proper job.'

'Laura's a pianist,' Harry said, diffidently. 'She was teaching piano and languages at a school in Nakuru while I was on the training course.'

Major Stafford beamed. 'Excellent. I hope you'll come to play for us one evening, Laura, we'd love that. Now, a few practicalities. You're expected to have gas masks here in the city, unlike up north, but the blackout's been relaxed now that Addis has fallen. And some news, Harry, I expect you've heard that the Italians are retreating towards Eritrea and we've captured Dessie now too.'

'That is good news. We're certainly winning through with the Italians.'

'Sad about their general, the Duke of Aosta. We were holding him here in Kenya, but he contracted malaria and has just died. Such a delightful man, immensely tall and civilised, educated at Eton and Oxford. He even fought with the British in the First World War and was awarded a medal for valour.

'Gosh, is that the time? Excellent chicken dish, dear. Najau, can you pass on our compliments to Murugi? A pleasure to meet you both,' the Major said, and hurried away to the door.

Beryl Stafford listened to the rumble of his departing transport then turned with a glint in her eye. 'Now, time to get down to the real business of the day! Archie thinks we care more about the Delves Broughton trial than the trials of war,' she said, slipping into first-name terms in her excitement, 'but Sir Jock has been *monstrously* treated in my view. It's a disgrace! He should never have been arrested, let alone had to endure *months* of languishing in jail before this interminable trial. It would rock this town if he's found guilty, I can tell you. At least a dozen people could have bumped off that amoral scoundrel, Errol, and that's a fact.' She was pink in the face with indignation.

'I heard in Nakuru that Sir Jock's wife, Diana, went all the way to Johannesburg to engage a South African barrister for the defence,' I said, 'despite her husband being tried for her lover's murder. A brilliant KC apparently, very flamboyant and forceful, and such a high-profile case, it must be a great incentive to win through.'

'Indeed. Well, he had just better deliver.'

Did I risk changing the subject? 'Would you possibly have the address of the Women's Emergency Organisation in Nairobi, Mrs Stafford? I'm keen to do some voluntary war work, as well as any teaching jobs I can find.'

'But that's excellent news! It was my dear friend, the then Governor's wife, Lady Brooke-Popham, who set up the KWEO right after Munich. It's Lady Moore at Government House now who thinks she's the cat's meow.' No love lost there. 'Anyway,' said Beryl, 'plenty of ways you can help, my dear. They're short at the crèche, and I'm sure the team serving meals to the German interns would love an extra pair of hands. You must certainly join my sewing group, of course. We meet here, Tuesdays and Thursdays, ten o'clock.'

If ever there was an order… At least there was the weekend…

'Siesta time,' I said, hanging on Harry's arm as we walked back through the beautiful, sweet-smelling gardens, 'and a long, lazy, sexy weekend ahead.'

*

Harry's days in Nairobi were speeding by. We often drove into town where the Chevvy had competition from Buicks and Fords as well as other Chevrolets. There were canvas-covered army trucks and green Humber Snipes lined up in front of shaded shops in Delamere Avenue, and we took in the imposing post office and Macmillan library next to the Jamia mosque.

There was a handsome statue of Lord Delamere seated on his lofty plinth in the middle of the roundabout at Hardinge Road, and one of Queen Victoria in a beautiful park with a bandstand and gloriously scented frangipani and jacaranda trees. We saw John Wayne in *Stagecoach* at the Empire Cinema, *Ninotchka,* with Greta Garbo, and Clark Gable in *Mutiny on the Bounty.* We shopped in the Indian bazaar, cooked macaroni cheese in our basic kitchen hut and made love.

Harry picked up his mail from the National Bank of India, the army's handling place. My mail too; it was being sent care of 2nd Lieutenant HA Werner now that Harry had his commission. He checked in daily about convoys; none on the move yet, but there would be little warning and I sensed Harry's need to do all he could for me before the off. He made enquiries about houseboys and we interviewed Kofi, a teenager who seemed very friendly and willing. He'd left school, since his mother couldn't afford the fees, and could start whenever we liked.

Harry was out doing his regular check-in over the convoy when Najau, the Staffords' head houseboy, appeared at the door of the cottage. 'A soldier officer has come to the main house, Memsahib, asking to see the Bwana. Shall I send him down? He has a dog on a lead.'

'Thanks, Najau, that's fine.' I smoothed down my blue-spot dress, ran a comb through my hair and took the African-print cushions out to the rattan chairs on the veranda. The latch clicked on our gate, it was Harry back and I grinned. 'You're just in time. Najau says there's an army chap with a dog here to see you and he's sending him down.'

The young officer rounding the trees with the *shamba* looked quite like Harry apart from the fair moustache. His dog, a mongrelly thing with black floppy ears, was straining on the leash. 'I'll do some coffee,' I said, but Harry wasn't listening. The dog was off his lead and shooting to Harry like a bullet, leaping up, barking, wagging his feathery tail as violently as if it had been a jockey's whip.

Harry squatted to be licked all over, with the dog's paws on his shoulders. It was the dog he'd adopted in Nakuru, of course. 'Hey, hey, enough,' Harry laughed, staggering to his feet. 'Laura, meet Toppy, oh, and Tim too!'

'I've heard so much about you,' Tim said, shaking hands, 'and I can see why.'

Harry grinned. 'How's life, old sport? Coffee? Tea? No luck in Nakuru?'

''Fraid not…' Tim grimaced. 'Tea would be great if it's no trouble.'

We still had only the two cups and a chipped mug. I filled a bowl with water for Toppy, made the tea and decanted the packet of cardamom biscuits we'd bought in the Indian bazaar. Harry and Tim went quiet as I rejoined them and set down the tray. 'What's up? Why are you both looking so sheepish?'

'It's Toppy. We were daring to hope that you'd be prepared to take him on?'

Would I? And if I had a job? Kofi could give him a run and he was rather adorable… 'The Staffords would have to agree, of course,' I said, cautiously, 'and the *shamba* might not take kindly to Toppy tearing through the flowerbeds…'

From the look of relief on Harry's face, you'd think peace had just been declared. 'Thanks, darling!' he beamed. 'I'll call Major Stafford in his office later, have a hunch that his may be the kinder, more doggie-inclined heart.'

Harry's hunch was right. Thanking Beryl, I assured her that Toppy was a good guard dog, which was a complete lie. He'd probably lick the hand of any intruder and lie down to have his tummy tickled.

Beryl's sewing circle was made up of the older-aged wives of senior army officers and the daughter of a senior railway official called Agnes. The gossiping over the clack of needles and whirr of sewing machines was at fever pitch, the group, as in Nakuru, completely obsessed with the Errol murder and trial of Sir Jock Delves Broughton. The verdict was expected that very day, 1st July.

The courtroom must have been packed to the rafters, unbearably stuffy, and Jock Delves Broughton feeling like a French aristocrat about to face the guillotine. Would Edmund Southan be there? He'd been staying with friends in Happy Valley country and was very likely to know Broughton, perhaps even be a friend.

Noontime came and it was good to get back to the cottage. 'This whole place smells of dog now,' I said, flopping into a chair, 'and you can stop prodding me about. Our little toto's probably no bigger than a prune, hardly going to pack a punch.'

'I just long to feel that first kick.'

'Another month or so. Stick around. Do you think Toppy has tics?'

'If he does, you'll find them. You're a very resourceful girl.'

After lunch, when Harry was out doing his routine check-up on the convoy, I read a book on the veranda, feeling sick to death of knitting. He was being a long time, but then the gate clicked and I relaxed. Only for a moment; Harry's face said it all. His leaving had always been imminent, but now it was happening, came as no less a shock. The loneliness, the worry; tears pricked and I looked away.

Harry said, 'I bumped into Tim at the barracks and he's feeling as low as I am. Hope you won't mind, but I've asked him to supper.'

'That's fine, but there's little to eat. It'll be a challenge for Kofi and only his third day!' We avoided any mention of the convoy. Kofi was a wiry, eager kid, likeable, a dog lover too, often stopping to pat Toppy as he whizzed about cleaning every cranny of the cottage. I wondered how long that would last. He was a Luo and spoke his native Dholuo. His Swahili was worse than mine, but he had a little English and we were managing quite well.

Kofi seemed surprisingly unfazed by the challenge of a lack of food. 'I cook chicken,' he said, his shiny young face lighting up, 'is nice dish.'

'But we've only got eggs, no chicken in the icebox.'

'I know where buy. Go now?' I eyed Harry dubiously, but at what unhygienic place?

'It's all right,' he muttered, 'but meat should always be well cooked or we end up with tapeworms. Best to wash fruit and veg in potassium permanganate ideally too, however much of a fag that is.'

Kofi's chicken dish, cooked with potatoes and milk, was tasty, and he'd thought to buy a pineapple and a slab of pound cake as well.

Tim and Harry put up a good show of light-heartedness over the meal, but having coffee out on the veranda, the mask slipped. 'Bad news, isn't it,' Tim said awkwardly, turning my way, 'and only two days till Friday.'

I pinched the bridge of my nose, trying to avoid wet eyes. There was the baby, Toppy for company, but the thought of all the long, lonely nights with no clue as to Harry's whereabouts, and always the dark buried fear of his non-return…

Tim left soon afterwards, telling me to be strong. We helped Kofi to clear up then, not feeling like talking, sat for a while, holding hands. We'd just gone inside to get ready for bed when there was a peremptory knock on the door. Harry raised his eyebrows, but I could only shrug, and he opened the door tiredly to see Beryl there with her knuckles poised for the next rap. Najau and the *shamba* were keeping well behind, with lanterns to see her back.

'Do have a seat,' Harry said, relighting the lemony candles on the veranda, 'and can we get you a drink or some coffee?'

'Whisky if you have it. Can't be doing with coffee at night, keeps me awake.'

She subsided onto a chair and took a breath. 'My dears, I just had to come to tell you, he's been acquitted! The verdict came at a quarter past nine. The jury were out for three and a half hours, but all twelve jurors were unanimous. For which, thank the Lord! I mean, just imagine the horrors of a whole fresh trial…'

'Well, Broughton will certainly be a relieved man,' Harry said, diplomatically. 'Thanks for coming down, so good of you…'

She talked on, wasn't letting up. No chance of downing her whisky and taking the hint.

'The jury foreman winked at Sir Jock, I'm told, as he said, "Not guilty," and the clapping in the courtroom hit the rafters. There was a great surge as Sir Jock emerged from the court, literally hundreds of people rushing forward, policemen too, which you must agree is very telling…' Beryl raised her solid chin, clearly feeling vindicated in her naturally sound judgement.

She stayed for over half an hour. Only the supreme frustration at having to hold on to our cool helped us to survive.

I'd grown closer to Harry by the day. We were comfortable in each other's company, interdependent, and his unexpected possessiveness was flattering in its way, making me feel wanted and loved. My love for him was of a different nature, nothing like the feelings I'd had for Bob, the tingling blood rush at the sound of his voice, the electric charge of his slightest touch, but it was still solidly based married love. Harry wasn't musical, but we liked doing many of the same things and our compatibility was growing.

I stayed outside for a few more minutes, explaining to Kofi while he cleared the drinks about Harry going. 'Bwana gone long time? Not see toto?'

I nodded, eyes filming. 'Perhaps Bwana will be back in time for the birth, perhaps.'

In bed, Harry made tender love and we talked late into the night. 'You'll write lots? It will mean everything, not even knowing where you are.'

'And you must too, daily. I'll live for any letter.' He turned to me and said with a hint of crossness, 'I wish you weren't so obsessively set on working. You need to think of the baby and rest up, you two are my whole life.'

On Harry's last evening, Kofi cooked spicy meatballs, boiled potatoes and peas. 'Peas are good,' said Harry. 'Anything that needs shelling or peeling means less chance of parasites and germs. Look after your health, whatever you do, darling.

'Now, can we talk names? I'm rather keen on Robert and Humphrey. Robert's my first choice. I like the idea of Bobby or Bob.'

We couldn't have a son called Bob... My heart fluttered dangerously. 'That wouldn't be my first choice, actually,' I said, dreading making Harry suspicious, hoping, in the dim candlelight, he wouldn't absorb my nervous smile. 'What I'd most love is a son called Andrew after my father. Be sure to be Andy, of course, which is fine. And his middle name, Harold, after you, darling... Andrew Harold Werner! It has a good ring and no problems with initials. Please say yes!' It took a little time, but Harry came around to the idea. He wasn't terribly interested in girls' names, but we settled on Lily or Louise. 'It's a lot of Ls with mine as well, but both lovely names. So, Andy or Lily, or who knows, I could be having twins.'

Harry left at first light, it was six o'clock, the early morning fresh-scented and cool. It must be even harder for Harry. I drove him to the pick-up point and we had a last quick hug and kiss before parting with shy smiles.

Toppy had seen the kit bag and preparations and skulked back miserably into his basket. He was still there when I returned. Kofi brought me tea, sensitively leaving it on the veranda, and pouring a cup with a shaking hand, I gave into tears. They kept coming with the thoughts of saying goodbye, people milling round, unspoken emotion; I couldn't stop. Toppy left his basket and came close, nuzzling my thigh insistently with his little snout. Wiping my eyes with the back of my hand, I recovered and smoothed his soft black head.

'Only you, me and the baby now, Tops. We'll just have to comfort each other and carry on.'

CHAPTER 29

Alone in the City

Harry had been gone over a month. At nearly five months pregnant, I was moving buttons on skirts to allow for extra inches. Being tall helped. Beryl said, 'Still no sign of this mythical bairn,' peering at me suspiciously, and I pulled my loose shirt tighter over my thickening waistline. But I'd look like a billowing tent soon enough and maternity dresses were next on the list.

Running up a couple of basic shifts would help to fill the long, lonely evenings. I'd bought two lengths of cotton, spriggy-green and a cornflower stripe, and Agnes of the sewing group had loaned me her Singer sewing machine.

She was the only member of a similar age, a pallid girl with short dun-brown hair and the sort of nose you saw before the rest of her. She seldom spoke, only sparked into life talking about her father and the Kenya and Uganda Railways.

'He's the deputy superintendent now,' Agnes said, on a coffee break, 'and you wouldn't believe the extra load with the war. You could say Daddy and the railways are keeping the whole army afloat! There's all the routine repairs and they're making bodies for ambulances, water tanks, gun carriers. I do feel proud.'

'And so you should,' I said dutifully, feeling the baby kick.

'It's such a famous railway,' Agnes said, 'think, laying all those lines from the Kenya coast to Uganda in the 1890s. Impassable country, hostile Maasai and Kikuyu – and the cost! It's a wonder it ever got built.'

'I love the story of the mad pioneer who faced down the Maasai,' I said, one that Agnes hadn't heard, to my surprise. He was determined to mark out a course for the railway, persuaded a few terrified Indian bearers along, made it as far as Maasai country, but then had to face the fearsome chiefs and certain death by machete. "Wait! I'm the magic man," he said, taking out his false teeth and shoving them in again. It got them through and on their way.'

'No wonder the railway was called the lunatic line,' Agnes laughed. 'The man-eating lions were the worst. When Nairobi was just a swampy spot to pitch a tent, one poor Irish railwayman was dragged from his tent one night and his wife, waking up to bloodcurdling screams, had to see him being eaten alive. People suffered a similar fate on the train from Mombasa. When it made its overnight stop at Kimaa – which means minced meat in Swahili – a lion would sometimes jump from a carriage with some poor man in its mouth.'

The weekend was stretching ahead with nothing to look forward to but sewing. I'd never previously minded my own company, but this was a new kind of loneliness, as blanketing as a blizzard. Missing and worrying about everyone at home, missing dear whacky Dolly with her warm heart, missing Bob...

And there was no Harry, no cosy companionship, shared meals, walks with Toppy, no sex; the marital loneliness was inescapable. It felt like being alone in the vast emptiness of the Sahara Desert or floating rudderless at sea.

I wrote to Harry almost daily.

*…You've left a gaping hole in my life, I miss you every minute
of every hour and dream of hearing that click of the gate and
there you are. I'm changing shape and our little toto is making its
presence felt, kicking like a billy goat. I'm sure, if you ever get any
leave, it'll be just when I'm at my porpoise-like fattest, rolling
about like those poor wives made to drink milk all day by the
early Bugandan potentates who liked their women elephantine.*

*I'm feeling fine, busy sewing and knitting, serving meals
to German interns at the Gloucester Hotel, and there's talk of
my language skills being useful elsewhere with the refugees.
Even the escaping Jews have to be interned, apparently, in
case of not being what they seem.*

The interns at the Gloucester were all male. There were many
resident Germans in Kenya, decent people, well liked, and any
who had two friends prepared to act as sponsors were being allowed
back into the community. But others had to be interned, and some
who made crude sexual asides in German had me incensed. They
never seemed to factor in the chance of anyone serving their meals
being able to speak the lingo.

Earlier in the week, their banal sniggering had really got to
me. A German farmer had muttered behind his hand to his mate,
looking straight at me, 'I'll take the juicy peach, she's ripe for the
fucking. You can have that other sow.'

I'd let fly and shot back furiously, '*Du sollst deinen Mund sauber
machen oder dein Mittagessen wird in deinen schoß enden!*' feeling
some satisfaction at telling him to clean out his mouth or have his
lunch end up in his lap.

Nervous giggles from the other interns and some slightly
suspicious looks from my co-helpers, but one of the overseeing
army officers had taken it in and later asked if I'd help with some
translating for the female interns, Jewish refugees among them.
He would be in touch via Major Stafford, he'd said.

The lengths of fabric draped over a chair back had an accusing air, but the maternity shifts could wait. It was Friday afternoon, just time to nip into town for any mail. None on Wednesday, but there must be some soon. Toppy was giving hopeful wags of his tail. 'All right, you can come too, and we'll go to the park for a run.' He knew the words *park* and *run* and let me know it.

Leaving and seeing Kofi asleep under a tree, I said loudly, 'Just going out for a bit.' He was a willing kid but mustn't start slacking without Harry around.

'Yes, Memsahib,' he said sheepishly, leaping up. 'I prepare vegetables?'

'And a milk pudding,' I said, 'good for the baby…'

I drove the Chevvy into town, parked outside the National Bank of India and checked my mailbox. My spirits dipped with nothing from Harry, but there was an airmail letter from Lil, which was cheering. She hadn't been in touch since our cables over the Café de Paris bombing.

With Toppy happily racing round in the park, I went to a bench with Lil's letter. She and Henry were thinking of getting married. He was everything she wanted in life, but qualifying came first for both of them and they felt kind of married already, studying together at Cambridge. Henry had met the parents at Easter, and she'd been to stay with his too, in Norfolk. I felt quite jealous; no long, lonely nights for Lil, although Henry, exempt from the call-up as a medical student, had had sleepless nights over whether to enlist or qualify. Doctors were needed more than ever, which had eventually swayed his decision.

Lil filled me in on the ghastliness of the Café de Paris disaster.

…We missed being bombed to pieces by only two nights! Even with the whole of bloody London strafed, we'd thought the Café was the safest, gayest place in town, 20 feet below ground! Survivors say there was an immense blue flash before

not one but two bombs whooshed down the ventilation shaft and exploded right in front of the fab Snakehips Johnson, the West Indies bandleader. He got the full force, his head blown clean off his shoulders. I have such an ache in my heart for that man, and the blast burst everyone's lungs at the nearest tables, but they'd have died instantly, thank God.

One rescuer said he tripped over a head rolling on the floor and looked up to see the girl's torso still sitting upright on a chair. And a man brought out on a stretcher said, 'At least I didn't have to pay for dinner!' which raised a laugh.

'Not sure how much of our news you get out there. Great to hear we've booted out the Itis and Haile Selassie is back in Addis, driven in triumphantly in an open car, flanked by our generals, it said on the news.

The tail end of the Blitz here, fingers crossed, the Hun shifting to the Soviets and Middle East, and we've lobbed a few back at last. Our pilots are the bravest, as well as dishy as hell, but bombing Berlin and Hamburg was at an awful cost, people say.

Bombing Hamburg, with all its heavy industry and huge port, was inevitable, but what about poor Bertha and Anna? They had to survive, and Frau Blohm. Were Mum and Dad safe with the bombing of the Clyde, Liverpool, Hull? Lil said they were fine and Dick was in touch, from somewhere out in the Atlantic, but weeks had passed since. It was wretched, being so out of touch.

Lil had added a PS…

Total despair here over Hamish – you know about him never coming back? No remains, nobody knowing a thing. His parents say there's always hope when people are missing, so that's a glimmer in the dark. He speaks fluent French – who'd have thought it – and he's such a good solid old plodder, our Hamish! Fingers crossed he'll be fine.

How could she have written in that light off-handed way? Just to put such terrible news in a PS? I was seething with fury, how could Lil have done that! She must have known how upset I'd be. There sounded little hope… And had Mum and Dad thought they were being kind, keeping it from me? Perhaps that wasn't fair, with no letter from them for weeks. I sighed. That last evening with Hamish, sitting in his freezing car after the Campbells' party, his moving declaration of love, it had lived on with me, even brought a small tear in low moments. *'I only want your happiness. As long as there's breath in my body I'd be there for you.'*

Was there still breath in his body? Had he been blown apart like the revellers at the Café de Paris? Was his body lying buried in a ditch? Was it under a heap of moulding bracken? Had he been captured? Tortured? If only I could feel half as confident of his survival as Lil.

The shadows were lengthening and few people left in the park. The smell of new-mown grass cuttings was painfully evocative of British lawns on Sunday afternoons. Homesickness overtook me and misery filled my heart.

Kofi had put lemony candles on the veranda and ice in the bucket, my slight irritation having an effect. 'And Toppy's water bowl?' Kofi was back in seconds with it and a big white-teeth grin.

He looked very smart in his crisp white high-buttoned shirt and black trousers. He wore a singlet and shorts by day but loved to dress up. A previous employer had given him two sets of whites, which he kept spotless. Good thing he seemed to enjoy washing and ironing with a baby on the way.

I seldom drank and smoked on my own, but felt so shaken over Hamish. There was a half-bottle of Gordon's gin, untouched since Harry left, and a couple of Schweppes tonics. Kofi brought slices of lemon and I picked up my book. It wasn't the evening for sewing with thoughts of Hamish so large in my mind.

The candles were keeping away the bugs, cicadas with their

insistent chorus, the exquisite scent of stephanotis and white jasmine; such stillness and calm.

I heard the click of the gate. Toppy pricked up his ears and growled; a low, suspicious rumbling. The lane only led to the servants' compound and a farm, where even a rattling truck was a rare event. It couldn't be Harry. He'd have bounded up the path; Toppy would have gone berserk...

Footsteps crunched and he shot down the veranda steps, barking. It must be a friend of Harry's, directed to the lane from the big house...

'Well, you've certainly tucked yourself away right down here!' I knew that tang of citrus, the foppish silk shirt... 'I'd have come sooner,' Edmund said, kissing my cheek as I rose, then plonking himself down on the rattan sofa without invitation, 'but I had a bit of business in South Africa.'

'How did you find me here if I'm so tucked away?' He was so charming and irritating...

'Easy peasy, not so many army-owned houses in this town, fewer still with guest cottages. I wasn't sure whether you'd have moved with your husband gone, but then there was that quaint cornflower blue Chevvy in the lane and bingo!'

'Not much detective work needed then. I should have been more circumspect, but since you're here now, I suppose you'd better have a drink.'

'I thought you'd never ask! Is that a gin bottle I see?'

Toppy was pressed up against me, still making throaty growls. 'Little chap's not much of a guard dog, is he? Far too soppy to get nasty. You need more looking after.'

'Did Mrs Stafford direct you down?' She'd have been riveted by a caller like Edmund, nothing if not a snob.

'God, no! Announce myself to old battleaxe Beryl and have all Nairobi knowing in seconds that I'd popped down for a gin with the most beautiful woman ever to be languishing alone?'

'I'm not languishing, far from it, and well able to look after myself.' Hard to see Beryl, who was always telling me to rest and wear good strong maternity bras in bed, making much of a scandal out of a social call on a pregnant wife.

Kofi appeared in his smart kit. 'I make cheese, pineapple, Memsahib?'

'Good man. And anything else you have in the canapé line.'

'Just cheese and pineapple, thanks, Kofi.' He looked so relieved. Such panic showing on his face that I'd had to smile.

'Sorry, Edmund, we don't run to caviar or cocktail sausages. You'll just have to hold back till wherever you're having dinner.'

'What, not here with you? Such a pity! Still, you must definitely come to lunch at the Muthaiga Club. Give yourself a break, you won't find La Beryl there taking all in with narrowed eyes and you'll enjoy the Club, it's fun.'

'Why shouldn't I find Beryl there?'

'She queens it at the townie Nairobi Club. The Muthaiga is more farmers and settlers from up country, more exclusive. A few people belong to both, but it's mostly one or t'other.' He was sounding as snobbish as Beryl.

I hesitated. The Muthaiga Club, with all its glamour and cachet was a tempting invitation, but Edmund was such a flirt, so flippant, I really rather disliked him.

'Thanks, very kind, but you don't want to be stuck with a pregnant woman.'

Edmund threw back a shank of floppy fair hair and laughed out loud. 'How come I never cottoned on that day at the doctor's, seeing how glowing you looked? And now, with this gorgeous velvety bloom, you're a perfect peach!'

'Isn't that rather overdoing it?' I met Edmund's eyes coolly. I'd been called a peach at the Gloucester; it felt like a warning.

Kofi brought the cubes of cheese and pineapple speared onto cocktail sticks. Wherever had he found those sticks? 'Anyway, thanks for cheering me up a bit. I was feeling low after a letter from home. A friend who was fighting in France went missing over a year ago, which I've only just heard about today.'

'And I intend to cheer you up a whole lot more,' Edmund said, leaning forward to pat my hand. 'I'll come for you at noon tomorrow and we'll have a nice long boozy lunch at the Club. It will cheer me up too. Every so often, I get a twinge of regret, guilt, whatever, about the army. Doesn't last long. If they won't have me with my gammy leg then tough titty. The business is thriving.'

'What happened with your leg?'

'I had a lion cub as a child that my parents let me keep too long. It got bigger, didn't take to being goaded and took a bite out of my leg. The leg healed, young bones, but has always been a bit shorter than the other. I had a frightful complex in my teens, but the girls seemed to find a limp quite sexy, so I soon got over that!'

'And the girls still do? Or are you married?' He probably was, must be well into his thirties, although marriage would mean little to someone like Edmund.

'Ah, marriage! I've tried it, not with a hundred per cent success. We're living apart, which seems a good compromise with a kid of three.'

Hard to see him as a father, and I imagined a sweet, serious blonde wife, too bland and pretty to hold him back. 'Is your wife doing war work?' She could even be one of the women I served with. We hadn't often exchanged surnames.

'God, no! Work, even with a war on, isn't exactly her line. Partying is… nightclubs till dawn.'

'So, you must keep seeing each other at them then.'

'Hey! I'm a quiet, retiring sort of guy, serious-natured. But we can't have a beautiful pregnant girl left alone and neglected with those,' he calculated, 'six long months still ahead of her.'

'Four, actually.'

Edmund looked suitably impressed. 'My, my! Well, better be off, since you don't run to more than a cube of cheese, off to a quiet dinner on my ownsome.'

'Something tells me you won't be eating alone.'

'Ye, of no faith at all,' he said, rising. He kissed my cheek. Was the citrus his soap or aftershave? He was tall, glamorous, and far too confidently aware of his own charms but knew now that I was five months pregnant, and wasn't that protection enough from unwanted advances?

'I'll come at noon. You'll enjoy the Muthaiga. It's a taste of Nairobi in its wilder days, a touch of glamour in these beastly times. Good to take your mind off that husband of yours too, risking all. It never does to sit around and mope.'

He slung down the two veranda steps unhampered by his limp and Toppy, who'd been treating him with wary caution, smartly saw him off the premises.

Edmund was probably right; it never did to sit around and mope. I had no illusions, positively disliked the man, and Harry would be jealous, certainly never accept that Edmund meant nothing. Still, the chances were that it wouldn't get back, and lunch at the Muthaiga Club would be an experience, a break in the loneliness and monotony of the past weeks.

CHAPTER 30

Invitations

Edmund was late, which seemed in character. I waited impatiently on the veranda, feeling edgy about Harry and cross with myself for taking so long to decide what to wear. The loose-fitting boat-necked navy and white had been obvious. Would I need a hat? Only my wedding hat really matched…

Toppy was giving me liquid-eyed looks, but he was out of luck; perhaps a walk later in the day. I'd just spent an hour de-ticking him and smothered myself in Schiaparelli's Shocking Pink scent, trying to kill the doggy smells. Dolly had made me buy it on our shopping spree in Cairo that day Mum had sent a surprise cheque. I'd written to Dolly, anxious for news of her father, longing to hear back. She and I were so close, able to share the most intimate of confidences.

The gate clicked and calling goodbye to Kofi, I hurried down the path, not keen for Edmund to become a known face. He kissed me on both cheeks. 'How lucky am I! You look gorgeous, a blooming beauty!' I grimaced.

He was in a light linen jacket and green-patterned tie, elegant as ever. I said, 'Is this a new car?' It was a bottle-green saloon with white wheels and looked gleaming. 'I'd have expected you to have a bright red coupe…'

'Me? A hard-working businessman and father? It is new, a Lincoln Zephyr, one needs a good, solid machine on these roads, living where I do.'

'Do I need the hat?'

'There'll be a few there, but your hair's glorious, never cover it up. Everything about you is glorious, except of course having that husband of yours. Is he an army regular? Did you marry back home? A child bride?'

'No, to both those.' I didn't want to talk about me and asked, 'Is Jock Delves Broughton likely to be at the Club? Beryl Stafford was ecstatic about the verdict, but with such divided opinions, I suppose there could be a few hostile stares.'

'You're right about that. He had a huge great party at the Club after his acquittal, which didn't go down well. The committee are very twitchy about their reputation with the war. I think he may be kicked out pretty soon.'

'It can't have been easy for him with his wife and Joss Errol flaunting their affair so publicly. I can see why people took his side.'

'Well, I'm not one of them. I've got zero sympathy for bloody Broughton. Joss Errol had many flaws, but it really bugs me that justice hasn't been done.'

Edmund was driving fast with his eyes on the road. His face in profile was straight-nosed, lean and tanned; his expensive-smelling aftershave and the aroma of new leather both appealingly masculine. He had long, tapering fingers and a heavy gold signet ring, inherited wealth and an easy life, but need looks and money have made him selfish, conceited and a probable cad?

The window was open, my hair blowing free. 'It's beautiful country round here with the flamboyants and Cape chestnuts in such lovely lavender bloom, I can see why the early settlers came out this way.'

'We're in the Muthaiga district now, almost at the Club. I'm very close by. You must come to see my house on the way back. It's what I call Nairobi Tudor, which was all the rage in my parents' day.'

'They've both died?'

'Yes, a car accident in England. I'd just started in the business. I have a sister who stayed on after the funeral, married an excruciatingly dull accountant and lives a screamingly boring life in leafy Surrey. I try to redress the balance. Here we are. Pink gins coming up and oodles of champagne.'

He parked facing the clubhouse, which was long, low and pillared and a delicious shade of pale pink. 'Who chose the lovely wall colour?' I asked.

'It came about quite by accident. When the group building the Club ran out of cement, someone who knew about lime brought rock from Kiambu and mixed it with murram, which produced this pink stucco.'

There were lawns, spreading trees, tennis courts and stables, Edmund showed me round briefly before going indoors. 'The Club's a bit reduced these days,' he said, 'with so many members away fighting, and probably still will be with fewer making it back.' I thought of Harry... 'So the committee's had to accept military members now and these guys come here on leave; loud, boozing and flouting all the unspoken rules, so the rules are unspoken no longer!' Edmund grinned. 'I miss the *ancien régime*. We still have our great chef, he's such a tyrant, even insists on French olives, as if Spanish ones wouldn't do!'

'How does the Club get round the rationing, the shortage of wine and spirits?'

'Probably best we don't ask. I'm told the club secretary tears his hair out, though, when people sign for twenty-four whiskies in a night. This is the bar.'

It had a cigars-and-brandy, polished-wood tang; swords, stuffed animal heads on the walls. Two men in military uniform leaning on the polished-wood bar top, each with a foot on a low brass rail, threw back their heads at some joke. They looked like settler farmers, as if they owned the place, slamming down their glasses and demanding refills. 'Lunch,' said Edmund, taking my arm.

The dining room was light and bright after the bar, swan-white tablecloths, sparkling glassware, bowls of Impressionistic tulips; high-pitched women with cut-glass accents, waiters in white cotton gloves hurrying between tables, attending to very vocal demands. Being shown to our table, Edmund stopped to speak to a couple to whom I took an instant dislike, Claudia and Charlie Loft.

Claudia was wearing extravagantly long ropes of pearls and dangling, glittering diamond earrings. She stared languidly with her cigarette holder carelessly held, and her husband, who looked a much-older overweight buffoon, was eyeing me up annoyingly. 'So, your husband's away with the KAR? He'll not have leave for a year at least, I'd say, ho, ho!' Charlie Loft chortled with his turkey wattle wobbling. I was incensed, but at least Edmund picked up on my fury.

'Now, now, Charlie, none of that. Laura's having a baby and coping all on her own. I'm just giving her a little break, taking her out of herself.'

'You'll do a good job there, old chap, very convenient, what!' The wretched man couldn't stop chortling and gave Edmund a hefty nudge as we left.

I was fuming, but waited till we were seated before exploding. 'How dare that man insinuate in that way. And please don't parade my condition again.'

'Sorry,' said Edmund contritely, putting up his hands. 'Only trying to kill any gossip.' He ordered pink gins and a bottle of champagne and laughed. 'Hey, such a fierce look!'

A waiter brought the menus and I looked down, worried about being seen to be having a tiff, which spoke of familiarity, and also about Edmund's mention of an influx of military members. Harry wouldn't take kindly if he got to hear.

Edmund said, 'I'd go for the pea soup and lamb cutlets, both good here.' He saw me glance at a woman in the jewelled headdress. 'That's Gwladys Delamere, she's the Mayor and Tsarina of this town, a bit bloated now, but an old flame of Joss Erroll's. She's sort of adapted to having a matronly, maternal affection for him, adapted to the bottle too.'

Edmund downed his pink gin and signalled for another. I stayed with the first. He knocked back the second gin and the waiter poured the champagne. 'And we'll have some red with the lamb, Odinga, the Bordeaux.

'Here's to friendship,' Edmund said, touching glasses.

I gave him a quizzical eye, still smarting, but the champagne was deliciously chilled – my glass topped up as soon as it touched the table – the soup was good and against my better judgement, I began to relax.

Edmund sat back and trapped my foot under the table. 'You're still cross, aren't you? Don't be, you're lonely, stuck in that cottage, you can't deny it, and if it makes you feel any better, I am too, single again and living out of town.'

'You expect me to believe that? This is a treat for me, coming here, don't think otherwise, but I'm sure there's a line-up of girls in your life and I'm fine, a happily faithful, pregnant wife.'

Edmund kept grinning. 'You're still looking solemn. Worrying about that husband of yours? It's Harry, isn't it? You mustn't. There's nothing you can do and he wouldn't want you to mope. Here's our lamb, I wonder if it's one of Mervyn Ray's prize sheep!'

'What's the joke?'

'There's been a big push to shoot as much wildlife as possible to feed the great influx of Italian POWs. Hunters are being paid to do what they love to do anyway, and one of our members saw what he thought was a distant herd of zebra. He went on shooting only to find that he'd shot every one of Mervyn's prize sheep!'

Mervyn was just a name to me, but Edmund was vastly entertained. 'I should write down some of these stories,' he said, 'like my mother's tales of the Prince of Wales. He was out here in the late twenties and stayed at the Club, and she was at dinners with him a couple of times. She said once one of his guests had to be physically removed, caught pushing cocaine to the Heir to the Throne between courses. Then another time, Gwladys Delamere started peppering the Prince with chunks of bread, only to miss and give Karen Blixen a black eye.'

It was well into the afternoon, the champagne finished, the Bordeaux too. Edmund, who'd downed most of both, seemed in full control, while I felt very mellow. Everyone in the dining room seemed well away; they'd probably start hurling bread pellets at each other soon.

Edmund ordered ice cream and hot chocolate sauce. 'Good for the baby,' he said rather ridiculously, but went on. 'I know all the best people if you need help with doctors and stuff. You just have to say the word.'

'Thanks, that's good of you.' I was besieged with offers of help. Beryl was full of strident advice and fellow servers of meals at the Gloucester were keen to help too. Most of them had Nairobi-based husbands, children, busy lives, but I'd made good friends with an older woman, Mrs Buckley, whose husband was serving abroad and her adult children doing war work at home. She'd even offered to come to live in for a few days when I was back from hospital, saying she knew how exhausted and terrified I'd feel in the early days.

I glanced at my watch, a present from Harry, bought in Nairobi before leaving, and felt a sudden desperate need to be gone from the Club with its brittle, rich socialites, gone from Edmund too.

I caught his eye. 'It's after four, I really must go. My dog's been cooped up all day.'

'You have to come to see my house on the way back, just a quick cup of coffee. Our coffee's world class, our sugar and tobacco too. I am in the business. And just for the record, you needn't think I'm going to pounce. I like your company, rather more than any line-up of girls.'

I blushed, couldn't help it; he wasn't going to let me off on that one.

Edmund's parents' house, in beautifully landscaped grounds, was vast with a steep pitched roof, tall side chimney and black timbers set in white stucco. Mock Tudor, just as he'd described. 'Don't you rattle around a bit in this magnificent pile?' I said, taking in a monumental stone fireplace and magnificent grand piano.

'I like having space. Your eyes went straight to that piano!'

'It does look very fine. Do you play?'

'No, my mother did. It's an American piano, a Baus. I think they went out of business in the Depression. Will you play something for me?'

I sat down on the stool and was instantly lost to a little Mozart, much as I wanted to go. 'It's a truly beautiful piano but, to be honest, does need tuning.'

'It shall be done. That was exquisite, though, amazing. Concerto number 21, wasn't it? We should have a musical evening here, I'll make plans.'

I was impressed that he knew his Mozart. 'We'll have coffee out on the terrace, Abshir,' he said, to a tall, chiselled Somali standing by.

The coffee was good, served in delicate Spode cups with serpent handles. 'Etruscan,' Edmund said, when I commented on them. 'My sister took a lot of the silver and china, but there's still masses of the stuff. The boys break quite a bit, but I see no point in keeping things locked away.'

I wasn't used to such a display of wealth or his easy off-hand attitude. Harry was straightforward, honourable, boyish; Bob, a truly decent man whom I revered, but instinct told me that Edmund was neither decent, straightforward nor honourable, and I'd do well to be on my guard.

'Must be off, but you really don't need to take me. I can easily get a cab.' It would cost a fortune but was a matter of pride.

'Don't be a ninny! I'm going into town anyway. The night is young!'

Driving fast, Edmund showed no effects of the quantities of alcohol he'd consumed. He said, 'I'll take you to a movie in the week and definitely another lunch at the Club when I'll have had the piano tuned. I'll organise a little concert soon too, ask a few friends who'd appreciate your exquisite playing.'

The chance to play was an irresistible lure, but I minded his presumption about taking me to a film and he sensed my resentment. 'You're lonely, stuck in that hut every bloody evening and you know it. Do you good to get out. I'll come for you on Wednesday, about seven.'

I left him feeling unsettled and a bit unclean, in need of a walk, a breath of air. Toppy waited excitedly while I changed into long-sleeved shirt and trousers; the insects would be biting in the half-dark. We went to the open land down the lane. It was a silky, seductive evening with a crescent moon low in the sky, and pushing through the rough, scratchy grass, I felt calmer, my head clearer.

Harry wouldn't wish long, lonely evenings on me. He'd like me to see Agnes, have dinner with army couples, even with trusted friends of his on leave, but not go out with Edmund. It was taking a risk; rumours could easily reach Harry, and all for the sake of playing a beautiful piano? But was it really such a sin to go out with the man a couple more times before my size set the seal on all that?

There would be no chance of feeling feminine and attractive any day soon, and the rewarding war work that I enjoyed would come to an end. My back would ache with the weight, breasts, limbs feeling extra heavy, and panic about giving birth had already taken hold. No Harry to rush me to hospital and hold my hand...

And always with the dark fear of all that could happen to him skulking in the shadows like a lion about to pounce. I had to stop imagining injuries, dysentery, malaria, mortars... It would be harder still later on, fears compounded by the terror and exhaustion of giving birth before the engulfing joy and petrifying responsibility of holding a tiny new being in my arms.

CHAPTER 31

Another Lunch

I agreed to go to the cinema with Edmund. It felt harmless enough and my evenings *were* very lonely. We saw *Shanghai Express* with Marlene Dietrich, who played the notorious prostitute superbly. The film had pace and plenty of high tension, when Edmund clutched my hand and held on tight. If I hadn't known better, I'd have thought he was genuinely scared.

Dropping me home, he didn't attempt to kiss me, simply smiled knowingly in the most infuriating way. I'd felt a flicker of physicality but couldn't have borne to have anything to do with Edmund. I wanted Harry.

In bed, sleepless for hours, I felt half a person, driftwood washed up on a beach. I missed Harry dreadfully, missed the sex. Stretching out a leg, feeling the cold emptiness on his side of the bed, my loneliness was unendurable. I missed Dolly too, who'd have bounced me out of my misery, so longed for my friend.

Two more weeks crawled by. Edmund was away, any further lunches at the Muthaiga Club overtaken by a business trip to South Africa, to my great relief. He'd pursued his idea of a little concert, which was incredibly tempting, but to go to the Club again with the influx of army members and all those brittle, gossiping women would, I knew, be a mistake.

I was in my favourite chair on the veranda knitting yet another pair of woollen socks for the war effort. The baby was showing, I had quite a bump, luckily neatly contained, but despite the glorious balmy weather, birdsong and the sweet scents of the garden, the days of pregnancy dragged interminably on with nothing to break the monotony. Casting off from a sock, I looked up to see the *shamba* waiting to give me a message. It was from Major Stafford. He had a free afternoon, he said, Beryl busy, complaining he was under her feet, and he wondered if I'd like to come to play the piano. I scribbled a reply, feeling elated. Music lifted me onto another plane; it was glorious balm to my senses.

I changed out of shorts into my most loose-fitting dress. It looked a bit twenties, raspberry pink and silver braided, but I was resisting maternity shifts for as long as possible. Would Major Stafford have any up-to-the-minute news, any clues as to Harry's whereabouts? Mombasa was under siege, Nairobi stocking up with sandbags. Were German and Italian planes about to swoop up the Nile and shed their load? The worry was ever-present.

He greeted me courteously with his sombre, kindly gaze and took me into the lily-scented sitting room. His shyness was very evident and I soon sat at the Blüthner piano suggesting a couple of Rachmaninoff Études. 'And perhaps Chopin's *Ballade number 3*?'

'I'd like nothing better,' he said warmly, drawing up a chair.

Soft sunlight filtering in, I was lost to the music and the afternoon flew by. It seemed no time before Najau was knocking and bringing in tea. Major Stafford said, 'That was lyrical, I could have listened all day.'

Beryl joined us with an accusatory air. 'Some of us have work to do, Archie, parcels to send…' She had a few cucumber sandwiches and a large slice of Victoria sponge before rising and saying pointedly, 'No free afternoon for me.'

'It's excellent, all the work you're doing, dear,' Major Stafford said, seeing her to the door. He joined me again with just the smallest hint of a twinkle.

I asked if he had any news he felt able to share.

'Well, we've had some heavy shipping losses off the coast at Mozambique. And the German General, Erwin Rommel, is a great worry. He's a wily old bird, great propagandist, a bloody so-and-so, in fact, if you'll forgive the language, and has full command in the desert now. Still, we're holding our own in Tobruk.'

Major Stafford looked at me kindly. 'You mustn't fret. Libya and Cyrenaica are a long way away from East Africa.' His voice was warm, he understood, but if he knew where Harry was based, he wasn't going to let on.

'Thank you,' I said, 'it's the not knowing that's so hard, living on hope.'

I played a little more after tea, some Mozart, but wanted to try to make the post office before closing and it felt like time to go.

'I'll walk you down,' the Major said.

Strolling through the gardens, he rested an arm on my shoulder. 'I've loved hearing you play, the most joyous of afternoons, and just wanted to say that if you ever need anyone to turn to for help or advice, I'm, um, always here.'

'Thank you, that's a great comfort,' I said, conscious of his lightly placed arm, 'especially since there seems little hope of Harry being back for the birth.'

'Yes, that's unlikely, I fear, doubt he'll have leave in under a year. I'm sure you've made hospital arrangements, but one of my chaps whose wife recently had a baby said how impressed they'd been with a nursing home out at Muthaiga. Only twelve beds and the midwife there was top hole, he said. If you would like me to find out a little more, it would be no trouble at all.'

I thanked him warmly, fending off Toppy, who'd come racing up and nearly toppled me. 'I haven't made any plans yet actually and been worrying a bit.'

'It shall be done,' the Major said, bending to pat Toppy then, lightly kissing me on the cheek, he hurried back up the garden. His shy brush of cheek made me smile.

I was just in time, the NBI closing its doors, and my heart sang to find a letter from Harry.

...Dearest one, there's a mail going soon so I must dash off a few lines. I hope my letters are getting through. Your last seems to have taken only two weeks and it was heaven to have it. Hearing about your changing shape and the first kick – how I wish I could have been there – and your description of love being capable of infinite growth is so true. I feel that too. Every day, I seem to love you more than the last, although I love you so completely that seems well-nigh impossible.

Life here is bearable, just! The heat is unbelievable. We hose each other down all afternoon as we're not too badly off for water, though it tastes vile, and have taken to wearing kikoys at times like the natives. It's an interesting uniform and no repercussions so far. The army can be sensible at times, but learning how to wear them without exposing the most tender parts takes practice!

Last week, there was a bit of a lull and we were housed in very unconventional quarters, a building that had been a brothel before the Italians left. We had the great luxury of showers and running water and who would have thought in that battled-scarred place we'd find a café with fresh limes and ice cream!

We're near a coast and I went bathing with some askaris in a tiny bay, little more than eight yards wide. Some locals shouted to us to get out, but we only took notice when we saw a shark's fin about a foot away… You nearly lost me that day. It had come within ten yards of land, in water a couple of feet deep, so the theory that they don't go into shallow water and near people making lots of noise is disproved! If we'd had a rifle, we'd have had ourselves a nice trophy!

I've solved the problem of finding a new batman after that last one took off with my watch and money, although where he could flee to in this barren land is hard to fathom. I have a prisoner of war batman now who speaks Amharic (a different dialect from the one I'd started to learn), as well as his native Italian, but we manage and he's very willing. He has every incentive to be, after all, or face a return to the prison camp smartly.

You asked about food. Dried peas and stew, more dried peas and stew. They give us pills to counter the lack of fruit and veg and we survive, but an askari was shot up the other day, trying to reach a watermelon through barbed wire. So sad. I haven't long – just time to say again how much I love you…

I folded the flimsy paper carefully back into its envelope and stored it in my bag. To think of him stoically ploughing on with the terrible business of war; I could almost smell the sweat and grime on his tanned body. It made me deeply proud. I would read the letter many times, but it couldn't sustain me for long. It was like the warmth of a lovely hot bath that dissipates in the chill of a draughty old Scottish home. It helped, but it wasn't Harry.

The weeks of pregnancy were excruciatingly long. At nearly seven months, the baby was growing fast and kicking energetically in its little interior cave. I was resting the knitting needles on my bump, round and hard as a football now, and felt a kick right up near the wishbone. Such a violent thump, it caused the needles to jerk and a few dropped stitches. Could it be its little heels, not fists, the baby upside down? It was a scary thought; best to see the doctor and be reassured.

I wrote to Harry about the Byland, the nursing home Major Stafford had recommended, having liked the sound of the place and not of the main hospital, but suspecting Harry would still push for a hospital birth.

Fears of any rumours reaching him were constant. Would a casual mention of Edmund be a form of insurance? My pen hesitated, but most things were better out in the open and it would get it off my chest.

> *...I went to the surgery for a routine check-up and got talking to a businessman with a limp... only a small white lie, implying it was in Nairobi ...who invited me to lunch at the Muthaiga Club no less! I was curious to see it and, goodness, it's a swank place. The women there were a whole other species, dressed to kill with great long ropes of pearls and, to quote Scott Fitzgerald, diamonds as big as the Ritz. Still, it made a break. I'm such a pregnant lump these days...*

Harry would probably fire off a string of questions, but I felt cleaner for telling him. Nothing had come of the interpreting work as yet, I said, knowing that would please him. Maddening how keen he was for me to stop work.

Glancing up, I saw the *shamba* at the bottom of the veranda steps. It was another note from Major Stafford who said a friend of his, Colonel Grant, had been in touch about my doing some interpreting for the interns. And just after saying the opposite to Harry. Colonel Grant hoped I could be at the George, the hotel requisitioned for female interns, at eleven o'clock the following day.

*

The George Hotel, in a northern province of the city, was more charmless than an army barracks, very down-at-heel. I crossed a sparse yellowing lawn with bald earthy patches feeling nervous, hoping my German, that had been fine dealing with the male interns, was really up to scratch for a proper interpreting job. Colonel Grant knew from the Gloucester that I was pregnant, but my bump was very evident in a loose apricot-cotton shift from the Indian bazaar and I felt a bit self-conscious. Anything to put off wearing home-sewn maternity shifts.

'Are you sure you're up to this?' the Colonel said solicitously, meeting me in the foyer. 'Don't hesitate to say if you find it the smallest strain.'

'No, really not, I'm a fit old horse, I assure you.'

'Hardly that. Now, let me fill you in. Astrid Sternberg, whom I need your help with, got out of Germany with her husband and children just in time. They had enough money to buy land and began farming up country, where Astrid had little opportunity to learn English. We have to intern these people, but she's gone completely to pieces, as far as I can gather, convinced we're maltreating her husband. So, anything you can say or do to reassure her on that score would be immensely helpful. Tell her that we're not like Hitler, only doing what we have to, and won't harm a hair of her husband's head.'

Colonel Grant was lean and dark with a small, slightly Hitlerish moustache himself and humorous deep-set brown eyes. 'Come on through,' he said. 'The interns are having coffee in the lounge. They're mainly Germans, a few Poles and Czechs, and most have a bit of English. The children are at lessons, it's a good time. Can you also explain that while the family can't return to the farm yet, there are group managers looking after the German-owned farms and theirs is in good hands.'

Astrid Sternberg was young and fair with a long, slender face, which was chalk-white and drained. She looked hunted and very puffy-eyed. 'Shall we get some coffee?' I said, unsure how to start. 'And there's a free table over by the window if we're quick!'

At the serving table with an antiquated urn and plates of biscuits, a yawning waitress told us to help ourselves. 'Do have a digestive,' I said, taking one. 'They're my favourite, though hard to pretend they're good for the baby!'

'First baby? My children are seven and five.'

'You look very young to have children that age.' I smiled, trying to relax her.

'They miss their father dreadfully,' Astrid said, her eyes filling, her wan cheeks already wet with tears. She was far from relaxed, tense as a string of my lute. 'You *must* help us,' she pleaded, looking warily at the two baby-faced soldiers on duty. 'They will torture my husband to find out secrets, but Walther is a farmer, he's innocent, knows nothing. We left everything we possess, fled the homeland. My mother wouldn't come, we haven't heard a word from her, I'm desperate…

'It's awful here, horrible, like being in hell. My children are teased and I have to live with these cold, sniggering women who loathe the Jews, who stare and speak to each other in English so I won't understand…'

I thought of Fraus Stürber and Meztger, sighed internally and said, squeezing Astrid's hand, 'You must hold on. I'll try to find out as much as possible, how soon you and your husband can return to the farm. Sad as it is, though, internment is just an inevitable fact of our two countries being at war, but you can absolutely rest assured that your husband isn't being harmed. That simply isn't happening.'

I kissed the girl's hot, wet cheek, urging her to stay strong and, promising to visit again soon, left the shabby lounge.

Colonel Grant, who was out in the hall, walked me to the door. 'It seems incredibly unfair, innocent Jews fleeing persecution,' I said passionately, 'having to be housed with Jew-hating members of the immigrant German community. It's criminally cruel. Those women are being vile, laughing and sneering in poor Astrid's face…'

'No other way, I'm afraid, but I'm sure the Sternbergs won't be detained for long, certainly not for the duration. It's just that wheels grind exceedingly slowly and caution prevails while the sifting process goes on. Only the hard cases, Germans who've expressed hostility to Britain, will be interned long term, with the women transferred to a camp at Mau Summit run by Lady Farrar and her FANYs. That's the First Aid Nursing Yeomanry, as I'm sure you know.'

'Yes. Thanks, that's some comfort. Can I visit again and keep trying to explain?'

'Of course, any time. I will make arrangements and give you a number to call.' He shook my hand. 'Thank you, this is just the sort of help we need.'

I drove home in a low state. Was there no end to the cruelty of anti-Semitism? Being confined, understanding nothing of the language, it must feel like blindfolded torture. Astrid needed a friend – and so did I.

*

I was sewing on the veranda a week later when Edmund slung up the steps looking tanned and glamorous. He kissed me on both cheeks and studied me with a great big grin on his face. 'Hello, gorgeous, I'm back from my travels.'

'So I see. Cup of tea? You seem to have had a good trip.'

I called for Kofi, brushing down my home-sewn green maternity shift, deliberately, very keen for Edmund to see my hard, round bump.

'Well, well, look at you, still blooming!' He smoothed over my mounded stomach with a lingering hand. It felt far too intimate a thing to do and I stiffened. The baby chose that moment to give a hefty kick, as if protecting my virtue, and Edmund laughed, depositing himself on the rattan sofa uninvited. 'Packs a hefty punch, the little chap, doesn't he! Now, about that lunch at the Club; what's best? Saturday? Sunday?'

'Thank you,' I said formally, resentful of Edmund's presumption, smiling at Kofi bringing the tea, 'very kind, but I'm a lumpen elephant, as you can see, and won't come this time.'

Edmund looked infuriatingly amused. 'You're no elephant, nothing more beautiful than a pregnant woman in her prime, and you can't sit around all day, pining. It's bad for your health.'

'People will assume the baby is yours,' I said, sure he wouldn't care a jot, quite enjoy his ghastly friends thinking he'd got me pregnant, in fact.

'Nonsense! Who cares anyway? And the piano's tuned now. You could have a practice before the little concert I'm planning. You're coming and that's that. Jock Broughton could be back from his travels, it'll be fun.'

Fun? It was wartime.

Edmund rested his chipped cup and rose, the issue of my coming to lunch resolved in his eyes. Not in mine. I had a last go at declining his invitation, still wistfully dreaming of playing his beautiful piano.

'No, you're coming and it'll do you good. I'll pick you up on Sunday at noon.'

*

In the harsh light of a hot midday, the Muthaiga Club had lost none of its charm, sheltered by graceful trees, the sun bleaching the stucco to the palest seashell pink. The place looked as settled and established against its brilliant azure backdrop as a Tuscan cathedral. *Shambas* were tending the grounds, washing the cars of the rich and privileged with uncomplaining care. It wasn't my world. I was more aware of that, more dispassionate, far from in Edmund's sway.

He took my arm going into the dining room where the noise levels were high, fine wine being poured down the thirsty gullets of all the languorous, blasé men and women, many of whom must be or have been part of the notoriously amoral Happy Valley set.

Edmund passed by Claudia and Charlie Loft's table again to my great frustration. Claudia was wearing a necklace of rubies the size of Victoria plums and she said, eyeing Edmund lazily with a knowing smile playing on her lips, 'You do love a little new blood, don't you, darling?'

'As do you, dear Claudia…' The look passing between them was unsettlingly intimate. She wasn't young, which was clear to see in the strong sunlight slanting on her well-powdered face, but with those high cheekbones and cold, piercing green eyes, had certainly been a beauty in her time. A past flame of Edmund's? Possibly still one? Perhaps she was just a knowing confidante now.

'And the father of this little tiddly-pop?' said Charlie Loft, smirking.

'Is my husband,' I snapped, while Charlie was guffawing heartily, 'who happens to be busy risking his life while you enjoy your lunch.' I'd almost swiped him.

'Touché! Spirited young filly, aren't you?' Charlie said, wiping tears of mirth from his wobbling, broken-veined face. 'Well, Edmund, my fella, I'd say you could have met your match with this one!'

Claudia's pique, if it was that at all, was well hidden behind her languid gaze. She wouldn't enjoy being out of the arc of male attention, though the eye contact with Edmund had been constant. How could she stand being married to that insufferable old goat?

It was my first question, reaching our table, and Edmund laughed out loud. 'Haven't you thought about those rubies the size of quails' eggs? Charlie's not the buffoon he seems, earned himself a tidy hand-out from De Beers, way back in 1914 when the Kimberly diamond mine closed, invested cannily and built himself a fortune big enough to buy Claudia whole treasure chests of jewels.'

The cocktails and champagne flowed, no nod from Edmund to wartime restraint… 'Jock Broughton seems to have got the message,' he said, looking around. 'He's staying away, but he'll hate being persona non grata, a thin-skinned fellow if nothing else.'

Edmund kept up a flow of witty, risqué stories. Was he trying to lure me like a fish to the bait of his silky insidious world? I wondered at him not doing something for the war effort. Joss Erroll had got stuck in; surely Edmund could too, with his business skills.

He was grinning. 'Penny for 'em?' he said, uninterested in any answer. 'I'll just sign and now that the piano's tuned, you must come to play for a while, which you do so very beautifully. Then I'll run you back. I've got work to do in the office and Sunday's much the best time.'

I needed to play, lose myself, let music blot out all the discordant stresses and soothe my soul. I knew the good sense of going straight home, knew it was giving in but, that beautiful piano… my fingers were already on the keys.

Leaving the Club, I knew too that I wouldn't come again. It had been an experience, the polished wood and cigar smoke, fragrant bowls of flowers, the scent of frangipanis. The Club had glamour and allure, but it wasn't for me.

Outside in the sunlight, feeling quite grateful, I softened. 'Thank you. I've really appreciated all your attentions, but it's high time you turned them now and I need to get ready for motherhood and apple pie.'

He pressed me to his side. 'The treats aren't over yet, your piano awaits!'

It played beautifully, tunefully; the music was as pure as a peat brook. I felt in thrall, mellow with champagne and the power and purity of the sounds at my fingertips. I forgot where I was, forgot about time…

The sound of clapping broke the spell and a voice calling out, 'Bravo!'

I turned from the piano and felt a scarlet rush of heat flood into my face; Claudia and Charlie were there. I hadn't heard them come in and faced them in an agony of fluster. 'Oh, I've got an audience, I didn't know… You didn't say, Edmund…' I didn't know where to put myself, feeling so furiously embarrassed.

'The girl's a genius,' said Charlie lazily, slumped back on a deep cushioned sofa.

Claudia was lounging in an armchair with her long, slender legs hooked over the arm; Edmund was standing beside the chair, idly cradling one of her feet. 'You played exquisitely,' he said, relinquishing Claudia's foot to help me up from the piano stool. 'Time for tea or there's always something stronger. We have excellent locally brewed tea and served slightly sweet, it's very refreshing.'

'Thanks. Certainly nothing stronger than tea or the room will swim! Then I must hurry home.' I caught the sly glance Claudia slid to Edmund with her cold, calculating green eyes. I didn't want to be there, only to get away, as far from the three of them as it was possible to be. At least leery old Charlie had an iota of warmth in his superficial soul.

We went out to the terrace where I'd had coffee with Edmund previously and sitting ramrod straight on the edge of a chair, I admired the evening light. It was filtering through the trees, casting soft, gilded shadows like a beautiful fan. Edmund handed me a cup of tea that I downed quickly, so desperately impatient to be away. The tea tasted sourly sweet, not the delicate flavour I'd anticipated, and looked slightly cloudy, as though the milk that I hadn't asked for had been off. Claudia, the detestable woman, kept staring at me too, with that disdainfully amused smile of hers. I felt angry and resting my cup, stood up abruptly.

'Thank you, Edmund, the piano played beautifully, but I really must go now, this minute, it's very late.' I must have risen too quickly, felt fuzzy, dizzy, and reached for the nearest chair back to hold steady. The dizziness overcame me, the lush garden seemed to be looping up, bearing down, the trees and bushes turning purple, the grass phosphorescent and every shade of pink. The baby! I panicked, terrified of going into premature labour. Could anything be worse?

The swamping panic faded away and everything was beautiful; the garden; the floating stars, crimson, vermillion and orange. There were smiling faces, blurry, but I reached out to touch them all the same, to stroke those beaming faces moving close to mine…

I felt breath on my cheek, heard a soft voice and put up a hand to touch the mouth and lips. 'We think you should lie down now,' said the soft voice. 'Lie down and take off your clothes, which will make it all better and better…'

My hand was being stroked. 'Feels good,' I said. Was I slurring my words? Had they come out right? I started to giggle, felt wobbly, felt myself being supported, too firmly. The colours weren't so bright; darker, deeper, purple as night. 'Lift up your arms and we will take off your dress, then everything will be beautiful…'

I was in a soft place. There were bodies, white shapes. Were there breasts hanging over my face? Were those stars right above my head? I was floating upwards, up from a soft surface. 'Like the pretty stars,' I said dreamily. 'All black now, just stars…'

Feeling hands. It felt painful, intense; it mustn't stop.

What was happening? Something hard, pressing, hurting, searing pain. I felt there and not there, in pain, not in pain. White shapes above me, white shapes by my side. This was hurting, horrible; slithery snakes, monsters with claws… I felt sick, sick and sleepy, and struggled to be free. Bodies pinning me down. Was this a nightmare? I wanted to wake up, get up, was I in a cave? Too much blackness. I could hear myself cry, felt adrift, out of space, the world, the whole of me draining away…

My eyes were focusing; I was in a dark room. 'It's almost dawn. How are you? Did you like it?' Edmund gave a cold smile. 'You seemed to, responded well.'

'We liked it!' I turned my head and saw Claudia; hateful, despicable woman.

'Where am I? What's happened?' I remembered then, playing the piano, the tea, and sat bolt upright. Surely, I wasn't still in Edmund's house? Had I not been home at all? I looked down and felt shock, revulsion, faint with nausea, bile swilling in my parched throat.

I was naked on a huge bed, with my pregnant bump, my whole body exposed. My hand went to my mouth to stifle a scream. Edmund and Claudia both grinning, standing by the bed fully dressed. This couldn't be happening; nothing could be this bad… I had a terrible headache, felt sick, sticky, but my mind was clearing fast, everything suddenly becoming horribly, shockingly clear. It was an outrage, unspeakable, a heinously revolting crime…

'Where are my clothes? What have you done? Raped me?' I mustn't give in, break down and sob, had to stay in control. I sat bolt upright, pulling round a rumpled sheet. 'Please give me my clothes back at once and leave the room. And call me a taxi this instant. If you have a shred of decency left in your criminal souls.' I swung down my legs and rose from the bed, pulling the silk sheet round me more tightly, trying to preserve some pathetic fragment of dignity. 'Go, go, will you, for God's sake? I think I'm going to be sick.'

'Bathroom's there.' Claudia inclined her head. 'Your clothes in there too. I'll say good night now then, dahling. It's late – very! Edmund will take you home.'

I made it to the bathroom and threw up, wiped my face, sat on the edge of the bath, nauseous and groggy, trying to contain the dizziness before struggling into underwear and a dress that I never wanted to see or wear ever again.

Had to stay in control… Swaying from one door to the next, out into the immense drawing room and seeing my bag, I grabbed it and made for the front door. Had to get out of the house and breathe the clean fresh air outside.

Edmund came out after me. A faint pink suffusing glow of dawn was lifting the night away. He put an embroidered silk wrap that smelled of another woman's sickly scent around my shivering shoulders and bundled me into his car.

'You drugged me,' I said dully, looking ahead, still battling with the nausea. 'I feel violated and defiled.' The thought of Claudia touching me… 'You took criminal advantage, let your lover abuse me and I suppose let that revolting letch have his way with me too… Have you no shame, no pity, no vestige of decency in your soul?'

'Charlie only watches,' Edmund said, as if that made it less bad. 'He likes to see women making love, gives him a kick. And you did enjoy it, you know, very sensitive to touch.'

I couldn't report them. It would be the ruination of everything; Harry, our marriage, my reputation. There was nothing I could do, nothing, nothing at all – as Edmund very well knew. Could any man be more hateful, caddish and cruel?

Some of the Stafford servants, possibly Kofi too who slept in their quarters, could be up by now and see me return. What would they think? Would anything get back to the Staffords? Would Beryl demand, in explosively shocked tones, to know what, in God's name, I'd been up to? Thank heavens for the baby; some women might envisage a seven-month-pregnant woman at a drunken druggie orgy, but not Beryl – or so I hoped.

What would I say? That I'd been playing at a small concert

put on by Sir Edmund Southan and fainted. Must have been the pregnancy, pushing myself too hard... Some kind people there had put me to bed and Sir Edmund, who had to be in the city very early, had driven me home.

A future of lies and half-truths lay ahead. I crept into the cottage, fell on the bed, buried my face in the pillow and sobbed my heart out.

CHAPTER 32

Toppy

The nights were the hardest. I was plagued with a recurring nightmare; a distorted face with huge crimson-rimmed lips and wide-open mouth were looming over me; crooked, skeletal hands coming closer; inch-long, blood-red nails about to claw… I couldn't scream, couldn't escape… I would wake up, bathed in sweat and terror, my head still filled with unbearable images and every pore of my body crawling with self-disgust. I would never be over the shame, never escape the sickening memories, the unendurable horror of it all.

To have been drugged into a spaced-out rosy otherworld, not knowing what unspeakably humiliating things were being done to me, even what I could have been made to do to myself, Claudia abusing me, directing my hands… Suppose I ever had to see Edmund again? How could I possibly cope?

I'd been ill after that night, feverish and vomiting, but refusing to let Kofi call a doctor. Now, three weeks on, late October already, depression had set in deep. I hadn't been eating and the lost weight wasn't going back on, which made me frightened for the baby.

I'd been having regular pregnancy checks with my doctor, Doctor Stout, and needed to see him now.

Driving to the surgery, the sun was exquisitely hazy as though with a covering of gauze, but nothing could lift the lowness and Doctor Stout, very thin himself, was bound to ask about the weight loss. I trusted him, but mentioning being ill with a fever would only make him wonder why I hadn't asked him to visit.

Worry over the position of the baby was a limp excuse for coming now, when the fever was gone, but it was genuine. I parked and went into the surgery.

A slow fan was barely stirring the stale air in the waiting room. My hands were clammy, nerves in pieces and my smile over-bright when I was called.

Doctor Stout said, 'Good to see you, Mrs Werner, pop yourself up on the table and let's see what's what.' He prodded about with sure, firm fingers and was quick to apologise when I shivered.

'It's just the fan,' I said, 'I'm not cold', but hands on my stomach directed my mind. Dressed again and beside his desk, he held my eyes. 'The baby's lying the right way, it's just a strong wee pair of heels giving lusty kicks. Tell me what's wrong, Mrs Werner. You've lost your colour, your spark, and the weight loss is indicative. You're showing every sign of depression. It often helps to talk a little and you can rest assured that nothing will go further than these four walls.'

I was grateful and had to say something, but could never speak a syllable of what had happened and muttered, 'I had a bad experience, but can we just leave it at that? I'll be over it soon, especially now you've set my mind at rest about the baby. I'll eat plenty of cake and put the weight back on again soon, I'm sure.'

He didn't press the point, sensitively moved on. 'I think you'll be fine at the Byland. It's a good nursing home and the midwife, Barbs Bliss, Mother Bliss, as we call her, is excellent. You have friends who could contact me if need, meantime? And someone to drive you in?'

'Major and Mrs Stafford could call for a cab, all's fine. Thank you,' I smiled, as Doctor Stout saw me out. 'I feel better already, which is just as well with so much still to do and no hope of my husband miraculously wangling any leave.'

I did feel a little better, less paralysed with misery, calmer, feeling able to face people again, and arranged to be back at the Gloucester, serving meals for two or three more weeks before the birth.

Everyone was very solicitous about my health. I assured them it had just been a fever, nothing much, though kind Mrs Buckley, who was coming to help with the baby, raised a quizzical eyebrow. She was grey-haired, grey-eyed, fond of grey cardigans, but there was nothing grey about her lovely sense of humour.

'Come to tea tomorrow,' she said, washing dishes while I dried, 'we can make plans and I'd enjoy doing some baking, put some colour back into those hollow cheeks.'

'My dog, Toppy, may be with me, but he can stay in the car,' I said disingenuously, hoping she'd let him come in.

'Nonsense, we can't have that. Toppy will be just as welcome.'

He trotted happily alongside me the next day while I peered at house numbers in the suburban street. I'd parked in the wrong block, but soon found no. 16, a squat, square, unexpectedly small bungalow with metal-framed windows. I'd expected a slightly grander home, but the garden was a restoring riot of colour and with the front door ajar, an irresistible smell of baking filled the air.

A large tabby cat slipped out of the open door, arching its back and hissing murderously at Toppy before shooting past into the garden.

'Oscar wasn't consulted,' Mrs Buckley said, laughing, coming to the door. 'But I take the decisions, no chance of mutual agreement in matters canine. Come on in and rest your feet, the last month is hell. Still, you're almost there. If the baby came tomorrow, you'd be fine. No one can truly pinpoint the dates, it's a myth.'

I sank down into a low-sprung armchair and Mrs Buckley poured tea from a flowered pot. She'd made cucumber sandwiches, scones, and dipping the point of a knife into a sumptuous-looking coffee cake, cut slices to gladden Dr Stout's heart. 'I had my full sugar ration, and we're lucky to have fresh eggs, not the awful dried stuff they have at home that my daughter, Loopy, says is like stale Bird's custard powder.'

'How is she?' I asked, fondling Toppy's ears. 'You must be incredibly proud of her.' I knew she worked as a warden and ambulance driver and was at constant risk.

'I am proud. She was such a wimpish child and now she's digging out corpses, dodging falling girders, rescuing cats. One of her fellow wardens was killed when his steel helmet touched a live cable. That really got to me.' Mrs Buckley sighed. 'Loopy says they drink gallons of sweet tea, and what she misses most, and this from a girl who sees one boyfriend in the week and another at weekends, is the sound of church bells! They're banned for the duration, only to be rung if there's an invasion.'

I talked about Lil and the Café de Paris bomb. 'The Café de Paris was a bear pit in the nineteenth century,' Mrs Buckley said, 'converted to a dance hall on designs modelled on the *Titanic*. How grimly prophetic was that?'

I told her how constantly guilty I felt at not being back home, sharing the load like Loopy, yet knowing I'd never have been a quarter as brave.

'You'd be just as game, shows in your eyes, and you're helping out here. You gutsy modern girls are doing as much in your way as our menfolk.'

She had a point there. 'You've cheered me up no end,' I said, 'but I really ought to make a move and give Toppy his w.a.l.k.'

'There's a park down the road, I'll come with if I may, and stretch my legs.'

We set off, pottering down the tree-lined suburban street.

Turning into the park, I caught sight of the Ngong Hills, radiant in the evening light. Harry and I had climbed the first peak, boiling hot with the exertion, hugging and kissing when we reached the top.

'What's Loopy's real name?' I asked, as we wandered over the scrubby grass, depressed by the amount of litter. 'Was she born here? Is this home?'

'She's called Delia, but it never suited her. My son is Douglas and I'm Rose, by the way. Both children were born in England but had a peripatetic childhood till boarding school age, such is army life. My husband, Roger, and I were in Aden, just pre-war, but my sister who was here in Nairobi got cancer so I came to look after her. This is her house. Then when war was declared and Roger recalled home, I couldn't leave her and after she'd died couldn't easily get back. There were ends to tie up here and Roger's in intelligence, closeted in some undisclosed place. Loopy was flat sharing, Douglas joined the RAF.' Rose smiled. 'He hasn't been shot down yet…'

'You have to keep the faith,' I said, my heart wanting to burst; Dick in the Marines, Jack just joined up… 'It's all we can do.'

We were back at Rose's gate. I looked round for Toppy; he'd been scampering ahead but was good at keeping to pavements and I'd parked in a block further down. He must have gone to the car. My anxiety showed and Rose came with me to check he was there. Toppy was squatting beside the car but didn't leap up when I opened the door for him, didn't stir.

'There's a bit of blood on his side,' said Rose. 'I think he's had a knock.'

It was hard to see much wrong, but his eyes had the plaintive look of an animal in great pain and I felt stricken. 'We should take him to my vet, Dr Vetch,' Rose said, helping me to lift him into the car. 'I'll come with, show you the way.' My hands were white-knuckled on the steering wheel; we couldn't lose Toppy…

We carried him into the vet's surgery in Victoria Street. The vet, talking to the receptionist, was old, white-bearded and stooped, his white coat hanging loosely on his frame, but he took charge immediately and soon had poor mute Toppy on a table, gently feeling him about. 'It looks like an internal injury,' said Dr Vetch, 'but I need to investigate further. Can you wait a while?'

He came to sit beside me on a waiting-room chair. The way he was looking made me blink back the tears. I said, 'Is it fatal? Please tell me honestly...'

'He's in a very bad state, hit by a car, I expect, and has broken ribs, but I can't tell yet whether a lung has been pierced or his heart. I'll let you see him now, but then it's better you don't come for a day or two – hard as I know that will be. I've given him an injection to stop the bleeding, but his breathing is difficult and the poor fellow can't lie down.' The vet touched my hand, a sweet, kind man.

Toppy was squatting on his haunches, just as at the car. He was all wrapped up in flannel bandages, his head swathed, and looking so pathetic that I covered my face with my hands. 'Is there a chance he will pull through?'

'A slim one. If you ring in the morning, I may know more.'

There was no change when I telephoned next day. I thanked Beryl for the use of the telephone and trailed back to the cottage with my fists clenched, praying. If I'd kept more of an eye... It was all my fault. Edmund was all my fault, accepting to go when I'd known better. Everything was all my own fault.

I sat down to write to Harry, painful as telling him would be. Spilling it out and taking responsibility was cleansing, but he'd been curt in his last letter, asking questions about the man who'd taken me to lunch.

...One of the chaps thinks it could be someone called Edmund Southan, a selfish cad and dodgy business dealer who hangs

out with the Happy Valley set. I'd be grateful if you'd tell me the name of this fellow who took you to lunch, and set my mind at rest.

I had to be straight and answer honestly, and on top of the news about Toppy, but there was no out…

…By the way, it was Edmund Southan who took me to the Muthaiga Club, but don't fret, my suspicious darling, I was far from doing any business deals and I'm so big now, only three weeks or so till I pop, he was hardly going to pounce! Anyway, he spent most of the time making eyes at a married woman at another table. It's you, my beloved, I long to be with more intensely with every hour that passes. I'm desperately lonely, wretched about Tops – he looked so pitiable, we must pray that he pulls through – and it's so close to the birth now, so scary, bringing this tiny scrap of ours into the frightening world. I feel miserable that you won't see the first days and weeks. When oh when will they ever let you come home?

Home? Kenya wasn't home. Harry's home had been a primitive shack in the Budongo Forest in Uganda, a place that he'd loved. Would we end up there, with paraffin Tilley lamps, marauding leopards and locusts? Squatting over a hole in the ground? The constant fears I'd feel for our child?

It was no use telling myself over and over that I'd known about Harry's job, the remoteness where he was living, and no excuse putting my impetuous decision to chase out after him down to teenage youth. I hadn't been a teenager in Cairo… Still, there was always hope, life moved on, Harry could be posted to other parts of the world, places with the chance for me to teach music and play the piano.

On Saturday, I visited Astrid at the seedy requisitioned hotel and poured out all my own anguish. She was sympathetic and concerned, better in herself too; she looked less like someone frozen in terror, face to face with a wolf. It was my third visit. I could come once more before the birth, hoping to have some solid news from Colonel Grant about when she and her family could return to their farm. I'd brought Astrid a small bottle of cologne, which delighted her. She immediately dabbed it all over her, scenting the dusty, fetid air of the lounge at the George.

On Sunday, Dr Vetch gave me hope. 'I'd say that Toppy is about half a percent better. Yesterday, my wife and I really thought he was going to die on us, his temperature was a hundred and seven.' Hard to know what that meant, but it sounded bad. 'We could see his heart beating through a hole made by a broken rib, though, and I will start to feed him artificially now.'

A few days later, visiting the vet's surgery after my final shift serving meals at the Gloucester, Toppy was on his feet. He was overjoyed to see me, pathetically affectionate. Dr Vetch still insisted he should stay for another ten more days for fear of the ribs being moved.

Back at the cottage, I felt a knife of pain, sudden, sharp and constricting. It was too soon to be the baby, surely; probably just a stitch. I'd had twinges before and decided a walk in the garden could help ease the pain.

Strolling over the fresh-mown lawns, I felt better; there were flame trees and swaying palms, roses, stephanotis, the incessant humming of a million insects. I sat on a bench overlooking the water garden where beautiful flat-leaved lilies floated on the still, dark depths. Three more weeks; it felt like being a child again, opening Advent calendar windows, wondering if Christmas would ever come.

I was collecting Toppy in the morning but would have to leave him with Kofi over the birth. The worry was that Kofi, who'd be at a loose end, would use the time to look for better-paid work and just when I needed him most. The kid was a bright fifteen-year-old, his father had moved on and his mother must be glad to have him in work, but it felt wrong that he couldn't afford school and was denied the chance to learn. Would offering to give him lessons after the birth help to keep him? I'd be tied with the baby, unable to work, and could easily teach him the basics.

A shadow fell over me and I looked up to see Major Stafford. I said, 'Hope you don't mind my wandering in the garden? It's so lovely here with the water lilies, the stillness and sense of peace.'

'Yes, isn't it? It gives me such pleasure to see you here,' he smiled, joining me on the bench. 'How is your little dog bearing up? I hear he was the victim of a hit and run incident, poor chap. I do miss my old Labrador. He had to be put down this year and I haven't felt up to a replacement. How are you getting on? Can I be of any help? I feel rather like a proxy grandfather to this infant! All fixed up for a lift to the nursing home, at night as well?'

I'd shut my mind to that possibility, but it was a worry... 'You've helped in so many ways and Beryl has kindly said she will call a taxi. The one worry I have is Toppy. Would it be a dreadful imposition to ask you look in on him occasionally? Kofi has promised to feed him, but I'd be so grateful if you could keep an eye.'

'I'll certainly do that, of course, and see the *shamba* does too. But we can't have you going in by taxi. One of us will run you in and Najau can take you if it's late night. Best to go in early, though,' he said, rising, 'and not be caught out.'

Kind, wise words. I'd had enough of being caught out, felt scarred and tarnished and always would, filled with self-loathing. All there was left to hope for now was a smooth, easy confinement, something going right at last.

CHAPTER 33

The Birth

The contractions came at night, thick and fast. I woke with a feeling like being squeezed by a boa constrictor and crawled out of bed bent over double and clutching my stomach in agony. The baby wasn't due for nearly three weeks.

Another band of pain. I hadn't the strength to stagger about trying to raise Kofi or Najau, just had to get to the nursing home. Everything was ready packed; soap, bandages, nightdresses, toiletries. Oh, God, another contraction. I grabbed my car keys and the holdall. The nursing home wasn't far, only a few miles. I could do it, had to.

Toppy was out of his basket, poised by the door as I opened it. 'STAY,' I said, sternly, nearly keeling over with another pain. 'STAY!' It was Sunday, Kofi's day off, but the nursing home could ring and dear, sweet Major Stafford see that Toppy was fed. 'Don't worry, all will be fine,' he'd said.

All wasn't fine, another pain coming… I was in a cold sweat reaching the car and started the engine only to lean over the steering wheel waiting for the contraction to pass. I had to do it, had to find the willpower and make it there.

Having the windows wide open meant that the large insects bombing the windscreen found their way into the car. I wound up the windows despite my desperate need of air. The handles were so stiff to turn… I was sweating and shivering, having to stop now and then with the pain, feeling in terror of wild animals.

It was four o'clock in the morning when I arrived, turning into the Byland's drive, praying the place wouldn't be in darkness. My breath was coming in short bursts as I grabbed my overnight bag and went to lean on the bell.

The lights were on, there were footsteps… The relief was indescribable.

A young nurse let me in. The night sister came and I was soon in bed in a small private room. All the pain and fear, bombing insects, the extreme terror of giving birth on a dark, deserted *murram* road became a distant blur. 'I'll bring you a nice cup of tea,' said the nurse, 'and a bell to ring if the pains start to come much more frequently.'

Abandoned then for a couple of hours, I had few contractions, but fear of giving birth was blinding my vision, making me feel hardly sane. Fear of the baby, three weeks early, being sickly and small; fear of the pain and indignities. I had never felt more alone.

Light began to creep round the curtains. Daylight at last. The young nurse brought me a boiled egg, tea and toast and sitting up in bed, contractions at bay, I felt a bit of a fraud. The room was small and surprisingly homely; beige curtains with large cabbage roses, two low visitors' chairs with wooden arms and mustard fabric seats, a bedside table with a small parchment-shaded lamp, dull blue lino that smelled of Dettol…

The midwife, Barbs Bliss, came to see me. She talked cheerfully of how contractions could ease up for a while, the whole process taking hours, but all would be fine in the end. People kept saying that. 'You need to be shaved and given an enema now,' she said. 'Nurse Maud will take you down the corridor.'

The enema with its snake-like rubber tube was an unspeakably awful procedure. Nurse Maud was over-keen with the razor. I smarted from the nicks and cuts and minded being shorn of my pubic hair; my mound looked as pricked and raw as a plucked chicken.

'Has to be done, m' dear,' Nurse Maud said, with little sympathy. She knew all about birthing, certainly more than I did, but had a maddeningly superior air.

Back in my room, another young nurse took over, gently rubbing oil into my swollen belly. 'What's that for?' I asked edgily, as she washed her hands.

'It's supposed to speed things up,' she said, sounding a bit dubious, 'and these,' she sprinkled round a handful of herbs, 'are supposed to help you to relax.'

The herbs had a clean aromatic smell, but the contractions, coming faster now, felt like a band of rubber being pulled steadily, mercilessly tighter. Surely the baby must come soon? I was helped to a table in the delivery room. There were steaming basins of hot water, towels, nurses, who urged me again and again to push. 'Push, push, push harder, you must push now!' I blinked back tears of pain, trying not to howl out loud, but couldn't do it. I was failing, a failure who couldn't give birth.

Doctor Stout came. He murmured about forceps while I clung on for dear life, clung to a nurse's hand, tighter and tighter, sweated, pushed and prayed.

Andrew Harold Werner was born at two o'clock in the afternoon. Tuesday 4th November 1941. We had a son.

It was a full three days before I was able to sit up in bed with a tray table and write to Harry, still feeling weak, exhausted and torn down below.

My darling,

We have our little Andrew, the loveliest little bundle you can ever imagine. He screamed so heartily when he arrived. It was the gutsiest, most glorious sound, full of the importance of living! All his little limbs were kicking, no half-heartedness about it. He was already trying to kick a football at five minutes old!

I leaned back on the pillows. It had been cruel, the way the nurses had whisked him away before even allowing me to caress his tiny head. Tears of frustration had sprung into my eyes, but I was just another exhausted mother in an emotional post-natal state. The nurses couldn't see beyond the system, and they were in charge.

It had been a full two hours before Nurse Maud, who'd been a great support, it had to be said, brought him back, bathed and swaddled in a pale blue shawl, and gave him to me to hold. His tiny face was peeping out and his eyes that were blindly wide open were more than a heavenly blue. They seemed to look straight into my own and I felt boundless wonder. It was the most piercingly emotional moment of my whole life.

'Time to take the wee one back to his bassinet now,' Nurse Maud had said officiously, making me feel waves of hatred. How could she deny me time with my newborn son?

I picked up my pen again, but said none of that to Harry and soon had to put it down; the Staffords were being shown in. I was delighted to see them both, and Beryl, who was beaming, laid a vast bouquet of peonies on the bed, but Major Stafford was called away minutes later. His army transport had arrived.

Not Beryl, she was in for the duration, camped out in the nearest visitor's chair, gossiping interminably about everyone's misdemeanours. A nurse came in with an embarrassingly large bunch of red roses and Beryl leapt up, taking the flowers from the nurse's arms to have a nosy read of the card. I knew instinctively who they were from and hid white-knuckled fists under the bedclothes, feeling chilled to the bone.

'Goodness me, Sir Edmund Southan sending you flowers!' Beryl exclaimed, handing over the card. 'Didn't know you knew him, dear?' I glanced at it casually, fighting the taste of nausea on my tongue. "*What a star you are! Love Edmund*".

Beryl's querying expression was under-laid with layers of prurient suspicion and curiosity. 'You must ask Sir Edmund to tea up at the house with me some time,' she said, the inveterate snob. 'I knew his parents, who were brave pioneers like my own, and must admit to being interested to meet him – despite all.' She looked at me with keen intent. 'He has a bit of a risqué reputation in this town, which you may not know. He's one for the ladies and people question how he's made such a formidable fortune. Archie is scathing about him, I can tell you, thinks he's a dishonourable cad for getting out of joining up, but then Archie is so *very* strict and proper. Personally, I don't begrudge people making money. My parents did. They saw the future and dealt in land, and I'm the lucky benefactor of a fine inheritance.'

As long as her parents made it by fair means… 'How do you happen to know Edmund, dear?' Beryl asked, with a determined look in her eye.

'Hardly do,' I said, in desperation. 'We chatted once at the doctor's surgery, so he knew I was having a baby, which perhaps explains why he thought to send flowers. He was probably amused by the idea of surprising me, but how did he know I was here!' I forced a smile, sick with nerves, sweat dripping between my breasts, thighs setting up a tremble under the bedclothes. 'To be honest,' I said, pushing my luck, 'I'm not madly keen on those sort of stiff-looking unscented roses. They always seem a bit over-ostentatious. Far rather your lovely, floppy double peonies, Beryl, which are my absolute favourite. I can't thank you enough.'

She looked pleased, if not entirely convinced, by the threadbare explanation. I smiled brightly and chatted, hardly hearing what she said, thinking about having the roses put out in the impersonal entrance hall where with luck they'd be dead or drooping by the time of leaving. 'Ah, here's my little bundle coming,' I said, taking Andy from Nurse Maud with intense relief, willing Beryl to take the hint and leave. 'Do have a peep. I can see Harry in him already.'

Beryl leaned and peered at the tiny face. 'Little cherub! Well, I'd better be off if you're about to feed the wee brat.' She heaved herself up from the chair, looked back from the door and said with knowing eyes, 'You do look very wan, my dear, not yourself at all. You need to rest up and take good care.'

I concentrated on feeding Andy, who always clung on like a little terrier, but the small room retained an aroma of Beryl's heavy scent and there seemed little chance of surviving her prurient interest. She wouldn't waste a minute in holding court with her circle of army wives. I could just hear her.

'Would you believe it! Sir Edmund Southan, no less, bunching my young tenant! I mean, one can't help wondering, can one?'

What I dreaded most – apart from Harry discovering about the flowers – was the gossip inevitably reaching Archie Stafford. He was a good man whom I wanted to think well of me, wanted others to do so too. News travelled, but gossip even faster, and with all the Staffords' army connections Harry was bound to get to hear. He knew about Edmund, the lunch at the Muthaiga. There was no escape, nothing I could do. How many more ways was Edmund Southan going to find to blacken my name and harm me? Tears welled before bitterness took over, but nothing could dispel the overwhelming sense of despair.

I laid Andy back in his bassinet and got on with my letter to Harry.

…Andy has really got the hang of sucking on a nipple now, a real grip after the first day of missing a couple of times! I'm

quite convinced he was born with wisdom teeth! By evening, the milk in my breasts has overflowed. They're huge and stiff as rocks. I'm told to feed him every three hours, as he needs the food and it will relieve me. He is a bit small, born three weeks early, but he fairly goes at it now, and looks up at me just as you do! It's so sweet of him to have enclosed such an intimate feature of you in his tiny self.

He was a little yellow on the second day, which often happens with the very small ones apparently, the immatures, as Sister calls them, but he's making good progress, sucking furiously. Sister says my milk must have alcohol in it, as he sleeps so soundly afterwards! I wish you could see him, he's so sweet, and the new-baby smell of him too, like rose petals and warm buns…

I was putting off mentioning the Staffords, but silly not to say they'd been.

…Mrs Buckley was my first visitor. She brought me this writing pad and has knitted the dearest little matinee coat and bootees. Wonderful she's putting her cat into kennels and coming to live in for a few days. And Major and Mrs Stafford have just left. They brought lovely peonies and Major Stafford has promised to keep an eye on Toppy. He's such a dear. I'll write again soon and send photos. Stay safe and PLEASE get some leave very soon…

A nurse came to wheel Andy away. 'Time to rub your wee back and put you down for sleepies!' The baby talk was infuriating, and why not leave the bassinet by my bedside? But I couldn't fight the system; the nurses had their routine.

Agnes visited and looked wistful. The poor girl so longed for marriage and motherhood. Two others from the sewing group came too. I wrote letters, tried to read books, tried to knit, but black thoughts of Edmund Southan crammed my mind.

A telegram came. *"CONGRATULATIONS STOP CLEVER DARLING STOP LONGING SEE."* News of the birth had taken its time to reach Harry. Was there hope that he could be spared the gossip and rumours? Little chance of that.

On the morning of leaving, I was packed and ready by ten o'clock, wildly impatient to go. So much advice and instructions; how to put the baby down, how not to over-swaddle him, the vital necessity of hygiene… Rose Buckley said dismissively that it was all just a matter of common sense. Fine while she was with me, but after that? No Harry to give moral support, the constant skimping to make ends meet and the awesome responsibility of caring for Andy on my own; he was my all.

Sister was extremely unhappy about my driving myself home with Andy in his Moses basket, but he'd be firmly wedged behind my seat. I needed my wheels and was adamant, ready to fight my corner when Sister came in.

'Andy ready? Can we be off?' I dried up seeing her expression and my heart began to pound. 'What is it? Not Andy, is it?' Please God, not that.

'No, no, Andy's fine, but we've had a message from army headquarters and I'm afraid Mrs Buckley won't be coming to help you. Her son's plane was shot down. He was returning from a successful mission but didn't make it home. The poor woman is distraught, urgently trying to make arrangements to return to England. I'm very sorry. I know she was a dear friend. The message said that she asked you to forgive her, but knew you would understand.'

I sat back down heavily on the bed. How many more mothers would have to lose sons before the war's end? Dear good, kind Rose, how was she going to bear a loss too unimaginably great to contain? There must be ways to offer solace and support. Should I go to the house? Would that just cause more pain?

The competent sister was reading my thoughts, seeing the painful indecision in my agonised, pleading eyes. She said, 'Give Mrs Buckley a day or so to mourn. The army will help where it can, but I doubt she will be able to return home right away. She will need a friend then, support and understanding, and that's when you should see her and fold her into your arms.'

Sister left and, alone, waiting to go home, I wept. What was my misery beside the loss of a brave son? I felt empty, gutted with grief, fearing for Harry, the family, Bob, Hamish. We had to win this war, for Andy, for all the babies, to have a future in a free world.

I would manage somehow. Harry would get leave eventually and have the magical moment of seeing his son, and in the meantime, it was down to me to nurture and protect our precious child.

PART THREE

1942-46

CHAPTER 34

Harry

Harry turned to lie on his back. It was a hot, windy night, the tent flap lifting and letting in gritty gusts of sultry air. He had the tent to himself, which felt like a luxury after having to share with a couple of heavy smokers, and any air, however humid and prickly with sand, was better than none. A zipped-up tent in that god-awful hellhole was hotter than a boiler room on a burning ship.

The bites on his legs were driving him to distraction. Sand-fly bites had a habit of coming out in livid welts and wields that went septic all too easily in that filthy place; must try to stop scratching them. The delay to his leave was a bloody bind, but if she saw him now, Laura wouldn't want him anywhere near her.

Still no convoy going south, and after being told he could go as soon as a guy with a shot-up arm was back from hospital. James had been back three weeks now. The frustration was all the greater with the amazing luck of Laura's friend Irene saying why not spend his leave holidaying in Tanganyika? She and her Swiss husband, Horst, were away for a couple of months, and their coffee estate at the foothills of Mount Kilimanjaro was there for the Werners to use.

Laura had gone on ahead by train, rather than drive all the way with Andy to amuse and the risk of breaking down in the middle of nowhere. Harry was glad to have the Chevvy waiting for him in Nairobi. He longed to be driving the distance, far from Djibouti, and they'd have the car then for the journey home.

He longed to be seeing his son at last; Andy was fifteen months now. Harry vividly remembered the tears, the emotional joy of knowing he had a son. He longed to be reuniting with Laura again. However bottled up with tension and stress, he ached for the touch of her, was exploding with need, but had to keep the lid on all his tortured suspicions and keep control.

People took their comforts while they could in wartime, but knowing what Laura's lover in Cairo had meant to her burned into Harry's sanity. He wanted her whole heart. She covered up her feelings like an elephant dragging branches over its dead, but elephants were never entirely over their loss and nor, he was certain, was she.

The Southan business seemed the final straw, a class-A shit like that would never have taken her to the Muthaiga Club out of the kindness of his heart. Harry's own only dalliance in eighteen months had been when the unit was sent to Nanuki for refitting, too far north to see Laura and the baby in the couple of days they were there. A proper bed and bath, two FANYs to make up a foursome for tennis… One of the girls, a pretty, flirty redhead, had been keen to make a night of it and taken him dancing at a seedy club, which had led them further on. It had been meaningless, a momentary release, and he felt little guilt.

He reached for the calamine lotion, which did little to soothe his infuriating bites. He had to be up at first light and what hope of getting any sleep?

*

It was another two weeks before there was a convoy south. Arriving shaken up from the journey and in a state of high tension, Harry took a taxi to the cottage, where the welcome from Toppy was overwhelming – his adoration at least was total – and fell into bed exhausted. He slept badly, even so, and was glad when daylight came. Kofi brought him breakfast, the Chevvy was in the lane and Laura had left pages of directions on finding the plantation. Harry did a fast round of shopping for presents and was on the road by nine o'clock.

He drove fast, concentrating, enjoying the miles shrinking as he travelled far, and given its impressive age, the Chevvy held up well. The interminable wait at the border was inevitable, but no less frustrating; a bureaucratic nightmare. How had Lieutenant Werner come by the petrol? Wife saved up coupons. Why wasn't the Lieutenant with his regiment in time of war? First leave for a year and a half. What was in all the boxes? Presents for his baby son, household things for his wife. And his purpose in Tanganyika? Holidaying in their wonderful country and, Harry added for good measure, perhaps they would care to accept the packets of cigarettes as a small token of his thanks for the opportunity.

The northern Tanganyikan countryside was hauntingly stark, mile upon mile of grassy plains dotted with lone acacias, beautiful in its way and never monotonous. Herds of elephant and wildebeest to be seen, a chain of ostriches loping across the rough road, bulbuls flitting by with their saucy flash of yellow under-tail.

It was late as Harry neared the estate; he'd made several wrong turns in the blackness of night, with tiredness smoking out his suspicions. He finally saw the high wooden gates that Laura had described. There was a pervading aroma of coffee and a big white sheet tacked onto the gate with "Welcome to our holiday home!" written in thick black marker.

Harry took down the sheet, unlatched the gates, closing them behind him, and drove uphill on a long, winding track. There must be a spectacular view of Mount Kilimanjaro from the other side. The tang of coffee on the air was potent; November, the arabica bushes would be in blossom, probably why Laura's friends, the owners, were able to go away, but with all the roasting and packing, the smell of coffee must be year-round.

The lodge loomed, brick-built, just visible with a dim light on the porch, a portico with wooden pillars. Harry parked, feeling an adrenaline charge, despite his exhaustion, and a jangling physical need. He had an overpowering longing for all to be well and arching his back, reached into the car for the bags.

The front door opened, light flooding out, and there was Laura. She was backlit, her chestnut hair haloed, and the rush of tender love that overcame him was more than his lurching heart could contain.

'Hello, stranger!' she said, coming close, stopping short when he stood rooted, a heavy bag in each hand. She was wearing an open-neck shirt – sleeves rolled up – and pale blue trousers. She was tanned, looking glowing, anxious when he didn't drop the bags and take her into his arms, vulnerable and confused. Eighteen months; he was sweaty from the journey, shaking with need of her, physical need, but still couldn't trust himself to move.

She came right up, staring with her anxious eyes, and touched his lips. He dropped the bags then and his arms enfolded her with a will of their own. His mouth found hers; it was contact and closeness at last.

'It's been a long time,' she said, dropping her head to his chest, speaking into his damp shirt, 'lots of catching up to do…' His fingers trailed her silky hair with all his long-compressed urgency feeling like a coil about to spring.

'Missed you,' he said.

Laura picked up what she could carry and led the way. The kettle was whistling, reaching its hysterical pitch, and she dropped everything. 'It'll wake Andy!' she said in panic, and raced off, leaving Harry to take in his surroundings.

He was in an enormous round living space, whitewashed and lofty with a stone fireplace and stripped-wood beams that curved up to meet in the ceiling.

There was a long sofa with bright cushions, reds, purples, yellows, a cut-down old threshing table piled high with books, toys and a scattering of bruised flowerheads. 'Andy loves flowers,' Laura said, coming back. 'And this is your moment, a first peep at your son. He's asleep – I hope – in a screened-off part of our room.'

Lifting back the mosquito net hung from a beam above the cot, Harry studied Andy's small sleeping profile. He felt an indescribable blend of love, pride and terror. The child looked so peaceful and pure, tucked up under a cotton blanket, so infinitely precious; Harry felt every protective instinct as a million harms flashed in, but children were tough, they survived, and he wanted a large family.

'It's lucky Irene had kept the cot and high chair,' Laura whispered. 'She has boys of six and nine and said you never knew about another one…' Harry wasn't listening; he was urging his beautiful Laura backwards towards the bed, completely uncontrollably overcome.

'Best not quite yet, darling, Andy's such a light sleeper…'

She was resisting him? The blood drained. Harry felt sickened, disbelieving, all the loving passion draining like sand through his fingers. Wasn't she feeling the same need, swept along on the same uncontrollable wave? Where was her passion and spontaneity? Didn't she want him even a little bit? Love him even less now than before?

He felt distant and hostile as cold anger took hold; Laura might be staring back with her pleading eyes, but she'd stopped caring, must have. All the rumours were horribly true. His shoulders slumped and he turned away.

'I've got a meal ready and you'll need at least a whisky or two after that drive.'

'Just coffee. I'll make it.'

'No shortage of that in this house!' Laura's lips had been trembling; he'd seen as he turned. He followed her into the kitchen. There was a bottle of Scotch, a carafe of water and a glass on a scrub-top table. Harry poured himself several fingers of neat whisky and knocked it back in two gulps. He poured more, sipping the whisky more slowly, saying nothing, watching Laura measuring out coffee with her back turned.

'We must talk,' she said, looking round with the kettle in her hand.

'Oh, yes?'

'I've been worrying about getting pregnant again, now, before we can be more together and even with luck in our own home. It's been hard this past year, it just feels better to wait a bit. I did talk about waiting in one of my letters, remember, only it wasn't resolved…'

'Oh, yes it was.' Harry glared, furious. 'I said, *remember*, only you don't choose to do so, how much Andy would love a sibling close to his own age. I was an only child, *remember*. I know all about the loneliness – and aren't children what we're bloody well here for? Well? Aren't they?'

He could hardly breathe for his anger, almost crushed the glass in his hand. 'This is all about the affair you've been having with Edmund Southan, isn't it? You needed a Dutch cap for that.' He fought an urge to shake the confession out of her, had to keep control. 'It got back to me, you know, the two dozen red roses your lover sent, and you wouldn't want to be tied now, would you, having another child?' He put down the glass and poured more whisky with a shaking hand.

Laura was holding on to the table, her head bent low. She lifted her head up and looked straight at him. 'Just for the record,

I was fitted with a Dutch cap the day before coming here. I should never have accepted Edmund Southan's invitation to lunch. He's a despicable man. I loathe him, loathe myself for having gone. It was silly, superficial curiosity, wanting to see the Muthaiga Club. I couldn't believe he sent those flowers, but we'd met at the surgery, he knew I was pregnant and probably asked the doctor's receptionist where I was confined. I haven't seen or exchanged a single word with him since that Muthaiga Club lunch.'

Laura was sounding really genuinely angry, hard to believe she was telling lies. Was it something the wretch had said or done? There had to be more to it. Why else would she feel such violent hatred? She had to be hiding something, talking in half-truths...

'How could you tell the man was despicable after a single lunch? You wrote about how entertaining he'd been, *remember*?' Harry rubbed at his eyes. 'Oh, forget it, forget the whole fucking stinking business. I need to crash out.'

He turned to go, but Laura came round the table and faced him, squaring up with her glistening, wet eyes. 'How can you choose not to trust me, not to believe a single word I say? I trust you, I don't question and accuse. Relationships are built on trust, from basement to rooftop, and you have none for me? You thought enough of my character to marry me...'

He kissed her then. Her closeness, familiar scent, eighteen barren months of loneliness... She felt thinner than he remembered. He couldn't get enough of her as she arched up her slight body to meet him. He tore at her shirt, but she forced away his hands, holding on to them, leading him to the bedroom with its four-poster bed, with their son sleeping lightly behind the screen. 'No noise,' she said. 'Just love me.'

Harry woke feeling stiff and hungover, blinking with the brilliant sunshine that was filtering in through the shutters. The light and dark bands falling across the bed were like a zebra's stripes. He put out a hand but was alone in the tangle of sheets. Laura must be up, seeing to Andy.

Feeling more awake and having arousing thoughts, the horror and shame of the previous night began to loom large. His head ached, he felt full of remorse, shocked at his appalling behaviour, but the guilt was short-lived. The terrible row felt like unfinished business; anger, hurt and bitter suspicions still lingered and a sense of being the one less at fault, his trust only partially restored, if at all.

Harry pushed back the mosquito net. His watch was still on his wrist; he'd never slept with it on before. Still ticking, thank God. Surely not eleven o'clock already? Laura must have been up for hours with Andy.

He crawled out of bed, showered and shaved, dressed in a green lumber shirt and khaki shorts and went in search of his wife and son.

They were out on a terracotta-tiled veranda to the side of the kitchen. Laura, in a yellow sundress, sitting on a candlewick mat with one arm round her knees; she was giving Andy wooden bricks to try to balance on the flat tiled surface. Harry took in the scene, even the design of palm trees and a sun on the mat, watching silently while Laura was absorbed. 'Clever boy! Now this one.'

She looked up then and Andy did too, staring up solemnly, warily, pulling at his mother's skirt. His eyes were a piercing sapphire blue.

'Hello, Andy, I'm your daddy who's been away.'

The child shook his little blond head vehemently from side to side then burrowed into his mother's lap. She laughed and gathered him up, struggling to get to her feet with his weight. 'He's a bit confused, but he'll be all over you in no time. You were done in so I left you to sleep, and now,' she kissed Andy's velvety cheek, 'it's sleep time for this little one. Give Daddy a big kiss hello.'

She held the child nearer, but he swung away. Harry kissed the top of his head, gossamer curls, the colour of sunlight, and said, looking up, 'He smells a bit rank! Your father has blue eyes, doesn't he? Andy's are as blue as the Aegean Sea.'

'You once told me your father's were too, but ours aren't, Andy's may change.'

Would he ever see his parents again? The war had to end sometime, but would they still be alive? Harry kept his sighs to himself, watching while Laura dealt with the stinky bottom and lowered Andy into his cot. The child wouldn't look at him even then, making him feel more brought down still. It was inevitable; he was a stranger, but it felt like a rejection and he couldn't help minding.

'Andy's good about his naps,' Laura said. 'Come and have some food. Anita, who does the washing, will be here soon, and she loves to look after Andy. Hungry?'

'Groaning, I hardly stopped on the way and food wasn't uppermost last night…'

He grimaced mentally, still tense with jealousy. She'd written often enough about Major Stafford and the interpreting chap; was all that half-truths too?

Laura cooked up a huge brunch; eggs with rich golden yolks, juicy rashers of bacon, mushrooms, tomatoes, crispy fried bread and good strong coffee to wash it down with. He hadn't seen a tomato or mushroom in months. 'Tell me some of the stuff you couldn't write about,' she said.

'I'm a dutiful chap, stick to the rules, can't say where we're based now, but it was Assab before, which is literally one of the hottest places on earth. The hardest bit was keeping up the troops' morale, and the very worst for me was when an *askari*, who didn't take kindly to a reprimand, shot the officer concerned. He had to be court-martialled, executed by a firing squad from our own ranks.' Laura covered her face.

'The *askaris* get into trouble with local women too – venereal disease, jealous lovers, one *askari* even murdered by a lover – so some of the battalions got together to organise camp brothels for the troops. It was a very popular solution till some bloody pompous politician got to hear of it and hit the roof!'

Laura said, 'I'm with the politician on that one...'

'You would be.' Harry was in his stride. 'I was in charge of a mortar platoon for a bit, sent on detachment to train up a new team, and had the smart idea, so I thought, of trying to get camels to carry the mortars, since the lads struggled under the weight. The camels passed the first test, quite unperturbed by close-up Bren-gun fire. We could load them up in seconds, but could we make them get up again except in their own time? A rocket under their backsides wouldn't have done it. More coffee?' Harry filled their mugs.

'There was another funny moment when we were on joint manoeuvres with a battalion from Tanganyika. I was at a waterhole with one of their men, an elderly black regimental sergeant major, and heard him counting the buckets of water in German. '*Eins, zwei, drei...*' He'd served with the German East African forces under General von Lettow-Vorbeck in the last war, he said proudly, and later showed off his medal ribbons earned fighting on both sides.'

Anita was at the back door, hesitating and looking scared. Laura said in Swahili, 'Don't be shy, come in and meet my husband. This is Anita, Harry, who's such a help to me with Andy.' She was a small, crinkled old lady who gave nervous smiles. 'Andy's lunch is under the fly-cover in the larder. Chopped chicken, potatoes and carrots,' Laura said. 'It'll need warming.'

They were free to go out for a bit; Laura wanted to show him round the estate and said he had a treat in store.

Coffee bushes stretched away down the hillside in virginal white blossom, looking beautiful as any bride. There were outbuildings for pulping, fermenting, milling and roasting; every stage of coffee production, everything orderly and spotless. 'More to come,' she said, taking him round to the back of the lodge, 'ice-cold drinks and the mountain, right up close.'

The sight of Mount Kilimanjaro rising up in all its majesty, almost in touching distance, left him speechless. It was breath-stopping, completely transporting, the beauty of the coffee bushes in glorious blossom entirely eclipsed. To be right up close to the highest mountain in Africa, the highest freestanding one in the world. 'Kilimanjaro translates as "Shining Mountain",' Harry said, 'and the sunlit snow on the peak is like a sparkling crown on a goddess. She's a mountain to be worshipped and adored.'

The lower reaches were clothed in forest green, pine and juniper, with the rich foliage fading to colours of mint and seafoam the higher the eye climbed.

He longed to be out trekking on the lower slopes. 'I suppose we can't go on any serious walks with a thirteen-month-old?'

'I've got a papoose. Andy can do an hour if I can get him to keep his sunhat on. You can always go off botanising, and I thought we could drive to Lake Duluti one day. It's a crater lake, no more than an hour away.'

They went to the lake and saw the Columbus monkeys that looked like nuns with their white wimples and long white fringes to their black coats. Harry saw a rare plant, senecio Kilimanjari, which was indigenous and gave him a thrill. 'Looks like a giant cactus crossed with a palm tree,' Laura said dismissively, jokingly, 'hardly like the little grey senecios in Dad's garden back home.'

Andy stole everyone's heart over tea at the lakeside hotel, even with the carpet of crumbs he bestowed to the under-table.

The sun was beginning to dip, exquisite light shafting through the woodland by the water's edge. 'Quick walk before home?'

Harry led the way, stepping carefully over obtruding roots, feeling his knotted nerves untangle, a loosening of all the tension. Then he stopped dead, still as a stone, adrenaline racing furiously as a deadly green mamba crossed their path. He shot out a restraining arm, feeling the cares of fatherhood in every fibre, but the snake slithered up a teak tree and was gone.

Laura talked about Astrid in the car and how quick Kofi was at his lessons. 'I mind all this British superiority, people like Beryl so shocked at my teaching him. It's Kofi and his peoples' country. We need to show them some respect, give them a chance of education or they will kick us out one day.'

'I wouldn't bank on it, can't see any change of attitude for decades.'

It took a few days, but Andy was soon giggling and giving his father smiles that were sunnier than the clearest tropical sky. 'Up, up!' he would say incessantly, and Harry would swing him high. It felt like shedding a yoke, a little hand slipped into his, the curl of tiny fingers in his palm. Harry's heart felt it would explode out of its ribcage. He wanted more children, many more, it felt right, his Christian belief. Surely, surely, Laura must feel the rightness of it now too?

Hours of playing with Andy, indefatigable with his repetitive games, trekking on the lower slopes of Kilimanjaro; it had been a heavenly holiday, but now the tension was building again, the stress and endurance tests of being back with his battalion, Laura on her own again for months on end, which preyed on his taut nerves.

He was sleepless in bed on their last night, unable to shake off the doubts and distrust, the sense he had of a missing piece of the puzzle. Nothing more was said about the Dutch cap. Harry felt almost certain that she'd given in and accepted his need for more children, but he was convinced she hadn't told him the whole truth about Edmund Southan. She'd been alone in Nairobi for a year and a half… How deep was she in with him, or had been? Harry lay wakeful for hours, hands behind his head, brooding and bitterly suspicious.

'I know you're awake, what is it? Don't bottle things up, please.'

'I was just wondering whether you're still so set on contraception.'

She gave a sigh that had a touching edge of sadness. 'I just thought you'd understand,' she said. 'It's the worry of bringing up children alone. Andy got jiggers in his foot here, just before you came. Thank heavens Anita knew exactly how to deal with them. She disinfected a sewing needle and had such a deft knack, said you have to catch jiggers quick before they turn into maggots under the skin!'

He sensed Laura's smile in the dark. She turned to stroke his cheek. 'Go to sleep now, darling, tomorrow's going to be a very long day.'

The misgivings and mistrust still lingered. He'd never thought of himself as possessive, but Laura had a streak of independence that he hadn't anticipated and found hard to accept. He wanted to feel her dependence on him, but she'd proved very capable of fending for herself. Shouldn't he be proud of that, the teaching jobs, concerts, driving herself to the nursing home in the dead of night – if she really had done… Southan could have driven her there… Such thoughts were pointless and counterproductive, Harry knew.

She was trying her best, had given in, given him the joyful hope of another child. And more… loving companionship and a beautiful son, the solid building blocks of a relationship that was far too precious to lose. 'Love you,' he said, reaching for her hand, and fell almost instantly asleep.

CHAPTER 35

Harry

The tea at breakfast was always tepid and stewed. Harry was used to that, nursing his third mugful in the mess tent, but the evaporated milk didn't help and the enamel mugs had worn-away black patches that gave off an acrid tang.

He needed to get going, the platoon was waiting, but he was thinking of Laura, feeling dejected and brought down.

He thought so often about her sad eyes, saying goodbye six months ago, her white face in that early-morning chill, their quick embarrassed parting kiss by the car. The pain of loneliness was constricting, pressing down on his windpipe like a flat iron; he missed her so very much.

Laura was five months pregnant, which made the long separation still harder to bear. She'd been coping with nausea, shortages of food and a fractious child; Andy cutting his eyeteeth and whinging, probably feeling out of it, not really understanding why he was less centre stage. She was alone and with no support, but there was nothing he could do about it, no way he could help. They'd had Andy christened in Nairobi, though, which had been a comfort on the long, dusty, thirty-truck strong convoy north to Abyssinia.

Hurrying out of the breakfast tent, squinting into the harsh white desert light burning off the scrubland, he cursed the war. He felt stressed out, weary, depressed and overburdened with officer responsibility.

The battalion had left Eritrea. They were blockading the frontier with Djibouti now, camped on scrubby desolate land, barb-wired and mine-strewn. Garrisoned a bit inland, further into British Somaliland with Dijbouti in the hands of the Vichy French, Harry's platoon routinely intercepted locals trying to break through the blockade. They could usually warn them off with little fuss, but there were more serious confrontations with armed groups of blockade-breakers. The Somali locals were a particular menace too, raiding the camp at dead of night, snatching rifles from sleepy sentries and even stealing revolvers from under the pillows of snoring officers.

The battalion had a good vantage point, camped on top of a stony hillock and able to see for miles over the endless arid scrubland; small outcrops of rocks in the parched valley were so bleached by the sun that they looked like ancient bones. Harry's patrol was eagle-eyed, straining out into the glare, and they soon spotted a group of armed insurgents who'd broken through the blockade. He asked his excellent interpreter, Abeba, to call down and warn them off, but the men took no notice and carried on tracking a path.

'You and I had better go down,' Harry said, 'intercept them and try to reason it out.' He felt a slick of fear; there was every chance the men would greet them with a hail of gunfire and turn tail and leg it.

'Sir, can I have a word? his Acholi sergeant said, looking anxious.

'Yes, Sergeant, what is it?'

'Sir, you must let me go in your place. I know these men and they're less likely to fire off without you there. I'm sure Abeba and I can settle this.'

'You're a good, brave man, Sergeant, but I couldn't possibly allow it.'

'You should let us go, Sir,' the interpreter argued, 'is better…'

They stood their ground and eventually giving in, Harry followed their path down the hillside, watching through field glasses with his muscles clenched. He saw them approach the seven heavily armed blockade-breakers whose guns were raised, and said a prayer. He saw the men's guns being slightly lowered as his two brave Acholi soldiers drew near. Saw Sergeant Otojok begin to talk earnestly, gesticulating, pointing up the hillside, probably persuading and reasoning with them rather than warning about what would happen if they persisted in breaking the blockade.

The men turned tail and began to retreat back to the border. Harry let out his breath and heaved a heartfelt sigh. He felt deeply indebted to Sergeant Otojok; there was a nobility about the Ugandan soldiers that was humbling. He held them in very high regard.

The platoon had a wearying rest of day, but back at camp and on his second stiff nightcap after a bearable meal of beef stew, life didn't seem so bad. The mess tent was hazy with smoke and there was a companionable rumble of convivial chat. Harry smoked his pipe and joined in amiably, feeling mellow.

Colonel Conway was coming over, probably with a few wearying extra chores or to complain about some slip-up or other, his face giving nothing away. He was a narrowly built man with a lean sculptured face, straight dark hair, domed forehead and a lively look in his eyes, however inscrutable his expression. He wasn't pompous, unlike others, had the sleeves of his khaki shirt rolled up as if about to do the washing-up, but his three pips were still hard to miss, gleaming in the fug of the ill-lit tent, and Harry sharpened up.

'I need a partner for bridge. You up for that, Werner?'

'Count me in, Sir,' Harry replied, mightily relieved.

Their opponents at the bridge table were two captains, Freddie and Cecil, both seasoned army regulars with fair moustaches; Freddie's large and luxuriant, Cecil's boyish and downy. Harry liked being clean-shaven, though getting hold of blades wasn't easy. Laura had just mailed him some more packs.

He and the Colonel lost the first game when Cecil successfully doubled the Colonel's rash bid of a slam. The captains won the next game, were on course to win the rubber, but Harry, not to be put off, bid five diamonds and made it. 'We're going to win this now!' Colonel Conway said confidently. He was a natural gambler, it seemed, despite looking more like a poet than a colonel on a desert mission, and when they won the rubber, and the next one, he was gleeful.

He bought Harry a drink, they found chairs, settled in, and taking sip of his Scotch and soda, the Colonel said casually, 'By the way, Werner, some news. I'm instructed by the powers that be to send you back to Uganda. Wild rubber is badly needed for the war effort and the head of the Forest Service in Uganda, chap called George Parker, has requested your release. He wants you back there to organise the rubber collection.' Colonel Conway eyed him. 'Sorry to be the bearer of bad tidings and all that. It's anyone's guess, though, when there's a convoy south, so expect you'll be with us a while yet.'

'Of course, Sir, understood,' Harry said, trying to keep the lid on his elation.

The Colonel rose. 'You're only on temporary release, remember, not demobbed yet... could be needed back here any time... Good game of cards,' he said, and went off grinning and laughing.

Harry soon turned in. He was fifteen shillings up on the night and went to his tent pinching himself. It wasn't only at cards that his luck could turn.

There was a mail next day, a letter for him from George Parker, saying he wanted Harry back in charge of the Budongo Forest as well, not just for rubber, and two letters from Laura. He couldn't wait to tell her his amazing news, suspecting she'd possibly be a little less thrilled than he was, given all the inevitable problems. There was the wait for his replacement and a convoy, the tricky decision of where she should have the baby. Nairobi? Kampala, with luck? They'd need help with Andy while she was confined, in whichever country, which had to be arranged as well.

There were the child-unfriendly hazards of the forest too. Laura took them far more seriously, while he, like a university student skipping lectures, clung to the principle that somehow one always got by.

Reading her letters in date order in the privacy of his tent, it was distressing to hear how bad things were in Nairobi. Still, she seemed in good spirits, filling him in on Andy's and Toppy's doings and talking movingly of Hamburg friends who had managed to get to Norway.

> ...Such heart-warming news, I was sure they'd have been put up against a wall long ago. ... The food situation here is dire. All the hawkers banned and I have to go to market to fight for such veg. as there is, just carrots and turnips and those only fit for mules. They upset Andy's insides too so I've put him on mashed potato and Marmite (for which, thank God!). Nairobi is making preparations in case the Japanese invade – have you heard anything of that?

Harry hadn't, but thought it very unlikely. Camp rumours about the battalion being sent out to Burma to fight the Japs there were far more believable. He thanked his lucky stars that a need of wild rubber was saving him from that particular fate. Turning to Laura's second letter, though, made him feel childishly cheated, momentarily deprived of the chance to tell her the news, but reading on, his heart soon swelled.

> *…I've just heard from Jane Parker that George has applied to have you return for rubber collecting! Please say it's for really real! Being back together again, I keep grinning in disbelief, so miracles do happen… And just think of all the contraceptives you could make in your new job!*
>
> *I'd resigned myself to a year or more in Nairobi, booked a place at the Byland again, and even found a cottage to rent with a bit more space for a second child. But if it's really to be Budongo then that's all out of the window. And this happening after my secret dread terror of you being sent out to Burma…*

Harry filled his pen and began to write, his emotions gushing out like a breached dam as he set about reminding her just how much it meant to him that she would happily live in the depths of the Budongo Forest if they could be together. *That* was the miracle, he said.

> *… I miss you most terribly in the evenings when I crawl into my lonely sleeping bag without you to hug. I miss you in so many ways: as my most darling wife and only mistress, my wonderful best friend and confidante…*

He couldn't end with a row of kisses with the new order just issued that was truly comic in its ridiculousness. "On no account will crosses denoting affection be allowed in private correspondence…" So that was that. But paper crosses were a poor substitute anyway, and he hadn't so long to wait now before having the real thing.

CHAPTER 36

Uganda

Harry was driving, bouncing the Chevvy along Uganda's dirt roads, and I was feeling every jolt and judder. The countryside was beautiful, undulating and peaceful, but rough terrain for anyone in the ninth month of pregnancy. I was bearing up, though, just, and the bittersweet memories of Kenya were softening like barren hills that looked lavender viewed from a greater distance.

I said, 'We were lucky at the border again, newlyweds last time, Andy's sunny smiles this time. He really won the hearts of those border police.'

'Anyway, you're finally fully legal, officially resident at last. And not long now till I can be carrying you over the threshold of our very own forest home.'

'Don't be daft, I'll hardly be a sylph. You can carry the Moses basket.'

The miles rolled on; would we even make the Kampala hotel by midnight? I didn't fancy giving birth in the dark on a lonely *murram* road. The memories of that terrifying drive to the Byland lived on.

I cradled my swollen belly, feeling in sympathy with Andy

who had cottoned on to saying *Wee, wee, Dada*, with monotonous regularity. I wanted one too. He had his favourite red fire engine but was squashed into a kind of padded chair that Harry had made out of a box, with the Chevvy's lack of a back seat, walled in between the piles of bulky luggage, Toppy's basket alongside, on top of a case, and they both needed a pit stop to pee.

'We're almost at Lake Victoria,' Harry said, 'where we stopped on the way out.'

'We were sprinkled with honeymoon glitter then and look at me now.'

'You look magnificent.'

'That's one way of putting it.'

Harry gave a quick glance as he swung off the road. 'No regrets?' He didn't wait for an answer.

'Don't get too close to the water,' I called, 'and keep hold of Andy's hand, and have an eye for Toppy.'

I found a bush to squat behind and hearing the whine and hum of insects, wished that I'd resprayed Andy. Thoughts of Harry's bouts of malaria brought shivers. Returning to the car, I leaned against the driver's door and gazed out over Lake Victoria feeling tired and nervous, sick with fear of the future.

The lake, in all its silvery beauty, was a calming sight. The sun was vanishing fast; a great, glorious fiery ball sinking below its watery horizon, bleeding its brilliance into a few light, low clouds, edging them with gold. The vast African sky was soon a glowing pink and apricot, the colours deepening to cardinal, crimson, plum and indigo as night descended fast. The African twilight was always short-lived.

'We saw tons of hippos,' Harry said, coming back with Andy on his shoulders. 'Curmudgeonly fellows, hippos, they'll have your backside off in a flash. There's a farmer here who once got too close to one and has a tin buttock now. It clanks like billy-o when he sits on a barstool!'

Even if I believed that, it was lost on a not quite two-year-old. Still, Andy giggled happily and made no objection to being settled back into the car. I gave him half a banana and we drove on in the dark. There were times when Harry seemed so boyish and uncomplicated and it was hard not to make comparisons, which he could probably sense and certainly mind and would only add to his bitterness.

He said, as the car hit a great rut in the road, 'I have such a sense of freedom, like a pardoned lifer must feel. No more reveilles and suffocating tents. I love Uganda and the foresting, and driving to Kampala brings back such happy memories. Waiting for you further down the lake, seeing you step off that flying boat with your golden smile; I was overcome, could have swooned like a girl!'

'You wouldn't, seeing me today, a great whale ready to pod.'

Harry reached out to touch my cheek. 'I do want you to love it here too. Sorry you have to be marking time in Kampala while I head north, but there's so much to do at the bungalow to be ready for the *memsahib*'s arrival. Finding a cook boy, making a cot-bed for Andy, seeing the place is all shining clean,' he gave a quick smile, 'and putting in fencing too. There's a steep drop on one side of the garden and if Andy goes chasing after any more birds, he could roll right down into the forest. Wasn't it sweet, the way he was so taken with that grey crowned crane?' Harry looked up into the driving mirror. 'Cheeky fellow that crane with his bright red bib, wasn't he, Andy?'

No sound. Andy was fast asleep, still clutching his stub-end of banana. He was slumped heavily sideways onto Toppy, but I couldn't, with my size, kneel up to settle him more comfortably and we had to stop again. It would be dawn before we were tucked up in our beds at the Imperial Hotel.

We were there not long after midnight. No punctures, no great dramas; we found our rooms and got in a few hours' sleep before Andy was up with the sun and bouncing on our bed, which we could have done without. Harry was off north that morning. He shopped for Tilley lamps, first aid kits, mosquito nets, and bought enough tins of Cow & Gate milk to feed the entire baby population of Uganda. He collected Toppy, gave me a goodbye kiss then was gone for a week.

The hotel was large and handsome with an arched porch and lawns where Andy could tumble, but the days were so long that it felt like time's mechanism was winding down. Even a frightful commotion at lunch one day, when Andy dropped a chip and a rat darted across the floor to swipe it, did little to break the monotony. The rat, or its cousin, visited our bedroom too and became a regular nocturnal visitor, eating the soap in the washbasin, since I'd made certain there wasn't a crumb of food to be had.

Harry returned, ranted to the staff about the rat, but he'd come to take Andy and the monthly nurse we'd just employed to the bungalow and was soon off again. The nurse, a South African called Miss Vorster, was a plain woman in her thirties who had seemed to know her stuff.

Alone, missing Andy, the first time we'd been apart, I felt even more desolate. No sign of a twinge or contraction. I was just stuck with my filthy rodent, waiting to give birth. Harry wrote, telling me to hurry up and produce Jamie/Louise so we could finally be together in our cosy forest home.

Remote, cosy forest home; I lived in terror of life in the Budongo. Compared with all the prowling wildlife, my ratty friend seemed very small beer.

I was sewing on the porch when a hotel boy came out for me. 'Mrs Barnes on telephone, Memsahib. You come?'

I heaved myself up wearily. Mary and Cedric Barnes had generously hosted the wedding reception, but however well-meaning, she was heavy duty, and talking to her took a slight effort of will. 'How are you, poor dear?' Mary asked, in tones weighted with solicitousness. 'I was wondering if you would care to come to stay for a few days. Cedric has had to go up country and it would be lovely company for us both.' There seemed no out, any excuse would sound churlish, and on the upside, they were unlikely to be overrun with rats.

'How very kind, if you're really sure it's no trouble?'

'Heavens, no! No trouble at all. It will be my pleasure, I assure you.'

*

Paying off the taxi outside the Barnes' squat brick bungalow with its tidy patch of garden, I tried my hardest to think positively. A boy came out for my case with Mary following. She said, 'My goodness, I was far bigger, having this one!' looking down fondly at her scowling pig-tailed four-year-old.

'Hard to imagine when you're so very slender!' Mary was rake thin, and colourless, conventional and dull… I felt guilty, had no business thinking in that superior way. She was being very good to me, kind and friendly. 'Come on in, let me show you to your room then we must have a nice morning cup of Bovril.'

Taken to a small back bedroom, I subsided onto the candlewick-covered bed, contemplating the politeness odds on asking for coffee or lemonade while Mary chattered. 'Betty and Rita are so looking forward to seeing you. We're delighted to have you back, and I've invited a few friends for tea, if that's all right.'

'Of course,' I said, feeling in ever-greater need of cold, fresh lemonade, 'lovely!'

Mary took me to the kitchen, boiled the water for Bovril and handed me a hot mugful. 'It must have been frightful, alone all that time in Nairobi,' she said, a bit slyly. 'But you had friends? Sympathetic company?'

Had rumours of Edmund even reached Kampala? 'Oh, sure, kind friends,' I replied, stoically sipping the Bovril, 'and I was lucky to rent a cottage from a major and his Nairobi-born wife. The Major was such a dear, kind man, looking after our dog while I was having Andy. His own dog had died and I bought him a spaniel puppy just before leaving.' Major Stafford had been moved almost to tears, which had more than made up for the expense and inevitable row with Harry.

'I made friends, doing a bit of war work too, serving meals to the interns and interpreting for refugees, as I speak German. I became close to one of them, a frightened young Jewish mother. We were good comfort for each other, and I also spent time teaching our houseboy the three Rs. He was quick to learn, which was satisfying, but inevitably soon found a better-paid job! Hard to blame him, and he still came to help me on his day off, even bringing me fresh eggs!'

'But you shouldn't be educating these boys, it can only lead to trouble. You really mustn't let them get above their station.' She did look shocked.

So many people thought like that – it was useless to argue the point – wouldn't change views, and I was a likely enough source of gossip already. Easy to imagine what Kampala's small prudish ex-pat community must be murmuring behind their hands. 'Shocking, isn't it? Laura Werner having a roaring affair in Nairobi while that poor Harry was away with the KAR. I mean, one can't help wondering about the father of this baby she's having…'

Inevitably, Plump Betty and Rita with her Pekinese nose were the first to arrive. They talked about untrustworthy servants, other wives, cocktail parties, the inflated price of sugar, with small children hanging onto their skirts. The effort of stifling yawns made my eyes water. A few paunchy husbands soon turned up, probably hoping that tea with its jam sandwiches and sponge would move seamlessly into gin and tonics. Which it did.

The days and purgatory of Mary's cooking eked by. She seemed to have less interest in food than the most absent-minded of professors. Her speciality was fish-paste sandwiches that smelled and tasted like the sole of an old boot. Cedric must be the most uncomplaining husband on the planet. I felt continually mean-spirited, but Uganda had no wartime shortages to speak of, and Cairo with its memories and sophisticated eateries was never far from my mind.

I escaped into town one morning to explore the famous old bookshop on Coleville Street. The packed shelves had a musty, evocative redolence and the coffee at the coffee shop in the building was good and strong. I had half an ear to the babble outside, the bartering and fights, tinsmiths' clatter and rattling carts; Kampala was lively and noisy, less filthy than Cairo and without Nairobi's ranks of army trucks, but its small ex-pat community wasn't the best…

Bob was in my thoughts. He shouldn't be. I'd stopped wearing his bracelet, hadn't hidden it, which would hurt Harry the more, but there must be a closing of the book now. The past had to be the past.

The baby was days late. I was expiring in the afternoon heat, though it was an excuse to rest in my room, frustrated and despairing, when the first contraction came. They came fast and furious then. I was staggering out into the hall, packed bag in hand, when Cedric walked in, returned from his travels.

'Good heavens above,' he said, taking in my white, sweating, pain-drenched face, 'best get you there right away!' I could barely get out my heartfelt thanks as he bundled me into the car and set off as fast as he could up one of Kampala's many hills to the main hospital.

He suddenly banged his head with a hand. 'Dear, dear, do believe I quite forgot to kiss Mary hello, in all the excitement. I hope she will understand…'

He drew up outside the hospital's main door, helped me out in great haste before rushing off home to make his peace with his wife. He was a good man.

Three hours later, James Timothy Werner arrived with flailing limbs and healthy cries and showed his tiny screwed-up face to the world.

CHAPTER 37

First Sight,
the Budongo Forest

The hospital was a long two-storey building, efficiently run, with a splendid view over the spreading city, but after ten days of confinement I was pacing the floor when Harry arrived to take us home.

I held out Jamie, loosely swaddled in a fluffy lavender shawl with his wrinkled little face peeping out. His father took him in his arms and the look on Harry's face said it all. 'No more wanting a daughter?' I smiled.

'I'll settle for this little fellow.' If he shared any fears about taking a newborn child to live in the depths of a jungle, there was no hint of a cloud showing.

Harry said, 'I've been shopping already. Bought a new battery wireless, gardening books and – wait for it – an actual fridge! And three pairs of curtains, which should be fine with the cream walls. The place is really beginning to come together.' Had there been no curtains before? My chest tightened.

We were soon on the road. Harry was driving with a slack hold on the wheel, leaning back and looking a bit shattered. 'You must have left before dawn. Shall I take over?'

'No, I'm fine, just gloriously unwound, out of the army and taking you home.' Home. My thoughts flew to the family, Scotland, grey skies, chill days, violent squalls. I had a sudden crippling urge to feel icy winds spiking my face, see a blanket of snow out of the window, the countryside silent and still. I'd been scared of the heat in India, imagining, in my small-child way, giants with hands like palm trees lifting me up into the burning sky. It was cooler in Uganda's northern forests…

'How do we get mail?' I asked. 'I feel so starved of letters from home.'

'We have a PO box in Masindi and either the Janssens or I make regular trips to pick up the mail. I cabled your parents about Jamie's arrival on the very day, so you should hear soon. Anke and Luuk Janssen are absolute bricks, by the way. They have two young daughters and live only a mile or so away. Anke keeps a cow – how she manages it in a tsetse fly area – and she's promised to let us have fresh milk.' Was Harry sounding a little on the defensive? 'George was up last week,' Harry said, 'and he wants me to supervise the rubber collecting as well as all my forest work in the Budongo. Seems like I'm going to be kept pretty busy…'

'Will I ever see you, my dear!'

I grinned, but Harry rightly sensed the implied loneliness. 'There's a Land Rover I use for work, you'll have the car, won't be trapped.' He glanced, as if to gauge my reaction, then said, 'I, um, think Jamie's beginning to stir…'

'Yes, we'd better stop for a feed.' As he was lifted out, Jamie searched the air for a nipple, his little mouth motioning sucking. I felt a great whoosh of emotional adoration, settling down by the deserted roadside and unbuttoning my blouse.

'Shouldn't you be doing that in the car?' Harry said, peering round as if half expecting to see a horde of his ex-pat friends looking on with horrified faces.

'It's hardly Trafalgar Square out here. Mary Barnes wouldn't approve, but I won't tell if you don't... Think local, the women here have it made, bare-breasted with just a colourful *kanga* slung round their hips.' Harry grunted, unsure quite how to react. The women looked so graceful with the baskets on their heads, slight hips swinging and a litter of near-naked children running around.

The villages we passed were just a collection of huts, goats, dogs and banana trees, but would our living conditions be so very different where we were going? Rain collected our only water in tanks, no electricity and the loo, the choo, as Harry called it, a nice fly-ridden cupboard-like hut over a hole in the ground.

Settling Jamie back in his Moses basket, I straightened up to find myself in Harry's arms. He kissed my mouth, pressing hard into me with lusting eyes, making his need of my still misshapen body abundantly clear.

'Can't properly yet,' I said, 'I'm a bit torn, only had the stitches out yesterday.'

'My poor, beautiful darling.' He brushed lightly over my lips with two fingers, slipping them into my mouth, feeling the wet of my lower lip and rolling it down.

'There's always improperly...'

He put his cheek to mine and I could feel his smile.

We drove on, the car eating up mile after mile with Harry telling of all Andy's doings, potty hits and misses, filling his toy wheelbarrow with off-cuts to try to erect his own fence, the trouble Harry had had trying to get him to eat his steamed pudding. Whatever had the monthly nurse found to do?

'How have you got on with Miss Vorster? Has she been much of a help?'

'Yes, and company of an evening. Andy's been fine with her,

no clinging when I've left for work, and she's been supervising the cooking. She thinks the cook boy's a dead loss, by the way. We may have to get a new one. She's reorganised the rooms too. The dining room is now Andy's bedroom and I get my office back when she's gone.'

'She sounds a bloody marvel. Are we nearly there?'

'Minutes away. It's forty steps up to the house. Shall I give you a push?'

'You'll do no such thing. A few steps are the least of my worries.'

'I know it's dark, but look to the right at the top just to get an idea of the garden. It's late summer, but there's always plenty of colour. The bungalow's brick and white painted now. I was taken aback, seeing it again after four years; no more the wooden thatched hut that I'd loved, but it's more solid and baby-friendly.'

The steps were unnervingly steep in the unlit dark. Harry was carrying the Moses basket and I was shining the torch for him, terrified in case he slipped. The darkness was alive; scuttles and rustles, large unseen insects buzzing round our ears and the usual cricket crescendo. Lizards with purple and orange heads darted in the torchlight. I could feel the shape of the place but see nothing of the garden, and where the forest must be there was only blackness.

Reaching the fortieth step, more exhausted than I'd let on, the house loomed. There was barking, light from an opening door, and Toppy flying out with his frenzied welcome.

Two boys flitted past and down the steps to unload the car. Miss Vorster appeared, stifling a yawn. 'Welcome back! There's cold meat, bread and fruit if you're hungry, but forgive me if I slip off to bed.'

'Of course,' Harry smiled. 'You shouldn't have stayed up, really no need.'

He took me into the marital bedroom, lit only by a dim Tilley lamp, but I was past taking anything in and had to feed Jamie.

Finding a chair and lifting him to the breast, holding him close, I tried to have brave thoughts about the forest.

After the long drive, the feeds, a bed that dipped in the middle, sleep was in short supply – and just when my eyes were drooping it was time for another feed. The stone floor was icy, the torch flickering. Harry didn't stir through the feed, but he'd had two extremely long drives. It was still dark and I used the pot, couldn't face the choo again with the teaming insects, fireflies and a chorus of ghostly grating howls that Harry dismissed as "just hyraxes being sociable".

I slept a bit then with a faint light of dawn showing through the unlined curtains, was glad to get up and dress. Khaki shirt and trousers, cotton socks, stout shoes; would I ever wear anything else?

When I crept quietly out into the living room, a boy in a singlet and loincloth appeared with a tray of tea; large yellow metal teapot, tin mugs, digestive biscuits and a punched-hole tin of evaporated milk. He set down the tray on a table and darted off before I could ask his name.

The strong tea was reviving and I went out to the veranda, cradling my mug with both hands. The sight of the forest, such an eerie menacing blackness, arriving late last night, now completely took my breath away. The rising sun, still hidden below the vastness of the forest, cast a pink glow that looked almost ethereal, like a dawn halo over the forest canopy. The myriad treetops were the deepest darkest juniper in the half-dawn light, stretching on infinitely, as far as the eye could see.

The sun rose quickly and the forest coloured fast. Trees became as green as a budgerigar's breast, leaves of lime and emerald, glints of citrus bouncing off the deep mahogany bark; it was mesmerising to see. But what swarming wildlife was out there? What petrifying silences? What terrorising animal screams?

Harry came beside me and rested his arm on my shoulders. 'All this and glorious birdsong too. Blue-breasted kingfishers, Rufus-red broadbills, kestrels. There's a long-tailed cuckoo that has a tuneful descending whistle and if it gets a response makes a constant three-note call. Vultures circle this hill, but it's worth the climb through the scratchy elephant grass to the top. The view's fantastic. You can see right over to Lake Albert and the Congolese mountains.'

He hugged me, I was shivering in the early-morning cold, and we went indoors. Andy was awake, we could hear his chatter, and I hurried to his room, hungry for a connecting hug after our first-ever separation.

Miss Vorster was getting him dressed. 'Thanks, sorry, I was out on the veranda,' I said, forcing a smile, frantic to be alone with Andy.

'It's what I'm here for,' the woman said with a friendly smile, making me feel a bit small. 'He's a bright little button, this one, can almost get dressed by his little self.' She did up Andy's last cardigan button and I had my hug before he was zooming about with his arms out like a plane, racing off to find his father.

I went to explore, following the irresistible smell of bacon coming from the kitchen hut. The door was swinging open on its hinges and I imagined beetles and rats running in. It was a big kitchen with a deep mottled butler's sink, chipped wooden draining board and a row of very antiquated saucepans dangling from a wormy-looking shelf. A stink of paraffin was hard to miss and a few indeterminate smells too, but the aroma of cooking bacon was making me extremely aware of how hungry I was.

The skinny boy who'd brought over the tea was sawing doorstep slices from a large white loaf. '*Jambo!*' I said, '*Habari gani? Jina Lako Nani?*'

'*Nze* Samson, *Nyabo*,' he muttered, understanding my Swahili, but saying his name in Luganda.

Nyabo was Madam, and the kid, looking down at his dusty bare feet, was nervous and ill at ease. 'Let me help with the breakfast,' I said in Swahili, smiling and taking over the bread knife. Samson toasted the slimmer slices I cut on the hot plate of an ancient Dover range where the bacon was sizzling in a heavy pan; he was young and scared, ragged in his dirty singlet, but I felt we'd get along.

'Here you are!' Harry said, coming in frowning. He spoke tersely to the boy in Luganda then turned to me. 'You should leave everything to him. You know that.'

'And you should go a bit easy,' I said, irritated. 'Samson just needs a bit of guidance. Why don't you take that tray with the plates and I'll be over soon?'

'You're too bloody soft,' Harry muttered. 'The boy will bring the trays.'

I stayed a few moments, watching Samson beat eggs and scramble them. I slipped in a pinch of salt and a few screws of pepper, which he absorbed, stopped him adding any evaporated milk, smiled a lot and left him.

Andy chattered while the adults concentrated on breakfast. 'Good eggs,' Harry said neutrally. I sipped the strong, hot reviving coffee then helped Andy down.

'Come to see your new baby brother, but tiptoeing in! He's still sleeping.'

Andy peered into the Moses basket studying the little swaddled mound then looked up at me. 'Not in tummy, Mummy. When can play?'

'He has to be walking first. You'll have to help teach him to crawl and walk.'

Andy stared, nodded sagely and pottered out of the room. I followed but left him on the veranda with Harry and Miss Vorster. It was time for a feed.

Miss Vorster was knitting, minding the baby, and Andy

having his nap. Harry took me to see his roses and a new vegetable patch; runner beans, lettuces, potatoes and more. 'You're not just a handsome birdman,' I grinned, and seeing a wooden plank bench under a jacaranda tree led him over to it. 'I want to have it out about Samson. Give it some time, he just needs a little encouragement.'

Harry, who'd looked impatient, wanting to get on, not sit on a bench, put up his hands. 'All right, you win, but that boy had better shape up.'

*

We settled into a routine. Harry was back at work, Miss Vorster proving her worth. Having the extra pair of hands gave me time to play with Andy, also take him regularly to his zinnias, his absolute favourite flowers, to see if any buds were out. Jamie was feeding well, putting on weight. It seemed no time at all before the month was up and Miss Vorster due to go back to Kampala.

Harry was driving her there and staying the night with his boss, George, which left me to face a night alone in the forest with Andy and a baby at the breast.

He and Miss Vorster left at dawn. I was up to see them off, just finished a feed and Andy woke soon afterwards. He was fractious with the disruption to his routine, whinging and difficult, hard as I tried to entertain him. He fell down in the garden and screamed his head off while I rushed him to the bungalow, trying to remember where the first aid kit was kept. Samson eventually found it.

We managed after that with Andy more his old self. I sprayed him obsessively with repellent, sprayed Jamie nervously too, and tried to communicate with Samson when he brought our lunch.

By the end of the day, having read to Andy till his eyelids, and mine, were closing, Jamie was in need of another feed. I was too exhausted to read or sew and anyway there was too little light from the Tilley lamp. I stayed out on the veranda. The crickets' racket was like a constant clack of knitting needles, insects whined round my head, but it was the howls and blackness beyond the garden that really spooked me.

The forest, shimmering and beautiful by day, seemed to have open jaws at night. I kept a broom close by in case a snake slithered onto the veranda, but what if a leopard caught my scent and came prowling? What about drunken local tribesmen? Would Samson come running if I called in distress? I was alone with no means of contact; Harry had the car.

Who was I to feel sorry for myself? There was a war on. Were we winning it? Losing it? A silly sob rose up from deep within my chest and when the sobs threatened to grow as loud as the howls in the forest, I crept off to bed to cry quietly into my pillow.

CHAPTER 38

Budongo 1944

The nearest town, Masindi, was an hour's run, but there was a good earth road, and driving fast, impatient to be there, I was hoping for any letters. Nowadays, a bus came with the mail and the local newspaper on Mondays and Wednesdays, but it was Friday and there'd been nothing in the week. We were low on stocks – meat, dripping, sugar, flour – and I grabbed the excuse to go. Letters were a lifeline to the outside world. Harry was home doing paperwork, meteorological stuff and plot data, but was pottering about in the garden, the work finished, so apart from a few ill-humoured scowls, hadn't really been able to complain.

Speeding along with a sweet sense of release, I slowed down, passing the Polish settlement on the edge of Masindi, curious to see a little girl squatting in the roadside dirt, staring in fascination at a pair of dead snakes, with others looking on. The huge snakes were entwined together like lovers, a deadly cobra and rock python, which was non-venomous but certainly didn't look it.

There were many Poles in the area, sent to the depths of Siberia, eventually released and left to travel where they could. The

Ugandan authorities had helped any who arrived in the country, clearing patches of jungle and erecting huts. Those snakes, though, and that blonde child with her big pink bow, were an unnerving reminder of the daily dangers of living in the bush. Not that I needed any reminders after the past year and a half.

Driving on into Masindi, I thought of Harry's longing for more children, how he'd have loved a pretty little daughter like that adorable child. If only he would try to understand, I couldn't face having another baby, not living where we were. We were both at fault. I'd been naive and unrealistic and we'd never really talked things through. I'd married into the Catholic Church, accepted the loneliness of the forest, even living without music, which was like losing my hearing, known what I was coming to, as Harry constantly reminded me, but his need for more children was the elephant in the room, and the tension getting to us both.

I parked in Masindi's main street and went to the post office first. There was mail, to my delight: a chunky letter from Dad – he'd probably sent photos – and a communication from the Governor's residence in Entebbe addressed to Lieutenant and Mrs Werner.

I did the shopping, bartering and buying in bulk then decided, a bit guiltily, to read the letters over a civilised drink at the Masindi, Uganda's oldest hotel. The town, which had been more of an outpost when Harry first arrived, had grown fast and was thriving. It had Polish policewomen, Poles teaching in the local school, still few shops, mainly shacks with corrugated tin roofs and Indian-run. Ugandans weren't shopkeepers but nor were they acquisitive or thieving. Our doors had no locks and Harry had never once felt threatened, weighted down by money bags on paydays.

The hotel was long and low, rather along the lines of the Mountains of the Moon Hotel, and sheltered by swaying eucalyptus trees. I'd worn an apricot halter-neck dress, needing a change from khaki trousers, and went into the hotel feeling suitably dressed and with a rare sense of independence.

The fans were turning slowly on the veranda, with the heavenly scent of frangipani trees banishing the slight muskiness of outdoor bamboo furniture. There were Europeans, sawmill and sugar-factory owners, tobacco barons, women in pretty hats at the rickety hexagonal tables, smoking and drinking gin slings. I sat down at a table, ordered a glass of fresh lemonade and saving up Dad's letter, opened the official-looking communication from the Governor.

It was an invitation to a garden party held in honour of the King's birthday on 14th December, taking place two days later on the Saturday. Harry would enjoy being asked. It would be a lovely break and chance to shop in Entebbe but meant an overnight stay in town.

The Janssens, Luuk and Anke, would have the boys, I felt sure. They were good, kind neighbours and I'd looked after Heidi, their twelve-year-old, when the younger daughter, Anne, had to be rushed to hospital with appendicitis.

Luuk was a saw-miller and Anke, who was in her thirties, now a good friend. She had been brought up on a farm and said her mother, who'd wanted a more sophisticated life for her, had dressed her up in sugar-pink frilly frocks when all Anke wanted to do was milk cows. She wore loose check shirts over her large bosom and had taught me plenty about survival in the forest. We'd had some good laughs, but she wasn't Dolly, who I missed so much.

I opened Dad's bulky package, which included photographs and a forwarded letter with an American stamp. Dolly's handwriting, and just when she'd been in my thoughts. Dad's letter was like soft spring water to parched lips, it was contact, closeness and connection. I could almost smell the pipe smoke on his tweedy old jacket, it lifted right off the page, and the yearning to be burying my face in that jacket was overwhelming.

The family photographs too brought smiles and wet eyes. Lil was married now and had just had a baby, "*a bonny wee thing called Angela*", Dad said helpfully, since I couldn't have told the sex or its bonniness from the wizened little creature in the photo. Mum was fine and would be writing, and the garden was quite a little jungle now, if hardly on the scale of the Budongo.

There was a photo of Jack in army uniform. I prayed he and Dick would be safe. Most of Dad's war news was out of date. I knew Paris had been liberated, that the Germans had surrendered many towns in Southern France and that Belgium was partly liberated too. I hadn't heard of the failed bomb plot against Hitler, though, with the bodies of the plotters hung up on meat hooks in public view. Field Marshall Rommel, who'd been one of them, had committed suicide to save his hero status, Dad said.

If only those good, brave Germans had succeeded… I touched lips to the letter and risking Harry's wrath, quickly opened Dolly's, late as it was.

Dolly's large, round handwriting brought her very close, but her brave update about Pete made sad reading.

> …*It's been bloody months since Pete's last letter, which was anyway like a wound-down clock. Saying he was war-worn! Some excuse! He prattled on about the victory parade in Tripoli with your Mr Churchill there. You'd have thought bloody Pete had taken the city single-handed. No lovey-stuff, just about battles, Sicily, Salerno, Naples, nothing about poor old me! I reckon the bugger has fallen for some hot little Iti number, all tits and pasta-curves, and hasn't the guts to admit it. He said the Hussars may be going to France next, which sounds dodgy, but what do I care…?*

Quite a lot. Poor Dolly.

…Anyway, I've picked myself up, no need to feel too sorry for me, I met the most amazing hunk on leave from his submarine and there's no stopping him. He can't have seen a girl for months, but I guess you don't, down there under the sea. I still pine for that so-and-so, Pete, had such dreams of cosying up with him and honeymooning in ye olde English thatched cottage covered in roses, and being able to see you again.

What news? I worry about you. You're mis, I can tell, stuck out there with the roaring lions and great big temperamental chimps. You have your two wonderful babes, but only I know what (who) you gave up and all you've been through…

I slipped the letter into my bag, but Harry wasn't averse to a casual rummage and it was so revealing and quintessentially Dolly, would need a safer home.

I was so late back, climbing the steps in the pitch black of night with my bare legs being bitten to bits and hearing shrieks and wails. Harry was going to be livid.

'What's all this racket then?' I called, racing in. Jamie was scarlet in the face, rattling the bars of his cot, tears streaming, Andy looking injured and defiant.

'Daddy said Jamie could have it in his cot, but it's my engine, mine!'

'And who hit his little brother and kept splashing him in the tub?' Harry was just as red in the face, yelling at Andy as he ran to me for a clingy hug.

'I fell down, Mummy, look! And we couldn't find Toppy for *ages…*'

'That's a very big plaster and I'm sure you were a very brave boy, but it's way past your sleep time, too late for stories, and no toys in bed either!'

'Sorry, darling,' I said, explaining about the drink with the sweetener of the garden-party invitation.

'You could have read the letters here. Leaving me in sole charge all this time…'

I resisted the temptation to say *just like you leave me all week*, and even felt a bit ashamed. Harry hadn't heard from his parents since 1939, no letters from them with photos and enclosures, not a word from Austria. He must feel desperately worried, not knowing how they were surviving under German rule.

Still, he needn't have worked himself up like a child. It took two stiff whiskies and a calming hour on the veranda before Harry could be halfway civil.

'Let's see this letter from the Governor then.' Looking up from it, pleased, he said, 'George will have been asked so I'm actually rather chuffed to be invited as well. Dundas is supposed to be a stickler for protocol, unlike old Mitchell, who had me over for drinks, remember, when he was staying near Lake Albert.'

'Remind me,' I said, making Harry scowl impatiently.

'I was newly-arrived, wet round the ears, and since the Governor's ADC had brought over the invitation himself and was so immaculately dressed it had felt best to wear a dinner jacket. Only to find old Mitchell in cords after a day's fishing.'

I smiled, it was a sweetly Harry story, and said, 'Sir Charles Dundas looks very impressive in the newspapers, in that plumed hat of his and all the finery.' He was a Scot and it was easier to picture him striding over the moors in kilt and sporran than hosting formal occasions in the tropics.

Samson, who was still with us – I'd won that battle – dished up supper: soup, cold meat and plum duff. Africans were good at the stodgy traditional puddings that Harry loved and he was in a much better mood afterwards, sipping whisky out on the veranda. 'Those bloody baboons have had all the pawpaws off that tree down the bottom, and when they were just coming ripe! I fired my rifle into the air, which I think was what made Toppy hide. He'd be a useless gundog.'

We heard a loud rumbling roar. Was it a lion? Coming from the forest? Toppy was growling, trembling from nose to tail. Were the boys safe in their beds?

'Hear that, darling? Sounds very close…'

'Do stop! You know it won't come up here.'

Harry's gun was beside him, a broom for stunning the puff adders that were a constant threat. I fondled Toppy's ears and said nothing.

*

On the day of the garden party, we left Andy and Jamie with the Janssens. Their house was built like a log cabin, which the boys loved, and Heidi and Anne were waiting excitedly by the gate, thrilled to be mothers to the boys. 'Come see the cow being milked, Jamie,' Heidi said, and he tottered off, clutching her hand, with Andy and Anne following. Neither boy gave their parents a backward glance.

The invitation was for four o'clock in view of the heat, which gave time to have my hair cut and shop for a new frock. I bought a silver-grey dress, sleeveless with a pearl-buttoned pleated bodice. A formal silk dress and jacket would have looked more the part, but with Entebbe like a cauldron, something sleeveless was cooler and easier to wear. With a wide-brimmed white hat, strappy high heels and the nylons Mum had once sent out to Kenya, it should just get by.

Harry was waiting by the car and kissed me on the lips. 'You've never looked more glamorous,' he said, as I righted my hat.

'Well, I am out from under! It's gone four, hadn't we better be going?'

The Union Flags were out in force, a pink-striped marquee sheltering dainty white-cloth tables with posies of flowers, staff standing by. The Governor's ADC, greeting all the arrivals, directed us to a long veranda where people were waiting to shake hands with the Governor and Lady Dundas.

We crossed the sloping lawns and queued. The Governor was perspiring, looking as if he couldn't wait for the last guest to be gone. He was in full uniform, a huge fine figure of a man with a good head of dark hair, parted and slicked down, a large intelligent face and a lot of chin. Lady Dundas, who was smiling, a little fixedly, had a slightly prominent nose, but her face was warm and open and she must be a great asset to him in his job.

'I hear you were married out here,' the Governor said. 'Fine thing, fine thing.' He smiled at me. 'Trouble making it out in wartime too, I don't doubt. You were coming from home? England?'

'Well, Edinburgh actually,' I said, anxious to avoid going into Cairo detail.

'Ah, a bonny Scotch lass, I should have guessed. We Scots get about.'

An extremely large woman, whose hat was a whole flower stall of blooms, its brim nodding under the weight, almost physically elbowed us out of the way. 'Ah, Lady Farmington,' said the Governor, taking her gloved hand.

'Your Excellency, what a simply splendid occasion this is, I do declare…'

Her cerise lipstick was bleeding into her upper lip lines, little beads of sweat visible on her brow. Other guests were lining up and when she started to talk at length about the King's birthday, the Governor took a hand. 'Now, my dear Lady Farmington, I'm sure there are a great many people here you're anxious to see…' It was hardly diplomatic and he chose not to notice his wife's sidelong glance.

Harry and I strolled about with sticky glasses of a warm, sweet fruit drink in hand. We spoke to Cedric and Mary Barnes and a friendly district commissioner whose wife was clearly feeling the heat, reeking of damp talcum powder.

The ADC came to chat. 'How about a cuppa while there are free tables in the tent?' He was stocky with fairish hair. He looked very sporty and fit and but for his impeccable British accent, could have been one of the many Antipodeans I'd met in Cairo.

He led us to the tent, pulled out a chair for me and summoned a waiter. 'I believe you knew a friend of mine in Nairobi, Mrs Werner, Colonel Grant?'

'Yes, we met when I was serving meals to the interns and he suggested I did some interpreting for the refugees.'

'He was here the other day and mentioned that. I think the Governor and Lady Dundas were most impressed.'

Harry picked that up and minded my having a hand in the invitation, I could see. He rose from the table, giving a stiff smile. 'Forgive me, but I've just seen my boss, George Parker, and his wife and should really go over to say hello.'

The tea was arriving and it felt only polite to stay a while. I smiled at the ADC, feeling a bit embarrassed, and said, 'You mustn't feel I need looking after, you'll have so many people to see.'

'Oh, please don't send me away! I've done my bit and these things run on oiled wheels. The staff enjoy them. They love to be on hand and dress up.'

'They do look very smart.' They were in crisply starched white tunics and red fezzes. Over tea, we talked about Tanganyika, somewhere the ADC knew and loved. 'Thanks,' I said. 'It's been such fun being reminded of our stay there and I've much enjoyed our chat, but had really better go to say hello to the Parkers too now. Do please remember me to Colonel Grant if you see him again.'

'Of course, he'll be pleased to hear word of you. Now, let me take you over. There are one or two here from Nairobi, actually, people you may possibly know, like Sir Edmund Southan over there, who's talking to the lady in the veiled hat. He's here on business, buying sugar and tobacco, beating down our poor farmers! We could say hello on the way if you'd like.'

I'd caught sight of Edmund just the split second before and my throat had closed over with the shock. I felt quite faint and had to grip the table to steady myself as the full implications sank in. Edmund didn't miss much, he'd have seen me but would bide his time like a fox with a lamb before making his move; no doubt in my mind that he'd make one. I could well imagine how much it would amuse Edmund to humiliate me in front of Harry.

'Are you all right, Mrs Werner? You've gone very pale. I expect it's this wretched humidity. Let me get you some water or would you like to lie down?'

'Oh, no, you're very kind, it's nothing really. I'll be fine.' I stared at the charming man, unable to smile. So much in need of his help, he was my only hope. 'I have met Sir Edmund but would particularly like to avoid him if possible. I do hope you understand.' How could he, though? How could anybody?

The ADC stared thoughtfully before giving a slight but reassuringly kind smile. 'I'll see what I can do. I'm quite good at steering people away!'

'I can't thank you enough, sorry to be so embarrassing, it's just that, well, it's a difficult situation.' Could anything be more revealing of culpability? I rose, a little unsteadily, murmuring renewed thanks, grateful to the wonderful ADC for escorting me over the lawns, more grateful than he could ever know.

The ADC stayed a moment chatting, with cultured charm, before taking his leave. 'Forgive me, duty calls. I've got a mission to fulfil.'

Harry's mood seemed amazingly transformed. 'Guess what? Fantastic news! George says we need a break and he's giving me some very generous leave.'

'You might think about South Africa,' said Jane. 'I know some good places to stay.'

'This is all so terrific of you.' I smiled warmly from one to the other. 'A family holiday, it's just what the doctor ordered! How can we ever thank you?'

I was being too effusive and relieved. Harry would feel resentful; he knew how desperate I was to escape the forest. And I couldn't help but keep looking around...

The strain was too much; I couldn't stand it. 'Would you forgive us if we made a move? We had a very early start and I'm feeling just a little shattered.'

Jane looked concerned, 'You are very pale, I expect it's the heat after Budongo.'

'It's time we went too,' George said, 'and no need to say our adieus, we can just slip quietly away.'

We were almost out of the gates when Edmund caught up with us.

'My dear Laura, what an *absolute* delight! The Governor's ADC was being most attentive, but seeing you were on your way, I just had to race over to say hi and bye. Now, you must introduce me to this famous husband of yours and these charming people.' He beamed, mainly at Harry, but including the Parkers in his arc with sophisticated ease. 'Laura was the most *adorable* of companions in Nairobi, Lieutenant Werner. I have a little-used piano at home, which she played completely exquisitely. She had me enraptured, completely spellbound.'

'And your guests too, I hope,' I laughed, but it was a tinny, hollow sound to my ears, resonant with terror and loathing.

'Indeed, and my guests,' Edmund said, adding with a lip-curling smile, 'on that occasion...' Could there ever be a more ruthlessly cunning implication of intimacy? At a single calculated stroke, he'd given Harry's jealousy raw red meat to feed on. I saw the shock and suspicious fury register on his face, saw him taking in Edmund's smooth good looks, the immaculate cut of his jacket, gold cufflinks, the foppish, floppy fair hair...

We got away. Perhaps the Parkers in their innocence wouldn't have read too much into it, but Edmund had managed to do irrevocable damage to a struggling marriage and ruin my life – all in a matter of minutes and purely for his own entertainment. It was evil beyond comprehension. He'd even managed – small consolation that he hadn't known it – to deny us the happy anticipation of an unexpected and much-needed holiday.

Harry drove to the Parkers' house, where we were staying, in complete silence. I stared out of the window. Would he ever get over his bitter suspicions that had just been increased 10,000-fold? We'd been living under such stress. What possible chance of recovery did our relationship have now, scored with still deeper cuts?

I felt weak, shivery, helpless and degraded, unable ever to breathe a word of the truth, say what had actually happened. Edmund could never be beaten; he'd won from the start and knew it. But a marriage could become frayed like a well-worn shirt and still not be quite ready for dusters. Could ours survive? We had to try, turn the collars, work at it, just do what we possibly could to find a way; there was nothing else to be done.

CHAPTER 39

Harry

Harry threw the Land Rover into reverse and parked under the covered stand at the bottom of the steps. At least Laura had remembered to move out the Chevvy. He climbed up the forty steps with a heavy tread. He needed a drink. Four weeks already. It had been the purest hell, getting through Christmas with all the forced jollities, and would he ever feel truly able to trust her again?

There was no way of knowing what had really happened. Laura clearly detested the man now, but there must have been intimacy at some stage. That snake Edmund had been keen enough to intimate that when he'd come chasing over with his fake, cold smiles. Laura had been looking so white and shaken…

Harry heaved a great sigh, crossing the garden. Perhaps the holiday in South Africa would help; he had to try to get over the whole thing somehow.

It was their last night in the Budongo Forest, which was a terrible wrench. George was relocating him to Gulu in the Acholi district right after the holiday. It was much more humid and tropical, a steamy heat that would sap them of energy and shore up their nerves. He was dreading it. Everything was packed, the whisky bottle drained, but there were still a few beers and he needed one badly.

He downed a beer and went to find Laura and say good night to the boys. She was putting two overexcited kids to bed. He read to them as usual, kissed them, and pulling the door closed, looked at Laura. 'Last drink on the veranda?'

She smiled and they went outside.

It was a still, scented, balmy night. The sounds of the night chorus seemed amplified, the vastness of the Budongo too. The forest had opened its arms to him. He had nurtured, planted, measured and tracked it, seen off the wily old witch doctor who spooked the field workers with his crazy spells. The Banyoro people had come to him with their malarial ills, and he and Laura had doled out vast quantities of quinine, Epsom salts for the malingerers, and driven the more seriously ill to Masindi. Were they really leaving? It broke his heart.

He said, 'Hear the francolin making its sawing noise and the bulbuls' chirping? And if I make a call like a nightjar, bet you one will answer.'

'Go on then.' Harry made a mimicking, churring call, relieved when a nightjar returned the calls, loud and clear. 'Okay, birdman, you win,' Laura said wryly.

She looked exquisite. Her skin had the glow of a perfect pearl, and there wasn't a woman in the tropics whose skin wasn't wrinkled and brown as a walnut. 'It's just the Tilley light,' she muttered when he said as much. He felt blameless, but guilty at how sad she looked and wanting her; it had been quite a while.

They would have neighbours in Gulu. There were seven British officials, including the District Commissioner, a doctor and nurse, but seven was still very few. One of the officials had his wife there, but the others didn't or were single and he'd be travelling a lot, leaving Laura on her own.

The holiday came first. George had given him a travel allowance and they were driving to Kampala, housing the car at a garage and boarding a BOAC flying boat to South Africa. Harry had never flown before and felt secretly scared.

'Funny to think the boys have never seen the sea,' he said, 'wonder what they'll make of it.' He eased his back; his muscles felt like knotted rope after a long, exhausting and emotional last day. They were leaving Toppy behind with Samson and the *shamba*, paying them extra for Toppy's keep, until Harry returned for him and to oversee the handover. He hoped his replacement would keep the boys on, Samson especially.

He reached for another beer. He wanted Laura, but it would be giving in and he was struggling.

'I'm on edge about Gulu,' he said. 'I'll so miss the solitude and my work here, you can almost smell the trees grow and mature. I'll have to get used to the Acholi too. They're very different from Banyoro in race, temperament, language. The Acholi are closer to the tribes of South Sudan. They make good soldiers. I was once with a recruitment officer in an area close to the Belgian Congo, and the Acholi there were naked and half-starved. They signed up with a thumbprint but did fine when trained.'

Laura looked out at the canopy of blackness. 'You must be so proud of all you've achieved and done for posterity here. I've been scared at times, worried for the boys, but I'll have happy memories too. The young leopard that crossed my path and didn't eat me, the termite hills, the choo… The pink dawns.' She smiled. 'It's bedtime. We've got the holiday and Gulu to come, but the Budongo Forest will always live on in our hearts.'

They made love in silence. Harry drove rhythmically into her body, feeling emotionally passionate and possessive. It was the release he craved and he clung to her afterwards, unable to pour out the battered love he was feeling, still mistrustful but knowing how much he still cared.

*

'There's the flying boat,' Laura pointed. 'I came here in one just like that years ago, it was so exciting. I know you and Daddy will love the ride.' Harry stiffened. The machine was the size of a blue whale and they were about to climb into its great belly; he couldn't believe it could skim the water and take off like a bird.

He fastened the seat belt and had to sit on his hands to stop the shaking, but lifting off – the speed, the people far below looking like tiny insects, Kampala a scattering of dolls' houses – it was petrifying, electrifying. Soaring higher, all the fishing boats on Lake Victoria were near invisible, tiny dots on the water's glistening sheen. He felt euphoric.

Nearing Mount Kenya, the view of the mountaintop against a clear blue sky was unsurpassable. Surely the plane would scrape on the jagged peaks. But they soared on and soon were flying over the majestic snow-capped Kilimanjaro. They were higher than the highest mountain in Africa, on top of the world.

'No more nerves?' Laura whispered.

'I know how it feels to be an eagle now.'

They touched down at Dar es Salaam then on to Lourenço Marques and Durban, where they were leaving the plane and staying overnight. The hotel had a dining room for whites and another for all the children along with their minders, all of whom, apart from Harry and Laura, were coloured or black nannies. The rigid segregation was disturbing but nothing new.

They went on by train to Somerset West, their final destination. Through yellow veld and farmland, there were unending rows of vines, purple hills, glorious views. Harry played rock paper scissors with the boys, but it was a long day.

Jane Parker had said that Somerset West was quite like an English seaside town, which was a perfect description. They had happy times, bucket-and-spade beach life with the children, and the small family hotel had an upright piano. Laura glowed. It was for the guests' use and she sat down on the stool immediately and played a little Brahms. One of the other guests, an old man in a striped blazer, was enraptured, watching her fingers on the keys. 'How can you play like that without sheet music?' he asked.

'It's like riding a bike. Once you've learnt a piece, it's just there.'

One evening, the hotel staff rolled back the carpet and Harry took Laura in his arms. It was the first time they'd danced since the Mountains of the Moon hotel.

They were having two weeks in Cape Town before returning to start their new life in Gulu. Harry had booked at a boarding house where the pudgy landlady, an Afrikaner with an accent so clipped it was often indecipherable, was never out of a wrap-around apron. She cooked hearty breakfasts and tasty evening meals and her son, who was a keen photographer, captured Andy and Jamie giggling as uproariously as if they'd just heard the funniest joke in the world. He developed his own prints and insisted on giving a set to Harry and Laura, absolutely refusing to take a penny piece.

Harry longed for his parents to meet the boys and see those smiles. He prayed they were still surviving in occupied Austria, sure there would be plenty of hungry German soldiers stripping them of every scrap of food they could produce on the farm. But his parents were strong and he felt they'd manage somehow. There was talk of peace being near...

They settled into the tiny ex-pat community in Gulu as best they could. The houses were laid out in a semi-circle, all bungalows – except for the District Commissioner's – well spaced with good-sized gardens and working plumbing, which, in Laura's eyes, made up for a lot. 'I don't believe it, an actual flushing loo!' There were offices and a medical centre, a few Indian-owned shops and Catholic and other Christian missions nearby.

The photographs of the boys were a perfect memento of a holiday that had been a happy and healing time. Laura had the best shot framed, but there was no mantelpiece in their new bungalow, nowhere to give the photo pride of place, and it looked a little lost on a bookshelf.

He planted zinnias for Andy and he and Laura got to know their neighbours. The Commissioner's assistant and his wife were opposite, a dull childless, Roger and Sarah Hilton, on one side and the nurse, whose name was Freida, on the other. 'But everyone calls me Freddie,' she said, with her infectious laugh.

Freddie fizzed with boundless energy. She was always calling by in her starchy white button-through nurse's dress, laughing and joking, never still for a second. She was short with stumpy tree-trunk legs, her hair a tight mop of ginger curls and every inch of her covered in freckles. No beauty, but with her green eyes and vitality, Freddie had sparkle and dash. Harry hoped she and Laura would hit it off and become firm friends; he would sleep sweeter on his travels.

Evenings with Freddie were never boring and there was also the considerable boon of her excellent working wireless. It was late April, dramatic events bringing relief and hope, Mussolini captured and executed, the Russians reaching Berlin and on the 30th of the month came the news that shook the world.

After five bloody years of inhuman cruelty, Hitler had committed suicide in his bunker, taking Eva with him. Harry felt unsteady on his legs, adrenaline tingling his spine, and he was overcome with emotion. The country had stood firm, fought on, so many brave soldiers had given their lives… 'It's over,' he said, hugging them both, tears in his eyes, 'we've won our hard-fought freedom.'

Everyone celebrated, but life went on as before. Harry worked, Laura filled him in on the locals. The bald District Commissioner was a pompous dry biscuit, his assistant "as shy as poor old Cyril in Nakuru". Lenard, the doctor, was sodden and unkempt, with nicotine-stained fingers. The Hiltons next door needed their gin, and the chief of police, a Scot with a wife and family back home, had quite a little thing going with Freddie. Harry hoped she'd still find time for Laura.

He felt picked up, excited about an imminent trip to his most westerly forest in the West Nile region of Arua, where he hoped to encourage the local chiefs to plant fast-growing species to provide fuel for the villagers. But the real thrill was the safari he was going on afterwards in the Imatong Hills that bordered Sudan. Two glorious weeks, camping and trekking with his shotgun, discovering new tree species in virtually uninhabited land, a forested paradise.

He got back to Gulu after dark; hot, sweaty and exhausted after the safari of his dreams, shooting and foraging for food, collecting the flowers of new species of tree, exhilarating proof of new discoveries that he couldn't wait to have officially recorded.

He was shattered, though, in no fit state to cope with any drama, but Laura was swaying in the doorway, white as a sheet. She had dark-ringed eyes, lank hair and seldom let herself go. 'Whatever's wrong? Is it the plumbing? Someone upset you?'

'Shh, for God's sake, Jamie's just drifted off.' She looked completely panicked. 'Andy's seriously ill. I'm desperate, frantic with worry…' Her voice was cracking and her hand went to her forehead as she leaned against the wall. 'He's finding it hard to breathe, his lymph glands are up. He's got the most terrible harsh dry cough that ends in an agonising whoop. Freddie says just a bad case of whooping cough, but it seems far worse than that. He isn't eating, being sick on nothing, and Freddie looked really subdued…'

Harry raced to Andy's bedside with his heart pounding out a drumbeat. The poor little fellow's face was like putty, lopsided with the swollen glands, eyes glazed and sunken. Harry smoothed the child's clammy forehead and knew at once that he had a raging fever, his temperature dangerously high. Freddie must have taken it, but it had to have climbed higher now. 'Can you say how you feel? Shivery inside? All hot and cold?'

The child hadn't moved, hadn't tried to sit up. 'Hurt, Daddy,' he whispered, lips barely parted, 'sick…' His breath was so short that his teary face went blue with the effort. He had a terrible rasping coughing fit then, as if sand were glued to his throat. He was convulsed and shaking, but no sign of mucus…

'You poor darling muffin, try to sleep a little now.'

They had a ghastly time with him all through the night, with his temperature rocketing off the scales. Andy was shivering violently, teeth chattering, and any fluids they begged him to drink he vomited up with the first sip. Harry felt tormented, tortured by his powerlessness to ease the child's pain.

By dawn, he had begun to feel shivery himself. He grinned wanly at Laura. 'Think I'm coming out in sympathy,' he said, crawling back to fall on the bed.

An hour later, when searing daylight was flooding in, agony even to his closed eyes, Harry had a headache that felt like a time bomb, like his head was about to explode. Only then did it dawn on him that he had malaria, and just how bad an attack too. As the room began to swim and a slew of sweat slake his shuddering body, Harry felt himself going under and despaired.

He was burning up with the raging fire of the fever, shaking so uncontrollably that the whole bed was rattling like a train, every muscle feeling pummelled by ton weights. He retched painfully, dreading all that was to come.

Somewhere in the dim recesses, he remembered Laura rushing out at first light to wake the doctor and Freddie. Were they closeted with Andy now? He had to get up, had to go to Andy, but couldn't lift his head from the pillow. The waves of nausea were suffocating, like an oily cloth stuffed down his gullet, and struggling to get up, he fell sideways back onto the mattress and passed out.

Semi-conscious again, he panicked about becoming delirious. What help could he be to Andy then? In his dazed state, something about the child's symptoms flashed in like a lightning strike; they were malarial. Andy had whooping cough, but malaria too, both at the same time. Could anything be worse?

'Laura, Laura, for God's sake, come quickly!' Could she hear? She *must* come…

He tried to focus on her misty figure in the doorway. 'Quinine,' he rasped. 'Andy needs quinine, tell Lenard. Andy doesn't only have whooping cough, he has malaria as well, I'm certain of it. Deadly serious, quinine desperately urgent. You *must* make that useless bloody doctor understand.'

CHAPTER 40

Andy

I put a teaspoon of sweetened water to Andy's lips, but they didn't move, not the slightest tremble. He was lying so still, hadn't had even a sip of water for two days. 'You must hold on, please, please, darling...' I mouthed the words, swaying with weariness. 'Don't leave us. You must find reserves; we can't lose you...'

I rested the spoon on the small table beside my chair. An upright chair and my limbs were aching, eyes sinking into my skull. I could hardly see for all the sobbing and giving into the strain. Sobbing fits that went on and on, shaking me like a violent tormentor until I crumpled, beaten by forces beyond my control.

I started shaking again, unable to grasp the enormity, the awful, unbearable truth, of being so close to losing a child. I buried my face in my hands. How could both Lenard and Freddie have missed the symptoms of a virulent attack of malaria? The manifestations of whooping cough had been clear enough, but it was perfectly possible to have both, and if Harry had seen it in his own malarial state, why couldn't that wretched sodden doctor have done so too and got the quinine into Andy at the very first sign?

Harry had begun to hallucinate now, mumbling gibberish, writhing and sweating as profusely as if his whole body was covered in Vaseline. He was past any more desperate attempts to get to Andy's bedside. The last time he'd tried his knees had buckled under him disjointedly like a little toy horse pushed up from its stand. I'd needed the houseboy's help to get him back onto the bed. I could hear Harry now and staggered up with bowed shoulders, needing to go to his side.

His eyes were open, cloudy, staring, ebony-ringed, his face streaming with sweat and the greenish colour of damp mould. The bedroom stank so badly of sweat, vomit and diarrhoea, I almost retched. But the fever had to run its course, there was nothing I could do, just pray for them both and bear my agony alone.

Andy's small form was completely still under the sheet, like a tiny shrouded statue. I sank down beside him again, going over and over every single minute since he'd first fallen ill. If only I'd insisted on his going to hospital, wouldn't he have had a better chance? But I'd listened to red-faced Lenard, whose breath smelled stale and whose hands had a whisky shake.

'He's too weak to withstand the stress of being moved, Laura, too frail to survive being shaken up on these roads. Far better he's here in the bosom of his loving family.'

I'd had to put my trust in that decrepit, dishevelled doctor, what else could I have done? The hospital could only administer quinine, he said, his syringes were sterile, he and Freddie doing everything they humanly could. But, why, why hadn't he seen, as Harry had, that Andy had malaria as well?

Freddie was back, her eyes liquid with sympathy, her forehead furrows of shared pain. She'd been taking Jamie to work, saying he'd be fine at the surgery, and he'd gone off happily with a big box of his favourite toys. He too had whooping cough, but a mild attack; no sign of malaria, thank God. And Freddie had closed her mind to his possible infectiousness, so great was the need.

The married couple next door, Sarah and Roger Hilton, had offered to have Jamie while Freddie was on her rounds, but it hadn't gone well. Jamie had made his unhappiness clearly known and Sarah was soon back with him. 'Sorry, but we've really no experience of toddlers. Tell me, how are the little patient and Harry doing? A bit better now?'

Couldn't the woman see the state I was in? Andy close to dying, Harry hallucinating, and she could ask after "the little patient"? But I had swallowed back a hysterical outburst and fondled Jamie's little sticking-up quiff as he clung to my stained, crumpled skirt.

It was the fifth day of my vigil. Andy's eyes had been closed for twenty-four hours. Was he in a coma? Harry couldn't be at my side, but a flash of self-pitying anger gave way to desolation and my chest rose and fell again with sobs of despair. Harry's hallucinations would be short-lived, but the disease had him in a vice-like grip and he needed me too.

I stood at his bedside, holding his clammy hand, feeling desperate beyond measure but powerless to help him through. I wrung out a flannel, laid it on his drenched forehead and left him again. Had Harry even been aware of me coming beside his bed and taking his hand? He'd stared wildly as I looked back from the door, dry lips moving. But his rantings had become more subdued and I had to keep vigil over Andy.

Lenard said Harry was strong and would pull through, but the clear implication that Andy wouldn't brought a fresh burst of racking sobs. It gouged out my heart. My throat was dry; I could hardly see for the red-rimmed puffiness of my eyes. Not Freddie, not Lenard, no one was finding it in them to tell me how close Andy was to the end. I imagined Harry's inner howls of grief to have been unable to be with his son for the final moments. His pain would be unendurable.

The hours crawled by. I needed Harry beside me, sharing the

agony and holding me together. All I could do was to watch over Andy, murmur my love and say prayers.

Lenard came, listened to Andy's chest, sighed, looked solemn and went away again. Freddie brought Jamie home and promised to be back within the hour. Jamie's glands were up and I could hear his coughing, the occasional whoop while Todo gave him his tea, but Jamie didn't sound too bad.

He pottered in before bathtime and stood staring at Andy's small still frame.

'What did you have for tea, Jamie, darling?' I asked, trying to distract him.

'Eggie on toast and ice cream. Want Andy better, Mummy, want him play.'

'He's very sick, darling. Come and give me a hug.' I held out my arms, needing to smother Jamie with protective love. 'You're going to be a big, grown-up boy soon, it's only three weeks till you're two years old! Andy may not be better. We're having a party on your birthday with balloons and a cake with two candles. You're a very special, much-loved little boy.'

Freddie was back. She held out a glass with a small amount of brandy, swilling the liquid round, warming it with her hands. 'Drink. Medicinal.'

I took a small sip. The liquid fired through me, burning a route to my gut. I arched back my aching shoulders, had another sip and focused on Freddie. My eyes felt like two stones in a well. 'Lenard wouldn't come out with it, but please tell me straight, Freddie. How long has Andy got? Is this coma the end?'

She sat down gingerly on the edge of his bed with a crackle of her nurse's uniform, the proper grown-up bed that Andy had been so proud of, his baby one with raised sides, Jamie's now. She lifted Andy's limp little wrist. 'His pulse is very weak, Laura. I don't think he'll live out the day. Try to prepare yourself. Sit tight and I'll see if I can get Harry up to be with you. I've just looked in on him and he's focusing again, gaunt and shaky but through the worst, I'd say.'

Freddie was back right away. 'Harry's asleep and it's the best thing for him, better he doesn't stir.' She stood by the bedside, felt Andy's head, lifted his wrist again, fingers on his pulse, then laid his frail stick-like arm gently down on the sheet again. Two tears dribbled down her freckled cheeks. She heaved her shoulders, gave a long, shuddering sigh and met my eyes.

'He's gone, Laura. I'm terribly sorry. There are no words.'

'I'll leave you a moment to grieve alone,' Freddie said, 'then get Harry for you both to have a little time with him before I go for Lenard. I'll bring you some sweet tea.' She came to stand beside me, stroked my bent head and left.

Alone, I laid my face down onto Andy's still, small, bony chest. There was no heartbeat, no life. My boy; my bright, loving, naughty angel child. He was dead. How could that be? I felt nothing, only numbness. Raising my head again, I picked up his cool hand and kissed it, leaned over to kiss his small ashen face. His eyes were closed; he looked so peaceful, like any sleeping child.

How could I carry on? How could you take in the loss of a son, your own flesh and blood; the bundle you'd held at the breast, heart swelling to bursting; the child that you'd weaned and nurtured and loved completely? It couldn't be, wasn't happening. But it was. Andy was gone from our lives forever.

I looked up. Harry had come into the room. He was swaying, as insubstanial as a shadow and ghostly pale, pain screaming out of his eyes. He dropped down onto the floor by the bed and I slid beside him too. To be where we could cling and hold onto each other, draw supportive strength. We clung on in silence then Harry kneeled up by the bedside, picked up his son's hand and shed soundless tears.

I had no tears. There was a blockage, something holding them back, a stopper like the little Dutch boy's finger in the dyke. I felt nothing, no emotion, only a void where any feelings should be. It felt like being outside myself, curious about the me on the inside, wondering at my strange inability to cry.

We had to carry on, Harry and I, do what had to be done and be positive, look after Jamie, thanking the Lord that his whooping cough was so mild. Harry couldn't be blamed for going down with such severe malaria, but he'd taken a week off, gone on safari, indulged his love of trekking and come home a malarial wreck. Dangerous bitterness crept in. Suppose he'd been back sooner, seen the signs and got the quinine into Andy in good time? Wouldn't the child have had a better chance? Wouldn't there have been a breath of hope?

No recriminations; such thoughts had no place in my mind.

I lived through another day, and another, then could stand it no longer and had to be out of the house, far away from well-meaning neighbours, far from everything familiar, every agonising reminder. I needed to be entirely alone and maybe, just maybe, find it in me to shed tears.

Harry was home. George had told him to go back to work only when he was ready. He was in the bedroom, sitting on the bed with his head in his hands. 'Can you look after Jamie for a bit? I want to go out, take the car, get some air…'

'You sure? Are you safe?' I nodded and turned on my heel. I had no plan except to let the car take me anywhere, nowhere, out into the steamy Ugandan countryside, down rutted tracks, somewhere, anywhere remote and far. I drove blindly, chest heaving as the memories swirled; Andy's sunny smile, how sweetly he used to bring me flowerheads, 'For you, Mummy.' His solemn little face, his fascinated excitement as his father pointed out species of birds…

My breath became jammed; I couldn't swallow for the lump in my throat, the piercing pain, my heart being torn from my chest and shattered into a thousand pieces. I couldn't see the way ahead, the muddy track, overhanging trees; everything was a moving blur. A scream was fighting its way up and the heaving sobs that had been blocked and stoppered by numb disbelief were unstoppable now, a great erupting flood, a tsunami, an ocean of howling tears.

I drove unseeingly and fast, lungs straining with the gasps for breath between sobs and howls, clinging to the steering wheel, wind blasting through open windows, whipping my hair all over my face and eyes. I swerved wildly to miss a goat. The car hit a rut and skewered off the track, front wheels hanging over a steep verge. The Chevvy stayed suspended, balanced miraculously, but for how long? Miles from home, no clue where I was, and the rustling jungle all around.

Would the car tip over if I tried to climb out? I couldn't stay in it, suspended over the ditch, and heaving and sobbing, crawled out and scrabbled up the bank. There was no way to get the car back onto the road, no way to get home…

A few small naked boys appeared out of the jungle and stood staring solemnly, first at my ravaged face, then the upended Chevvy. They vanished again but returned with three skinny older boys who also stared at the car and me.

'My little boy died,' I said helplessly, in Swahili. They nodded solemnly, opening the car doors and pushed and heaved, levered, sweated and hefted and finally had the great heavy machine back up onto the level. They had broad white-teeth grins of achievement, broader still as I thanked them emotionally, eyes streaming with fresh tears. They refused to accept any of the coins that I tried to press into their hands.

*

Harry and I covered our son's little body with his favourite zinnias and laid a wreath of zinnias on his coffin that looked heart-wrenchingly small. Harry had been in contact with the Catholic mission over the months and it was there where Andy was laid to rest, nestling among the flowers that he'd always loved so very much. Members of each of the Christian missions, all of whose establishments were within a few miles, carried the coffin. It was a touching show of solidarity and Christian care and I was comforted.

Harry couldn't speak, couldn't mumble the responses to prayers, and I too was silent, holding Jamie's hand tightly as the coffin was lowered into its tiny grave.

CHAPTER 41

Harry

Harry would never be able to come to terms with the loss of a son, the cruelty of it, the intensity of the pain; it was too overwhelming. He could hardly bring himself to speak to anyone and felt constant bitter guilt at having recovered when Andy with his whole future ahead of him had faded.

Laura had drawn within too and they were better able to survive without communicating. Andy's jollity had been like a lightning conductor, protecting them from the worst of all the tension and rows. She was being brave and strong, disrupting Jamie's routine as little as possible and still giving him the promised little birthday party. There were no other children – which was a pity – but Freddie came, Lenard too. Sarah and Roger looked in briefly and the District Commissioner, who turned out to be not such a dry old stick after all. He was the unexpected life and soul of the party, had Jamie in fits of giggles with his antics and gave a little extra puff from behind, helping Jamie to blow out his two candles with delighted chuckles.

The nights were the hardest, with hour upon hour of sleeplessness. Harry found it easier to cope at work, where everyone sensitively avoided any mention. George, who had been a rock, coming over from Entebbe for a few days to lend a hand, was about to retire as Uganda's Chief Forest Officer to take up a lecturer post at Oxford University, which had been a blow. Another loss; George had been such a good friend to him over the years, an amazingly understanding boss.

He was in the office, thinking about George, when the phone rang. George said, 'Can you drive over here tomorrow? I've got a bit of news for you.'

'Of course, I can be with you by noon.' Harry had an idea what the news might be, but didn't want to get his hopes up; he never did.

*

Stripped of its familiar clutter, George's small fuggy office looked drab and soulless. 'Uganda's going to miss you,' Harry said, 'and we will most of all.'

'I don't know about that, but it's going to miss you too for a while, Harry. You're due for home leave, which you'd have been expecting, but you can take a postgraduate year at Oxford as well if you'd like.'

'I'd certainly like! Thanks, that's the best news ever, totally unexpected.'

'Don't get too excited. It's lousy pay, you'll have to find lodgings – which won't be easy with a family – and work bloody hard too.' George wiped his brow. 'God, this place is an oven and Jane's expecting us for lunch.'

They drank beer and over cold beef and salad, Harry was animated for the first time in weeks. 'I should get back,' he said. 'Thanks for lunch and it's wonderful to think we may be crossing paths in Oxford and this isn't a final goodbye.'

He shopped for the food Laura wanted, bought a toy truck for Jamie and drove back to Gulu.

Jamie loved the truck and went straight out into the garden to fill its container with earth. Harry said, 'Here we are. Bacon, sausages, flour and beans,' handing the carrier to Laura, 'oh, and we're going home on leave.'

He told her about the post-grad year and her eyes filled with tears. 'Sorry. It's wonderful news. It's just the thought of leaving Andy, not having him close.' She stared, wet-eyed. 'Mum and Dad would so love to have known him…'

Harry put an awkward arm round her shoulders and folded her against his chest, feeling her stiffness, all the conflicting emotions. She'd longed so much to go home, never been happy, neither in the forest nor in Gulu. He said, 'We'll be back here after the study year, it's only extended home leave.'

Would they really want to return, bring Jamie back to that steamy malarial outpost? The thought filled him with dread. He stroked Laura's soft, shiny hair. She hadn't given a thought to how she looked, but seemed now to be doing her best to get on with life. 'We have to try,' he said, tightening his hold.

*

A month later, they were on the shores of Lake Victoria, a small family of three waiting to board a BOAC flying boat to Cairo. His nerves were long forgotten, but watching the cumbersome plane skim the shimmering lake brought back memories of their South African holiday, with both boys so giggly and happy. He fought the lump in his throat and picked up Jamie as they began to board the plane.

The state of the interior came as a shock. The rows of seats had been stripped out to allow for cargo and reduce weight; passengers had to make do with narrow benches up against the sides of the hull. The war was over, but not the aftermath, and they'd be living with hardships for years.

Laura said, 'We're like pieces of freight, in for a miserable old flight. Good thing I brought sandwiches and pop.' She shifted on the seat. 'I'm missing Toppy dreadfully. He absolutely knew, didn't he? Do wish he could have come with.'

'He'll be fine. Freddie loves him, she's not just being kind.' He was irritated, felt cut up and bereft, but what was the point of saying so? They'd given Freddie the Chevvy too and she'd promised that both Toppy and the car were only on loan, but it would be over a year and the car on its last legs. Toppy would be hers too by then, and heartless to reclaim him.

The hours dragged on. They read to Jamie, sighed, stood up to ease numb bottoms. The benches were no wider than a floorboard, like kindergarten seating, and the roar of the engine's noise made talking near impossible, even had they wanted to chat to the other passengers, who were mainly army personnel. An exhausted mother with a small baby too, and a couple of large garlic-chewing, buttock-shifting Egyptians.

The heat and stale air in the plane weren't being helped by the stink of a very toxic nappy, and the baby's constant crying got on everyone's nerves. Jamie put two stubby little fingers in his ears. 'Why can't it stop?' he wailed, which caused a few smiles. To be overnighting at Khartoum was a palpable relief to all.

They were in Cairo the following afternoon. The Forest Service had booked them into Shepheard's Hotel, to Harry's delight. 'Goodness, the scale of the place! And it's very buzzy, isn't it?' Even as the words left his lips, he realised all the memories the place must have for Laura…

'Yes,' she said, not quite meeting his eyes, 'but it's a bit of a mausoleum.'

Her tension was unmissable. How could she let in even the smallest thought for her Cairo lover and be so affected as to let it show? They were grieving for their precious lost child, for God's sake. Shown up to their room, Harry banged a case down onto the bed, hating her at that moment, almost wanting to lash out.

The hotel was overbooked, heaving with army officers and their families. There were correspondents, diplomats, everyone scrabbling to beg, bribe, do whatever it took to land one of the few passages home. The army had priority now, though. Harry was a civilian and way down the chain.

It was nearly time for dinner and he needed a drink. Jamie was asleep upstairs, a maid keeping an eye, but there were no free tables on the terrace. He saw the cooling fans, palms in urns, all the army officers, men like Laura's lover there, lounging about and ordering gin slings. 'Is this the scene of your affair?' he asked coldly, leaning against a pillar, eyes skinned for anyone leaving.

'No.' Laura stared at him with sad eyes and looked down. He flushed and cursed himself for coming out with it.

They slept far apart and by day Laura was remote, Jamie whining and bored. They kept up a front, went to the archaeological museum, the bazaar, saw beautifully decorated mosques. All of it was new to Harry and he was humbled by the sight of the stupendous pyramids. But the extreme August heat got them down, the sand and filth, the poverty, limbless beggars; he felt lonely, bitter and broken-hearted.

Another week crawled by, and another. Harry fought valiantly for passages home, but he wasn't alone. People almost came to blows. He and Laura were living with tragedy, it was shared pain, but the distance between them was growing. He could sense their relationship failing, the cooling of his feelings, his eyes on laughing, pretty girls. Cairo was full of them.

There was the horrific news of the Americans dropping an atomic bomb on Hiroshima. Then the shock of another bomb dropped on Nagasaki. Was this what it took to draw a final line under the most terrible of world wars?

*

The long wait for a passage on a troopship was finally over, but the ship was more crowded than Brighton beach in a heatwave. Women, children and army officers had the luxury of a cabin, not so other ranks and civilians, poor buggers like Harry who were issued with hammocks and told to sleep in the hold. It was worse than dossing down in the boiler room. Worse still, the Colonel in Command, whose lined, sun-tanned face was ghostly with weariness, ordered that all deck space was for the use of cabin passengers and out of bounds.

Harry led a revolt. To be denied a chance to sleep on deck and breathe fresh, clean sea air was a step too far. He and a few others simply went ahead and slept out under the stars. The boards were hard as concrete, but the Colonel turned a blind eye or was far too tired to notice.

They docked at Liverpool in chilly, windy weather, where Jamie too led a mini revolt. 'No, itchy, itchy,' he screamed, flinging his chubby little arms out of the sleeves of the Fair Isle cardigan that Laura was urging him to wear. He'd never worn wool before and fought so hard that she held up her hands in surrender.

'I think he's won that battle, just hope he doesn't catch a chill...'

Seven years since Harry had set foot on British soil, five for Laura. It took sharp-elbowed determination to push through the scrum of heaving, kit-bag-toting troops to get ashore. Civilised restraint got you nowhere.

The man on the customs desk, narrow-eyed and pasty, asked, yawning, 'Anything to declare?'

'Everything,' Harry said, taking some satisfaction from the useless sod's double-take. Did the bloody man think they were returning from a summer holiday? 'This is all we own. We've been out of the country since before the war.' Not strictly true in Laura's case, but near enough.

Out of the terminal building, Jamie was fractious, shivering in his shirt and shorts, Laura white-faced and tired, all three of them were, joining the long snaking shipload all queuing for a taxi. Rubbish was gusting down the streets, smuts landing on their long-unworn clothes. The dusty, inhospitable wind wasn't much fun and it was two hours before they reached the front of the queue, but they were home.

Harry had yet to meet his parents-in-law. He felt quite nervous about it on the train to Edinburgh, and the cruelty of losing Andy was never out of his thoughts. Would reuniting with family and the homeland be a chance, however slim, to pick up the pieces and begin anew? They had to try.

CHAPTER 42

Buffy

The train was late. Buffy kept looking down the track, but no sign. He felt weak, coughing and in pain. The platform was draughty, gritty with coal dust, and he was shivering in a thick pullover, tweed jacket and cashmere scarf, though it was only September.

The station was busy with so many soldiers coming home, and the two benches on the platform were taken. Buffy wished someone would get up and leave; he felt exhausted. Edith sensed it and before he could stop her, went over to speak to a woman and young lad sitting at the end of the nearest bench and when the boy stood up hurriedly, signalled to Buffy. He felt embarrassed but grateful; his legs were about to give out.

Three to six months and a steady decline. He knew he was capable of staying positive and cheerful. He had the love of his family, birdsong, the beauty of the garden, Mrs Hodges' cooking – though he couldn't eat much, the weight disappearing like melting snow – and now he was about to have his beloved Laura home again, more than he'd dared hope for.

She'd been through so much that he was determined she

shouldn't know of his cancer, not just now, home and reuniting with the family. Edith had promised to tell her at the first sign of his fading. Surely that was the better way?

Edith's gentleness and concentrated care over the past weeks had been wonderfully heartening. He'd known how frustrated she felt at his insistence on coming to the station, but she hadn't tried to stop him. They knew what mattered to each other. They'd had a good marriage. He cherished the feelings of trust they had and sense of belonging, the cornerstones of love, and never more than now.

He worried about Laura and Harry, and tried to picture the stresses of living in the Budongo Forest with two small boisterous boys. No piano, no chance to play – Laura needed the release of her music – and not even basic sanitation. The tragedy of Andy; that had surely taken its toll on the relationship. There was no crueller fate than losing a child.

They'd obviously had a grim time in Cairo, though Laura had made light in a letter posted from Malta. Harry sounded a decent chap, but Buffy knew how much she'd cared for someone in Cairo, which must have brought back difficult memories. He hoped Laura would feel able to confide about marital problems, but knew he couldn't really be of any help.

The train finally steamed into the station an hour late, cranking to a noisy, squeaky halt. There they were, climbing down, and his heart gave a leap of joy. Edith took his arm and they hurried to hug their precious darling daughter and meet her small depleted family. Laura had grown into her looks. She was more womanly now lovely as ever, but tellingly pale; he could see the sorrow behind her smiling eyes. Harry was carrying Jamie and put him down to shake hands.

Buffy liked his direct look. Harry seemed a straight, honest fellow on first impressions. Jamie looked like neither of his parents, staring up with big solemn brown eyes, and he considered for a while before taking his grandfather's hand. 'That's very grown up, shaking hands,' Edith laughed, mussing Jamie's hair.

'I've missed you both dreadfully,' Laura said, her voice muffled as Buffy held her close. His heart felt in danger of cracking wide open with the joyful wonder of being able to see and hold her again before the end. She stood back, looking full of alarm. 'There's nothing of you, Dad! Is it the war? Rationing? How have you got so terribly thin?'

'It's just old age! Shall we be off? I'm sure you must both be in need of a large drink after that journey, and I should think it's Jamie's bedtime too.'

'It'll be a squash in the car with the luggage, but we'll manage,' Edith said, leading the way with the porter. Harry picked up Jamie and caught up with her, while Buffy shuffled along slowly with Laura, keeping his arm tucked through hers, as much for the support it gave.

'You shouldn't have come, Dad. You're obviously not well, it's madness.'

He squeezed her arm. 'Fire, flood and raging tigers wouldn't have kept me away. Promise you're keeping your head above water? Jamie needs you now, more than ever.'

'I know. And, Dad, I can't tell you how much this means, home again and seeing you and you getting to meet him at last… But you do badly need fattening up!'

They had reached the car. Edith was driving and Harry, under pressure, sitting beside her in the front. 'This takes me back,' he said, peering out of the window at Edinburgh's stern suburbs. 'Remember, darling, our first meeting in one of these tall, solid old houses all those years ago. I couldn't take my eyes off you. I was staying with Alan Woods and you came over with a few friends.'

'Of course I remember,' Laura said, subdued, which made Buffy anxious.

Clear of the city, the harvested fields looked like a Turner painting, soft and bathed in an amber haze. The hay bales looked sentinel, like the statues of Easter Island, and the sinking sun fringed the clouds in gold. Buffy pointed out some sheep. 'See their woolly coats, Jamie? They're sheared of their wool in the spring to make cosy jumpers for us all, but they need those new coats now.'

'Jamie refuses to wear his woolly cardigan,' Laura said. 'He's being very stubborn – you must think of the sheep, darling, and be grateful.'

At home with all the family there, any homecoming celebration was tempered. Buffy heard the whispered condolences about Andy, saw sympathetic looks, which must only serve as reminders. Poor Laura and Harry. 'Great to have you home, Sis,' Lilian said, 'and this is Angela. She's a year old already.'

'Does she get those buttery blonde curls from Henry? I'm longing to meet him.'

Jack said, giving Laura another hug, 'It's more than great, having you home! I can hardly believe that after five long years we're all here together, unscathed.'

It wasn't his most sensitive remark, but she'd know how innocently it was said. The sadness of Andy couldn't be blamed on the war. Buffy thought of the boy Jack had been when she'd left; a handsome grown man now, war-weary, aged beyond his years. 'How you doing, Dad?' he said, glancing. 'Time to slip off to bed?'

Buffy silenced him with a look. Jack's career in the army was a source of great pride, a major by the end of the war in Europe, speed of advancement that was well earned with Jack's bravery and commitment. The fear of his being sent to Japan had thankfully passed, and feeling comforted, Buffy put down a hand to Max, who was nudging his thigh. The poor old dog, half-blind, very slowed up with old age, had made such an excited fuss of Laura, pawing and nuzzling her. A dog's memory and sense of smell seemed to go back years.

Next morning, making for the kitchen, Buffy hung fire in the doorway, enjoying seeing Laura and Mrs Hodges reconnecting again with touching warmth. Mrs Hodges had lost her husband in the first war. She had her sister and always maintained the formalities, but was such a much loved member of their family.

Laura was handing over a box of dates with a lovely smile. 'I brought you these in Cairo on the way home.'

'Oh, my, you shouldn't have!' Mrs Hodges exclaimed, wiping her hands on her apron. 'We've felt for you most terribly… and that on top of the war and all…' She didn't know how to express her sorrow, none of them did, it was impossible.

Laura said, 'I worried so much about you all at home. We were spared the rationing, but how have you coped and cooked all your delicious meals?'

'We got by – oh dear.' Mrs Hodges fished for a hankie in her apron pocket and blew into it as loud as a trumpet. 'Look at me, blubbing, and everyone wanting their breakfast.' She turned to Buffy, leaning on the doorframe. 'Best take your father to sit down now and I'll have breakfast on the table, quick as a flash.'

Laura took his arm and they went into the dining room. 'Dad, what's going on? You're wafer-thin and nobody will give me any proper answer. I'm not a child. I think you should tell me what's wrong.'

'My lungs aren't great, darling, but I'll be fine, just need to take things easy for a while. I'm far more worried about *you,* do want you to find somewhere in Oxford and be settled as soon as possible.' Buffy fondled Max's ears, who thumped his tail. 'Then perhaps when Harry's busy studying, you and Jamie could come up here sometime for a week or two?'

'We'd love that, Dad, more than anything…'

Laura was looking so suspicious and anxious that he was glad when Edith came into the room. She said, with a glance at him, 'Breakfast! Laura, can you round up Harry, Lil and the kids and I'll see how Mrs Hodges is doing?'

Buffy gave his wife a grateful smile. 'Oh, and Fudge, Mum and I found an ancient Arran jumper of yours in a trunk this morning. You used to look such a little lamb in it. I'm sure it will fit Jamie and it's not itchy at all.'

'That's not strictly true, Dad, but I'm sure if you say so in your most grandfatherly way, Jamie will believe you.'

CHAPTER 43

Oxford, October 1945

Jamie and I went out after breakfast as we did every day. Being out of our two cramped fusty rooms, out in the cool fresh air, helped me to keep more in control. I pushed the dilapidated Silver Cross pram till we were in the beautiful heart of the city then lifted Jamie out to let him walk for a while, keeping hold, steering the pram with one hand. Lil had the pram that had been Jack's, but the Silver Cross with scratched navy paintwork and rusty wheels that I'd found in a junk shop was still well sprung.

Harry and I had eventually found two furnished rooms and a box room that we could just about afford. We'd settled in and it was possible to put up a front. I could smile at our landlady, Mrs Cooper, and her aged husband, smile at passers-by when out with Jamie, and had even made a friend, but it was all a façade, as flimsy as a Japanese screen.

I'd been so close to breaking down over breakfast but felt better now, looking up at Oxford's mellow historic buildings. The glory of the architecture was wonderfully calming. I pointed up to the Radcliffe Camera's dome with its mother-of-pearl sheen.

'Look, Jamie, see how magnificent and gleaming it is?' He couldn't have any concept of grace and design yet, but perhaps a little of such things filtered in.

We walked past colleges with stone frontages that glowed honey in the autumn sun. It seemed a miracle that Oxford's historic heart had survived the war unscathed. Hitler was supposed to have wanted to make the city his capital, but how could anyone know?

Jamie's little legs were tiring. I lifted him back into the pram and we carried on to the River Cherwell to join up with Connie, my new friend. Connie was petite, about five foot two, with caramel-coloured hair and the sweetest nature, uncomplicated and kind. She was married to a surveyor, Chris, who'd been called up just after qualifying and was now very junior in his firm and underpaid.

Connie and I met at the Cherwell most days. Jamie loved to throw crusts to the swans and play with Connie's son, Billy, who was a month younger; a funny little fellow with a pugnacious face, squashy nose and sticky-out ears. He adored Jamie and wasn't at all pugnacious, in fact, just a lot better at kicking a ball.

As if to disprove that, Jamie kicked the ball out of the pram. It rolled into the road and was swiftly retrieved by a student, who grinned and kicked it back into the pram.

'Say thank you, Jamie.'

'Thank you, thank you!' He giggled and his sunny expression was so alarmingly like Andy's that my throat closed over.

Connie was waving to us. I lifted Jamie out and the two little boys raced along the towpath, bumping into each other with giggles and tumbles. It was a fine late October day, cold and clear; there were rowers on the Cherwell, swans looking piqued at being disturbed. The leaves were in glorious colour – crimson, parchment, mustard – fluttering everywhere in the light breeze. The towpath was slippery with them.

We watched the boys, picking them up from falls and sorting out any wails. Connie sighed. 'I long for more children, and you must have another, Laura, in time. A new baby wouldn't diminish the memory of your lost son. It would be a little person in its own right and a sibling for Jamie.' I smiled and said nothing. Not wanting another baby was at the heart of my misery and fragile state. There were other reasons, not only the depth of grief, but none that were easy to share.

Connie said, 'My problem is living with Chris' parents. He wants us to have a place of our own first and, of course, there's the lack of money. His parents have a large Victorian semi with a big garden. Billy can run about, but my mother-in-law is always hovering, so this is my escape, coming to the river, and a lovely bonus meeting you.'

'It isn't easy, is it, sharing?' I said. 'We're paying little rent and can use the kitchen, lucky to have found anything at all, but the house is cramped and narrow and right on top of the railway line. Still, there's a back yard with space for the pram.' I didn't go into the dank mustiness of our rooms, two armchairs that sagged like spent elastic and the reek of over-cooked vegetables always filling the hall.

Connie had brought a thermos of Camp coffee and sipping the hot sweet drink in companionable silence, we were lost in our respective thoughts.

Harry's need of more children was in his every gesture and glance; it was an immovable boulder, a fallen tree in our path, a dividing wall in our skimpy, lumpy double bed. He was still bitter about the Dutch cap and on the rare occasions he rolled me into his arms, our lovemaking was silent, mechanical coupling. Was I struggling to keep hold so rigidly, so woodenly, that he'd had enough?

Harry was suffering too, just better at containing his pain. He didn't have the same sense of claustrophobia, the head-pounding need to rush blindly out of the house, run to anywhere, an alley, public lavatory, bus shelter; any anonymous place where my jangling nerves and tear-blotched face would go unobserved. I'd given into the need a couple of times, leaving him to see to Jamie.

It wasn't only the agony of Andy, the vision of his still small body that never left me; it was Dad, who was obviously extremely ill. What wasn't I being told? Was the illness terminal? Cancer? I couldn't lose him, not Dad, my rock and support whom I loved absolutely.

It was the future too, and the past. Had Bertha and Anna survived? Bertha lived in the suburbs. Wouldn't that have been some protection? Had Ava been rounded up and gassed? We'd been still in Uganda as news of the unconscionable horrors meted out at the hands of the Nazis, which had defied belief, had unfolded. It had been impossible to fully absorb the scale of such crimes against innocent humankind.

And there was Hamish. Still no word, no clue, no closure. Mum said his poor family never stopped praying and hoping that somehow, against all the odds and length of time, he would return.

I was plagued unceasingly by thoughts of Edmund too, the blind hatred and guilt, the hurt I'd caused Harry, the harm to our marriage, which was fundamental. Edmund was evil, but I had only myself to blame.

Jamie and Billy had tired of playing a game with twigs and were scuffling their shoes in the leaves, demanding attention. Connie said, 'Time to make a move?' I nodded, shaking the plastic stacking cups free of drips as we began to pack up.

'I'd love it if you could come home for lunch,' she said, 'My mother-in-law's happy and there's a spare bed in Billy's room. The boys could have their nap and a runabout in the garden when they were fed.'

'That would be terrific if you're really sure? Such a treat, Jamie's a bit cooped-up in the afternoons with no garden…'

Not Jamie, I was the one forcing back sobs, straining to be out of our musty rooms. I hoped Connie wouldn't sense how close I was to falling into a black hole. Lines of Tennyson sprang to mind. "Always I long to creep/ into some still cavern deep/ there to weep, and weep and weep/ my whole soul out to thee". I remembered earnestly discussing his poems with Harry. 'Don't you love the depth of sorrow and passion in Tennyson's *Maud*?'

'Up to a point, but it's quite ironic at heart,' Harry had said, lying me back on some grassy bank and smiling into my eyes, 'you soppy old thing!'

Connie asked, a bit telepathically, 'How's Harry getting on with the studying?'

'He says it's okay. He's working for a doctorate on top of the postgrad course, and the title for his thesis is a real mouthful. "*The Determination of the Rate of Growth in Tropical Unevenaged Forests in Relation to the Regulation of Fellings*". He wouldn't hear of shortening it!' Harry's irritation when I teased that it hardly tripped off the tongue had been typical; he knew I took his work seriously.

'It'll be a lot further for you to go home,' Connie said, as we walked on. 'Why don't you get the bus, leave the pram and pick it up tomorrow?'

'Thanks, that's a very kind thought. It would be a great help.'

A vague idea was forming. I'd never allowed in thoughts of Bob, which would be even more dangerous now, hanging on by my fingernails, but he'd said he would always be there for me, and just to hear his voice…

He had written his mother's address and telephone number on a scrap of paper that I'd slipped into a book of Tennyson's poems, probably why Tennyson had been in my mind, since that scrap of paper was in my handbag now. Couldn't I call his mother on the way home? So much easier without the pram… Ask if she could possibly let me have Bob's address…

Bob would talk sense into me, tell me that however much I

was in free fall now, things could change. Life took many turns. I imagined Bob urging that Harry and I would work things out, one way or another. He'd tell it like it was, help me to see the way forward. Nothing could be more unwise, as I tried to tell myself firmly, but how else could I carry on?

CHAPTER 44

Mrs Sims

Connie's mother-in-law drove us to the bus stop. Jamie was excited to be going home on a bus and I thanked her warmly. 'And for that delicious shepherd's pie.'

'You must come again, any time. We loved having you.' She was a pallid, rather fussy-looking woman. Her husband was always at work or playing golf, she'd said, a little sadly, when she and I were washing up and Connie in the garden with the boys. It was easy to see why Connie needed to escape to the river.

Walking home from the bus stop, I knew it would be terribly wrong to take Jamie into a telephone box to ring Bob's mother; it was a call to be made alone.

Not having made it, though, the evening was even more of a strain. I couldn't concentrate on my book, couldn't face sewing, constantly framing what to say to Bob's mother in my mind and burning for a chance to be out of the house alone.

Harry didn't seem to notice. We were stressed out enough already, but perhaps he'd sensed the extra tension. He left in the morning without finishing his coffee in his keenness to get away.

Jamie played with his cars on the lino while I washed up breakfast. He was under my feet and already a bit bored; I had to think how to amuse him.

Mrs Cooper, our landlady, came into the kitchen. 'Shall I dry?' she said, 'Mr Cooper's gone for the paper.' She was shrivelled and stooping, with swollen arthritic fingers and joints, but kindly and uncomplaining.

I turned, smiling. 'Thanks, that's good of you, sorry if Jamie's a bit in the way.'

'That reminds me, something I've been meaning to give your little boy…' She plugged the tea towel into its suction holder and was soon back in with a large cardboard box. 'I've been saving some of our Reg's toys,' she said, as I hurried to help with the heavy box, 'don't reckon he's going to be giving us any little ones now, more's the pity. The war did for him, he's gone a bit funny in the head.'

'I'm very sorry,' I said, 'but there can always be medical breakthroughs. You mustn't give up hope. Thanks for these. Jamie will love to play with them, but they'll always be here for Reg.'

'Yes, well, that's as may be.' Mrs Cooper fidgeted awkwardly. She knelt down with cricking knees and began to take pieces of train track out of the box, showing Jamie how to join them up.

'Um, would it be all right, Mrs Cooper, if I left him with you for a few minutes and popped to the chemist? I really won't be long.'

'Of course, deary, take your time. We'll be fine, me and the little one, won't we, poppet?'

I rushed out without a coat, bought some Aspirin, asked for change for the telephone and went to the box. I inserted the pennies with shaking fingers, lifted the receiver and when the call was answered, froze.

'Hello? This is Mrs Sims. Who is it? Who's there?'

My fingers were so slippery that I had to use one hand to help the other to push button A, willing her not to hang up… 'My name's Laura Werner,' I said breathlessly, getting through at last. 'I'm calling from Oxford, terribly sorry to be bothering you, but I was a friend of Bob's in Cairo and he gave me your telephone number... I just wondered if you had an address for him... You see, I, um, lost a child to malaria a few months ago and...' She didn't need to know that. Whatever had possessed me? The blood rushed to my face. 'Sorry, forgive me, it's just very hard to explain, but Bob was so good at helping me to see...' I started to cry, fumbling for more coins; loud, untidy sobs and Bob's mother was hearing it all...

'You mustn't worry about being upset. It's always difficult to talk on the phone. I live near Didcot and there are plenty of trains from Oxford. Why not come down? I could pick you up at the station.'

'Oh, that would be incredible – thank you so much. I have a two-year-old, but think I can leave him with a friend. Would Tuesday be possible? I could look up train times and ring again over the weekend.'

'Tuesday is fine,' she said. 'It will be lovely to meet you, but I'll wait for confirmation of train times.'

Hurrying back, shivering, I found Jamie and Mrs Cooper still happily playing trains on the kitchen floor. Mr Cooper was there too, down on his aged knees, and he'd managed to get the train up and running, wobbling along on its tracks. I thanked him excessively and he beamed, before having a wheezing coughing fit that got me quite alarmed.

Jamie and I soon went off for the pram. Connie's mother-in-law insisted we stay for lunch again and, choosing my moment, I mentioned, not entirely disingenuously, that the mother of an old friend of mine had asked me to visit.

'Jamie could come too, of course,' I said, 'but it would be a bit boring for him, and you must say if this is at all a bother, only I wondered—'

Connie's mother-in-law interrupted. 'But we'd love to have Jamie, wouldn't we, Connie?' She smiled and agreed with positive warmth, though it meant having to be with her mother-in-law all day.

*

The weekend passed in a haze of high-wire tension. Out with Jamie, I checked the train times – couldn't have not – and took him into the phone box with me too.

Tuesday came and I sat ramrod straight in the carriage with my coat folded over my knees, a camel coat with a tie belt that Mum had given me when just home from Uganda. I shouldn't be seeing Bob. It was deeply disloyal to Harry, and Bob was probably married. It was unfair to him, dreadfully wrong. He and I had loved each other, briefly and gloriously in Cairo, but there was no going back.

Mrs Sims had said her car was a red and black Austin 12, registration JM 7931. I didn't need to look for it. The woman with iron-grey hair in a chignon who was scanning the passengers had to be Bob's mother. She had his lean face, high-boned cheeks and rather severe features, and there was a kindness about her face too, a softness so reminiscent of Bob. My heart began to flutter.

She came up close, holding out her hand. 'It's Laura, isn't it? You're just as I imagined!' She smiled, a small smile, but a warm one. Her eyes were brown, not Bob's. 'Thank you for coming. I'd somehow felt in my bones we'd meet one day.'

'This is terribly good of you,' I said, flustered. 'I felt so dreadfully guilty and shy about telephoning, worrying that old friends can so often just be in the way.'

'I understood that, and your need. I lost a child too, Bob's sister, when she was seven and he only five.' Having Bob home now, though, and the war over, must be a great comfort to her. Was he married to Coral? Did he live nearby…?

'I've got a bit of lunch ready,' Mrs Sims said in the car. 'just soup and cheese and chutney.' She glanced with a quick smile. 'I grow fruit and veg to make a few jars of jam and chutney, as far as the sugar ration allows, that I sell in the village shop. It's hardly any money, but helps to keep busy.'

'Yes, being busy would help me too. I long to be teaching music again. I have a baby grand at my parents' house, but there's nowhere to have it in Oxford.'

That was of no interest to Mrs Sims, just chatting, trying to break the ice. She couldn't have felt less like a stranger, though, Bob's mother who seemed to know all about her son's relationship with me in Cairo.

Mrs Sims turned up a narrow rural lane with a pair of farm cottages on the corner, steep hedgerows on either side, and slowed in front of a long, thatched cottage with steps cut into the verge. Parking in front of a garage, she took me up a few steep steps to the aged-wood white front door. Turning to look behind us, I couldn't believe the beauty of the view. It was extraordinary, glorious, and I exclaimed. 'You can see for absolute miles, the whole way over the Thames valley!'

'Yes, I love looking out from my bedroom window, it's so calming, makes one feel at peace with the world.' We went indoors. The hall was low and beamed with a row of hooks just inside the door. Let me take your coat,' she said, 'and come into the kitchen where it's warmer and we can have a nip of sherry.'

Copper pots hung from a huge ceiling beam, lines of Kilner jars on shelves, bunches of herbs drying over the stove and the irresistible smell of fresh baked bread. The kitchen had a modern picture window that looked out over a long back garden, autumnally colourful with bronze and red foliage, a last few roses, and there was a vegetable garden and fruit-bush cages beyond.

'However, do you manage it all?' I asked, in awe.

'A big strong fellow comes to help now and then. It's hard for these chaps back from the war to find work.'

She poured two small glasses of light dry sherry, the colour of topaz, reminding me of Mum, who liked the same sherry, and we sat at a scrub-top table. I took a sip and felt the burn of the alcohol, but was already on fire with anticipation. How could I possibly cope if Bob walked through the door?

His mother, who was opposite, was looking at me searchingly with anxiety showing in her eyes.

She said, 'I have some sad news. It wasn't easy to tell you on the phone, but Bob died. He was killed in the war.'

The blood drained. It wasn't true, couldn't be, not Bob. It was a shock too great for my heart to contain. Andy and now Bob, it was the end; I couldn't cope. I'd loved Bob, been sustained by the good in him. He'd been lover, mentor, and for the many years when I'd tried so hard to wipe all thoughts of him from my mind, still always there for me somehow, still my invisible support and guide.

Bob was gone. He'd been a war correspondent, out in the field of battle, recording the horrors; he hadn't needed to join up. Why? Why couldn't he have thought of his mother – and *me*? What crazy sense of duty to King and country had led him to fight and join the ranks of the fallen, destined to be just another statistic of war?

Mrs Sims reached over and covered my white-boned knuckles with a cool light hand. She transmitted boundless shared pain and understanding. 'He loved you. He couldn't have married Coral, whom I believe he'd talked of to you, and Coral knew that, deep down. She was engaged to a local doctor by the time Bob came home and his relief was palpable. He'd felt dragged down by a need to do his duty by her, but no longer. That's when I heard all about you. It made me feel better, glad that he'd known what it was to love, proud of him for putting you first. I'd wanted him to marry, longed for grandchildren, but he did what he felt was right and best and that he must go to fight in the war.'

I covered my face with my hands. Mrs Sims had lost her husband, daughter and now her good, brave and only son. She would understand more than anyone my mute agony and incomprehension, but it didn't lessen the pain.

It took supreme effort of will to face her and ask questions, but I had to know. 'Can you tell me what happened, if you can bear it, how he died?'

'Bob had joined the Brigade Group when he came home, trained at Tidworth and fought in the Tunisian Campaign before being transferred to Italy. He fought in the terrible battle of Monte Cassino, survived that, only to be shot by a lone German sniper at Liri Valley right at the end of the war, which seemed a particularly cruel twist of fate.'

I crumpled again and Mrs Sims put her arm round my shoulders. 'You have a young son,' she said. 'You're married to someone whom Bob felt was more your age and would be home and on hand once we were through the war. Tell me, what's gone wrong? It's more than the loss of your precious son, isn't it, that led you to telephone and feel in such need of Bob's support? Is it something you can talk about? It helps to open up and share the pain.'

I met her sad, sympathetic eyes. 'I'm dreadfully sorry, I should never have made that call and got in touch, shouldn't have needed to lean on Bob and make you have to tell me. I feel terrible.'

'Don't feel that, lean on me a little more instead, it does help to talk.'

I hesitated. It felt wrong to burden her, but her small half smile was gentle and encouraging, and I was in a wretched emotional state. I took a breath. 'Forgive me, it's hard to explain, particularly being married to a decent man – and he feels our loss as much as I do – but that doesn't lessen the tension. We had a good marriage, happy companionable times. It's just that we're struggling now. You're right, it's not only about losing a child, it's my not being able to face having another. Harry has always wanted a large family, he feels bitter and the distance between us is growing. My father's dying too. I know it and love him so much. I've been having a sort of little breakdown, but it's self-inflicted, all my own fault.'

'I can't believe that. Why should you feel you're the one to blame? There must be a reason. Can you talk about it?'

'Harry was away with the KAR for a year and a half. I was pregnant, living alone in Nairobi, coping and doing war work, but then I had a traumatic experience with a man, which was as bad as it gets. I couldn't tell a soul about it, least of all Harry, without being pilloried and disbelieved. Harry sensed I wasn't being open and that as well as setting my face against another child has soured our relationship ever since. So, you see, it is all my fault…'

Mrs Sims shook her head and rose. 'No, it's not, it's just sad, dreadfully difficult circumstances, the misfortunes of life.'

She warmed up the soup. I couldn't eat, could think only of the cruelty of war and my desperate devastation at Bob's loss.

'I hope you'll come again one day,' said Mrs Sims, 'and do bring your son. I'd love to meet him, completely understand if you'd rather not, but you looked at the piano in the sitting room as we came in…' had I? I'd been so ratcheted up about seeing Bob '…and Bob had said you're a concert pianist, I'd love to hear you play.' She smiled with moist eyes then looked away, collecting herself. Turning back, she said, 'Bob left you a note in case you ever got in touch and anything had happened to him.'

How could he have known that I'd need to turn to him one day? and My lips trembled and tears filled my eyes as Mrs Sims went to get the note.

She returned with a light blue envelope, which I slipped into my handbag feeling an unbearable sense of connection, 'Would you mind if I read it alone?'

'Of course not. Now, shall I take you to the station?'

The note, written in ink in Bob's clear, free-flowing hand, was an anchor, a rope to give me a surer footing. Reading it on the train, oblivious to others in the carriage, I felt it distilled our love into such an essential element of itself that I could cope the better and bear his loss. I felt as if he were with me, holding my hand, giving restorative strength.

My darling Laura,

People die in wars. I've chosen to join the fight, but I couldn't have taken this course without being sustained by my love of you. I'd felt close and in love with you on the ship, confirmed in that love the first time we were alone together in Cairo. I felt complete. I knew I could never love anyone with the same intensity of feeling, the soaring emotions that overcame me those few times we were together that I had to try to keep light, knowing you loved me too. I'm writing this now to leave something of myself if I don't return from this war.

If you should ever have cause to read this note, it will be because you have some need of me; for that reason and because it's important to me to feel that even not being there in an hour of crisis, you will know how completely and gloriously you were loved. How you were always with me, in my heart and spirit and understanding – with me to the last. If this is any comfort, as the comfort it has been to write it, then I can feel that our love hasn't died with me. I like to think that you will tuck it away, keep it safe and bravely carry on.

With all my love, Bob

*

In the next days and weeks, fresh grief settled around me like an invisible shell. I felt shielded from exposure by a hard, protective crust; I could lift my head, tortoise-like, to communicate with Connie, who knew nothing of Bob, and when it came to Harry, who did know, was able to withdraw within.

Jamie was holding us together. Harry and I could talk of his little doings and at other times, the many hours when Harry was in libraries or at lectures, the fault lines lay hidden, but we were growing ever more remote. The tension was most evident in the long evenings. We were civil, even friendly, but with none of the normality of married life; fights, laughter, teasing and shared bitches.

I visited Mrs Sims often, taking Jamie, who was fascinated by a rocking horse that had been Bob's. She suggested he might like a ride on a real horse. A friend of hers had a beautiful bay and ran a little business giving rides.

The friend, Mrs Jones, lifted up Jamie, and sitting high up on the bay with Mrs Sims, his cheeky face was one big grin. He would tell his father, but I was entitled to have an elderly friend and didn't think Harry would even ask who it was.

Mrs Sims said her niece's daughters were coming to stay at the start of the Christmas holidays, that their mother was keen for them to learn the piano and would I give them lessons? The younger girl was musical, rewarding to teach, and Mrs Sims kept Jamie happily amused. She had a marvellous capacity to make life worth living, although being with her always brought Bob too close.

Christmas came. We had it in Scotland with my family. The house was festive, scented with fresh-picked holly and ivy and candles. We marvelled at the piquant-smelling oranges that Dick had got from a Canadian airman.

Dick said, 'He was stuck here, waiting for a passage home, and his family sent over a hamper. I swapped the oranges for a bottle of gin!'

Lil played records, Bing Crosby's *White Christmas* and *I'm in Love with Two Sweethearts*, sung by Issy Bonn, a Jewish survivor, and Jamie and Angela jumped about to the music, holding hands.

'No turkey again this year,' said Edith. 'I've wheedled a couple of scrawny little chickens out of dear old Mr Frazer in the village. Anything other than this ghastly "murkey" on sale!' It was sausage meat moulded to look like a turkey.

'Glad you spared us that,' Lil laughed.

Dad had a sad setback. His faithful, old half-blind Max had become terminally ill and it was time for a visit to the vet. Dad insisted on taking him, weak as he was, and returning, leaning on Mum's arm, he wiped away a tear. 'Do you know, Max wagged his tail cheerfully all the way to the end, which is just how I plan to go too.'

I spent a lot of time with Dad. He was hoarse, coughing, emaciated, his skin drawn tight over high cheekbones that had bright pinpricks of colour on the bone. When the drugs kicked in, his eyes were dilated and large and he talked obsessively about his favourite foods.

'I'm dying, darling Fudge,' he said, one day when we were alone. I may have a couple more months, but who knows? Will you and Jamie stay on for a week or two in the New Year? Harry has to be back for the Hilary term, but if I'm right about you both, perhaps a break won't be a bad thing? And to have you here for these last weeks would gladden my heart.'

'Being with you, Dad, will more than gladden mine. This is the only place in the world I want to be.'

CHAPTER 45

Father and Daughter

It seemed poignantly coincidental that I should be staying on in January with Dad, just as back in 1940, before sailing for Cairo. Those days seemed an eternity ago, a time of hopes and dreams.

And now he was a very sick man with little time left. The pain of losing him was physical, a tightening of the chest, a pulse beating fiercely in the temple. I felt chilled throughout, wearing extra woollies. He was the most loving and supportive of fathers, not yet sixty; it was unendurably sad.

Mum had been devoting herself entirely to looking after him, but now, with me home and Mrs Hodges helping with Jamie, she was working at her Edinburgh clinic again. She'd achieved her goal, opened a clinic for women and families in need and took obvious justified pride in its reality.

I heard her car and she came in. We'd moved Dad's bed down into the sitting room and since he was asleep, we went to the kitchen to be quiet. Jamie was out in the snowy garden with Mrs Hodges' nephew, she was helping them make a snowman, and Mum said, holding out a letter, 'It's most peculiar, this came for you, sent care of me at the clinic. It has a Swiss stamp.'

'Can't think who'd be writing from there,' I said, curious. It was from Ava. She was alive. I remembered her boarding the *St Louis* bound for Cuba just before the start of the war, all its Jewish passengers with their valid visas denied entry and the ship forced to return to Europe. How had she escaped the concentration camps and as was known now, a gas-chamber death. Reading her letter, it seemed nothing short of miraculous that she'd survived.

…I knew your mother was a doctor, managed to locate this address and do hope this letter finds you. I'm hoping to reach Britain or America, but with so many of us living illegally here in Switzerland and all desperate to do the same, it's a slim chance! Still, to be free to write and post a letter… I thank God!

You heard about the fate of the St Louis? We docked back at Antwerp. I eventually made it into occupied France but had to keep running, half-starved and frozen stiff. Someone had told me about Chambon, a remote village in the Auvergne with a history of helping fleeing Huguenots and whose villagers were said to be sympathetic to the Jews. The village was right over in the east, high on a mountain plateau, surrounded on all sides by forest, but it seemed my only hope.

God knows how I got there, I collapsed on the steps of the church and the Protestant pastor, a most marvellous man called André Trocmé, and his kind wife, Magda, took me in. The villagers hid me, fed me, built up my strength and helped me to set off across the Alps. There was no more testing and terrifying a journey, but I was eventually smuggled into Switzerland where there were other Protestant resistors prepared to help.

I'm bowed down with grief for the murdered millions, never thought I'd be glad that my mother had died in my arms on that ship. I do all I can with my undercover practice here to treat people in need, but every case is a knife-edge risk, the locals are watchful, and I need to get to England or America somehow.

I expect you're married by now and a mother, possibly still in Africa? I hope so much this reaches you and you can write with your news…'

I wrote to her that afternoon. Mum said that displaced people, mainly Jews trying to reach Britain, were not helped by the Government's fear of establishing a precedent. Still, doctors were badly needed and she'd do what she could. Cases were being dealt with on an individual basis and having a job to come to would be a great help.

Ava's letter crystallised my feelings about Uganda. The risks for Jamie were too great. I couldn't return and wrote as much to Harry, relieved when he responded in a surprisingly measured way.

…I feel just as anxious about Jamie. I may have to go back alone since my prospects are far better there than anywhere else. Also, not to go would mean having to resign from the Colonial Forest Service, which would be a big step to take. I'd forfeit all pension rights for a start, having served less than ten years. Still, I'll put out feelers for other jobs, scout about for good references and with great good luck even find a research job here at home…

He asked after Jamie and my father, but his very reasonable letter was passionless, the hairline cracks in our relationship were becoming a chasm. It felt like being on opposite sides of a fast-flowing river with no way of getting across.

Buffy was going downhill fast, couldn't walk, couldn't even stand now. Mum and I alternated being with him, constantly keeping an eye and chatting when he was wakeful, as brightly and positively as the lumps in our throats would allow.

Jamie wandered in at times when he tired of being in the kitchen with Mrs Hodges and he had taken to staring at his frail, skeletal grandfather, who would smile and tell him a story before sinking back on the pillows and closing his eyes.

'Granpy got malaria, Mummy?'

'Not malaria, darling, but he's very, very sick…'

Afternoons were Buffy's best time. Before settling down by the bed, I would build up the fire and stroke the undeserving Tabitha, who had the pick of the armchairs, her purring was as loud as a lawn mower on a sunny afternoon. Buffy would never mow his lawn again, never feel the warmth of summer sunshine.

'Love you, Dad,' I said, picking up his ice-cold hand lying limply on the counterpane. I couldn't talk about my marriage, it would be insufferable extra strain, but the longing to lean on him and open up my heart proved too much and I weakened. I told him nearly all. 'Harry's going to try to find work here, but that's a long shot and if he goes back to Uganda alone and we drift ever further apart…'

'You're not yet thirty, Fudge. You have Jamie, you're an exceptional musician, your whole life ahead of you. Believe in yourself and the future. Life won't be all bad, there'll be changes, things happen. It's all going to get better soon.'

'Oh, Dad, I love you so much. I should be comforting you! Lie back and rest now.' I stroked his limp white hair, kissed his chill, frail cheek. His skin was parchment-pale, transparent as tracing paper. 'Mum will be in soon and she'll read to you.'

*

February came. Halfway through the month, Edith called the family together. We both knew it was time. Lil, Dick and Jack came in stages, each preparing themselves in their own way. Harry came. He said he couldn't have dreamed of a kinder, more charming father-in-law or one with a gentler sense of humour. That did for me and I crumpled. Harry took me awkwardly into his arms.

The next day was black and heavy, with menacing clouds that exploded into a hailstorm. We all had our private moments with Buffy, didn't gather in a crowd round the bed. It was a pattern that we slipped into. I knew Dad was going to die in hours. I felt the blockage when I tried to swallow, the constriction in my chest, the blood in my veins turning to ice.

I played with Jamie, waiting to go into Dad who had slipped into a coma that Mum said could last for a couple more days. She was being a practical, experienced professional doctor, never allowing her emotions to show. After nursing Buffy for many months, she was as prepared for loss as any wife would ever be, but when the moment came, I was sure it would hit her as hard as if he'd been a fit well man.

When I went into the room to be with Dad, some sixth sense, an inner voice, was telling me that he had minutes left, not hours. I drew up the chair to his bedside, struggling to hold on.

Hearing was the last of the senses to go, people said, and clinging to that, I brought my face close to his and said, 'I love you, Dad,' as clearly and unfalteringly as possible. 'I love you with all my heart and always will.'

Jamie was pushing open the door and heard me. 'I love Granpy too, Mummy.'

He sang it out light-heartedly and Buffy opened his eyes. He stared into mine. Was there an infinitesimal movement of his lips? Had he heard? I kissed his white hair and lifted his ice-cold hand to my cheek. 'Love you, Dad,' I whispered again before my throat closed over. He gave me a blue-eyed stare before his eyes slid lightly closed and his chin dipped. I knew he was dead at that moment and sat rigid, still holding his chill hand, feeling an inestimable sadness. Buffy had fought in one world war, lived through another, but the cancer had got him in the end.

I leaned over to kiss his forehead and led Jamie out of the room. Jamie had seen two people die, two people he was close to, whom he'd loved and laughed with, and he was not yet three years old. Edith was outside the door. My face was enough; she paled and hurried to Dad's side while I went to call the rest of the family.

I could manage my grief, feeling the stronger for the talk I'd had with Dad, the simple support he'd been able to give me in his last conscious hours. But I knew there would be times when, as with Andy, the pain of loss would come to me in the small hours and I'd see that momentary connecting blue-eyed stare, clear as a bright cloudless sky, and my own eyes would fill and my chest tighten round the void. I would bleed for my father then, love and mourn him. Love him for the rest of time.

CHAPTER 46

Carinthia, August 1946

It was late July, hot and humid, the academic year over and we were still in our two rented rooms. I was cutting Jamie's breakfast toast into squares. Harry had resigned from the Colonial Forest Service. George had given him an extremely generous reference, considering the difficulties of his leaving, and Harry had been appointed mensuration officer at a new forestry research station in Hampshire. The job was technical and precise, but the pay was a pittance, and no help with housing.

Not being due to start till September, he was furiously working on plans to get to Austria via Switzerland, to see his parents. He was incensed at being refused Austrian visas, which seemed cruelly unfair since the war was over and he hadn't seen them since 1938. The plan felt fraught with difficulties, with little chance of success, and we'd be away the whole of August with no time to find anywhere to live near the research station on our return.

Harry wanted to try before leaving, but what we'd find with such funds as we had would be no more than a chicken coop. He'd bought a car, an old Ford Anglia, but the money only went so far.

'I'm off house hunting,' he said after breakfast, picking up the car keys. 'I'll find something by the end of the day, in the country probably, property's cheaper there. Be a good boy for Mummy, Jamie.' Was I to be given no say in our future home? Harry hadn't even suggested our coming too.

I said we should. 'It's my home too and if it's out in the sticks and you take the car, how do we get about? Jamie needs to start nursery school and make friends.'

'I'll be quicker on my own. Let's see what I come up with first. There'll be a bus or something, don't be so bloody defeatist.'

'Perhaps *you* could get the bus,' I called angrily as he left, bitter about his need to go alone. I found as many excuses to get away. We did try to be conciliatory at times; it was just that our efforts never seemed to coincide.

The day stretched ahead. Connie was away visiting relations and it felt best to begin packing for Austria as a way to keep Jamie engaged. I brought the battered old leather suitcase out from under the bed. 'We'll need to take your Grandpa-woolly, Jamie, jumpers for us all. It can be quite chilly in Austria. And after we've packed, we should start sorting all the books and your toys to have ready for when we move and have to say goodbye to Mr and Mrs Cooper.'

'But can I keep the train?'

'Well, it really belongs to their grown-up son... We'll see.'

I took Jamie to the library, where he loved all the picture books. He chose *The Little Fire Engine*, by Lois Lenski, taking it up to have stamped all on his own.

We played games at home, went out again for a walk. If only Harry would try to understand that I couldn't face another child. Andy couldn't be replaced. Harry must see that, and with the way things were between us, I dreaded being further tied. I loved Jamie with so great an intensity, such unfathomable depths of love, that the pain could take my breath away. He was my all.

I read to him at bedtime, kissed him good night; he smelled of apples and soap and looked very small and vulnerable, curled up on his side, sucking the satin edge of his torn-off square of blanket. My heart swelled to bursting.

It was ten o'clock before I heard Harry on the stairs. I put down my darning. 'Any joy? Are we the proud owners of a home of our own?'

'Yep. I've bought a house for nine hundred and eighty pounds.'

'But that wouldn't even buy a broom cupboard!'

'It's bought a nice brick bungalow, no electricity or mains water as yet, and it's in a hollow, but a home of our own…'

'We might as well have stayed in the Budongo,' I muttered, yet feeling a bit of a heel; Harry's job being low paid was no fault of his own. 'Is it furnished? Out in the country obviously. How do we heat it – and wash?'

'We'll manage. Not furnished, but doesn't your mother have beds in store? It is in the country, but you could stay protected from the wind,' he grinned. 'Being in a hollow does have its upsides. You'll be able to have your baby grand there too.'

I was ahead of him on that. Music was my survival kit, which would be needed.

*

We left for Austria via Switzerland, though I couldn't see Ava. She was on her way to England and thanks to Mum, joining a doctor's practice in Birmingham.

In Zurich, we discovered there was a through train to Prague and no trouble over visas for Czechoslovakia. We could have transit visas for passing through Austria too, where we hoped to slip off the train and avoid having to show our papers.

We almost missed the train, with all the checks of visas and passports. 'It's because of all the war criminals and displaced people on the move,' Harry said.

'Still, bureaucracy gone mad.'

The train rumbled on through the night, reaching Zell am See in the American occupation zone in Austria by dawn. Quite a few people were leaving the train and we mingled in, stiff in every joint, trying to look like an American family. A yawning official waved us through. We were visa-less, but on Austrian soil.

Klagenfurt, where Harry's father had given him the address of a British major, was a slow local train ride away. The train had hard wooden seats, stank of urine and was packed. Harry unchivalrously grabbed two places when the occupants needed a stretch, and Jamie immediately fell asleep across our knees. No one checked our papers, remarkably, and eighteen interminable hours after leaving home, we stumbled out blearily into the bright sunlight in Klagenfurt.

The city had been badly bombed. There were grand buildings still standing, but distressing gaps and sad shells of houses with waving shreds of wallpaper on exposed walls. No taxis anywhere, and asking any passers-by for help with directions they just shrugged sullenly and walked on.

Harry carried Jamie while I lugged the suitcase. Finding the address Harry had for the Major was like reaching a waterhole in the desert. Could any dilapidated office block have ever looked more welcoming?

The Major stood up from his desk. 'However, have you managed to make it all this way?' he asked, looking astounded. We didn't bore him with the saga.

He was clean-cut and slightly paunchy, weary eyed in that drab, miserable place, but he couldn't have missed our great state of exhaustion and stubbing out a cigarette, told the corporal to rustle up some coffee fast, milk and biscuits for Jamie.

'I can give you a permit to work on your father's farm, Mr Werner, but Eis is thirty miles on and the only way is by rattle-bus.'

The bus was certainly a bone-crunching antiquity, but the countryside was beautiful. I stared out of a filthy window at softly mounded apple-green hills on the far side of Lake Wërthersee, almost forgiving the bus its slow, cranking progress. It took us on through swathes of pasture; there were copses of pine and a whole network of sparkling streams that Harry enjoyed. 'Dad said they're all stuffed with trout, and the Security Service chaps lob in a hand grenade or two to bag them for breakfast. Hardly sporting…'

At Eis, speaking German, we gave a local lad a few coins and asked him to go to the farm and say we were at the bus stop. Harry's parents arrived in a horse-drawn wagon soon afterwards. They were as astounded as the Major had been.

I stood by shyly while they hugged their only son with outpourings of emotion. It had been eight years. They were both white-haired, haggard and heavily lined, wearing painfully shabby clothes.

'We've been living under such stress,' Harry's mother, Marta, said, once we were unwinding in their ramshackle kitchen. 'The war may have ended, but there's no money for repairs.' I'd seen that as Jamie raced round after unending hours on train and bus, exploring all the sorry dilapidated outbuildings.

'Being one of the most productive farms in the region saved us from being interned,' said Harry's father, Wilhelm, 'though every scrap of food we could produce was commandeered. I wasn't allowed a car and had to report twice a week to the nearest police station, an hour's walk away. Not much fun with snow and ice on the road. We're virtually self-sufficient again now thankfully. Still no car, but my eyesight's failing anyway.'

We sat on narrow benches at a scored wooden surface, more chopping block than table. Misshapen pots, panniers of earthy potatoes and gruesome bits of pig dangled from hooks in the low rafters. Marta poured tea from a balding enamel pot. She cut hefty chunks of fresh-baked bread and there was home-churned butter and rhubarb jam.

'We have a good labour force,' Wilhelm said, 'plenty of temporary help, mainly the sons and daughters of local peasants who like to be paid in farm produce. Even the doctors and dentists will accept a block of butter or ham hock as payment. Our wagons are horse-drawn, as you saw, and our one small lorry runs on beech chips from our woodlands. We're milking, haymaking and harvesting cereals again, growing flax for shirts, producing leather for shoes and saddles, and still all done by hand! We're the lucky ones, alive and doing fine.'

The days slipped by. I walked for miles in the idyllic countryside while Harry helped on the farm and Jamie played with the labourers' scruffy children. He was sleeping ten or twelve hours a night with all the fun, fresh air and exercise. I wondered if Harry's parents had picked up on the strained relations. Pointless to speculate; and I was rested and more relaxed. I drank the farm's rough, strong cider and listened to Wilhelm over the evening meals.

'The Nazi SS regularly searched the premises for anything not surrendered, and had they found gold, jewellery or any other valuables, the penalty would have been death. And we had to billet a constant stream of arrogant German troops on the farm. I suspected one or two in my labour force of being Nazi informers, and hearing that some bright spark had nicknamed a large fat sow, "Nazi", had her despatched to the slaughterhouse double-quick!

'We'd just seen the back of the German troops when in came the armed Yugoslav partisans, who've always claimed this corner of Carinthia as their own. They constantly try to sabotage the region, suborning any Slovene speakers, and are either bandits or freedom fighters to the villagers. But even the Slovenes are divided and have a job to know whose side their neighbours are on. A woman caught tipping off one of the partisans narrowly avoided being executed.

'With the end in sight, it was hard to keep up with the stream of fleeing troops and civilians. We gave temporary shelter where possible, which was permitted, but feeding anyone or giving the children milk was strictly *verboten*. Needless to say, we weren't going to let people starve. Then came an influx of trigger-happy Bulgarian troops, who were the worst; drunk, unpredictable and dangerous, demanding accommodation and forcing me at gunpoint to unlock the cellar and hand over the keys.'

'Wilhelm was so calm and brave,' Marta said. 'As soon as we heard the British troops had reached Carinthia, he scribbled a note about the Bulgarians and sent our most trusted groom on horseback to deliver it to the first British soldier he found.' She smiled at her husband. 'It was a chaotic time, all those Nazi officers and commanders hurtling north to Berlin, leaving their wives behind, but our groom succeeded and a British patrol turned up to help. Even with the language difficulties, they got across that the farm was under British protection and those drunkard Bulgarians had just better mind their p's and q's!'

'I had a good laugh,' Wilhelm said, well into the rough cider and loving reminiscing, 'meeting the British Military Governor appointed to this part of Carinthia. He told me that as MG he'd taken over the luxurious villa that the fleeing Nazi commander had occupied and found the wretched man's poor deserted wife still there. She begged to be allowed to stay, promising to cook the MG a nightly hot meal. There was all her husband's fine wine and champagne, she said, his car too... The Governor soon had to move on from that house, but still returned in the evenings to claim his dinner and wine!'

As August drew to its close, it was time to go home. Harry was far too taken with life on the farm, despite the conditions, and even talking of our settling there permanently. It was a huge relief when his father warned him off with the threat of Soviet occupation and we hit the long, rattling journey home. First to Oxford for all our belongings, which somehow had to fit into the car, say our goodbyes to the Coopers and make our overloaded way to Hampshire and our future home. Making it one was going to be a challenge; a waterless, electricity-free bungalow, which even by Harry's own admission was in a damp and gloomy hollow.

CHAPTER 47

Hampshire, October 1946

Another boiled-egg supper, another evening alone. Harry had been on a three-month secondment to Cyprus. He was due back the following day, but my heart was heavy with foreboding. I'd hardly heard from him in all that time, just a couple of duty letters, which was in sad stark contrast to the stream of loving correspondence of our KAR days…

Harry seemed to grab any chance to travel. He'd been to Bavaria with forestry professors from Munich University, to Baden-Württemberg, where he'd had lunch on the princely estate of the Markgraf von Baden, whose houseguests, Harry said, had been addressed as *Royal Highness.* And in the last of his rare letters from Cyprus, he'd mentioned the possibility of another trip.

The real sadness was my not minding his being away. Having the piano was salvation, losing myself to the music, soft and soothing as a Scottish burn, and I was giving piano lessons to the older siblings of Jamie's nursery school friends. I had the car, could drive to Didcot to see Mrs Sims, take Jamie to Oxford for a day with Connie and Billy. Connie was still living with her in-laws, but ecstatic about a new baby on the way, and having a mother-in-law to help couldn't be so bad.

There were troughs, times when dread of the future would invade and shrivel my skin. The cracks had become rivers, and the cliffs and heights of our marriage crumbled to the shore. Agreeing to have another child would make Harry happy, but he'd still find every reason to be away.

I brewed a pot of coffee, hoping it wouldn't keep me awake, and sipped it slowly, cradling the mug to warm my hands. It was over a year since Carinthia. Memories of Oxford had faded like a sepia photograph, but the move to Hampshire with all the troubles and tribulations was still in razor-sharp focus.

The bungalow was a charmless brick square; two bedrooms, living room, kitchen and dining annex. It had been a building site when we arrived. No chance of starting a garden with the rubble piled high, and the builder, a scrawny, surly, flat-faced fellow who lived in a nearby shack, had taken weeks to shift it.

I'd said dryly we should name the house *The Dip*, and we'd settled on *The Hollows,* which, along with my baby grand, raised the tone just enough to mask the lack of water and electricity when nursery school mothers brought children to play.

The research station had been hardly up and running when we arrived; Harry hadn't even had a table and chair. He'd felt very spare and gone off to Dingwall in Scotland to work in the field with some mensuration foresters – back just in time to return there to have Christmas with my family.

It had been the first Christmas without Buffy. We'd tried to be jolly and make it special, but all missed him acutely. I could never forget his startled clear-eyed stare the second before he died. It would come to me queuing in the bakery, on buses, waiting to pick up Jamie from nursery school. It would wake me up in the night and my throat would close over, the tears leaving my pillow damp.

Another Christmas without him wasn't so far off now. It was October, cooler, the evenings drawing in, and I shivered. The previous winter, our first at *The Hollows,* had felt as great an endurance test as any climb of the Himalayas. January, February and even into March, it had been the coldest winter since 1895 and unlike the pain of childbirth, I could remember the agony of it, the depths of snow, the challenges, in every bitter detail.

Chilblains on my toes and fingers, the green logs that wouldn't burn, Harry's sullen frustration at being snowed in, frosted ice on the inside of windowpanes, frozen milk bottles on the doorstep, the tops pecked by poor hungry birds, and the awful stink of the paraffin heaters that had no hope of shifting the chill. We ran out of water more than once, the tank was too small, and Harry had to trudge off, cap in hand, to a local market gardener and haul back supplies.

When a May heatwave broke more records and Harry was doing a water run almost daily, his curses were a match for all the Tommies in Cairo. The council had suggested digging underground for a second tank, only the cavity was so badly shored up that it collapsed before completion and brought a corner of the house down with it. It had been almost funny.

Now, a full year on, we were going onto mains water and electricity. I wasn't looking forward to all the mess and upheaval, but having Harry at home would help with that. It would be good, too, to have a few weeks together before Jamie and I left for Scotland.

Mum had asked us to come and I was eagerly looking forward to seeing her and my own chance to get away. Jamie could easily miss the last week of nursery school. Mum was so self-sufficient that I worried whether she had some particular reason for needing us there and how she was bearing up. I couldn't bear her to be ill.

Harry returned from Cyprus looking tanned and fit as a yachtsman. 'Welcome home, stranger!' I said, hurt by his chaste kiss on the cheek. Three months he'd been away, and not even a proper hug and kiss. 'How was it all? From the look of you, it was certainly sunny.'

'Not bad. Hard work. I suppose Jamie's asleep in bed? I've brought him some picture books and a camel.'

'He's fast asleep but dying to see you. I don't think we'll get much of a lie-in in the morning. There's supper when you're ready…'

'Sorry, I'm really not hungry. It was a lousy flight and I'm dead on my feet.'

'Sure, of course.'

I toyed with a bit of fish pie, alone, feeling rock bottom, and inevitably my thoughts turned to Edmund Southan. He'd left me bitter, damaged, defiled, destabilised, my marriage was disintegrating, but was he really the sole cause? Harry and I had grown closer again in South Africa, and been managing better before Andy's loss. If only Harry could have propped me up for just a little bit longer… No excuses, we'd both suffered, had so much to drive us apart, but the rot had started with me alone, I was the one to blame.

Jamie was irrepressible in the morning, loving his presents, noisy and bouncy at breakfast. 'Come see my seeds in the garden now, Daddy!'

'Finish your cereal first, and it's very nearly time for nursery school.'

But he was down from the bench, leaving his half-eaten cornflakes, pulling on his father's hand. It was a job to get him into the car and away. I saw him in, watched him race up happily to his friends then drove away feeling on edge. Harry was at home for the morning and we needed to get onto some sort of wavelength. I opened the door to a rich aroma of coffee. Harry was in the kitchen and held up the pot. 'Want some? It's good stuff. I smuggled a packet in.'

'Thanks, smells great.' He was at the table, didn't get up, and I slid in opposite.

He was watching me over the rim of his mug, looking about to say something, so why didn't he just get on with it? *The Times* was on the table – the paperboy biked it out daily – and eyeing the headlines, I did my best to be chatty.

'The USSR boasting about its new eastern bloc will certainly please EH Carr!' Churchill's fury at *The Times'* deputy editor siding with the Greek communists had been news even out in Africa, with *The Times* tagged *The Threepenny Daily Worker* for a while.

'Hmm,' Harry muttered, not listening. 'Um, sorry, darling, but I'm off again on Monday, just for six days. It's Italy this time, finding flora in the Abruzzo region. I know it's short notice, but perhaps if Jamie could stay with a friend... Would you, um, like to come?'

Harry bloody knew I couldn't, not with the works starting on Monday, which we'd only just talked about at breakfast. Muddy trenches, electricity wires chased into the plaster, and he knew there was no one to have Jamie for six days.

I said coolly, holding his eyes, 'I have to be here as you know, with the builders starting on Monday. You'll probably pass the men on the path.'

'Oh, yes, sorry, but think of the benefits! Running water, light at the flick of a switch, and it will make the house easier to sell...' He blushed and looked away. His tanned face had turned the burnished red of a pomegranate, and my insides turned to ice.

'I'll get the mail,' he said, making for the door, 'just heard it drop. And I should see what needs saving in the garden before they start to dig.'

Tears prickled. I could be wrong. And anyway, what could I do? Walk out because of a blush? I sat at the kitchen table feeling raw with misery, chilled to the marrow. It felt like the end; a long, lonely, unrecoverable finality.

Harry was out for ages. He'd left the mail on the shelf in the small hall, mainly bills, but there were two letters for me, surprisingly; one from Germany, the other from the States. I went back to the kitchen with them, poured more coffee and dreading the news from Germany, opened Dolly's letter first.

…You'll never guess! I'm getting married, soon to be Mrs Hank Gregory, and there's never been a more fab army lieutenant in the whole world! Hank the Hunk, I call him. He's all rippling muscles, loving and kind, sweeps me right off my feet. Literally, he swings me up like a two-year-old! And, best ever, we're going to have our honeymoon in Scotland! Hank's mother has an aunt in Dundee, so you can bet that old bottom dollar how hard I'll be pushing to see you. I'm head over heels, skittering about like a spring lamb – just want you to be happy too. And you will be, I swear, somehow, sometime…

Dolly was still teaching, but longing to have a string of mini Hanks soon.

I was happy for her, feeling warmed. Less so, fingering the letter from Germany, having had no reply to any of my letters to Bertha or Anna. I'd written to my old tutor, Frau Blohm. She could have moved away, anything could have happened, but the writing looked familiar and the letter felt like a reply to mine.

It was. Frau Blohm was very sorry to be the bearer of bad news, but Bertha Schulz had been killed in the war. One could only hope she died instantly; she'd been queuing for food with all of Hamburg half-starving and when the siren sounded, in the crush of people, hadn't been able to reach the shelter in time.

Anna Lange had lost both her parents and gone to live with her grandparents in Holland. She'd left no forwarding address. It was all very sad, Frau Blohm said. She thanked me for my kind enquiries; she and her mother were battling on and sent their warmest wishes.

It was a hammer to my heart. Tears dribbled down my cheeks and dripped onto the page. Dear, sweet Bertha, queuing for food for the family; could any death have ever been more pointless or more desperately poignant and cruel?

Harry came in and was solicitous. He collected Jamie for me and over lunch, tried to be more friendly; probably as much for Jamie's benefit as mine. But he left for the research station in a great hurry then, unable to hide his relief to be getting away and leaving me to the piano lesson I had to give to a nine-year-old girl who had no interest in learning. And whose mother outstayed her welcome over tea.

The images were there, insidious jealousy leaking into the bloodstream like poison. Harry collecting plant samples, meeting another's eyes amidst beautiful autumnal flora in the mild Italian sun. I could see it all.

Our own loving looks were long gone, tenderly wrapped up in tissue like wedding lingerie, now lying forgotten in a bottom drawer. Did Harry still have fond memories of our better days? Would this affair, even if it was one, be short-lived? Papering over marital guilt took guile, and Harry was too honest to dissemble. Did we just soldier on, meantime, and live our lives? What else was there to do?

*

Mum was on the platform. Jamie and I clambered down from the train and he raced over. 'Gransy, Gransy! Is it going to snow?'

She swung him up into a hug. 'I'm not sure when, but an old man in the village has assured me that the snow is on the way. It'll be here very soon.'

I said, 'Thanks for meeting us, Mum. I've been so longing to be here, longing for the chance to look after you too for once.'

'We'll look after each other. Isn't it great news, water and electricity after the horrors of last winter? I've been so worried how you were coping.'

'The works have been hell, such chaos – it's lovely to be here with you now!'

'I helped dig a ditch, Gransy,' Jamie cried, leaping about. 'Did it, did it!'

It was past his bedtime. He ran off some exuberant energy before having his supper and being hustled into bed, his eyelids drooping all through the story. I kissed him, smoothed his tuft of hair that refused to lie flat and crept out.

Downstairs, I felt Dad's absence intensely. Seeing the sitting room without my piano, with none of his scattered newspapers and books, no drift of his pipe tobacco, but he was there, in the room, in my heart, always.

'You're thinking about Dad, aren't you?' Edith said, coming in.

'Yes, it's difficult not to here, as you must find too. You're working and busy and seeing friends, I hope, Mum, but the long evenings can't always be very easy.'

'Sometimes it's comforting just to be here on my own,' she said, with a tear slipping out. I needed a hug, seeing that tear, and drank in her special smell. She was an intelligent, still-handsome woman of fifty-five with a career, a mission in life, but she'd lost the husband she loved and my heart ached for her.

Over supper, she said. 'Are things still very bad? I couldn't miss the tension when you were last here, and it's been hard to miss too in your letters. Try to think positively, you'll ride out a bad patch. It's war, life, upheaval.

'But now,' she said, lifting her wine glass with a purposeful smile, 'I've got some news for you. It's all rather unbelievable and I need to fill you in.'

'What sort of news?' I felt anxious and on edge.

'It's Hamish, he survived the war. He's here, home again, alive but damaged, which is why I didn't want to tell you in a letter. He's, well, difficult to reach.'

'But that's inconceivable! I mean, it's a whole two years since the war…' I'd thought of Hamish often, feeling his loss profoundly, all the more so for his sad, embarrassing declaration of love before going to France. 'That's the very last news I could have expected, Mum, impossible to get my head round…' I stared at her, trying to disentangle my feelings; disbelief, joy, relief and so much more.

'How badly damaged is he? It would be too cruel if he's survived only to have a life not worth living. Why is he only just home? You must have some clue.'

'I don't, he's extremely uncommunicative and surly, hardly says a word even to his parents, though of course he's never found it easy to talk to them. His father's such an old stick-in-the-mud, bit of a tyrant too, and Margot is in Angus' sway. I know Hamish was very attached to an elderly French cousin of Margot's and spent most of his childhood summers with her in France. He speaks French like a native, which I suppose is how he managed somehow or other to survive.'

'Please, Mum, please tell me everything you can. I need to know…' Was I sounding as desperate as I felt? Hamish was a friend; he mattered to me.

'He was trying to reach the beaches at Dunkirk, he's said that much. I suppose he was wounded, very weak, no one saw him fall in those ghastly circumstances and he was eventually recorded as missing, just one more sad statistic of war.'

'But why hasn't he been in touch till now? That's what I can't understand.'

'It could be short-term memory loss, anterograde amnesia, which can be caused by physical injuries and shock, psychological trauma too. He won't say a word about the recent past, just shrugs and says he'd been close to death, crawled into a wood and been found by a woman walking her dog.'

'But he must have got his memory back, by the very fact that he's here.'

'You're right. And I'm sure he knows more than he's saying.'

She looked at me thoughtfully. 'He asked after you, wanting news, so he knows about Andy and also just possibly picked up that there were a few problems…'

'What exactly had you been saying then, Mum, for God's sake?'

'Nothing, but Hamish is sensitive and astute – and you know how he feels.'

I did. I still couldn't believe that it was pure intuition on his part and deeply resented the intrusion into my private mess. But would Mum really have alluded to marital difficulties? 'Please don't talk about Harry and me, not to Hamish or anyone else,' I muttered, and burst into tears, heaving sobs. I couldn't stop.

Edith jumped up and put her arm round me. 'Darling, darling, don't keep it bottled up. It's good to cry and let it out. Is it very bad?'

I sniffed, wiped my eyes and recovered a bit. 'I think Harry's fallen for someone. He keeps going away. I'm mainly to blame, but we're so distant now…'

'Forget the blame. Break-ups are hardly ever one-sided.'

'I don't know what to do, just keep muddling on?'

I felt at my lowest ebb. There was no answer, no soothing balm that Mum could give. Harry and I were half separated, but we'd made vows, had to go on. Perhaps when Jamie was away at school – Dad had left money for his education – I could get a proper job, have a life of my own…

Mum said, 'I'll support you in whatever you decide. Harry may get this woman out of his system, and relationships can mend. You'll be together over Christmas, see how things work out then. He'll be trying his best, and meantime you and I can be company and prop each other up.

'I have to be at a conference in Oxford for a couple of days and do ask Hamish over then. He's awkward company, swears a lot, but you may be able to unlock something. He's always loved you after all.'

CHAPTER 48

Full Circle

The snow wasn't long coming. Jamie came racing into my room in the early morning when a faint pink glow in the dawn sky gave just enough light to see the snow lying thick and heavy, weighing down branches of leafless trees, bending shrubs low. 'Snow, snow, Mummy! Can Gavin and me build a snowman?'

'Not before we're dressed and have had breakfast. Gavin and Mrs Hodges have to get here too, and it may take them quite a bit longer with the snow.' Mrs Hodges' great-nephew and Jamie becoming such good mates was a boon.

The sun was soon up, sparkling the snow with icy crystals like thousands of land-lying stars. I made the porridge, which had Mrs Hodges tut-tutting when she and Gavin came into the kitchen with pink cheeks and steamy breath. She hurried to take over, cooking bacon and eggs and conceding that my porridge wasn't bad. I said I'd learnt at her feet, and her pink cheeks turned pinker.

After breakfast, Gavin's second one, Mrs Hodges said, the boys were uncontainable, prancing around while we tried to get them coated, gloved and scarved. 'Can we 'ave a carrot and two coals for the snowman's eyes?' Gavin said, his own eyes bright and dark as two little coals themselves.

'What about its mouth?' I said. 'Perhaps a row of red beans?'

I helped them to build the snowman, played games, threw snowballs and took them into Edinburgh to kit them out with skates in case there were hard frosts and the ice on the canal became thick enough for practice goes. The skates were a pre-Christmas present for Gavin, I said, shutting my mind to the cost.

Mum left for her Oxford conference, since the trains were running and the lane to the main road salted. She pressed me to give Hamish a call and ask him over.

I spent the day clearing snow and getting in more coal with Mrs Hodges. When she and Gavin left, Jamie and I did a jigsaw in front of the fire, a picture of swans on a lake. We put the pieces on a tray and rested it on the footstool.

I didn't call Hamish, putting it off, though I wasn't sure why. Perhaps worrying how difficult it would be, seeing him again and reconnecting? I was cross with myself, all the same, and tucking up Jamie in bed later, wished I had done.

I'd just kissed Jamie good night when the doorbell rang. I hurried downstairs, sure it would be the neighbours bringing the pot of plum jam they'd promised and it was a shock to see Hamish on the doorstep instead. His left-hand coat sleeve was hanging limp. Mum hadn't told me he'd lost an arm.

'I know Edith's away,' Hamish said, 'heard her saying she couldn't play bridge with my mother today. Can I come in?'

'Of course! Quickly, out of the chill. I was going to call and ask you over, you've beaten me to it,' I said, feeling guilty. He'd think I'd been putting it off, as I had been.

'As you were told to do?' He gave a raised-eyebrow look. I felt even worse.

'Yes, you're right. Mum did suggest it, but I wanted to anyway, to say what unbelievable joy it was, knowing you'd survived. It just felt a bit pressurising and intrusive to call and ask questions when you weren't giving any answers.'

Hamish stared but made no comment. He'd come in dragging his leg slightly, but had no stick and looked in pain. I thought fleetingly, sickeningly, of Edmund, whose limp had seemed to come and go. Hamish shrugged off his coat, hung it on one of the hooks in the lobby and we went into the sitting room.

'Whisky?' I was at the drinks trolley and poured a few fingers into a glass. 'I reckoned no water,' I said, bringing it over to him, moving a small side table to the other side of one of the armchairs. 'You are right-handed? Managing okay?'

'Driving's off the list, most things are. You get to a point of not caring whether you live or die.'

'But you do care, you wanted to survive.'

'Yep, that kicks in. I was lucky only to have an arm blown off, unlike all the other poor buggers, left to rot in France.' His gaunt, hollow face was chalky grey, his cheekbones like coat hangers holding up the paper-thin skin. Hamish's large brown eyes, once annoyingly beseeching, were angry and penetrating now.

He drank some whisky and reached to put down the glass. From the set of his shoulders and drained, sunken face, he seemed in a state of such complete exhausted, helpless despair that I dropped down onto the footstool and touched his hand on the chair arm. If our old familiarity still held good, there must be some way to reach him. I wasn't the smug, self-obsessed young girl he'd known, probably still too self-centred, but older and I'd suffered in my own way too, had had my fair share of life's knocks.

'Tell me what happened. It will go no further if that's what you want. Tell me about the woman who found you. Did she hide you all through the war?'

Hamish reached for my hand, which he held in a painful

clutch. 'I don't want to talk about the war. No point, can't recall much anyway.'

'Yes, you can.' He wasn't suffering from memory loss; that much was clear as daylight. 'Your parents never gave up hope. We were all willing you to survive.'

He let go of my hand, struggled up to go to the drinks trolley and looked back.

'Of course, have as much as you like,' I said. 'I'll have some too.' He brought me over a glass, going back for the soda I wanted then back again for his own glass. I didn't try to help; he must loathe being made to feel dependent. 'Did the woman keep you hidden all that time? Was she married?'

Why ask that? Stupid question. 'But could you not have been found?'

Hamish studied the whisky that glowed gold in his glass, downed it, gave a sigh from the depths of his being and fastened his eyes. The force of his stare was very unsettling. 'Yes, she was married and did hide me. She was called Yvette.'

'Go on. I care, need to know, and it won't go any further, as I said.'

He kept staring, but as if torn in two with indecision. I imagined the horror, the intense pain it must be, even to speak about being close to death, but longed to find a way to build his trust, a bridge of understanding. I got up to jiggle the fire, sat back, stroked Tabitha, now sharing the seat, and withstood Hamish's stares. I felt a grain of hope that he'd open up, that he needed to and it would help him.

'You really want to hear? It's not a pretty story, left me in this mess… The woman, Yvette, was living alone. Her husband had been sent to prison, God knows what for, but not before he'd beaten up one of her brothers, the youngest and very backward, but whom she'd loved dearly and cared for. That brother, poor sod, had dragged himself off, never to be seen again.' Hamish pressed his hand to his furrowed forehead. 'I can't go on, it's too tedious. Tell me your news.'

'None that you haven't heard. Mum told you about my losing a son in Uganda. I'm sure it would help if you felt able to unload a bit, help me too, and I wouldn't say a word if that's what you want. Can't you trust in me as a friend?'

He gave me another sullen-eyed stare. 'A friend? Is that what we are, friends?'

He looked down then went on. 'I can remember every bloody thing, every last sordid detail of all those filthy, fucking seven long years. It's grim stuff.'

'Tell me all the same.'

'Well, I owe my life to Yvette, for what it's worth. She knew the risks and took them. Her dog found me, but she ran off then. Must have decided I was a goner, I assumed, but she was soon back with a big, busty, brassy blonde. They were close friends, worked at a hairdresser's in St Omer, and between them managed to drag me to Yvette's house, a tatty new-build on the edge of a hamlet.

'It hadn't been such a totally impossible risk for her to take. France had just capitulated and feelings were running high in that tiny village. The local doctor even took out all the shrapnel and cleaned and dressed what was left of my arm. Yvette still had her poor loopy brother's identity papers. His photograph was blurred, my French good, and I could just about act the part when the Germans came snooping. I looked weird, armless and wobbly, and Yvette said it was a farming accident. The Germans didn't speak French, but she mimed it.'

I got the whisky decanter, refilled Hamish's glass and sat down on the footstool again. 'It was still early on in the war. What happened when you were stronger?'

'Took me two years to recover and I couldn't have got anywhere anyway with the war on. Yvette nursed me. She needed the companionship, sex too, when I was eventually able to make it.

She was wiry and plain but had taken risks, lived on a pittance and was keeping me. I owed her. I chopped wood with my one arm for old people in the village, just as her brother used to do.'

Men fell in love with the women who nursed them. I had no business minding his being virtually married to Yvette, but I did. 'Why stay on after the war, though? Surely her husband had done his time by then and come home?'

Hamish seemed to be looking right into my skull; his eyes burned in. I held them. He said, 'You really want me to go on? Well, I was better, stronger, desperate to get the hell away the moment peace was declared. I kept saying Yvette's husband must be due home soon and there'd be trouble, but she didn't seem to know when they'd let him out and clung onto me, begging me to stay. She had her arms round my neck when that evil cur walked in the door.

'He was a brawny little runt, her husband, a pig-eyed violent bastard. He grabbed the poker and beat me relentlessly; head, legs, shoulders. I was in a pool of blood, losing consciousness. He gave me a last crippling kick then turned to start on his screaming wife. She'd seen it coming, though, and was out of the door. I was just aware of him making off after her before blacking out completely.

'He probably didn't find her and went to a bar, since Yvette must have come back with her hefty blonde friend, Bruna – second time of them saving me from dying – and got me to Bruna's house, which was rank. It was revolting, peeling pink wallpaper, cheap scent, and that was where I stayed.'

Hamish reached for my hand again, fingering it absently. 'Bruna had been left the house. Her father had died in the first world war, mother from cancer. I think those two women got a weird kick out of shielding me, a frisson, sexual to Yvette, and Bruna loved being in on the act. I was in as bad a way as when they'd first found me and didn't give much for my chances. If you think I look bad now, you should have seen me then; pulpy bruises, broken ribs, gammy leg gammier. I was weak with pain, gagging on the smells, sweat, cooking and mouldy, damp walls.'

'Why couldn't you have had the doctor and found someone to call home?'

'The old doctor had retired by the end of the war and his replacement was a snotty, officious little bugger who demanded to see my papers. So, I had to act the poor brother, not easy when half dead. Successfully, except that having convinced the man I was the village idiot, he could hardly bring himself to touch my pulped, battered body. Didn't even ask how I'd lost my arm.'

Hamish dropped my hand, racked by a cough. 'Can you understand how I can't face telling the parents any of this? It was months before I could move, all my hopes of freedom gone up in a puff of a filthy French Gauloise. Yvette was always round too, being crude. I don't know how things were with her violent thug of a husband. She had bruises, but it didn't put her off coming to see me. The best thing about her was how she'd cared for and really loved that helpless brother.

'I lay in the dirty sheets in that revoltingly boudoir-ish house, concentrating all my energies into how to escape. You were the spur. I had you in my mind night and day, the burning need to see you. I slowly grew stronger and with cruel bad luck when I'd been escaping and halfway down a lane was spotted by that thug of a husband and beaten up again. If it hadn't been for a couple of farm labourers who pulled him off and told him to get lost, I'd be dead. The good luck was the thug not going to the police for very good reasons of his own. Anyway, I managed to stagger on, lost, sleeping rough, living on scraps from strangers, one of whom was kind enough to loan me the money for the ferry when I got to Calais and that was it.

'I heard about your father,' Hamish went on. 'I'm sorry, I know how much he meant to you.'

I thanked him and we sat in silence. I knew everything now.

It had been incredibly painful even to hear him out, but he'd had the guts to tell me.

The fire needed attention. I got up to see to it, thinking of Hamish saying that I'd been the spur, although the need to survive was primeval, as he himself had acknowledged. I watched the flames flicker and respond then turning back, looked over to Hamish, who rose with the help of his one arm and came to face me. He was staring and I smiled back, embarrassed. He was embittered and distrustful, living with pain, but his love for me was unquestionably still there, plain to see, deep and heartfelt as it had ever been.

I said lightly, 'Will you stay to eat? There's only cauliflower cheese and not much of that. We can have it in here on a tray. How are you getting back? Taxi or will you telephone home? I can't leave my son or I'd take you.'

'Where's Harry?'

'In Hampshire, where we're living now. He's been away a lot, but since his last trip, staying put a while, busy doing research and trying to finish a doctorate.'

'So why are you here then and not there?'

'It's just… I'm having a break, being company for Mum.' Silly, that hesitation.

'Oh. And your son who's four, called Jamie? Does he look like you?'

'Not much. Do boys often look like their mothers? You don't look like yours.' Hamish shrugged and I turned back to the fire to stoke it up with more coal.

'I can do that.' He took the shovel from my hands.

'I'll go and hot up the food. Have another whisky and there's some open wine.'

In the kitchen, I took the cauliflower cheese out of the warming oven and gave it a blast under the grill. The Hamish of old, cautious, conventional – though had he really ever been? –

bound for a solid position in his father's solicitors' firm was no longer. He was scarred mentally and physically; would he ever recover enough to have any chance of a normal decent life?

I got a tray ready and watching the cheese bubble under the grill, remembered him once saying that but for the coming war, he'd hoped to travel.

'It's your own fault, being stuck with me all evening,' Hamish said, giving me a start. I looked round. He was leaning against the doorframe.

I said, 'Have you been there long? Come and sit down.'

The oven cloth was on the cooker rail and I took the dish over to the tray and picked it up, ready to return to the sitting room.

'Sorry, I can't carry that tray, bloody useless to anyone these days.'

'But you can bring the wine.'

We went back to the fireside and sat with plates of food on our knees. Hamish had got the fire going nicely. 'What are you going to do now you're back?' I asked. 'Join your father's firm?'

'No, not the firm, my father has his views and they're not mine. I've got out from under now. I'm due a bit of loot from the army so there's no rush. I have an idea for a book – nothing to do with my experiences. Perhaps I'll join another firm sometime, possibly somewhere further south.'

I didn't ask about his idea for a book; he would have given one of his shrugs. I said, 'Come over tomorrow if you're at a loose end. We can have a walk.'

'Won't your son take fright at the sight of a one-armed shell of a man?'

'Shouldn't think so. Time will tell.' I smiled.

'I suppose you'd say I should call for a cab now?'

'Well, it is quite late.'

We went out together to the telephone in the chilly hall. The taxi would be ten or fifteen minutes. I was glad, not irritated as my teenage self would have been, stuck with Hamish still hanging around staring. We went back to the warmth of the sitting room where he took hold of my hand and touched lips lightly.

'You'd say I shouldn't have done that.'

'I'd say I'm a married woman.'

'Only up to a point…'

He grinned unexpectedly and returned my hand. 'Thanks for letting me in the door tonight. Sorry about the bad language. It gets to be a bit of a habit after where I've been. Must try harder,' he touched my cheek, 'in many ways…'

I separated, but smiling inwardly, looking forward to seeing him the next day. We waited, anticipating the doorbell, but both jumped when it rang. Hamish told the driver he'd be out in a couple of minutes. I helped him into his coat and he took my hand again. 'Ten o'clock tomorrow? Morning coffee? No good regretting asking me, I'm coming anyway.'

I stayed in the hall listening as the taxi drove away then cleared away the dishes, put the guard in front of the dying fire and went up to bed.

What did I feel? Hamish had loved me from the start. 'I'll always be there for you,' he'd said, that night of the Campbells' party, before leaving to join up and become a pawn of fate. And tonight, saying I was the spur, fixing me with that piercing stare. Did I care too, now? Certainly, more than before. He was haggard, damaged, brittle enough to crack like thin ice, but alive. I wanted to talk and discover more about him, about my own feelings, try to get used to how changed he was and possibly even unload some of my troubles.

Nothing was going to happen in a hurry. There was Jamie, my life to sort out, so much uncertainty. Harry and I could yet find a way through. And if we didn't? We had to try. We'd taken vows. I'd lost Andy, Dad, Bob, friends in the war, but that night, lying awake for long, electrified hours I thought of Bob saying, a little tritely, that life took many turns. My lids were closing and, finally settling on my side for sleep, for the first time in years I had hope for the future.

Acknowledgements

First and foremost, my most heartfelt thanks above all to Antony Hummel, who so kindly entrusted me with a number of files of his parents' wartime letters and allowed me to create this fictionalised account of their lives during that eventful, historic time. It has been a joy to work on this book, and he and his wife, Margaret, have been wonderfully patient and supportive throughout the long process.

I owe thanks to my late agent, Michael Sissons who sadly died after reading a few early chapters of *Love at War,* but his very positive response at the time was all the encouragement I needed.

Warmest thanks too, to Trevor Bell, who I think will agree that we've done a great job of encouraging each other in our respective bookish endeavours.

And very many thanks are due to Aidan Hartley, who was so generous with his time when I was in Nairobi, giving wonderful insights into the Kenya, Nairobi and Muthaiga Club of the '40s along with immensely helpful suggestions of interesting and instructive books to read that gave great insights into wartime life there at the time.

My tthanks to Celia Goodhart for sharing childhood memories of her very early years in Uganda and her brother, Nico Hemmingford, too who kindly sent me his memoir about living there in the late 30's and at the start of the war when his father was headmaster of a school for boys.

The team at The Book Guild have been terrific, guiding and advising me so soundly and wisely and getting this show on the road. I am greatly indebted to Rosie Lowe, managing production, Meera Vithlani, trade marketing specialist, Jack Wedgbury, who designed the cover and was always so wonderfully patient with my wilder ideas, Philippa Iliffe publicity specialist, Joe Shillito, production controller, Hayley Russell in editorial and Lauren Bailey who will be on hand to help me after publication day.

Enormous thanks to all my wonderful friends for putting up with my repeated excitable descriptions of my characters' true lives, I know I must have bored you all to tears.

And finally, boundless thanks to my family as ever, my fantastic children who have been so constantly supportive and encouraging, Sholto, Nick and Larissa and their respective partners, Alex, Conrad and Betsy, all of whose advice has been invaluable too. I am truly blessed with my wonderful son and daughters-in-law. And I can never say a heartfelt enough thank you to my husband, Michael, ever my rock and guide. His uncomplainingly loyal support and patience over my writing has been unbelievable, he is my beloved all.

Bibliography

Best, Nicholas, *Happy Valley: The Story of the English in Kenya*, Thistle Publishing 2013

Boyd, Julia, *Travellers in the Third Reich*, Elliot &Thompson 2017

Cooper, Artimis, *Cairo in the War 1939–1945*, John Murray 1989

Fox, James, *White Mischief*, Jonathan Cape 1982

Halson, Penrose, *Marriages are made in Bond Street: True Stories from a 1940s Marriage Bureau*, Macmillan 2017

Hummel, Fred, *Memories of Forestry and Travel, passages* from which I have quoted directly, Radcliffe Press 2005.

Jaffa, Richard, *A letter from Oggi, The letters of Olga Franklin*, The Book Guild 2015

Markham, Beryl, *West with the Night*, Virago Modern Classics 1984

Mills & Vetch, Stephen & Yoyo, *Muthaiga: The First One Hundred Years, 1913–2013*

Moorehead, Alan, *The Desert War*, Penguin 1989

Nicholls, C.S., *Red Strangers: The White Tribe of Kenya*, Timewell Press 2005

Ranfurly, Countess of, *To War with Whitaker*, William Heinemann 1994

Reynolds, Vernon, *Budonga: Of Forests and its Chimpanzees,* Reynolds 1965

Stanley, Wendy, *A Tame Colonial Girl,* KDP Amazon 2017

Steward, Andrew, *The 2nd World War and East Africa Campaign*, Yale University Press 2016

Stewart, The Rt Rev C.E., *28 Years of Happiness in Africa,* personal memoir

Thompson, Gardner, *Governing Uganda: British Colonial Rule and its Legacy,* Fountain Publishers 2003

Tugendhat, Julia, *My Colonial Childhood in Tanganyika,* the Choir Press 2011

Vickers, Hugo, *Cecil Beaton,* Weidenfield & Nicholson 1985

Fiction

Atkinson, Kate, *Transcription,* Doubleday 2018

Brett Young, Francis, *The Crescent Moon,* Penguin 1938

Gee, Maggie, *My Driver,* Telegram 2009

Harris, Robert, *Munich,* Hutchinson 2017

Larson Erik*, In the Garden of Beasts,* Crown Publishers 2011

Lively, Penelope, *Moon Tiger,* André Deutsch 1988

McVeigh, Jennifer, *Leopard at the Door*, Penguin 2017

Manning, Olivia, *The Levant Trilogy*, Penguin 1982

Shand, Rosa, *The Gravity of Sunlight*, Soho Press Inc. 2000

Wollaston, Nicholas, *Café de Paris,* Constable 1988

For writing and publishing news, or
recommendations of new titles to read,
sign up to the Book Guild newsletter: